Lying in Wait

OTHER BOOKS BY LAUREL OSTIGUY

THE ONONDAGA STATE SERIES

Last Goodbye
Longing to Be

Lying in Wait

LAUREL OSTIGUY

Visit my website at www.LaurelOstiguy.com

www.facebook.com/AuthorLaurelOstiguy

http://twitter.com/authorlaurelo

Email: authorlaurelo@gmail.com

Cover Designer: rba designs: romantic book affairs

Cover model: Kathryn Foucha

Photographer: Lindee Robinson Photography

Editor and Interior Designer: Jovana Shirley, Unforeseen Editing, www.unforeseenediting.com

ISBN-13: 978-0-692-19937-4

Dedicated to
Diana M. Kupillas and her one true love.

Prologue

I had been working under Professor Tucker as a DJ at the college radio station for the past two years, and the best he could give me was some lousy explanation and a week's notice. It's a wonder I didn't quit right there on the spot. But I love it too much. Unfortunately for me, it's not the only thing I love, which is why this hurts so badly.

Damn you, Laura Chase.

I pace my room, trying to consider my next move. I'm interrupted over and over as my phone rings again and again. Whoever is calling me is not getting the hint that I don't want to talk! After the fifth ring, seriously agitated, I grab the receiver, practically knocking the phone off my desk.

"Yeah?" I bark.

"Colin, it's Sean. You have to come to the station. She...she..." he stammers.

"She what? Slow down," I say, quickly changing my tune. My heart rate has picked up significantly. And I feel a heightened energy like nothing I've experienced before coursing through my veins.

"She was attacked by some guy! Get over here!"

Before I can respond, I hear someone crying in the background, and then the phone goes dead.

Oh my God! Laura! No! my thoughts scream in my head.

I, without even realizing what I'm doing, drop the receiver, throw open my door, and run at top speed back to the station.

Not Laura! Please, God, don't let anything bad happen to her. I'll die if anyone's touched her!

Panic ensues. Either that or I'm having a heart attack at the ripe old age of twenty.

I pump my arms, trying to gain speed. My breathing is heavy. I attempt to maneuver my way in and out of the students shuffling out of their afternoon classes. I almost knock someone over.

"Sorry," I yell.

I push my way through the side entrance to the Student Union, near the mailboxes, and sprint down the hallway toward the station.

I burst in. "Where is she?" I can't help my voice from quivering.

Patrick points down the hallway toward Studio B. The look of sheer sadness on his face is enough to make me want to burst into tears.

"Holy shit," I mutter as I run down the hallway.

Without even knocking, I rush into the room. Sean and Ryker are hovering over a frail figure sitting in the chair. The blinds on the windows have been drawn.

My mind is racing with all kinds of horrific thoughts. I hear the cries of a woman in agony. With shaky hands, I reach out to put my hand on Ryker's shoulder, so I can move him out of the way. I need to let her know I'm here. I need her to know I'll protect her and do anything I can to help her. I'll make sure she is safe in my arms. Tears start to well in my eyes as I hear her whimper in pain.

As Ryker steps aside, I whisper, "I'm here."

One

THE AUDITION

Laura takes a deep breath and holds it before pulling open the door. The thumping in her chest can undoubtedly be heard by anyone within earshot. Her nerves are on high alert as she steps into the room and gradually releases her breath. No one turns to her as the door slams shut. She stands there, fiddling with her résumé in her hands.

A young man sitting at a desk near the window turns toward her. He peels off his headphones and pushes his black-framed glasses back up on his nose. "Can we help you?" he says with little enthusiasm.

"Yes, I'm here to speak with Professor Tucker." Laura's voice cracks.

"Yeah, this way."

He gets up and wanders down the hall. She follows him. He knocks on a closed door at the end of the hallway.

"Come in!" a bellowing voice yells from behind the closed door.

He opens the door a crack. "Someone is here for you."

"Laura. Laura Chase," she says.

"Laura Chase," he repeats.

"Yes, please have her come in. Thank you, Patrick."

Patrick opens the door all the way, and Laura passes by him.

She turns to him as he starts to close the door. "Thank you, Pat—"
But, before she can get it all out, he's already closed the door in her face.

"Ms. Chase, please have a seat," Professor Tucker says.

From what little information Laura could gather about her interview, she knew that Professor Tucker was a tenured engineering professor at Onondaga State and also the manager of the on-campus radio station WOUR97. He is a distinguished-looking man, appearing to be in his late forties, with spiked, dark hair and a goatee showing early signs of gray hair.

He also happens to be close friends with Professor Rhodes and Professor Cooper, from the Marketing Department, both of whom put in a good word for her. Hence why she was able to secure this meeting halfway through the first semester.

"Thank you," she says.

She sits as he motions for her to do so. She places her book bag next to her and then hands her résumé to him. She notices the corner is wet from her gripping it so tightly. As he glances at it, she nervously tucks her short brown hair behind her ear.

He then pointedly asks her, "What makes you believe you'd be a good DJ for our station?"

Bree Van Tousen, Laura's floor mate and close friend, spent the better part of last week rehearsing and going over different questions and answers. Laura anticipated a question like this would be asked but not so soon in the interview.

"I love music," she begins.

She watches as he leans back in his chair. He now appears disinterested.

She channels Bree's confidence and then adds, "But I'm sure that is what everyone tells you when they come in here. Loving music is only a fraction of what a DJ should be interested in."

He leans forward. "Continue."

She slants over and takes her notebook out of her bag. "I listen to the station every day, and there are opportunities to get more listeners by introducing some new programming. Anyone can pop a CD in and listen to their favorite band. There should be a greater need—a reason, if you will—as to why the students have to turn on the station and listen."

"What do you propose?"

"I, for one, read *The Weekly Blue* each week. But, exactly like the title indicates, it is printed only once a week. What if the radio station did the campus news each day or a few times each week? Open discussions, hot topics, students calling in to talk about what is happening in their community."

"And you deduce this will get more listeners?" he says, rubbing his goatee.

"Yes—or at least, it is worth a try. Programming can always be altered or changed. For example, surveys and polls. The school has them all the time for the best cafeteria dessert or best place to eat downtown. I don't see why the station couldn't be polled, too."

He nods his head.

Laura adds with a confident smile, "Don't college students have more opinions than they know what to do with?"

He starts to chuckle, and for the first time since coming in the room, Laura's shoulders relax.

"I suppose you are right on that. Well, Laura, you've put some time and thought into your ideas."

She glances down at her notebook. She rips out the pages with her outline. "You're welcome to take a peek at my ideas." She eagerly hands them to him.

His face perks up. "Thank you. I appreciate that. Have you been informed by Professor Rhodes that we have only the late shift available at this time?"

"Yes, I'm aware of that and completely fine with it. I'm a bit of a night owl, myself."

"Okay then. Why don't we have you go into the booth, and you can show me what you've got?"

With an excited sensation flowing through her, she follows him down the hall toward the studio.

"Ready whenever you are," Professor Tucker says.

"I'm ready," she says with confidence.

He gives her the signal, and off she goes. She does exactly what she practiced with Bree and nails her audition. Her voice is clear and concise. It is obvious by her choice of words that she has not only studied how to blend in with the station, but she's also added her own flair, making her style be known.

He slightly smiles as she turns toward him. "Thanks, Laura. Why don't you come back to my office?"

"Of course," she says as she gets up from the chair.

He enters his office. He doesn't sit in his chair. Instead, he stands before his desk and leans on it. Laura comes in the room.

"I must say, Laura, I'm not only impressed with your delivery, but I also like your ideas."

"That's great to hear," she says, trying not to seem too excited.

"I'd like to offer you the night spot. Starting next week."

"Wonderful."

"Is that a yes?" he says with a smirk.

"Yes, Professor Tucker. Yes."

"Great. Here is what it pays."

He hands her a few pieces of paper. She reviews them and agrees. It's not much, but it will sure give her that spending money she needs for school supplies and what will remain of her social life.

He leans over and extends his hand to her. She takes it.

"It will be awesome for the station to have a female DJ," he says with a smile.

Her cheeks pink. She had no idea that she would be the only one.

"Do you mean, this year?"

"No, Ms. Chase. In the last ten years. It's been a long time since we had a female on staff. Welcome to the station."

She can't help but feel elated as she gathers her bag. But she has to ask, "Really? Why is that?"

"That is a great question. It hasn't been for a lack of recruiting. I suppose we all assumed the right woman would come along eventually. You really need to want to do this job. It's long hours and late nights. That doesn't always appeal to college students."

Laura chuckles. "It's appealing to me! Thank you for the opportunity, Professor Tucker. I'll catch you next week."

"And please, in the station, call me Tucker—which is fine with me."

She smiles wide as she pulls open the door and enters the hallway. As she passes by all the guys sitting at their desks—some with headphones on, others answering calls—Laura can't help but puff her chest. She pulls open the door to the station and boasts as she leaves, "Bye, guys. See you all next week!"

Laura makes her way through the Student Union and back to Willis Hall, the dormitory she lives in with her roommate, Abigail Price. She also hit the jackpot when it came to dormitory floor mates, too. Jen, Casey, Bree, Melissa, and Maddie have all become very close over the past several months. They have come to rely on one another like sisters would as they charge through their whirlwind freshman year.

On top of the world, she enters Willis and takes the stairs up to the sixth floor. She passes Jen and Casey's room.

"Well?" Casey says with her Southern drawl as she peeks out of her room.

Laura simply smiles.

"Jen! Come out here!" Casey yells as she follows her down the hallway.

Laura knocks on Bree's door.

"Come in!" she yells.

Laura enters with Casey and Jen hot on her heels.

"Abigail, Melissa, come here!" Jen yells down the hall.

Abigail pops open their door. "What is it?"

"Laura is back."

Abigail hurries toward Bree's room. Melissa is close behind.

Abigail bursts into the room. "Well?" she asks, tucking her long blonde hair behind her ear. Her navy eyes are wide as she anticipates Laura's answer.

Everyone is surrounding Laura, but the smile alone totally gives her away. "I got the job!"

"I knew it," Bree exclaims.

"Laura, I'm so happy for you!" Abigail says as she throws her arms around her roommate.

"Laura, that is awesome!" Casey joins in on the hug.

"Want to know the best part?" Laura says as they release their embrace.

"What?" Jen asks, resting her hands on her shapely hips.

"I'm the first female DJ the school has had in a decade!" she says, barely able to contain her excitement.

"Holy shit!" Jen blurts out. "That is incredible!"

"We need to market this all over the school," Bree, the budding marketing major, says as she goes over to her desk and pulls out a notebook and pen. "This is a big deal, and we need to make certain everyone at the school knows about it."

"I know a girl on the school paper," Jen chimes in. "You know, from doing interviews with the soccer team." Jen has had her name in the paper a fair share of times, considering what a damn good midfielder she is.

"Great. We'll start there," Bree says, taking total control of the situation. "Jen, can you give me her name?"

"Absolutely. She's very cool. I'm sure she'll eat this story up, Laura," she says, turning toward her. She goes over to Bree's desk and writes her information down on the notebook. "Proud of you. This is such a huge step, and considering it is 1995, it's about damn time they had a female DJ!"

"Right!" Casey yells, pushing her chin-length, wavy reddish-brown hair back off her face. "Girls, tonight, we are going out to celebrate Laura!"

They all file into the stairwell and make their way down to the main floor of the dormitory.

Bree holds Laura's hand as they start to stroll out into the late fall evening. "Wow, you did it," she says.

"Thanks to all the coaching you gave me," Laura responds, her hazel eyes softening.

"I know," Bree says with a laugh, "but you were a good student."

"And here I thought, I was the one who was minoring in education."

"Ha! Me as a teacher? Highly unlikely. I have no patience for anyone," Bree retorts with a laugh.

"I know you'll make us proud," Abigail says with a genuine smile as she links arms with her roommate.

Laura is getting nervous as she anticipates the reaction from the school, the newspaper, and her all-male coworkers. *Will they welcome me into the station or hate the idea of me?*

Independently, the women at OSU will soon discover, just as Laura and her friends did, that this institution has not had a female DJ in a very long time.

Can I fill these shoes, and can I compete with the men who have dominated this role for ten years?

I can't believe I'm doing this. Pretty soon, everyone will know my name. Am I ready for this?

Two

AND SO IT BEGINS

"Laura, here is the studio you'll be working out of at night," Tucker says as he opens the door to Studio B.

Laura tries not to gasp as she steps in and lays her virgin eyes on the glorious display of microphones, buttons, and the classic On Air sign hanging on the wall.

"I'm curious, Laura. Why you didn't tell me who your father was?"

She whips around. "How did you know?"

"I had a feeling you knew your way around a studio all too well."

"I wanted to get the job on my own. And, with the help of Professor Rhodes and Professor Cooper, I suppose I wanted to see if I could do this."

"It wasn't hard to figure it out. Rick Chase was a pioneer for college radio back in the '60s."

"Yes, my father did love being on the radio. He called me to say he was very proud of me."

"I'll be proud of you, too, if you follow in his steps," he says with a laugh.

"Let's hope."

"Okay, a few key things before you start tonight." Tucker takes her around the room.

Thankfully, Laura spent the past week with Tucker, getting prepared for her first shift. She is comfortable with the panel; however, her nerves are still surging through her body at a rapid pace.

"You ready?"

"Yes, I am." She lets out a deliberate sigh as she smooths down her pale blue V-neck sweater.

He smiles, trying to reassure her. "We loved the article written about you in *The Weekly Blue* this week. Certain to grab some more listeners for the station."

Laura smiles. "To say my friends were a tad bit excited for me would be an understatement. They were adamant that *The Weekly Blue* write that article," she says with a laugh.

"It's good to have friends who care about you and support you. This will be a whole new chapter in your life. Pretty soon, you'll be a campus-wide name."

"I think that's why I'm nervous."

"I know you'll do great." Tucker glances at the clock. "Why don't you get settled? I'll be right in the room with Patrick." He points to the control room that is separated from her by only a pane of soundproof glass.

Once Tucker leaves, Laura wanders around the room, running her fingers over the panel and touching all the cataloged music, eagerly anticipating her first song. She sits and adjusts the height and the balance of her microphone. The rack mount feels natural to her as she leans over the board to make sure she can properly reach all the buttons.

Her heart thumps loudly as Tucker comes into the room across from her. He is with Patrick, and they get prepared on their end to hand the airwaves over to Laura. The clock on the wall says it's three minutes before eight.

She places her headphones on her ears and watches as Tucker sits down in front of the computer board. He locks eyes with her as he switches on the Silence light. She cues up her first song. Then, she takes a deep breath and releases it.

Tucker points to her and counts down—three, two, one. The On Air light illuminates.

In a concise, clear voice, Laura begins her radio career. "Good evening, Hawks. This is your newest and only female DJ, Laura Chase. I'm excited to be coming into your room tonight or wherever you might be listening to WOUR97. Hit me up at 555-WOUR and let me know what you'd like to hear. Until then, I'm going to start off the night with one of my favorites." She starts the music. "Here is 'Wonderwall' by Oasis."

Tucker and Patrick are both smiling. Tucker gives her the thumbs-up.

The next two hours go smoothly. She gets call after call, some girls congratulating her on the job and others calling in for their favorite songs.

Laura leans back in her chair as the next song plays. She's more comfortable with her surroundings as time passes.

It helped that her father had been on the radio in college and then on a local station in Upstate New York. He'd reminisce about his days as a DJ. His excitement was infectious.

"Okay. Well, I suppose I should be leaving," she says with an equally soft voice.

"You should," he says, unable to take his eyes off hers.

She brushes past him, and she opens the door to the station. As she closes it, she faintly hears him mumble. As she passes by the window, she notices him standing in the same spot where she left him, shoulders horribly hunched. She pauses and contemplates returning to the room. Then, she observes him start to pick up the mess he made, and he throws it all in the trash. She watches him with despondency, only she is unsure of why.

She pushes open the glass door of the Union and faces the cool, crisp November evening. She is no longer marinating in the excitement of her first day as a college DJ. All she can think about is her coworker back in the studio, basking in his own misery.

What has gotten you so distraught, Colin Reed?

Three

SWING AWAY

Laura arrives early at the station to give herself enough time to get prepared for her second show. She catches Tucker as he is coming out of his office and toward the control room.

"Laura, how are you?"

"Great. Hoping I might catch you for a few minutes before my shift."

"Of course. I'm about to finish up in Studio A. Come in here for a minute, and we can talk," he says, pushing open the door.

He gives the thumbs-up to the DJ, and Laura turns to see none other than Colin in the seat. He catches her eye, and she blushes. He nods to her.

"You guys meet?" Tucker asks.

"Um, yes, we did, the other night."

"Great. You need anything, you can ask Colin. I trust him fully."

She can't help but hesitate before she responds, "Yes, of course, I will ask him."

"So, how can I help you?"

"Wondering if you got the keys for me so that I can lock up tonight?"

"Shoot. I was supposed to do that today, wasn't I?" He pauses. "But don't worry; we can fix that."

"Okay, no problem. Also wanted to know if the station had any objections to playing live music…um, bootlegs, if you will. I have a few in my own collection I'd like to bring in."

"Right. Well, there doesn't seem to be much legislation around it. Consequently, if you purchased it, for now, I'll tell you that you can. I know kids come on campus and sell a lot of bootlegs. The legality of such remains a mystery for now."

"Got it. Appreciate it." Laura glances at the clock. "I'm going to get ready," she says as she turns to leave but not before glancing over at Colin as he takes a call.

He smiles slightly at her. She pulls open the door and ducks out.

Laura enters Studio B and waves to Patrick in the control booth across from her. He waves back.

She adjusts her seat and gets comfortable. She fine-tunes the microphone and cues up a few songs she brought with her to play. A few minutes later, Patrick gives her the countdown, and then she switches on her microphone, illuminating the On Air sign.

"Good evening, Hawks. This is Laura Chase, your one and only female DJ. Can you believe they allowed me to return?" She laughs. "I'm excited to be coming into your room tonight or wherever you might be listening to WOUR97. Hit me up at 555-WOUR and let me know what I can play for you. Until my first call, I get the distinct pleasure of picking my favorites. Here is Mad Season with 'River of Deceit.'"

She has another flawless start. She gets a lot of calls. Melissa, Jen, and Bree all call in with requests. She can't help but laugh as Melissa requests the only country song of the evening.

"I'm happy to play that for you, my friend from Texas. So, for all of you into grunge, enjoy a little Johnny Cash."

An hour into her show, Laura gets a call from a rather oblivious student. "Hey, can I order a large pepperoni pizza?"

"Will that be delivery or pickup?" She jokingly takes the order and says she'll drop it off after her shift.

She glances up as she laughs, playing Sublime's "Smoke Two Joints," and notices Colin standing in the control booth, smiling at her.

At the end of her shift, she hears a faint, "Hey, Laura." His voice is more formal than the other night.

She can imagine that he must be humiliated.

"Hello."

"Great job."

"Thanks." She tries to smile at him, but it is difficult to get a read on him.

"I told Tucker I'd lock up tonight."

"I see."

He stands before her in silence. He appears as though he has something to say, but instead, he turns and pulls open the door. "Take your time," he murmurs as he ducks out.

"Okay," she whispers.

She finishes shutting down the boards and cleaning up coffee cups and other assorted snack wrappers. She shuts off the lights and crosses the threshold of the main office. Colin is at his desk, working on his homework.

She clears her throat. "Late night for you?"

He spins round. "Yeah, it's quiet here. I can usually get the most work done."

"I see. I will leave you to it."

"Wait," he says with a louder tone.

Laura turns back around.

"I wanted to say that I'm sorry about last week."

She takes a step closer to him. There is sadness in his eyes. "I'm not going to lie. You scared the crap out of me. But I hope you are okay."

He smiles faintly at her and then nervously runs his hand over his face. She doesn't know him well enough to conclude with certainty that he is exhausted, but it also doesn't take a genius to know it is a fact.

"I'm sorry about that. I obviously wasn't thinking clearly." He pauses and then leaves little room for her to reply when he says, "You did really great tonight." His comment seems out of the blue.

Wanting desperately to ask him what his issue is but feeling the compliment overtake the moment, she replies, "Thanks. That means a lot. I'm still, you know...nervous, I guess."

"Don't be. You're killing it."

"Thanks. I hear you're—"

"The bit with the pizza was funny," he interjects.

Laura says with a laugh, "I hope whoever that was isn't still waiting for it."

Colin smiles wide. She is taken aback by his striking expression. It's the first time he has seemed happy or perhaps relaxed for that matter.

Laura glances at the clock on the wall. "Well, I should head out. Long day tomorrow."

"Right. Of course. I'll catch you on Wednesday."

"Good night."

"Good night, Laura," he says with cheerlessness as he turns back toward the papers on his desk.

She reaches for the door handle and hesitates for a brief second

"You forget something?" he asks.

"No." She pulls open the door and walks to the west exit of the Union.

She knows it is none of her business, but the morose tone of his voice bothers her. When she has heard him on the radio, he seems so full of life. She wishes she could stop thinking about it, but she can't seem to shake him from her mind.

When she gets back to her dorm, Abigail is fast asleep. After washing up in the bathroom, she switches on the lamp on her desk. The best part about their dorm room is the three-fourths dividing wall that separates the sleeping area from the front study area. She grabs her work notebook out of her bag and attempts to create a playlist of songs.

She stares out at the empty campus and relishes in the serene calmness these grounds exude late at night. No students to bring it to life, virtually empty walkways, lit by the old lampposts, which are perfectly aligned across the gardens. She can't help but feel somewhat lucky that she chose OSU. Considering the friends she's met and now the job at the station, she is happy—despite her puzzling encounters with Colin.

She yawns as she switches off the light on her desk. She shuffles to her bed, and with a tired mind and body, she pulls her covers up to her chin and closes her eyes.

After dinner on Wednesday with her floor mates, Laura heads over to the station early to pull her playlist before her shift.

"We'll be listening tonight," Abigail says as the girls head back toward their dorm.

Laura and Bree walk to the Union.

"What is going on with the internship? Anything new?"

"Thank God I'm done reading those boring essays," Bree says with a roll of her beautiful eyes.

Bree, in her own right, has some recognition on campus as the freshman who landed the prestigious marketing department internship. Not surprising to those who have gotten to know her over the past months. She is determined and confident.

"Finally, I'll be working on a new project. Should be much more interesting."

"That's great, Bree," Laura responds as she pulls open the door to the Union.

The two unlock their mailboxes and pull out whatever is inside.

Laura stuffs her mail in her bag. "Want to grab a coffee?"

Bree glances at her watch and then out the window. "Shoot, I can't. I've gotta run to my internship. Sorry! Next time." She pulls her coat tight around her waist as an early snowfall trickles down from the sky in front of the Union. She turns on her expensive heels and heads down the hall toward the back exit.

"Okay!" Laura yells after her.

"Good luck tonight," she says as she pulls open the back door and hurries out into the brisk evening.

Lying in Wait

Laura enters the station. Most of the staff have left for the night, and there is only one programmer and one engineer left. She knocks on Tucker's office, but there is no answer. She goes over to Studio A and opens the door to the programming room.

"Hey, Patrick. Professor Tucker gone?"

"Yeah, but he left the keys on your desk. And he is cool with you calling him Tucker."

"Right. I know. Hard to get used to, but thanks."

She peeks into the booth, and Colin is staring at her.

"See you later."

She heads to Studio B. She switches on the radio and listens to Colin's show. After about an hour, she is ready for her own shift. With her headphones on, she swings around in her chair and leans into the microphone. With the seconds counted down from Patrick, the On Air light is on.

The phone lines immediately light up.

She smiles as she opens up her introduction by taking a caller. "Hello, this is Laura. What can I help you with this evening?"

The caller bursts out, "My stupid boyfriend dumped me after a year." The girl on the phone starts to cry.

"Wow. Sorry to hear that."

"He did it over the phone!"

"I can't be certain, but it sounds like he did you a favor."

"A favor?" she asks.

"Yeah. Who wants to date a guy who doesn't have the gall to break up with you—after a year, no less—to your face?"

In the background, she can hear the caller sniffle.

"Yeah, I guess you're right."

"Keep in touch and let me know if I'm right."

"I will."

"Good. This song is for you. Here's 'You Learn' by Alanis Morissette."

After she plays the song, the phone lines stay lit almost the entire evening. She gets into a rhythm of answering calls and chatting with the listeners. She fluidly goes from one call to the next, and before she knows it, her time is up.

"Last caller. Good evening."

"Hey, Laura. Can you play 'I'll Stick Around' by the Foo Fighters for my girlfriend, Shannon?" the male caller asks.

"You've got it. A perfect song to end the night. Thank you all for listening, and I hope you'll come back next time. Good night."

She switches off her microphone. She whirls around in her chair, claps her hands, and starts to get up. "Whoa, another night done. Success!" she says in a whisper to herself. Quickly she realizes she is not alone.

"I guess we're even now," Colin says with a smile. He is wearing a well-fitted T-shirt and jeans. His hair is pushed back off his face, allowing his eyes to be the main focus.

"You startled me," she responds. She can feel the heat make its way into her cheeks. She nervously tucks her hair behind her ear.

"Sorry. I wanted to come in and say congrats on a good night. You had a lot of callers."

"Thanks. It felt good tonight. I'm, you know, slowly finding my rhythm."

"You are. And if you stick with it long enough you can get moved out of the crappy late night shift. We've all been there. We've all had to do it," he chuckles.

"I don't mind it so far. I'm sort of a night owl anyways." She smiles at him. "You were good tonight, too."

"You listened?"

"Yes, of course." She nervously pulls at the string on her OSU Hawks sweatshirt.

"Cool. Thanks."

"Is Patrick still here? I want to—"

"No. I told him I'd lock up."

"I have keys now."

"Yeah, I know, but I figured someone should at least take you through all this," he responds with a boyish smile.

"Right. Sorry. Of course. Thank you."

His gaze forces her to lower her eyes. "Whenever you're ready," he adds as he turns and opens the door to the studio.

After she gathers her bag and notebook, she enters the main area. Colin is standing in the room, leaning on his desk. Headphones around his neck, backpack slung over one shoulder and a skateboard sticking out of it.

"I'm ready," she says as she pulls on her jacket.

"Great. We keep these lights on over here on night mode. Tucker asks that we lock his office, the two studios, and the main door. That way, all the equipment is somewhat under lock and key should anyone not authorized get in here."

"Okay. I locked Studio B already."

"Great. I checked the rest. All we need to do is lock the main door."

Laura follows him out, and he turns to lock the door behind them.

"Thanks, Colin. Appreciate you staying."

"Of course. Where do you live?"

"In Willis. You?"

"In Simmons. But I'm hoping to get into Parkers Village next year. Or maybe off-campus. Basically anyplace but the dorms."

She chuckles. "What year are you?"

"Sophomore."

"Oh," Laura says. She was half-expecting him to be older by the way he knew his way around the studio.

"Hey, let me escort you to your dorm."

"No, you don't have to do that."

"I know. But it's late, and I'd feel better about it."

"Okay…thanks."

They exit the doors of the Union.

"How do you like working at the station?"

"It's good. But, I don't really know anyone."

He laughs.

"You know, besides you, Tucker, and Patrick, but he hardly says a word to me."

"The engineer guys are all like that. The DJs call them *the quiet ones*," he jokes. "They are not as interested in chatting it up like we have to. It's nothing personal. Patrick and Ryker are cool, and Sean, the other DJ, he's a good friend of mine."

"Honestly, being the only girl can be intimidating."

"I can imagine," he says with sincere eyes.

They cross over the street toward Willis.

"Thank you for taking me home. I do appreciate you looking out for me."

"Anytime." He smiles. "Hey, this Saturday, a bunch of us are getting together down at Monroe's before the holiday. You should come. It will be a good way to get to know the guys."

"You think it will be okay?"

"Okay? Of course. You're one of us now." He smiles as he takes his skateboard out and puts it on the ground.

"I suppose I am. Do I need an ID?"

"Nah. Come around eight. Tell them you work at the station, and you shouldn't have a problem."

"Okay then. I will meet you all on Saturday."

"Night," he says as he pushes off on his board.

"Night," Laura calls after him. She watches his long body weave from side to side as he glides on his skateboard back through campus.

She unlocks the door to Willis Hall. She is about to pull the heavy metal and glass door open when she hears a distinct rustle in the bushes embracing the cement wall of the dormitory. Her skin prickles.

She calls out, "Hello? Someone there?"

She squints in the darkness to try to get a better look, but the dull neon lights of the building are overtaken by the darkness of the late evening hour. The movements stop. Suddenly, through the dark, a figure of some kind is hugging the wall and escaping into the campus grounds. A creepy sensation runs up and down her body. As quickly as possible she yanks the door open and hurries inside.

Four

HERE COMES TROUBLE

Colin enters Monroe's about quarter of eight. A few of the guys from the station are already in the back, playing pool.

He grabs a beer from the bartender. "Hey, Bones. Our newest DJ is supposed to be joining us tonight."

"No shit. Laura? She's awesome."

"Yeah." *She sure is.*

"Cool. No problem."

"Thanks, Bones." He heads back to meet the guys from the station. "What's up?"

"Not much," Patrick says, pushing back his glasses. "Want to play next?"

"Definitely."

Once Ryker, Patrick's engineer buddy with the deep blue eyes and wavy brown hair, sinks his last shot, Colin racks up the balls to play Patrick. As he leans over to break, Laura comes in the door. He tries to concentrate, but he is immediately struck by how gorgeous she is. She has on a little more makeup than usual, and he kind of likes it on her. She seems nervous as she tucks her hair behind her ear and eagerly glances around the room.

Colin leans back up and hands the cue to Sean, his muscular sidekick with a sharply defined jawline. "Hey, man, play for me, will you?"

"It would be my pleasure to kick Patrick's ass." He takes the stick.

Colin meanders toward the center of the bar. He watches Laura spin around. She gives him a striking smile. His breath catches.

"Hey," she says over the music.

"Hey. Glad you could come. Want a drink?" he asks.

"Sure, that sounds good."

Bones, the bartender, immediately comes over. "Hey, Laura."

Colin can tell she is not used to being noticed. Her cheeks become rosy.

"Hey," she responds shyly.

"Congratulations on the gig," he adds.

"Thank you." She lowers her eyes.

"What can I get you?"

"I'll have a Natty Light."

"I'll take another one, too," Colin adds.

Bones pops the caps on the beers.

"Come on. The guys are going to be psyched you came." He motions for her to follow him to the pool table.

"Hey, guys," she says, removing her coat.

Colin tries not to stare as he admires the tight white long-sleeved shirt she has on and the jeans resting low on her hips.

"You play pool?" he asks.

"Sort of."

"Okay, well, sort of is better than no. So, next game?" he asks hopefully.

She smiles. "Why not?"

"Laura and I have next game," Colin announces.

He watches her out of the corner of his eye as she nervously tears at the label on her beer bottle.

"You ready for the break?"

"Yeah. A few more exams, and I'll be ready to get out of here."

"Where is home for you?" he asks.

"Stockbridge, Massachusetts. You?"

"Saratoga Springs, New York."

She chuckles. "No kidding. My roommate is from Glens Falls."

"That's cool. Small world sometimes, right?"

"Yeah, it can be."

"Come on. Let's play." He grabs a pool cue.

After three long games of pool, she says with a laugh, "Should we give up the table? I'm terrible, and these poor guys have been waiting so patiently. I couldn't win if you handed it to me."

Colin laughs as he returns his pool cue. "It appears so." He asks the group, "Another beer, anyone?"

Sean nods his head.

"I'll get them. It's the least I can do," Laura says.

She goes over to the bar, orders a few beers, and brings them back to the guys. Colin starts to grab the beer from Laura's hand when he freezes. With narrowed and hate-filled eyes, he stares across the room at something...or someone.

"I'll be right back," he growls.

Sean and Laura watch as he storms off.

"Oh boy," Sean whispers. "This ought to be good."

Colin approaches a table with three girls. He turns to the pretty girl with long chestnut-brown hair.

"Hey, Colin."

"Joey, what are you doing here?" he snarls. He is not holding back his feelings whatsoever.

"Having a drink with Amanda and Nicole, obviously." Her voice has the usual bitchy edge to it.

"I can see that."

"Hi, Colin," Amanda says coyly.

He clenches his fists as he focuses on Joey. "Can I talk to you…alone?"

"I'll be right back," Joey says to the girls.

Colin marches toward the back part of the bar. Joey is hot on his heels.

"What the hell are you trying to pull?" he starts.

"You won't see me, and I knew you'd be here with the station guys for your holiday soirée. I had to come here and try to talk to you before the break. You've left me no choice."

"Of course I won't see you." He tries to contain his emotions, but he is like a caged tiger.

"Colin, I miss you, and I feel remorseful. Don't you know that?"

"Remorseful?"

"Yes, I'm sorry." She caresses the collar on his shirt.

He grabs her hand. "Don't."

"Please, Colin, let me at least try to make it up to you. You can't shut me out."

"Says who?"

"You. I know you, Colin. This is not you."

"Do you, Joey? Because maybe, if you did, you wouldn't have…"

"Please let me try to explain. After that, if you don't want me anymore, then fine. I'll walk away."

Her sad, big brown eyes soften, and he unexpectedly feels his heart start to soften, too. He doesn't want it to, but it's happening regardless.

He glances over at his coworkers. They are all enthralled in their own conversations, including Laura.

The alcohol clouds his judgment. Joey's blouse is open at the top, and his mind floods with memories of some of the good times.

"Fine. One chance to explain, Joey," he barks.

"Let me grab my coat," she says as she saunters over toward the table with her friends.

He grabs his jacket from the peg by the front and holds open the door as he allows Joey to go ahead of him.

Once outside, she says, "Come back to my place, okay? My roommates aren't home. We can talk there."

"No," he says.

It's freezing out, but she is hot. That doesn't make it easy on him. Her coat flaps open in the wind, exposing her tight body.

But that's not her problem. It's mine.

"Joey, I'm here to talk. That's it." He shoves his hands deep into his pockets.

"I know," she says softly.

"Fine," he repeats. Colin's chest heaves as he envisions the last time he was in her room. It was the time he caught her in bed with someone else. "This was a mistake." He tries to turn and leave.

She steps in front of him. "Colin, please don't go. I slipped up, and I want you back."

"You cheated on me." He can hardly lock eyes with her.

"I know," she says, lowering her head.

Joey is gorgeous; anyone with eyes can see that. But she lacks a sense of compassion that Colin could never quite place before. There is something very cold about her. They dated for over a year—which, in college years, it might as well have been ten years. She is a year older than him, and for some reason, her popularity as a party girl on campus and him as a DJ on the radio made for a good but, at times, crazy relationship.

"How can I possibly take you back?"

"It was a stupid, drunken night, and I regret it with every muscle in my body." Tears start to form in her eyes as she gazes up at him. "Please, Colin, you didn't even let me try to explain…"

"Explain," he responds in a loud voice. "What is there to explain?" He is too drunk to be doing this now. He should have known better.

"Colin, please," she coos as she slowly places her hands around his waist.

He twitches at her touch. It's been weeks since he's touched her. Touched anyone for that matter.

"Joey, don't."

"Don't what?" she whispers.

"Do what you are doing…"

She releases her hands from around his waist. He glances in the window of the bar and contemplates his next move. His mind wanders to Laura. He feels badly for leaving his station buddies.

He starts to turn. "I think I—" He stops and watches the confident smile spread across Joey's face. As though she knows he'd be a fool not to take her back. She gets what she wants. Always.

This irritates him and is very typical of her. She thinks she can do no wrong. He flips a switch.

"Joey, I am asking you to give me some space," he whispers, shaking his head. "I was trying to have a nice night with my coworkers, and you took that from me, too."

The harder women like Joey make you fall, the harder it is to get over them. That's Joey in a nutshell. She makes damn certain that you can't walk away from her. Little did Colin know that, when they met his freshman year, she'd cause him so much pain today.

She calls after him as he walks up the hill and away from the bar. He knows he can't stay if she is in there. He also knows he doesn't want Laura to see him pissed off. No one wants that at a bar. They are all there to blow off steam and get to know her. He can't let his drama get in the way of that.

Colin arrives at Studio A with only fifteen minutes to go before his shift.

"You're late," Tucker says.

"I know. I'm sorry."

Professor Tucker narrows his eyes at him. He knows it is unlike Colin to be late—that is, until these past few weeks of school. His mood and behavior have become unpredictable. Much like the rumors about his relationship with Joey.

"Want to talk about it?"

"No."

"Things with you and Joey okay?"

"No, not really."

"Anything you need from me?"

Colin shakes his head as he avoids meeting Professor Tucker's eyes.

"Okay. All I ask is that you make sure it doesn't get in the way— whatever it is," he adds as he leaves the room.

Colin mindlessly goes through his shift. At one point, Patrick gives him a questioning expression as he plays Nine Inch Nails' "Closer" when a caller asks for something completely different. At the end of his shift, he throws his headphones down as Patrick comes in the room.

"Dude, rough day?"

"Shit. Sorry, Patrick. I'm having an off day. Totally my bad."

"It's okay. It happens."

"Hey, where's Ryker?" Colin asks about the other engineer.

"Oh, man, wicked sick. Has the flu."

"Bummer. Right before the break."

"Yeah, I'm pulling double duty tonight," Patrick says with a yawn.

"Let me help. I was going to stick around and study anyway. So, what can I do?"

"Really? That would be huge. I've got to finish my final project."

"No worries."

"Let me get Laura all set, and I'll grab you in a few."

The sound of her name runs a chill down his spine. "Cool. I'll be at my desk."

Colin will do anything at this point to come up with an excuse not to be in his place. He has felt conflicted about his breakup with Joey. When he left the bar the other night, he wondered whether or not everyone deserved a second chance or if this was simply the perfect opportunity for him to walk away. But, despite him asking for space, Joey has continued to call him, leaving messages of apologies.

What if she really is sorry? We all make mistakes, don't we?

He sits at his desk and listens to Laura take call after call. She is on point tonight, far better than he was.

About an hour into her shift, Patrick comes in. "You mind keeping an eye on the board for the rest of her shift? She's in good shape. I don't foresee any issues."

"No problem. It will be fine."

Over the past year and a half, Colin has learned how to work the boards as well. Tucker taught everyone here how to maneuver their way around all the systems. He always says they are one big team, not a group of individuals.

He takes a deep breath before opening the door to the sound room. He can feel his cheeks flush as she catches sight of him. He feels terrible for the other night and hopes she is not pissed he left her with the rest of the guys.

Why would she be? She works with them, too. She probably didn't even realize I'd left.

As the hour winds down, he is in awe of how well she handles the callers. In the last month, they have certainly seemed to take a liking to her. She is massing quite a following.

As she switches off her mic and the On Air sign goes off, he gets up, and with hesitation, he enters Studio B.

"Hey."

"Hey," she says softly back.

She looks awesome tonight. Tight green sweater with low-cut jeans. Her eyes are bright and alive, her hair perfectly smoothed behind her ears.

"Great night," he says, barely able to meet her eyes.

"Thanks. Um, what are you doing here?" she asks.

"Sorry. Patrick needed to leave to get some work done."

"Okay. I'll hurry, so you can get out of here."

"No, it's just that…"

She leans up against the desk.

"You know, the other night at Monroe's…"

"Yeah, you left." Her voice is agitated, only he is perplexed as to why.

"I know, and I'm usually not like that…leaving without saying anything."

"I know. Sean told me." Now, her eyes look sad.

"He did?"

"Yeah, I'm assuming she's the reason you were upset that night."

If she only knew.

"See, I…we…"

Her eyes get larger as he says *we*.

"We had to talk about something," he mumbles.

"You don't need to explain. It's fine," she says.

"I was hoping to stay."

"Okay," she says, with a tip of her head to the side.

"But I didn't, and now…well, I suppose—"

There is a quick bang on the glass. Startled, Colin whips around. Standing in the booth, glaring in at the two of them, is none other than Joey herself.

She pulls open the door, and with the fakest smile, she says, "Hello. Am I interrupting?"

"Joey?" he stutters.

Laura stands there, frozen, and he feels terrible that she is out of sorts.

"Uh, Joey, this is Laura, the new DJ—"

"Yes, newest female DJ, of course. The whole campus knows about her, Colin." She steps forward and reaches out her hand to Laura. "Nice to meet you."

"You, too," Laura says.

"How did you get in here?"

"You gave me a key, silly," she boasts.

"Oh shit. Right. Tucker wants that back," he lies.

She narrows her eyes at him, clearly disapproving of his remark. "Wasn't your shift over a few hours ago?"

Colin grits his teeth. "Yes, but I'm still working."

"No problem. I'll wait while you finish, and I can drive you home. We can finish our conversation."

He turns to Laura. "I have some things to do here…"

"It's fine. I'm almost done anyway." She picks up her notebook and bag and starts to shut down the lights in the room.

"Joey, I'll have to call you later, okay?"

Joey stands before him, sexy, demanding, and clearly without boundaries. He is trapped with no way out.

She stares him down for a moment, and then, like a switch flips, she says, "Sure thing. But please do. It's important." She spins on her heel.

Laura and Colin watch as she leaves the room.

Once she is gone, Colin turns to her.

He starts to say something when Laura quips, "I've got this. Really, Colin. Don't worry."

But I want to worry. He searches her face. He steps toward the door and closes it. "Listen, Joey and I used to date, and...well, the night you and I met, I'd found her in bed with someone else."

She gasps internally at his admission. "I see. I'm very sorry to hear that."

"So, as you can imagine, I've been having a rough time. God, that is hard to admit." He plops down in the chair. "We were having so much fun at the bar. Then, she came along, and it just ruined my mood," he confesses. "So, I left."

"You needed to be alone. I get it."

"She can get the best of me. She doesn't always take a hint. She has very few limitations."

"I can see that," Laura adds. "It seems like this break from school is coming at the perfect time for you."

"Yes, it is. And I guess I just wanted to say that I'm sorry I just took off. I've not been quite myself lately."

"Understandable." She tries to smile, but the air in the room is thick with sadness.

"Can I walk you home?" He smiles as he stands.

Laura gets the sense he needs to walk her home more than she requires it. So, she graciously replies, "That would be very nice of you."

They exit the Union to the beauty of newly fallen snow. Not a single person is in sight on campus as they walk toward her dormitory. In silence, they stroll down the brick walkways and arrive at her door.

"Hey," he says as she puts the key in the lock. "I appreciate you listening."

He leans down and gives her a hug, much to her surprise. She hugs him back, and she feels his shoulders relax.

He releases her. "I'll talk to you after the break."

"Merry Christmas."

"You, too." Colin starts to walk away when he turns and says, "Practice your pool game during the holidays. I'm going to need you to step it up." He chuckles.

Laura smiles and waves good-bye as she enters her building. As Colin treks back toward his dormitory, he pauses in the middle of the deserted campus and glances up toward the sky. In childlike fashion, he reaches out his hand and catches the falling snow. He smiles as he enjoys a much-needed moment of peace.

Five

ROUGH NIGHTS LEAD TO BETTER DAYS

Laura has spent the first month of second semester heavily involved as a math tutor at a local school for fourth-grade kids. She is earning extra credits toward her major since, sometimes, her class and work schedule at the station aren't always in sync. Her academic advisor has been willing to work with her because of her excellent grades and her job at the school.

"College is meant to teach you about life," she said to Laura one day. "And that means, finding a balance."

She was getting into a rhythm and thought she had found equilibrium in her life. That was, until Valentine's weekend when Laura's otherwise happy world with her floor mates abruptly came crashing down around her.

As they all gather in Laura's room, they could not have prepared themselves for the news they were about to hear.

"Abigail, what is it?" Laura asks.

Her head hangs low as she whispers, "I left the party last night, alone. I wanted to go see Nathan."

"Abigail, you're scaring us. What happened to you?" Melissa's caramel-colored eyes are wide.

"I could faintly hear other students leaving the party. I could hear the sounds of their feet on the hard snow. And then he called my name." She is barely making sense.

"Who did?" Jen asks.

"I-I kept my head down and tried to concentrate on the path ahead. The trees were thick, so it was hard to see, and my foot throbbed more and more as I stepped on the heavy snow." Her chest starts to heave.

"Abigail," Laura pleads, "please tell us what happened."

She starts to shake. "He told me to wait for him. I started to turn toward him, but he violently threw his arms around me and pulled me back, forcing my body against his. I went to scream when he clasped his other hand over my face. It was hard to breathe. He told me, if I didn't shut up, he'd hurt me more."

"Holy shit," Casey mumbles.

Abigail cries, "I started to scream, so he knocked me back and pushed me up against a tree. He yanked open my coat. He…he ripped my shirt. Then, he grabbed my hands and jerked them behind me."

Laura rushes to the bed and envelops her broken friend.

Through muffled sobs, she admits, "He kissed me, hard, and I wanted to shout or struggle, but ultimately, I was paralyzed with fear."

"How did you get out of there?" Jen asks.

Abigail peers up. "Tank. It was Tank. He saved me by knocking the guy to the ground."

Tank—her boyfriend, Nathan's, football teammate—is a massive human being. There is little doubt that the guy he struck wasn't hurt badly.

"Thank God!" Melissa gasps.

"He carried me to Nathan's and called the police."

"What did the police say?"

"Not much, but I got the feeling there is more to this…"

And there is more. Much more.

The campus is abuzz with rumors of a serial attacker wreaking havoc on university grounds all over New York State. There have been a few articles written in *The Weekly Blue* about attacks at other universities, but now, it extends to OSU. Unfortunately, the volume of girls coming forward—saying that they, too, were assaulted—is astonishing. It's no longer their dark secret to keep. The ugliness is being exposed. College life as they have all known it is quickly changing, and there is nothing anyone can do to stop it.

That is exactly why the campus feels different now than it used to merely a few short months ago. Now, women travel in groups. It's rare to see a woman alone. And men who are out, unaccompanied, are eyed suspiciously by any passing group. Athletes are being questioned by their coaches and some by local police. Everyone's whereabouts are in question; no one is exempt. Mix the staggering cold February air that has graced New York State with the uneasiness on campus, and the school feels like it is in the beginning stages of a bona fide lockdown.

Lying in Wait

On this particular night, Laura, Melissa, and Maddie enter the Union. They've decided to escort Laura to her shift for the next couple of weeks until things settle down. More importantly, Laura tries to keep an irregular schedule, as suggested by campus security.

"*Don't be a creature of habit. Make different changes each day, but more importantly, stick together as friends and members of this campus community,*" their dorm monitor, Brittney, read verbatim from the paper at a floor meeting last week.

"Thanks, girls. Appreciate you walking me. Patrick said he'd take me back."

"Okay, cool. Good luck tonight. We'll be listening," Melissa says with a smile.

"Thanks. And you'll check in on Abigail for me?"

"Of course."

"Great. Appreciate it."

She pulls open the door to the station, and much to Laura's surprise, Joey is marching out.

"Hey, Laura," she says with a sickly sweet smile.

"Hey, Joey." As she passes her, she gets a funny feeling in the pit of her stomach that she can't place.

Laura heads down to Studio B and switches on the lights. She sits in her chair for a few minutes before turning on the equipment. Her mind is racing with all sorts of thoughts about her friends and what's happening on campus. She starts to ponder her playlist. She wants to try to lift up the campus, not keep it down with sad and depressing songs. But sad and depressing songs are all that keep popping into her mind.

She switches on her microphone. She glances up at Ryker in the booth and then says, "Good evening, Hawks. This is Laura Chase, and thanks for listening to WOUR97. Call me at 555-WOUR and let me know how I can raise you up. Until then, here is Radiohead with 'Creep.'"

An appropriate song title, unfortunately.

Ryker gives her the thumbs-up as the phone lines light up like a Christmas tree.

"Good evening. This is Laura."

"Hey, Laura."

"Hello, caller."

"Um, hi. This is Tiffany. How do I get a guy in my class to notice me?"

Laura can't help but chuckle. "I'm no expert, but what I can do is play a song for him."

"Okay."

"What's his name?"

"Justin."

"Okay then. I hope you're listening, Justin. This is for you." She switches on Matthew Sweet's "Sick of Myself."

"Hello, caller. You are on the air."

"Hey. I'm worried about all these attacks on women that I'm hearing about on campus," the caller begins.

"I know. We all are."

"What do we do about it?"

"Well, for one, we must all be diligent with being aware of our surroundings."

"Yeah, I guess. I'm scared, if I'm being honest."

Laura looks up and catches Ryker's stare. His expression is gloomy. He gives her a slight nod to continue.

"I know. We all are. So, we need to be on alert and not let our friends go places alone." She pauses and starts to reflect on how maybe she has been given a golden opportunity to keep the campus from falling into a deep depression over things no one can control. "But you called me because you want me to try to make you feel better, right?"

"Yeah, we could all use it."

"Agreed. Therefore, I'll play Joey Lawrence's 'Nothing My Love Can't Fix.'"

Laura hears laughter, and then the caller says, "Seriously?"

Laura starts to laugh, too. "Absolutely not."

Instead, she plays "Cannonball" by The Breeders. She looks up. Ryker is laughing hysterically. She smiles wide as she sits back in her chair.

After her shift, Ryker comes in the room.

"No Patrick tonight?" Laura asks, as he is supposed to bring her home.

"No, he covered for me a few times, and he needed to get something done tonight."

"I see. Cool."

"Hey, I'll let you finish up in here," he says as he exits.

Laura finishes cleaning up and shuts down the equipment. She is about to turn off the small light near the desk when she hears, "Joey Lawrence? Really?"

She whips around. "What's wrong with Joey Lawrence?" she tries to say with a straight face.

Colin smiles. "Oh, nothing. I'm his biggest fan. The guy is awesome."

"Wow." She smiles wide. "We finally have something in common." She can't help but laugh.

"It only took us four months to figure it out."

He looks good tonight in his blue-and-green-striped sweater and jeans. His hair is longer, and it suits him. She grabs her backpack. He holds open the door for her and allows her to go out first. As she passes him, she catches his cologne and gently closes her eyes as she takes it in. It's crisp and light, like jasmine or citrus bound to a hint of leather.

She enters into the main room to find no one is there. "Where is Ryker?"

"He left."

"Oh," she says with obvious disappointment.

"Need something?" he asks.

"Patrick was going to bring me home, and then I thought that maybe he told Ryker—"

"I've got you," he says, grabbing his jacket and bag. "Chopped liver at your service."

Cheeks fiery red, she says, "Oh no, I didn't mean it like that."

"Of course you didn't," he responds with a wink.

Something about the way he looks at her with his bright crystal-blue eyes makes her skin tingle.

"Right," she says quietly as he starts to turn off the lights.

Practically in the dark now, the two find themselves facing one another in agonizing silence.

"Ready whenever you are," he says softly.

"Of course." She turns on her heel and heads toward the door.

The Student Union is empty as they stroll down the hallway toward the west entrance.

"Brace yourself," he says. "It's cold tonight." He pulls his knit hat out of his bag and goes to put it on.

Laura pulls the collar on her jacket up over her ears

"No hat?" he adds.

"No. Forgot it."

"Here, take mine."

"No, I wouldn't dream of—"

But, before she can finish, he steps in front of her and gently places it on her head.

"Cute." He smiles wide at her as she bashfully lowers her eyes.

It's the way he eyes me. I can't explain it, but I just know, every time he does, I get goose pimples.

"Now, let's do this." Much to her surprise, he takes her hand in his.

She can feel the warmth of his skin on hers. He pulls her toward the door.

He is right; it's freezing out, and the wind makes it feel about thirty degrees below zero. The cold air catches her breath as she steps out of the Student Union.

"This is the coldest it has been so far," she remarks. Her eyes water as a brush of stony air whips across her face.

"Yeah, it gets cold here."

They head down the walkway and toward the cafeteria.

"How are things?" Laura asks.

"Things are good, I suppose."

"I saw Joey leave the station. Everything okay?"

"Yeah, I guess. She had to ask me something."

"Did she forget there are telephones for that?" Laura replies, trying to lighten the conversation.

"Right?" He laughs.

"Well, at least she seemed like she was cheery."

He cocks his head to the side, and with a confused expression, he asks, "She did?"

"Yeah. I mean, to me, she seemed fine. But what do I know?"

"Can we talk about something else? How are you doing?"

"Sure. I'm good. Lots going on with friends, school and all that."

"I know; you seem very busy. Don't be afraid to let off a little steam now and again. It's good for you."

"I know. It's just, sometimes, the days seem to fly by with homework, the station, and lately, my friends…"

"Sounds like you need another night out at Monroe's."

Laura gives him a quizzical glance. They cross the street and head toward Willis Hall.

"Next time everyone goes, let me know." She takes off his hat. "Here, for your walk back."

His expression is one of anguish, and he slowly reaches out and takes the hat. "Well, that's kind of what I wanted to ask…"

Laura glances past him, toward the front door of her dormitory. She notices Abigail hurrying through the lobby of their dorm, hysterically crying.

"I'm so sorry, Colin. I have to go," Laura blurts out.

"Oh, right. Okay. Well, I was hoping I could ask you—oh, good night."

Laura already has the first glass door to her dormitory open. It shuts behind her as she pulls open the next one. He watches her for a moment as she runs up the stairs. By her sudden movement, it's clear to Colin that something is very wrong.

Laura sprints up the stairs, two at a time, trying to catch up with Abigail. She finally catches her in their room. She is wiping her eyes with a tissue.

"Abigail, what is it?"

Abigail turns to her with bloodshot eyes. "I'm afraid I've lost Nathan—for good," she blurts out.

"What? Why?" she asks.

Deep down though, she has a funny feeling that she knows why. Over the past few months, Abigail has developed this peculiar relationship with Nathan's teammate, Tank.

"I don't know," she lies.

The thing about Abigail is that she is a terrible liar. Laura can see right through her. But, in order for someone to come clean, they have to be ready to.

"Okay. What did he say?"

"He was mad about me going out the other night with Tank, and you know what he did?" she states, raising her voice. What she failed to truly state was how late she had been out with Tank and how stinking drunk she had been when she finally returned to the dormitory.

"What?" Laura says with wide eyes.

"He got Tank kicked off the football team."

Laura gasps, "No way. Not Nathan." *Because he just might be the nicest guy at school.*

"I know. I almost can't believe it. But it's true. He could lose his scholarship and everything. All because of me."

"Because of you?" Laura can hardly believe this crazy tale.

"Yeah, I guess they told Tank that his friendship with me was causing too many issues for the team and that he needed to cool down and get it together."

By issues, she means, the late nights with Tank, the major attitude problem Tank has toward just about anyone, except Abigail, and Tank's clear inability to stay sober enough to think for himself that his scholarship might be in jeopardy due to his actions and his actions alone.

"That seems a little far-fetched to me."

"What?" she says defensively.

Laura nervously tucks her hair behind her ear. "Do you actually believe the coaches care about what happens in the players' personal lives?"

"They must, Laura, or this wouldn't be happening," she responds with frustration and then collapses back on her bed. "I screwed up, Laura," she whispers.

"Screwed up how?" Laura asks.

"I can't explain it."

The silence in the room is thick. The continuous web of lies Abigail has spun is the reason she is where she is today.

How does she not see this?

"Can I say one thing, as your friend?"

Abigail sits up, propping herself on her elbows. "Sure."

"Ever since Tank came into your life, he has brought you nothing but trouble."

I've seen him try to put a wedge between you and everyone who loves you, including me. He treats me like dirt, and I barely know the guy. Laura wishes she had the balls to say that.

Abigail's navy eyes grow increasingly wide, and then they fill with tears. "He-he saved me that night," she cries. "I can't forget that." The pain in her voice is real.

Laura comes close to her bed and gently lowers herself next to her. "I know," Laura says as she pulls her friend in for a deep hug. She holds her tight. "But it is much more than that, so much bigger than you and him."

Abigail pushes Laura away. With an indignant expression, she implores, "Look, there are things about Tank that I can't tell you or Nathan or anyone, and I know it's not right, but until I figure it out and feel comfortable doing so, then…well, I guess I'm just asking that you trust me. I thought Nathan would. But all he can see is jealousy, and he has nothing to be jealous about."

"Really? You don't have feelings for Tank?"

Abigail inhales sharply, and Laura knows she has hit a nerve.

"Only as a friend."

"To the outside world, it doesn't seem that way," she presses.

Shoulders hunched, Abigail whispers, "I know. But it's true."

"I'm sorry you are sad."

There is nothing for me to do. I can't help you if you won't let me in!

"I just need to figure this out…on my own."

Laura, defeated and blue, simply gets up and makes her way down the hall to the bathroom. Her eyes fill with tears as she thinks of her friend Abigail and the heartache she is feeling after losing Nathan.

Laura has always had difficulty with not being able to solve an issue on the spot. Hence her wanting to major in mathematics. One correct answer at a time. Simple.

But what she cannot comprehend is Abigail's inability to lean on a friend in her time of sorrow. There must be more to this. It's not simple. It's complicated.

Lying in Wait

The next morning, Laura stares out the window of her classroom, clearly unable to concentrate. She is merely waiting for the time to pass. She hoped that Abigail would confide in her about all the secrets she'd been keeping. The secret nights out with Tank. The book with the drawing and love letters. Hell, even the flowers she'd gotten from him for Valentine's Day that she tried to pin on Laura right in front of Nathan. She hated being looped into her lies, particularly to Nathan. He is such a great guy, and Abigail is a fool if she pushes him away.

She has the power to stop this, but why won't she?

Laura heads back to her dorm after her last class. She enters her room to find that Abigail is not there. She locks up their room and decides to head to lunch, alone. Unlucky for her, she runs into Bree in the hallway. She looks pale, like maybe she has been sick or something.

Laura is about to ask her if she is okay when, in typical Bree fashion, she snaps, "I guess I can go to lunch with you." Bree, ever the bitch when the wind takes her.

Laura is in no mood for her today. It happens. She's human after all. Laura's blood starts to boil, and she is about to say, *I didn't invite you,* but instead, she pacifies her inner self, faintly smiles, and responds, "Sounds good." Typical Laura.

They enter the cafeteria and don't say another word to each other as they go their separate ways and get their usual lunches. Meeting back at the table, Bree loudly puts her tray down. Laura jumps. She glares at her through the corner of her eye.

Laura picks at her sandwich, taking small bites, as she has most definitely lost her appetite. She watches with complete annoyance as Bree stabs her fork in her salad but never once eats a single bite.

Laura sighs.

"What is your problem?" Bree barks.

In no mood for her bitchiness, Laura quips back, "What's wrong with you?"

She can tell she has shocked Bree, and for once, she doesn't care.

How come no one ever asks me how my day is going? My floor mates are so consumed with their own issues that they think they can just toss me aside when I'm not needed. Abigail and Bree are supposed to be my best friends and yet they are so absorbed with their own drama they stopped asking me how I'm doing. I'm tired of being in second place around here.

"What, did your dog die or something?" she snarls.

"Me, huh? I'm the one with the problem. Maybe if you actually cared to ask," Laura hisses back.

"What is that supposed to mean?" she says in an equally prissy tone.

"You don't care about anyone but yourself," Laura blurts out as she abruptly gets up and leaves the table.

She puts her tray on the conveyer belt to the kitchen and busts out of the side door of the cafeteria. Not wanting to go back to her dorm, she heads to the only other place she knows where she can find some peace—the station.

She finds it quite busy for this time of day. Ryker and Patrick turn to her as the door shuts.

"Hey, Laura," Patrick says.

"Hi, guys," she says on the verge of tears.

"They are cutting some promos in Studio B, so unfortunately, it is preoccupied," Patrick says.

"Shit," she whispers under her breath.

Afraid she might burst into tears, she hurries down the hallway to Studio A. Laura rushes into the control room of Studio A and is thankful no one is in there. She turns into the corner of the room and starts to cry. She is exhausted from schoolwork, math tutoring, late nights at the station, and the drama that consumes everyone at college. She wishes she could just snap her fingers and make it all go away. She has continued to watch her friend Abigail spiral into a deep hole, and she hasn't been able to get through to her. She knows she has failed. On top of that mess, she hates that she yelled at Bree. It's unlike her to lash out like that.

What is causing all of this? she wonders as she stands with her hands over her face. She hunches deeper into the corner as she sobs without control.

She closes her eyes and takes a couple of deep breaths, attempting to collect herself. Wiping the tears from her tired eyes, she turns toward the center of the room and slowly opens her eyes. She starts to smooth her hair behind her ears when, through the glass in Studio A, she sees Colin standing there, watching her. He's crushed. Her heart wants to burst in her chest as he pulls open the door, and with two long strides, he is standing before her.

"Laura, what is it?" he whispers.

Colin, the boy who keeps coming in and out of her life. One of them always seems to be around right when the other is crumbling or at their worst.

"I didn't know you were here," she breathes out. Yet, now, she feels relieved he *is* here.

"I hate for you to cry," he responds.

He reaches up his hand and runs his thumb over a tear on her cheek. Again, she feels the warmth of his hand on her skin. She didn't forget about holding his hand the other night. It felt good, natural.

"I only want to help."

"I know. It's…"

"What?"

Before Laura can even realize what she is saying, she blurts out, "I'm so tired." She peers up at him through misty eyelashes.

"Come here," he says compassionately as he steps toward her with arms open wide.

She lowers her head and steps into his arms, burying her face into his chest. He wraps his arms around her and tightly holds on. The feeling of being touched by him continues to be a welcome craving. He reaches one hand up and softly strokes her hair. She squeezes her eyes shut and lets the tears drip down her face.

He whispers, "You're too wonderful of a person to cry."

She picks her head up off his chest and glimpses up toward him. "What did you say?" she whispers.

He does not let her go.

"You are incredible. I hate the thought of you being sad. You're so perfect," he gushes.

She steps back from his embrace, and with a slight roll of her eyes, she says, "I wish you wouldn't say that."

He takes a step toward her, closing the gap between them again. "But why?"

She swallows hard and has difficulty with meeting his eyes.

"Laura, I wanted to tell you the other night. I thought a lot over the break, and I'm over Joey."

"What?" she whispers.

"Yes, I definitely don't want to be with her anymore." He reaches his hand out and gently takes hers.

"But I saw her, all happy…leaving here the other day."

"I'm sure. She puts up a good front. But I told her to stop coming to the station and that she will just have to accept that we're through. Done."

"Oh." Now, Laura can feel the heat rise in her cheeks as he desirously gazes at her.

"I know it's been a strange time for me. And I've just had to get through some crap in order to see past her."

"I didn't know you felt that way."

"I'm not great with this kind of stuff. I'll be the first to admit that. I had a lot of emotions to get through, and it was way harder than I'd thought it would be."

"I do understand. It cannot be easy."

"No, but that night at Monroe's, I felt free again. Happy. And I realized I hadn't been happy, not in a long while."

Laura swallows hard at his confession. "You deserve happiness, Colin."

He smiles wide and then pulls her in closer. With his other hand, he tucks her hair behind her ear, and then he draws her face up toward his. Without saying a single word, he lowers his tall frame to where his lips are only centimeters from her. She can feel his breath on her face as she closes her eyes. She gets the warm touch of his soft and full lips at first, but then, with more passion, he kisses her deeply. Her knees weaken as his lips are all over hers. He runs his hands through her hair. She puts her arms around his waist, delicately touching his soft skin under his sweater. As her fingers trace his hips, she can hear him moaning deep in the back of his throat. He swiftly pulls back from her. He smiles.

Her heart is pounding. "What?"

"I want to do that again," he responds slyly.

He draws her face into his again, and slowly, with great care and sincerity, he kisses her. All her worries and sadness, like passing time, start to fade away.

Six

I'LL TELL YOU MY SECRET

"Tucker, you wanted to talk to me?"

"Yes, Laura. Please come in."

Laura goes into his office, closes the door behind her, and takes a seat.

"I've thought a lot about how I want to handle this…" he begins.

Oh shit. How did he find out about me and Colin?

"When you first interviewed over five months ago, you said to me that you had ideas of where you wanted to take the station. I admired that, and more importantly, I liked your concepts."

She exhales deeply. "Okay…"

"I don't like where things are headed on campus. Women are scared, and men are being scrutinized if they are wandering about alone. In times like this, all we have to give them is music."

Laura nods her head.

"But what we *need* to give them is the news, information, a way to connect us together."

"I agree. I get a lot of calls, looking for information. Sometimes, Patrick or Ryker have to screen them out; otherwise, I'd have no time for music, only talking."

"Right, but I see nothing wrong with that, and I'd like to ask you to come up with a news model. Have it on my desk no later than next week. Can you do that?"

"Yes, absolutely. Not a problem." She can hardly contain her excitement. She rises.

"But, Laura, keep this between us for now. I don't want word getting out to the others yet. I'll be bombarded with ideas and suggestions. This is yours to own. It was your idea, and I want you to possess it."

"Understood. And thank you for this opportunity."

"You got it. Now, have a great shift tonight."

"I will. Thanks!"

Laura leaves his office and can't help herself as she passes Studio A. She peeks inside and sees Ryker working the board.

"Hey, Ryker," she says cheerily.

"Hey, Laura. He's having another killer shift," he says, looking back at Colin in the studio.

"I know," she says as she glances at him, her cheeks pink, resembling a late October sky.

Colin waves slightly to her as he continues talking to a caller.

Ryker looks at Laura, then at Colin again, and then back at Laura.

"What?" Laura asks.

"Nothing," he says with a smile and shake of his head.

"Okay then…I'll catch you later."

"I'm working a double tonight. Thanks for asking," he says sarcastically as she starts to close the door.

She swings it back open, and says, "Large coffee, one cream, two sugars."

"You *do* know I exist!" he says, laughing.

She rolls her eyes at him. "I'll be back with your coffee."

After Laura gets coffee and delivers it to Ryker, she gets settled into her chair and makes all her adjustments. This time though, she has next to her a folded copy of the latest *The Weekly Blue* and a notebook to jot down all the questions she might get from callers.

She switches on the microphone, and away she goes.

Within seconds, the board lights up with calls.

"Good evening, Hawks. This is Laura, coming to you live from Studio B at station WOUR97. I'd give you my number, but by the looks of these phone lines, I'd say some of you have me on speed dial. Hello, caller, you're on with Laura."

"Hey, this is Sam. "

"Hello, Sam. What can I do for you?"

"Can you play 'Pass the Mic' by the Beastie Boys?"

"I'd be happy to." She glances up toward the booth as Ryker steps in from finishing Colin's show.

Colin is standing next to him, smiling wide. Laura motions for Colin to come in as the song is finishing.

"Aren't we lucky tonight? Everyone, Colin Reed is joining us!" Laura laughs as she hands him headphones. "Caller, you are on the air."

"With both of you?"

"Yes," Laura says.

"Yes," Colin says into his microphone.

"Wow, cool," the female caller says. "I want to dedicate a song to my boyfriend, Kevin. Should I pick Nirvana's 'Heart-Shaped Box' or The Lemonheads' 'Into Your Arms'?"

In unison, they both say, "Lemonheads."

Laura hits the button and plays the song.

"Funny," Colin says as he gestures with his eyes back toward Ryker.

"Well," she whispers, "if you're going to stand there, you might as well join me."

He smiles wide at her, and her heart skips a beat.

About halfway through her shift, Colin gets up. "Hey," he whispers, "I have got to get some homework done. I'll see you after, okay?"

Playing it cool in front of Ryker, she just nods as she picks up another call.

By the end of her shift, Laura is ready to call it a night. She arrives in the main office after locking up. Colin is at his desk.

"Thanks for waiting," she says softly.

He turns around and smiles at her. His hair falls softly to the side, and Laura has an urge to run her hands through his hair. But she resists trying to play it cool.

"Of course. You mind waiting for a few minutes while I finish this?" he asks, pointing to his paper.

"Sure. What class is this for?" she asks, realizing they spend most of their time talking about the radio station, not school.

"My computer engineering class."

"Ah."

"Tough class but required."

"You want to be an engineer?" she asks.

"That's the plan," he says with a wink. He turns back to his paper and continues writing. "Hey, you never told me why you were upset the other day. You said you were tired, but it had to be more than that."

"Right. You remember that," she adds shyly.

"Of course I remember it," he says with a devious glance.

She blushes a deep shade of red. "Oh, right." *How could I forget that kiss?*

"So?"

"You see, my roommate, is—was dating this guy, and she has been acting very strange over the past few months."

"Strange? How so?"

"Like hiding things, making up little lies to her boyfriend to kind of cover for his teammate—"

"Hold up. Teammate?"

Laura's hazel eyes get wide as she realizes what she is doing. "Never mind."

"Not so fast," he says with a smile as he puts down his pen and slides his chair closer to her. "You already gave up the goods. It won't be hard to figure it out, and don't you think, at some point, I'll be meeting her anyway?"

Laura tries to hide her smile, but she can't. "Well, I guess."

"You can trust me, Laura. I won't say a word. Besides, what I'm interested in knowing is what got you so upset and how I can maybe help you."

He caresses her cheek. She notes how soft and warm his hand is.

God, is he sweet.

She locks eyes with him. "Okay. She told me the other day that her now ex-boyfriend might or might not have tried to get his teammate kicked off of the team because his relationship with my roommate was getting in the way of the rest of the team's success. This is according to the rumors swirling around on my floor."

"Really? Seems unlikely."

"That is what I said! And, besides, knowing what I know about Nath—" She abruptly stops and places her hand over her mouth.

"Nathan. As in Nathan Ryan. QB1. No shit. So your roommate is Abigail? Everyone at school knows who they are."

She unclasps her hand and nods her head.

"You mean to tell me that Nathan Ryan got one of his teammates kicked off of the football team because his teammate had a thing for Abigail?"

Laura cringes as she tells him the story. "He does act weird around her, like he has a thing for her but in a different kind of way."

"This other guy have a girlfriend?"

"Yeah, sort of."

"Abigail tell you she likes the other guy?"

"No. She insists they are just friends. But, man, he is super protective of her."

"Huh. You try talking to her?"

"Yeah, and she won't tell me anything. Says she can't. She is distant and lonely and scared and…"

"Scared?"

She can't tell him about the attack. It isn't well known on campus. Only within their circle of friends.

"Yeah, you know, like her world is spiraling out of control and how Nathan isn't there for her. I don't know what to do. I tried to talk to her, but she avoids me and stays out late. She doesn't eat, sleep, nothing, and she is such a lovely person. I truly care about her."

"Then, go to him."

"What?"

"Yeah. You can't get through to her, so go tell Nathan."

"Should I?"

"You said he is really nice, right?"

"Yeah, considering what a big deal he is around here. He's, like, one of the kindest people I've met at school."

Colin clears his throat and then playfully winks at her.

"Aside from you, of course," she says with a wide smile back. "Should I talk to him?"

"Let me ask you this. Would you want someone to come to you to tell you what you couldn't see right in front of you?"

"I suppose I would."

"He's not over her, right?"

Laura can't help but laugh a little. "In my opinion and from what I've seen firsthand, I'm guessing no."

"Give it a shot. Can't hurt."

"No, I guess it can't." She mulls over all the things she could say to Nathan. Her head starts to spin. As she gazes at the ground, the following words simply fly out of her mouth, "Can I ask you what you said to Joey to make her understand it was really over?"

Now, it is his turn to stare at the ground. Laura waits patiently as he collects his thoughts.

"Yes. I told her that I thought I knew how to be happy, and that meant not being with her anymore. I think she kind of always felt she could do no wrong, and I'd just be there for her. But I told her I wanted to move on. I didn't say this to her, but in the end, she did me a favor.'

Laura tries not to gasp and blush at the same time, but she does regardless. "Ouch, Colin. That must have been an awful conversation to have."

He meets her eyes. "Yeah, but I suppose that's why it didn't hurt me to be honest with her."

"I'm glad you were."

"Am I saying too much?"

"No, it's...I'm sorry for you but not sorry," she says with a slight smile.

"Neither am I."

She can feel his hand on her leg.

"I'll be fine. Now, come on," he says. "We spend enough time in this place."

"But what about your paper?"

He stands before her and offers his hand to her. She takes it, and he gently pulls her toward him and into his arms. He hugs her tightly. "I can finish it later."

She closes her eyes and breathes in deep. "Okay and thanks, Colin, for the chat," she says quietly.

"Thank you." He slightly draws her back and then leans in and gives her a soft, delectable kiss.

His kiss makes her forget all about her problems. His lips slowly release hers but not before he grazes his teeth along her bottom lip. A welcome sensation rushes over her. She wants to stay in his arms where his embrace shields her from all her friends' secrets. The kind of secrets that can destroy two lovers with the lash of a tongue—or worse, break a friendship clean in half. Either one could be irreparable should the damage be great enough.

Seven

THE SECOND COMING

Laura nervously enters the office of *The Weekly Blue* in the Rounds Hall, located on the opposite side of campus.

Part of her proposal to Tucker was to team up with *The Weekly Blue* to gain access to additional sources and to fact-check her segments before going on the air. She was surprised by Tucker's reaction to her suggestion. He filled her in on the years of animosity between the two media sources and the countless battles with administration for funding.

She hears the clicking away on keyboards and is alarmed by the number of staff who are sitting at desks in the main area.

Sure takes a lot of people to run a student newspaper. Wish we had half of this staff at the station.

A young guy rolls his chair close to her, practically bumping into her. "How can I help you?" he says with a slightly suggestive grin.

"I'm here to speak with Travis."

"Lucky him," he says. Then, he yells, "Travis!"

Laura is not prepared as Travis—a tall, well-dressed guy with windswept, dark hair and big blue eyes—comes waltzing down the hallway. Although he can barely get down the hall with everyone trying to get a quick piece of him.

"Travis," one girl says, "can you look at this?"

He takes the paper and barely glances at her. He scribbles something on it and then tosses it back to her.

Another guy approaches. "Travis, this needs your approval by four thirty."

He grabs that as well, eyes it, scrawls something across the top, flings it back to the guy, and then continues down the hallway.

Laura blinks several times.

"Laura, hello," he says. "I'm Travis Taylor." He extends his hand.

Laura swallows hard. She takes his hand. He shakes it firmly.

"Hello, Travis. Laura Chase. Professor Tucker arranged a meeting through Professor Campbell."

According to Tucker, this little arrangement was not met with open arms by Travis or the paper. The station, as Travis put it, should stick to what we know—music. Not the news. It was made very clear to Laura that she was stepping on toes. But Tucker encouraged her to continue to step; otherwise, she'd never get where they needed to get. Plain and simple.

"Of course. Please, we can meet in my office."

She watches as he ambles back down the hall toward an open office. He exudes tremendous confidence. From what little she knows about Travis, he's a junior at the school and has been involved with *The Weekly Blue* since his first day on campus. Professor Tucker said he was the second coming of editorial perfection at the student paper and revered among the faculty.

"Laura, please have a seat."

His office is merely a small room at the end of the hallway, but considering where the rest of the kids are sitting and typing feverishly, some might consider this a big deal.

"Thank you."

"How can I help you?" he says assuredly.

"I am going to start a news segment on the radio."

"Professor Campbell mentioned *that*."

"I was hoping to solicit some help from the paper or its staff to try to gain a wider perspective on the ins and outs of campus life."

"I see." He looks across the desk at Laura with a peculiar smile.

"But what I'd like to do and what I consider important is to include input from *The Weekly Blue*. Legitimate resources to make certain the students know that what they get from us is real and accurate."

He rubs the scruff on his chin and contemplates something. His icy-blue eyes narrow at her. "I must ask, how else would you get your information?"

"Pardon me?" Laura says with a cock of her head.

"Is the radio station now in the business of investigating the news?" He crosses his arms over his chest.

She takes a deep breath. She moves to the edge of her seat. For the first time since entering the room, she truly locks eyes with him. Despite the butterflies in her stomach, she finds the courage to say, "Travis, there is a man—and I use that word loosely—terrorizing our campus and, from what little I know, at least a half dozen other campuses in the state of New York. I am proposing we—meaning you and me—use our resources to give the students and people of this community the best and most accurate information possible."

As he blankly stares back at her, she feels her anger rise. And not just anger toward him. Anger with a lot of things, one of them being that the asshole in question has in fact attacked her own roommate.

When she doesn't get even a slight retort back, she rises to leave. Before exiting, she blurts out, "And, yes, we at the radio station have the audience and capability to reach people every single day of the week. Not merely *once* a week."

He gives her a sly smile as she starts to leave the room.

"Wait. Laura, wait."

She doesn't turn right away. Finally, she glances over her shoulder.

"What are you proposing?" he asks.

She doesn't smile as she faces him. In fact, her expression is void. "I would like to develop a new topics segment, one which is vetted and given full credit to the appropriate staff members of the newspaper. But I'd like to open the discussion, encourage questions on news that is happening on a daily basis to *my* audience."

"How many days are you suggesting?"

"A few to start, and then *if* it is successful, further discussions can be had."

"Okay, and how will we work together?"

"Your team submits information to us, touchpoints we can elaborate on and have educated discussions about."

"Okay, and what do we get?"

"You can quote callers and me in your articles to bring the circle back around. Link the two of us together…"

His eyes rise.

"Let them see us as two interconnected sources to get their information," she adds. "Not the paper once a week and then in between the radio station getting a bunch of concerned callers, with little resources to get their questions answered properly."

"Are you planning on having guest speakers from the paper?"

"With your permission. Absolutely. We'd welcome that."

He leans back in his chair. It's obvious he is thinking about something. He jots down a few words on a piece of paper, folds it, and then places it in his breast pocket. "I have a few things I want to run by Professor Campbell."

Laura, at the ready, reaches into her bag. "Here is my proposal. Please tell Professor Campbell that this has been evaluated and approved by Professor Rhodes and Professor Cooper in the marketing department as well as Professor Tucker."

He grants her a sideways smile. "Okay, I will," he responds in a slightly mocking tone.

Laura's want to leave his office is overpowering her in this very moment. This is not at all how she envisioned her meeting taking place.

What is this guy's problem?

As if a fire were lit under her, she squarely faces him. With the same authoritative tone he granted her, she says, "I'd like to imagine that both of us have the same goal in mind."

"And what's that?" he says. His tone and demeanor are both cocky.

"That we both give enough shit about the students on this campus. That connecting with them, no matter the forum, is the only end result we truly care about." She again gets little reaction from him. So, she steps toward the door. "You know, Travis, I'd be willing to bet that you were once just like me, trying to make a difference here. Wanting to bring together a campus that is in trouble. Far more trouble, I'm guessing, than either one of us could have imagined. You know how hard this will be." She shakes her head.

His mouth drops open slightly. But he says nothing.

Laura yanks open the door to his office, only to find a long line of conformists waiting for the great Travis Taylor, the so-called messiah of *The Weekly Blue*.

If only they knew.

Laura stops by the station on her way to the cafeteria. She is hoping more than anything to catch Tucker and let him know about her meeting with Travis.

She enters the station. She opens Studio A and peeks her head in. Ryker is at the board.

"Hey, Laura. Here to see Colin?" he asks.

With a furrowed brow, she says, "I wanted to stop in and say hi."

"Right. Totally."

Laura peers into the studio. Colin waves to her. His smile is sincere.

"See you," she says as she starts to closes the door.

"Cool. See you later."

She knocks on Tucker's door.

"Come in!" he yells over the radio.

"Hey, it's Laura."

"Laura, how did your meeting go?"

"Oh, fine." She enters his office and shuts the door behind her.

"Let me guess," he says. "He acted as though he was the god of who knows what!"

Laura can't help but smile. "Yes, he truly did," she responds as she starts to laugh.

"Good. I'm glad you recognized it, too."

Surprised, Laura gives him a quizzical glance.

"Now, that needs to be put aside. If Professor Campbell says he's good, he must be."

The corners of Laura's lips start to turn. "He was...is, um, quite pompous."

"Exactly, but unfortunately for us, we need to go through him. Student to student. I'll deal with Campbell. What is your next move?"

Laura leans forward. With all the bullshit she has endured, she is more than ready for this challenge. "You asked me to do this news segment for a reason."

"And that reason being?"

"That I can handle a guy like Travis. I get him. He's me two years from now, only he hasn't learned that you don't get there by treating people like shit. You get there by remembering where you came from. Today, he looked at me like I was a peon. He's not that old to forget."

Tucker sits back in his chair. His eyes dart back and forth. He's giddy, only he's not sure why. "Like I said, what is your next move?"

"Let me open a segment next week. Introduce it and see how it goes. By next week, I can identify a person, a source, to help me corroborate and identify some of my stories and topics."

"Okay. I agree."

Laura claps her hands. "Great. And can I just say, Tucker, when I interviewed for the DJ job months ago, all I really ever wanted to do was this. To report the news to the students. To bring a voice to the stories that surround us. Little did I know then that there would be so much to take into account. With the recent crimes on campus, we need this now more than ever. So, I thank you for taking a chance on me and letting me do this."

"You are most welcome. I knew you were the right person to do this when you brought the idea to me. First female in over ten years and now the first to report the news. This truly is a unique time for all of us."

"Thank you. I won't let you down. So, when are you announcing this to the guys?"

"Soon."

For many reasons, this does not sit well with Laura. "Okay, but will I be doing this during my regular shift? Or adding on a second shift?"

"For now, I'd like to switch you and Colin."

Laura is certain the word *Colin* comes rolling out of his mouth in slow motion. She stares at him. Tucker doesn't know they have started to get closer. And by closer, she means, heavy make-out sessions in the station after her shifts. So, it is clear that Tucker doesn't know that she has feelings for Colin, beyond that of a coworker. Worse, Colin doesn't know she is doing this, and now, Tucker just asked her not to tell anyone.

What the fuck have I done?

He looks back at her. When she doesn't respond, he says, "Do you understand?"

She shakes her head again. "I'm sorry. Understand what now?"

"I'm going to switch you and Colin. We need the news to be during the day, so students can tune in and get a sense of what is going on. Your shift is perfect for social and party-type requests. This news needs to take place during the afternoon."

Laura's heart pumps hard. One heavy beat at a time.

I can't screw over Colin! I can't. All the guys at the station have worked so hard for their spots. Their schedules revolve around their shifts at the station. Colin even mentioned in jest about how I got the crappy shift. The night shift that no one wants…ever. This will be a major disruption. But how can I get around this? The news does need to be on during the day. This could be a game changer for the school. I know this.

He chuckles and sits back in his chair. "What do you think? You ready to make your mark, Laura Chase? Follow in your father's footsteps?"

Follow in my father's footsteps? Make my mark?

Her head is nodding, but her mind is screaming, *No, no, no, not like this! Don't make me be the reason Colin gets kicked out of his spot!*

"Yes," she says as she tries to prevent her bottom lip from quivering.

She feels like she could burst into tears. Even if she tells Tucker about her feelings for Colin, that won't change what needs to be done. She has been working toward this since the day she started, and Tucker is taking a chance on her. *How can I back out now?*

"Okay then. I'll let Colin know after his shift today to give him a week to get ready for the switch, and then, Laura, you'll be ready to roll."

"Great," she says halfheartedly.

I think I'm going to throw up.

Eight

THE ROCK IS CRUMBLING

Laura, unable to face Colin, hurries into the cafeteria to find all her floor mates starting to eat. That is, everyone but Abigail.

With a plethora of emotions swirling throughout her, she decides to grab a quick sandwich instead of waiting in the other long line for whatever special hot dinner there is tonight. She's afraid that, when she sits with her floor mates, they will undoubtedly see right through her.

"Hey." She puts her tray down and slides into the chair next to Jen.

"How are things at the station?" Jen asks.

"You know, busy as ever. But good."

"Where is Abigail?" Casey asks.

"Don't know. You guys know? I just came from the station."

"No, haven't seen her." Melissa says with sadness in her voice.

"She's probably studying," Maddie adds.

"Perhaps," Bree adds with an edge.

"Anyway, Jen, are the girls at the soccer house having a party for Spring Fling this year?" Casey says, trying desperately to change the subject.

"Spring Fling?" Maddie asks.

Jen and Melissa almost simultaneously sit back with a gasp. Jen motions to Melissa to speak first.

"You do know what Spring Fling is, right?"

"I've heard about it, but…"

"No *buts*! It is *the* party weekend of the year around here," Jen says with excitement.

They all nod, except Maddie.

"Really? Tell me more."

Jen begins, "From what I know from one of the seniors on the soccer team is that the Spring Fling tradition started years ago as the weekend in which everyone—including the school—sort of knew that the very first weekend of May could potentially bring chaos to town."

"No kidding. Like what?" Maddie leans in further, eyes wide with excitement.

"Well," Casey says, "I heard last year where everyone threw their beer bottles around at this one party. Catapulting beer bottles…flying glass everywhere. Stupid, right? But, man, imagine if you were there and survived it?" she laughs.

Jen is eager to add, "Then, there was the time when police—in riot gear, mind you—marched the streets, trying to prevent people from burning couches and all kinds of things. Students just walking to a party and watching couches burn along the streets."

"It is just party after party, one crazier than the last," Casey says.

"Believe it or not, this sometimes noiseless campus gets its name in national magazines as another party school without an off switch," Jen adds.

"How has this gotten past you?" Casey asks with a laugh.

"No idea," Maddie responds.

"Don't worry, Maddie; they are all just Neanderthals. So immature," Bree scoffs.

"This year, the soccer house, men's ice hockey house, and the football house are all having a block party. Live music all day. It's going to be awesome," Jen says.

"Count me in," Melissa says. "*That* is where I'll be."

Laura silently eats her dinner. She notes the cool vibe Bree is emanating. She is here, but it's clear she does not want to be.

"You're coming, too, right, Laura? Won't Abigail and Nathan be at the football house?" Melissa asks.

She glances up from her plate. "I'm sure of it," she lies with fake enthusiasm. She can tell by the question that Abigail has yet to confide in the others about her breakup with Nathan.

"Cool." Changing the subject, Casey asks, "Any of you know what movie is playing tonight in Montgomery Hall?"

"Is it *Billy Madison*?" Melissa says.

"Yeah, that's right. Anyone want to go?"

"I have to get some studying done," Laura chimes in.

"I'll go," Bree responds, which surprises everyone. They all look up at her. "What? I go to the movies, too," she says with a flip of her hair.

"I'll go, too," Jen says.

"Great. Let's head over, so we can get good seats," says Casey.

"Sure." Bree peeks up her big brown eyes at Laura. Her sadness is more apparent now, but before Laura can react, Bree stands and quickly follows the others out.

"See you later," she calls after them.

Laura sits at her desk and looks out the window, aimlessly flipping through her textbook.

After about an hour, she grabs her wool sweater from inside her closet. She tightly wraps it around her and then plops on her bed with several weeks' worth of *The Weekly Blue* newspapers. She starts reading through them again.

There are a few articles written about attacks and sexual assaults on other campuses in New York. But, with the lack of solid evidence and little police reporting, the articles in the newspaper are sporadic enough that it seems to be more aligned with random acts of violence on campus. Not the work of a serial rapist. There is one article written in September, urging new students to be aware of their surroundings and to engage their dorm monitors about campus safety but nothing more than that.

What amazes Laura the most is the apparent lack of input from the school administration. Most of the articles are written by student writers, merely encouraging students to be cautious and diligent on campus as they embark on their four-year collegiate journey. There is very little sense of urgency. This alarms Laura and sets a fire in her to make sure the school and students take these attacks far more seriously.

An hour passes when she unexpectedly detects a very faint knock on the door. She gets up, wondering if her mind is playing a trick on her. She lends an ear to her door.

Then, a voice whispers, "I know you're in there."

Laura whips open the door, and without warning, Bree falls into her arms, sobbing like a child. Laura's heart begins to melt as she strokes her friend's long brown hair.

My goodness. This must be bad if she is crying like this.

She waits for a while and then finally says, "Bree, you have to tell me what is wrong, so I can help you."

This stunning woman, the model who has graced covers of magazines, looks up from Laura's embrace, makeup all over her otherwise flawless face, and Laura knows what she is about to tell her will not be good.

Bree, through inconsolable sobs, tells Laura of her life-changing first night at college, "He lured me into a path, and I soon realized there was no way out. He pushed me on the ground and tried taking off my clothes."

Laura almost goes into complete shock. She cannot believe that not one, but two of her closest friends were attacked by the same asshole by happenstance.

"I struggled and fought as hard as I could, but then I went into shock and felt completely frozen as he hit me over and over again."

"Oh, Bree, I'm so sorry...so very sorry," she cries.

"By some small miracle, Laura, he just stopped. As though my will to stop fighting turned him off. He just got up off of me and disappeared. So then, I ran. I ran as fast as I could back to the dorm."

"Thank God you were able to get away."

"Laura, all excuses aside, I just needed someone to know what my days have been like. I have not always handled myself in the best way, and I know I let my bitchiness get the best of me. But you guys aren't like my friends back home. You are all so sweet and kind, and...I'm grateful for that. And I just wanted to say, I know I haven't always treated you guys fairly."

"Oh my God, Bree, don't even say that. College life in general is confusing and hard. But this is just horrible. No one can expect any more from you than you can give in the moment. Anyone who truly cares for you, that is."

"I know, and poor Abigail. I have been mad these past few weeks, considering her. The way I treated her, and then she unknowingly drops the biggest bomb on me when she told us she was attacked. I felt a thousand times worse than I ever thought I could. Had I said something, maybe they would have caught that jerk earlier, and she never..." Bree trails off.

"Oh, Bree."

"After hearing what happened to Abigail, I decided I should have spoken up. Being afraid of what others might think is...maybe I cared too much that I...I don't know..."

"Now, wait a minute, Bree. *He* is the reason this has happened, not you."

"The police believe they caught him."

"Really? God, I hope that is true."

"Yes, but for now, the police are trying to keep it under wraps and not make it public. You know how the media can convict someone before the courts do. I know they have not made an arrest. The guy is in the hospital, and they need someone to positively identify him first. Guess he looked bad enough that it would make it difficult to do so right now."

"Good," Laura adds with a firm nod of her head.

Lying in Wait

The girls discuss the situation at hand for another hour. Laura is tempted to tell Bree about Colin and, more importantly, about how she has to take his spot but doesn't want to.

Should I let my feelings for him get in the way of a great opportunity? she ponders as she listens to Bree talk about her own heartbreak.

Finally, as she realizes the depth of what Bree has been through, Laura considers if there is truly a destiny that we are all unaware of. It makes Laura contemplate whether or not Colin is her destiny. Or worse, whether or not he'll feel that way about her after he finds out about her new role at the station.

When there is a lull in the conversation, exhaustedly, Laura says, "Bree, you can sleep in here tonight. Abigail left a note saying she will not be home."

"She with Nathan?"

"Something like that," Laura says with a slight smile.

Bree curls back up on Laura's bed, and Laura pulls a blanket over her. Laura goes over to Abigail's bed, climbs in, and shuts off the light.

"Good night, Laura, and thank you for being here for me."

"Good night, Bree," Laura whispers as she tries to close her eyes and let her brain rest.

She wants badly to fall asleep and let this all be just a terrible nightmare. Wake up tomorrow and have all her worries be washed away. But all she can feel in her heart is sadness. Today, in particular, she doesn't feel like things will get easier, only harder.

Abigail is hurting, Bree is still hurting, and I'm about to hurt Colin. Could this be any worse?

Nine

IT ALL CHANGES

Colin opens the door to Tucker's office. "You wanted to see me?"

"Yes, come in. Have a seat."

Colin takes the seat across from Tucker's desk. "Sure thing. What's up?"

"We are going to start additional programming at the station."

"Okay," he responds with cautious excitement.

"It's a news segment, and we plan to be on the air during the day. In your time slot."

Colin's eyes narrow. "Um, okay. But what does that mean?"

"It means that, for now, we are moving you to the eight o'clock time, and we are moving Laura into your slot."

"Laura?" he says, trying not to sound hurt.

"Yes, she will be doing the news."

A number of emotions washes over him. He can't tell in the moment if he is angry or sad or dejected, but whatever this feeling is, he hates it. And he hates that it has to do with Laura.

"I see." Colin is unsure of how to play this because he doesn't want to be mad at Laura. However, he is saddened that she did not say a word to him about it. *No heads-up?*

"Look, Colin, we didn't want to upset anyone. We believe this will be great for the station and the community."

"I don't doubt that. I guess I don't know what to say right now other than I'll just need to readjust what I've been used to for almost two years."

"I completely get that this will be an adjustment. But we don't have much time. With the news coming at a rapid pace and with the attacks becoming better known and statewide, we have to act. I hope you can understand."

"I'm trying, Tucker. I'll do what is best for the station."

With a sad expression, Tucker replies, "Of course. I knew you would."

Colin stands, and before pulling the door open, he says, "When does this go into effect, the schedule change?"

"One week from today."

One week? That gives me no time at all to change my schedule, but maybe no one cares about that.

He goes down the hallway and immediately out the door. He can't let the others know that this bothers him. He can't face *her* either. Not yet. He desperately needs time alone to digest this. Confused and disappointed, he goes back to his dorm room to try to get a grip on his emotions.

Why wouldn't she have told me? He paces his room. *Why didn't she at least give me the heads-up that she was stealing my spot? The spot I'd worked hard to get. Could she be that cold and not know it?*

He watches as the sun starts to fade over campus. He sits at his desk for over an hour and stares out his window. He tries to comprehend the news he just received and not let it get in the way of their budding relationship. He doesn't want it to change things between them. He wants to believe that she didn't have a choice in the matter.

Right?

The phone rings in his room, and he doesn't answer it. He doesn't want to talk to anyone. He leans back in his chair and contemplates his next move with Laura.

The phone in his dorm rings again. He regards it with a scowl.

"Stop calling," he mumbles. "I need a second to breathe."

With his head in his hands, he closes his eyes. Taking in a deep breath, he slowly lets it out.

The phone rings *again*.

Clearly agitated, he grabs the receiver. "Yeah?" he barks.

"Dude, it's Sean. You have to come to the station. She...she..." he starts to stutter.

"She what? Slow down," he says, although his own heart rate has picked up significantly.

"She was assaulted by some guy! Get over here!"

Before Colin can respond, someone is crying, and then the phone goes dead.

Oh my God, Laura. No! he screams in his head.

As though a thousand knives were pressed into his chest, Colin, without even realizing what he is doing, throws open his door, barely closing it behind him, and runs at top speed back to the station.

Lying in Wait

As he pumps his arms and breathes heavily, he maneuvers his way in and out of the students, trying not to knock someone over. He pushes his way through the side entrance to the Student Union, near the mailboxes, and sprints down the hallway toward the station.

He bursts in. "Where is she?" he asks, his voice quivering.

Patrick points down the hallway toward Studio B. The look of sheer sadness on his face is enough to want to make Colin erupt into tears.

"Holy shit," he mutters as he runs down the hallway.

Without even knocking, he throws open the door. Sean and Ryker are hovering over a frail figure sitting in the chair. The blinds on the windows have been drawn.

Colin's mind is racing with fear, and his hands are shaking as he reaches out to put his hand on Ryker's shoulder. He needs to get a better look at her and to let her know he is here. She is safe now. Tears start to well in his eyes. He can hear her crying.

"I'm here," he whispers.

Sean looks up and moves out of the way.

Joey jumps up and throws her arms around Colin. He gasps when he realizes it is *not* Laura. A horrible wave of gratitude washes over him. As Sean watches the two of them embrace, he can't help but give Colin a questioning stare.

Joey? he mouths to Sean.

Sean nods his head and then lowers his stare to the ground. Colin, still holding her, realizes that it categorically doesn't matter who it is.

Right?

He is glad she is safe now.

Sobbing, she whispers, "I didn't know where else to go."

"It's okay," he says, stroking her hair.

"I'm scared," she whispers.

Is she hurt? he mouths to Sean.

Colin is paralyzed by fear, waiting for the answer. Sean shakes his head.

"She is shaken up badly," he whispers. Then, he says to Joey, "Can we do anything for you?"

"I can't be alone," she says with a whimper.

"You won't be," Colin says as he holds her tightly.

Joey continues to sob as he embraces her. No one notices Laura standing in the open doorway, clearly unaware of what is happening.

"Laura," Sean whispers.

Turning as he still holds on to Joey, a rush of emotions comes over him as he locks eyes with Laura. Her face twists with anguish as she looks at the scene in front of her.

"I-I can come back," she says, barely able to get the words out. She looks at Colin and then down toward Joey. "I'm so sorry," she whispers.

"Please tell her to leave," Joey cries as she shields her face from her.

Embarrassed, Laura turns on her heel and hurries back down the hallway. Colin motions to Sean to go after her.

"I'll be right back," he says.

"Tell him to shut the door," Joey says with an angry tone.

"Holler if you need me," Ryker adds as he, too, exits, shutting it behind him.

"Laura, Laura," Sean whisper-yells as he rushes down the hallway after her. He finds Laura in the main room, about to leave. "Laura!" he barks. "Hold up."

She whips around with tears in her eyes. "What?" she says.

"Come here for a minute." He gestures for her to follow him to a private room.

She passes by as Patrick gazes sympathetically at her.

Once inside, Sean quietly closes the door. "Listen, Laura, Joey was assaulted..."

Laura places her hand over her mouth. Eventually lowering her hand, she says, "Oh my God, Sean. How horrible."

She considers her friends, Abigail and Bree, and now Joey. She is almost consumed with sadness and horrid fear. This is a campus epidemic running rampant right in front of her very nose.

"She came here and said she had nowhere else to go. She asked for Colin, and I called him," he says as he steps closer to her. He reaches his hand up and gently runs it over her arm.

With numerous thoughts swirling in her head, she doesn't react to the way he is looking at her.

"I'm sorry."

"Me, too," she whispers. "I don't know what to do."

"Listen, I'm good friends with Colin, as you know. So, I know what is going on with you two."

"Oh."

"So, they need some time, I suppose. He needs to help her. She is pretty shaken."

"I can imagine." She pauses. "Well, I should go. I just came to..." *Tell him I am truly sorry for taking his spot. It was never my plan.* "Oh, never mind."

"I'll call you," Sean says kindly.

"Thanks." She opens up the door and exits the station.

"Joey, what happened?" Colin whispers.

He releases his embrace and pulls back from her. Her hair is messy, and there is dirt on her face. Thankfully, there are no real visible wounds. He takes his thumb and forefinger and gently touches her chin, turning her head from side to side, trying to get a good look at her.

"I don't want to talk about it."

"Okay. Did you call the police?"

"No," she says with heavy tears filling her eyes.

"Okay. We should report this. Maybe, if we do, they can find this scumbag," Colin says, trying to hold his anger in. He reaches for the phone in the booth.

She grabs his arm. "Please, Colin. I can't. Not right now."

"How can I help you? I mean, what do you need from me?" He releases his hand from the phone. "Are you hurt? Do I need to take you to the hospital?"

"I don't think so. I'm..." She starts to tremble, unable to finish her sentence.

"I'm sorry, Joey."

"I'm scared."

"I know. I can only imagine."

"Can we leave? Please," she begs.

"Do your roommates know?"

"No. I don't want anyone else to know." She glances up at him with a pleading look in her eyes.

"Okay." Colin is unsure of what he should do next.

"Can I stay with you?"

He realizes that he is hesitating but quickly snaps back to reality. "Of course. Whatever you need."

"Thank you."

He takes her hand and leads her toward the door. She buries her face in his chest, trying to shield herself from any onlookers. He is praying in this moment that Laura is gone. He doesn't want her to witness this. In fact, no woman should have to see this.

"Guys, I'm taking her to my place," he says to Sean and Patrick, who are standing near their desks, whispering.

They both nod their heads as Colin and Joey leave.

Once inside his dormitory, Colin leads Joey directly to his room.

"What do you need from me?" he asks.

"I'd-I'd like to take a shower," she says in a soft, low voice.

"You sure that is a good idea? Are you positive you don't want to talk to the police?"

"Colin, *please.*"

He puts his hands up. "Okay, okay. I had to ask again. I want to know you are thinking clearly—as best as you can."

She stands before him. Not moving. He goes over, grabs a clean towel, and hands it to her. She leaves the room and goes down the hallway to the showers. She knows her way around his dorm, having been in it a hundred times with him.

Within minutes, she is back, carrying her clothes with the towel tucked under her arms and knotted in the front.

"Here, you can wear this T-shirt." He gives her one of his shirts. "Stef won't be home tonight," he adds, referring to his roommate.

"Oh, okay."

"I'm going to go grab us a few drinks."

"No. Please don't leave me," she says, shaking.

"Joey, I'm going down a few floors, and I promise I'll be right back."

"All right."

"Lock the door behind me, and I'll knock when I return."

Colin leaves and hurries down to the lobby and into the common area to grab a couple of bottled waters.

When he comes back, he knocks, and then Joey asks, "Colin?"

"Yes, Joey, it's me," he replies.

She opens the door and peers around the corner of the door. He pushes it open and then closes it behind him. Her frail body is standing there in his T-shirt, her hair wet and unbrushed. He feels sad for her but can't find the words to express it.

"Here, drink some water." He hands one to her.

She takes it with shaking hands.

"Come, lie down." He guides her over to his bed. "You should get some rest."

She lowers her body on his bed and lies back. He pulls the covers up to her chin. He strokes her wet hair.

"Thank you," she whispers, closing her eyes.

"Rest, Joey. I'll be right here with you," he adds with trepidation.

He gets up and goes over to his desk. Sitting down, he switches on his desk lamp and opens his textbook. Only he can't study. He gazes out the window and down on the campus below. Hurt washes over him with anger flowing not far behind. He watches a few men move from building to building, and he wonders who is terrorizing this campus and hurting women.

Who could be cruel and ghastly enough to hurt innocent women?

Lying in Wait

The phone rings, and he picks it up, hoping not to wake Joey.

"Hello?" he says in a hushed voice.

"Hi, it's me...Laura."

Colin lets out a deep breath and reluctantly says, "I can't. Now is not a good time."

"Oh, okay. Sorry. I'll talk to you soon."

Before he can say anything, she hangs up. His heart drops for the hundredth time today.

He catches a faint cry from the other side of the room and gets up. Joey is crying in his pillow.

"Joey?"

She picks her head up, and with just a look, he knows she is not okay.

He crawls into the bed alongside her. His head rests on the cold metal headboard as he gently places his hand over hers. "I'm here, Joey. I'm right here."

Ten

UNDECIDEDLY OVER

Back at the station the following afternoon, Laura sits at a desk in the front room, staring into space. A few minutes later, there is a slight knock on the main door.

No one moves, and the guys wait for the door to open. Patrick turns as a tall guy enters the room.

"I'm here for Laura."

Laura turns around. Travis is standing in the room, looking particularly handsome today. He is wearing jeans and a red button-down flannel shirt.

He looks respectable in red, she thinks.

"Hi, Travis."

"Hey. How are you?" he asks.

"Good," she says with uncertainty.

He cocks his head to the side.

"Oh, shoot. Forgot we were meeting." She scrambles to her feet. "We can meet down in Studio B."

He smiles tenderly and nods. "I'll follow you."

She pushes open the door to Studio B, switches on the light, and pulls up another chair to the desk. She searches through her desk drawer for her notebook.

"I hear you got the go-ahead to start next week. Congratulations?"

She's startled by his kindness. Her cheeks turn pink as she says, "Oh, yes, next week, and thank you for volunteering your time to help me."

He smiles wide as he takes a seat. "Welcome. It's been a while since someone has put me in my place. I admire that."

Did I?

Something has changed in his demeanor. She suspiciously eyes him and then attempts her discussion by asking, "So, I guess we can begin with some of the hot topics that keep popping up at the paper."

"Obviously, there are the arts and entertainment announcements. We have a few headliners coming for Spring Fling in May. Those always drum up interest. People like to know about the events all weekend long. I'll leave you a list of bands, the locations, ticket prices, and so forth."

"Okay," she says, jotting down notes.

As he observes her, she gets a peculiar sensation. She bites nervously on the end of her pen to try to thwart his stare.

He continues, "The president of the school is having an open Q and A session in the Union next month. You'll get a lot of calls about that, I'm sure. We always do." Travis continues to fill her in, and he shares notes and articles for her to brush up on. He leans back in his chair. "But, obviously, the most important is the campus assaults and attacks on women here and at other schools in New York."

She pauses and looks out toward the control room. A shiver runs down her spine. She says softly, "I know. Awful."

"Right now, we are investigating a few more leads ourselves; therefore, I can't talk about those. But feel free to mention that we're continuing to keep it a top priority."

"Of course, I will."

"If you don't mind me asking, what do you plan to say about it?"

"I went back through some of the papers and started archiving my facts and descriptions. I only want to report on what I know—accurately. Here," she says, handing him a few sheets. "I have started drafting and compiling my own timeline."

He contemplates the sheet handed to him. He rubs his chin as his eyes dance over the outline. She nervously awaits his reaction.

"Wow. I'm impressed, Laura. This is pretty detailed."

"When you can't sleep at night, you tend to work the mind till it's tired," she says with a half smile.

"I hear you on that."

"Can I ask, has anyone at the paper interviewed any of his alleged victims?"

"Yes, we interviewed one woman because she knew of a few others, and there had been no reports or movement by the police. She wanted to know we were on top of it, thinking maybe we could scare the guy out of here. But my sources tell me that is not happening despite our best efforts."

Travis could not be more accurate. In the past month, Laura alone has learned of three women who have been attacked.

This is absolutely crazy.

She tries not to make eye contact with him, for fear he might know this is way too close to her.

"It's hard to put into words how scary this is."

"Would you like to see if she'd be willing to do an interview on the radio?"

"Seriously?"

"Yeah. Obviously, she would be anonymous."

Laura's skin crawls at the mere thought. *What questions would I ask? How could I find the words or the nerves to interview her?*

But then something inside of her bursts. Three women she knows have been attacked by this predator. She has the power of the airwaves to bring more attention to a horrible epidemic on campus. It is her duty to do so.

"Yes, I'd like to speak with her."

"Okay, let me see if my source can arrange it."

"Thanks, Travis. I appreciate the support."

"I know," he says in his infamous, cocky tone that Laura remembers all too well.

She laughs for the first time in the past few days. "Of course you do."

He chuckles. "I'll have someone drop my notes off to you. Take a look and let me know if you have any other questions."

"Okay, I will."

"Oh, and one more thing that has been the topic of conversation."

She looks down at her notebook to start writing, but he doesn't say anything. She glances up at him. A smile spreads across his face.

"What?" she asks.

"The paper is curious about the woman who finally got the radio station to launch a news segment. That has gotten some buzz around the office."

Laura feels her cheeks turn fiery red. Then, with a smirk, she quips, "Maybe, someday, they will get a chance to interview her."

"Very smug. I like it."

He starts to stand, and she rises as well.

Suddenly, the door to Studio B opens. Colin is standing before them. He glances back and forth between them like a tennis match.

"Um, Colin, hi!" Laura says in an unusually high-pitched tone.

"Sorry to interrupt. I thought you were alone. I can talk to you later."

Travis steps toward Colin. "Hi, I'm Travis."

Colin gives him the eye up and down and then says with zero enthusiasm, "Oh, hey. I'm Colin."

"Of course. From the radio."

"Yeah, that's me," he says, only he doesn't smile. He turns and nods at Laura, who appears frozen "I'll leave you guys."

"Actually, I was about to leave. Right, Laura?" Travis says as he heads to the door.

"Yes, thank you. I'll talk to you soon."

Travis turns. "I'll let you know what my source says. Bye." He turns to Colin. "Nice meeting you."

"You, too."

Travis heads down the hallway, leaving Laura and Colin in terrible silence.

She steps toward him. "Hi, how are you?"

He shuts the door and then turns halfway back toward her. "When were you going to tell me?" he says in a low audible tone.

"What?" She comes closer. "How is—"

He abruptly turns. "When, Laura, were you going to tell me about your new spot here?"

She feels the crush of her heart as he finally locks eyes with her. He is hurt. Badly.

"I couldn't say anything. I didn't know how to tell you, and Tucker felt that he wanted—"

"This was Tucker's idea?"

"No, it was mine really."

"It was your idea to do this?"

"Yes, I suggested it a while ago."

"But you never once wanted to fill me in and let me know about how you wanted to change things. For all of us?"

"All of us?"

"Yeah, Ryker, Patrick, Sean. This will affect all of us. And we find out at the last minute. My whole schedule has to change now."

She gets closer to him. She tries to take his hand. He pulls away.

"Colin?"

"What, Laura?"

"You seem…I don't know. Are you okay?"

"I'm not positive. How do you expect me to be in this situation?" He lowers his head.

"How is she?" she asks, barely able to squeeze out the words.

"Awful."

She puts her hand over her heart. "Oh God, it's horrible."

"It is," he whispers. "I don't know what to do."

With a myriad of emotions coursing through her, she remarks, "I know, and I'm hoping I can help."

"Help?"

"Yes, you see, Travis and I—"

"Yeah, who is that guy?"

"Oh, that is Travis from *The Weekly Blue*."

"Travis from *The Weekly Blue*?" he repeats.

"Yeah. He is going to help me with my—"

"Ah, I see," he interrupts. "He is going to help you with your new role."

"Yeah, Tucker—"

"Tucker? *And* Travis? He can help you with your radio segment better than say, Ryker, Patrick, Sean, or me, who live and breathe radio?"

Laura steps back, eyes wide. "Colin, I never meant to...I believe what I can do for the women..."

"What, Laura?"

She starts to stutter. "I plan to interview—"

"You're going to talk about it? Drag a girl through the mud!"

"No, of course not, but I—"

"You know nothing about it," he barks.

"Colin?" She wants to scream that she *does* know about it—all too well in fact. But she would be spilling Abigail's and Bree's darkest secrets simply to prove a point, and that is not who Laura is. Not at all. With a hurtful glance, she asks, "Why are you mad at me?"

"You still don't get it." He starts to turn, and with his hand on the door, he says, "I need to go back and take care of Joey."

"Oh, right. Of course. Are you going to her place?"

"No," he whispers. "She is staying with me."

Laura can't even hold her reaction in. "She is, um, staying with you?"

She watches his shoulders hunch.

He can't even look at her as he says, "Yeah, she needs me right now."

"I understand," she whispers.

He slowly turns his head to glance at her, anguish on his face. He opens his mouth to speak but says nothing. He pulls open the door and exits abruptly, leaving Laura standing there, broken and confused.

She hangs her head. *What just happened? Are we already over before we even began?*

Eleven

THE SOFTER SIDE OF TANK

Laura is sound asleep, and she doesn't hear her door open. Abigail enters the room and switches on the light near her bed. She reaches out, gently touching Laura's leg. She stirs slowly and finally wakes. They lock eyes. Laura scrambles to sit up.

"Hi." Abigail smiles brightly.

"Hi. You're back?" Laura has not seen Abigail or spoken to Nathan since she called him the other night to tell him that she'd been worried sick about her.

Abigail sits at the end of her bed. "Yes, and I had to wake you, so we could talk." Abigail moves closer to her. "I had to say thank you."

Laura whips up her head. "Thank you?"

"Yes. I know you tried to bring Nathan and me back together."

Laura sighs with relief. "I have been worried about you and this whole saga with Tank and Nathan. I had to step in."

"I know. I've been worried myself, to be honest."

"Are you and Nathan okay?"

Abigail smiles widely. Her cheeks are pink and warm. "We are better than okay, Laura. We are back together and happy again."

"Oh, Abigail," Laura gushes as she throws her arms around her neck. "You guys belong together."

"I have you to thank…and Tank, too."

Laura releases her arms. "Tank, too?" She tries not to frown.

"Yes. He went to see Nathan, just like you did, but he wanted to apologize and try to make this all right again."

"Really? Wow."

Not how I imagined this story unfolding.

"Yes, there have been a lot of confusion and rumors and hurt feelings and all because of me…" Abigail starts to cry.

"Please don't cry. You're happy again. That's all that I care about."

"Thank you, Laura. I am happy. More than happy."

Laura's heart softens as she looks at her friend. At this point in her life, she has little to be happy about, but this, this renewed love, does make her content. For now.

A few days later, Laura arrives at the Union with Abigail. Knowing the importance of both Tank and Nathan in Abigail's life, Laura needs to come full circle with Tank. And Tank just might be the one to shed some light on the creep he beat up, so it is a win-win for Laura to make nice with him.

"I don't know why I'm nervous," Laura says as they approach the couches near the fireplace. She apprehensively tucks her hair behind her ear.

"Don't be. Please trust me. He is a good guy."

"If you say so."

"I do." Abigail motions to Laura to sit at a few chairs placed in a corner. Abigail looks around. She spots Tank and waves for him to come over.

With his head hung slightly, he makes his way through the afternoon student crowd and toward their secluded spot.

Laura immediately notes how much better he appears. He is clean. Hair perfectly pulled back in a ponytail. His physique is stronger and more upright than in the past when he was slumped over and inebriated.

He smiles warmly.

"Hey," Abigail says sweetly.

He gives her a friendly hug. "Hey. How are you?"

"Great."

He turns. "Hi, Laura," he says kindly.

"Hello, Tank." She tries to keep her eyes steady, but it proves too difficult for her. "Nice to see you."

"You, too."

Laura watches as Tank drapes his arm around Abigail's shoulders and gives her a welcoming squeeze. Their interaction completely mesmerizes her. It is obvious that they have quite a loving friendship.

"I'm going to grab a coffee, and I'll be back a little later. Cool?" Abigail says as Tank unzips his football warm-up jacket and sits across from Laura.

"Okay," Laura responds.

Tank smiles at Abigail as she turns away. "How are you?" he asks.

"Fine. And you?"

"Hanging in there." He pauses and then continues, "I hope you don't mind that I asked Abby to bring you here, so we could talk."

"Of course not."

"Good. I want you to know that I'm sorry that I was rude to you. In fact, looking back, I was a real jerk." He pauses. "But, all excuses aside, I have had a very difficult few years and…"

Laura tries to put herself in his shoes. He was seventeen when he found out his best friend had an inoperable brain tumor, and he sat by his side as he passed away. It's tragic.

"Tank, I do understand—or at least, I'm trying to. I can't imagine what you must have gone through."

"This past year has been so hard. But I feel like Abigail, Nathan, and I are finally on solid ground. But it wouldn't feel right if I didn't have your friendship, too. Abby means that much to me. And the people in her life mean something to me as well."

The sincerity in his voice is enough to stun Laura.

"I can tell you mean that."

"I do, Laura," he says as he slides forward in his seat. He rests his arms on his knees. "I want you to know that I'm in a good spot now. I'm back on the team and refocused. I won't screw this up again."

"That is great to hear. I'm happy for you."

He smiles sincerely. "I feel like a weight has been lifted off my shoulders," he confesses.

She slightly lowers her head. "I wish I felt the same," she mumbles.

"Everything okay?"

"Oh, yeah. I have this new spot, I guess you could say."

"On the radio?"

"Yeah, and I was hoping I could ask for your help."

"I'm intrigued." He leans in closer to her.

"I am working with the newspaper and would like to talk about the attacks on campus."

"Okay," he says, rubbing his chin. A spark ignites in his silver eyes.

"Have any reservations about me interviewing you?"

"Live?"

"Yes, of course. About everything that is happening here and your perspective on what we as a community could perhaps do to stop this."

His eyebrows slant as he tips his head to the side. "You know the police believe they've caught him? The night I hit him, he went and got medical help about an hour from here, and he has been under surveillance in the hospital ever since."

Her skin prickles. "Are you positive? There have been no such reports."

"Confident. The night of the Black Hearts party. Don't you remember?" he says, giving her a confused expression.

But Joey's attack happened after the Black Hearts party.

"Yes, but I thought he was still out there—"

Tank cuts in, "Unless they really got the wrong guy. But, from what the police have told both Abby and me, they believe they have their man. So, in order not to scare him, they are building their case while he recovers in the hospital. I'm deducing they have a lot of files to go through, and I hope they take as much time as they need. As long as that guy is off the streets, then they should keep it quiet until they are ready to blow the lid off."

Laura's mind races backward as she tries to remember the sequence of events last week.

Could Joey have been attacked by a copycat? Or did they get the wrong guy? Is this campus that unsafe?

"I see..."

"Laura, you all right? Something else going on?"

"I don't know. Maybe, in all my research, I might have gotten some dates or something mixed up," she lies.

She knows exactly what is happening, and she is positively too frightened to tell Tank. She has to find Colin and tell him.

"But, to answer your question, as long as my lawyer says it is okay to speak about it, then I will be happy to shed light on what I know."

Laura panics. If Tank talks about what he knows and she knows that Joey was attacked after, no doubt those surrounding her at the station will swiftly realize they have another creep on campus.

"Thanks, Tank."

"Welcome. Have you told Abby about your plan to interview me?"

"No, I haven't had the chance. As you know, things have been a tad upside down in our world, so I plan to tell her before I go on with the interviews."

"Interviews?"

"Yes, we have a girl who gave an interview to the paper and might be willing to talk about her story on the radio—but only if she is willing."

"In my experience, people tend to deal with a crisis in copious ways. I have realized there is no formula for how to handle tragic situations."

He speaks from experience.

"Thank you for saying that because my goal is to be sensitive to everyone, but I don't want to assume that each person automatically prefers not to talk about it. Some people need to in order to heal."

"Completely agree."

Abigail is making her way back from the coffee shop. She waves slightly.

Tank turns to regard her and then turns back around. "Cool, and like I said, happy to help in any way I can."

"I appreciate that, Tank. I plan to tell her as soon as I get my facts straight."

They watch as their friend approaches.

"Hi," Abigail says sweetly.

"Hi," they both respond.

"Good talk?" she asks with hope.

Tank eyes Laura. "Yes, it went very well," he says with a wink.

Laura nods, but her mind is racing with so many other issues than this newfound friendship with Tank. "Yes, everything is good."

"Oh, good. I'm glad to hear that," she gushes, placing her hand on her chest.

Laura glances at her watch. "Hey, guys, sorry to cut this short, but I have a ton of work to catch up on."

Tank spreads his massive arms out, and within seconds, he is enveloping Laura completely. She laughs as he squeezes her. She returns the hug.

"Thanks, Laura."

"Thank you, Tank. Thanks for keeping Abigail safe."

In hindsight, upon learning of Bree's situation, Laura now knows just how safe he kept her. It could have been far worse. It could have been devastating.

"Thanks for being a good friend," he whispers.

They release their embrace.

Abigail is smiling with misty eyes. "You guys made my day! My two friends are now friends. Yay!" She laughs.

With a chuckle, Laura says, "On that note, I'd better go before I ruin it."

"Nothing could ruin this," she exclaims. "Nothing."

Twelve

ALL THE MEN

Laura spots Colin as she heads down the hallway to the station. She is about to yell his name when Joey comes around the corner and catches up to him. Her heart sinks as she watches the two of them side by side. She lowers her head, hoping to get inside first, but the three of them simultaneously reach the station door.

Trying to be upbeat, she says, "Hey, how are you doing?"

"Fine," they both mumble.

This is the worst situation to be in, and Laura is cringing inside. Colin releases the door and holds it open for the two of them. The entire team turns with pained expressions as they watch the unlikely threesome enter the station.

Sean in particular eyes Laura and then Colin and slightly shakes his head.

"Hey, guys," Laura says.

As Laura heads down the hallway to Tucker's office, she senses someone behind her and turns slightly.

She can hear Colin say to Joey, "I'll be right back."

Her heart skips a beat as he approaches.

"You meeting with Tucker?" he asks.

"Yes," she says, barely able to speak.

"Oh, okay. I'll wait here."

About to knock on Tucker's door, Laura turns. "May I please speak to you in private first?" she says pleadingly.

His tall frame hunches slightly. "Okay."

She opens the door to Studio A. He follows and shuts the door.

"What's up?" he asks as though he were speaking to one of his skateboarding buddies.

Laura's hazel eyes grow wide. "Colin, what can I do to make you realize that I did not mean to hurt you?" she blurts out.

"Nothing," he snaps as he runs his hand through his hair. He looks handsome today despite the tiredness that has set in his eyes.

"Nothing? There is nothing I can do?" Tears start to fill her eyes as she realizes she is in a no-win situation.

"I have too much going on right now," he adds.

"I can see that."

"Can you? Because it doesn't feel that way."

Laura starts to sense an unexplained anger brewing inside her. "I have tried calling you, talking to you, but you've stopped letting me in."

"I've stopped letting you in? Is that how you see it?"

"Yes. You've basically cut me off because I got a new opportunity."

"One that stepped over me. All of us in fact."

"That is fair, but you never even bothered to try to have a conversation about it."

"Like I said, I have a lot going on right now."

"I know, and I'm understanding of that."

"Are you?"

"*Colin.*"

His eyes flash wide at her.

She continues with a smidgen of anger in her voice, "You honestly believe you are the only one this has affected?"

He stares at her, saying nothing.

With sadness in her voice that cannot be masked, she adds, "Joey isn't the only one who could use a friend."

He lowers his head, unable to meet her eyes. She brushes past him, reaching for the door.

Hastily, he grabs her arm. "Laura, please," he begs.

She stops. "You don't want to keep her waiting," she says as a tear falls on her cheek.

He pulls her into him.

She puts her arm up to steady herself from getting too close to him, pressing it on his chest. "*Please don't.*"

"Laura, I need to tell you something."

Bracing for the worst, she can barely glance up to meet his eyes. He takes his hand and draws her chin up to look at him. She swallows hard. He wipes the wet from her cheek. He searches her eyes with desperation.

"What?" She feels the tears beginning to sting again. When he doesn't say a word, she pushes off of him and leans in to open the door.

Without warning, he is drawing her back toward him in a body-hugging embrace. He leans in and kisses her. He eagerly runs his hand down the back of her head, tightly holding her face to his. She can feel the passion, confusion, and desperation swirling between them, and the next thing she knows, she is kissing him back with a longing she has never known to exist before.

Then, without warning, they hear someone yelling down the hallway, "Colin? You in here?"

Colin releases Laura. Her eyes fly open in a stunned fashion. He gives her a sorry expression. Without warning, he turns, shielding Laura from the hallway, and rapidly exits.

Through the door, his voice carries. "Oh, hey. I had to finalize a few things in my studio "

"Oh, is that what was taking you so long?" Joey asks.

"Yeah," Laura hears him say as he hurries back down the hall.

Laura, too shocked to move and feeling weak in the knees, stands there, alone, in Studio A with her heart on her sleeve.

Laura waits a few minutes before exiting Studio A. She sneaks out and gingerly steps down the hallway.

Part of her is thankful to find that both Joey and Colin are gone.

As she enters the main area, Sean motions at her. "Hey, can I talk to you?" he asks.

"Of course."

She starts to follow him down the hallway when the door to the main area of the station opens. Laura turns. Travis is standing there.

"Oh, hello!"

"Hey, got a minute to talk?"

Sean whispers, "We can talk after."

Laura turns to Travis. "Of course. This way."

He follows her down to her studio.

"What's up?" She tries hard to smile.

"I wanted to check in to see if you had any last-minute items you wanted or needed to go over."

"Oh, gosh. Thank you, Travis." She scrambles for her notebook. "I do have something I'd like to run by you."

"Okay," he says, removing his coat.

The tight long-sleeved shirt he has on and the well-fitting jeans are a major distraction. She gets a sensation she tries desperately to shake off. It would be a lot simpler for her if some of these men around her weren't so handsome and brooding.

Focus, Laura!

They both sit near her desk.

She concentrates. "Can you take me through the events that have happened since February, to your knowledge, of the attacker and reported crimes on campus?"

He narrows his eyes, unaware of where she is going with this, but he proceeds anyway, "Yes, of course."

For nearly an hour, he goes through the past seven-plus months' worth of reports from sheer memory.

Stunned, Laura asks, "How do you remember all of this?"

He shakes his head as he says, "Laura, how could anyone forget?"

There is a softness in him that he doesn't often show.

"Right. Of course," she says.

"But here we are today, and thankfully, we're in a much better place."

"You believe it is over?"

"Yes. We have not heard a peep in over two weeks now. Trust me, this guy does not lie in wait. He was active, bold, and aggressive. Moving from one campus to another and another and then back to us. He slipped in and out of sight with ease."

"Hmm."

"You don't seem convinced."

"It's not that. It's just…"

"What, Laura? You okay?"

"Oh, yes, I'm fine, but—"

"Listen," he interjects, "you can tell me things, and I won't tell anyone. I can't really. It's a code we have at *The Weekly Blue*. We don't burn bridges for information."

She takes a deep breath and contemplates her next move. Something has been eating away at her, and she needs to get this off her chest. "I might have heard of another attack, less than a week ago."

His eyes light up at first and then narrow directly. "I see, and you think they are connected?"

"Connected?" she asks.

"Yes. I came to tell you that I just got the inside word that the police have made an arrest. We won't be able to print it until next Wednesday. So, I'm giving you permission to tell everyone. We'll still run it in the paper, and by then, we'll know more details, but I say, go for it, Laura. The people are waiting to hear this. They need to know it."

Laura can feel her skin crawl. "You think I should?"

"Yes, but I'd keep it for last in case you get a lot of questions you can't answer. Tell them you'll have more to come as the process unfolds. The NYPD does not want to make a wrong move and blow this."

"Wow."

"Yeah, some football player, McPherson. They call him Tank. He hit the guy. Valentine's Day weekend. Guess he was pretty banged up, so they had to wait to make their move."

"Tank's a friend of mine."

"Oh, yeah? Ask him about it."

"I did. He said he'd do an interview if his lawyer lets him."

"Oh, perfect. Can I be here to get a few quotes and ask him some questions for the paper?"

"Of course. As long as he is okay with it," she replies.

"Naturally." He pauses, searching Laura's face. "But still, there is something bothering you?"

"It's this other incident. Could there be a copycat on campus?"

He contemplates that for a moment. "Honestly, I can look into it."

"No, it has to remain a secret."

He chuckles. "Everything I do is a secret until it is published in the paper. Believe me, it won't be known."

"Oh, right. Okay."

"Are you afraid, Laura?"

"I'm confused." She unfortunately means this in several aspects of her life. "How could this happen a few weeks after he has been in the hospital? Has everyone gone mad around here? Is the campus that unsafe?"

"Listen, Wolfie is my best reporter. Well, for the sake of argument, let's call him a reporter. He has been all over this story since the moment it broke. If he doesn't know anything about this, he'll find out. Trust me. I'll get back to you soon, okay?"

"Appreciate it."

"No worries, but until then, you are in great shape for Thursday."

"Really?"

"I know so. You'll kill it."

She lets out a long sigh of relief. "Thank you for the boost of confidence."

"Anytime." He starts to stand, and Laura scrambles to her feet. He reaches out his hand to shake hers. "But I got the sense from our first introduction that you don't need a boost of confidence." When she takes his hand, he holds on a tad longer and gazes directly in her eyes. "I'll be in touch."

She swallows hard. "Okay. Thank you, Travis."

"Welcome, Laura."

He lets go of her hand and turns toward the door. Laura drops back in her seat, and with her head in her hands, she considers the afternoon she's had.

Thirteen

WE ARE IN THE BUSINESS OF THE NEWS

With the support of her floor mates, particularly Abigail and Bree, Laura enters the station on Thursday afternoon for her first official shift as OSU's WOUR97 college radio station on-air news correspondent. She is dressed in her favorite bright blue button-down shirt and skintight jeans, with tall brown leather boots on her feet. She spent extra time on her makeup, as Travis alleged the paper planned to send a photographer down to the station for some photos of her on air.

Unfortunately, she has a very heavy heart as she pulls open the door. She has not heard from Colin since they were lip-locked in the studio two days ago. But she did overhear a conversation between Ryker and Sean in which Sean said that Joey was still staying with Colin until the landlord changed all the locks on her house. Laura has also tried to put herself in his shoes. He will now be following her in a different time slot. It hurts her that he got switched, but at this point, her hands are tied.

Tucker peeks in. "Hey, you good to go?"

"Yes," she says with her usual confidence, only this time, she doesn't feel it inside.

"Great!" he says enthusiastically.

"Who is manning the board?" she asks.

"Patrick volunteered."

Relieved, she says, "Oh, great. Thank you."

"Okay. Now, we go live in five minutes."

"I'm ready."

Five minutes flies by, and she finds herself sitting in her chair, headphones on. Within a few seconds of a countdown by Patrick, she is live.

"Good afternoon, Hawks. This is Laura Chase, bringing you our campus and community news. Call me at 555-WOUR and let me know what you'd like to discuss regarding this week's top headlines.

"But, until then, let me begin this segment with our Greek news. Delta Sigma Theta is currently under charter review for an alleged hazing incident last week. Sorority president, Sasha Wilson, says—and I quote—'*The women of Delta Sigma Theta take any incident of hazing or misconduct very seriously. We are cooperating with the university on this matter.*' I received an update from our friends at *The Weekly Blue* that a meeting is scheduled between the school review board and the Greek life president, set for April 23. To read more about the school policy on hazing and Greek life, you can view our handbook under Student Activities. I will keep you updated on any new information about this meeting at a later segment.

"In local news, for those of us who love the downtown bookstore, it is in jeopardy of closing if the school doesn't decide to buy it and make it a part of the campus. They are asking all supporters of this transaction to sign a petition at the bookstore no later than April 18 if the bookstore is to become an official downtown store of OSU.

"I am encouraging all our listeners to show up and support this school landmark, aptly named the Unofficial School Bookstore. The proprietor of the bookstore is James Montgomery. His great-grandfather, the late Walter Montgomery, donated money to build what is now Montgomery Hall. Let's keep the Montgomerys in mind when signing the petition and make another great establishment live on at OSU."

She pauses for a moment. "Caller, you are on the air."

"Yes, hi. I agree with you about the bookstore. The owners are awesome, and they always stock all our textbooks and at the best prices. I plan to bring my roommates and go down there to sign the petition. Hopefully, the school will buy it."

"One can only hope. What we need to do as students is show the university that we want it to become a part of the school. Let's hope they listen. Thanks for calling. Next caller."

"Hey, Laura. This is cool. I'm glad the station is doing it."

"Thank you. Appreciate the call. Please give us your feedback on this segment by dropping off your comments in the box posted outside the station."

Laura flips the page of her notes and then continues.

"And, now, to sports. The men's hockey team is playing in the semifinals on Saturday. Tickets are still available but going fast. Don't forget to wear your school colors. The Union is selling OSU winter hats and scarfs at a discounted price this week. Grab yours and wear them to the game. The women's swim team is coasting to another spectacular season, as they crushed the Orangemen for the fifth year in a row. Katie Donahue currently holds the school record for the fifty-meter butterfly. Next home swim meet for the Hawks is Tuesday night at eight p.m. The men's baseball team kicks off their season on Saturday after a less than stellar preseason in which they finished two and eight. But Coach Christian truly believes that, with the help of freshman phenom Jake Wilson behind the plate, the Hawks can only get better. Game time is at one p.m. this Saturday."

The show continues for another thirty minutes as caller after caller adds their two cents on the news she has already mentioned. A few people call in to talk about sports. With the help of Jen, Laura lined up Katie Donahue to call in to talk about her school record and her time on the swim team.

Then, with a deep breath, she adds, "In final news, the campus police have reported that they have a man in custody that *they* believe to be the perpetrator who has been attacking women on numerous campuses throughout New York. It's reported that OSU is being revered as the reason the Campus Creeper might have been caught on Valentine's Day weekend. Further details to come in the next few weeks, so please stay tuned."

She pauses as she watches the lights blink on the caller board. "Caller, you are on the air."

"Thanks, Laura. I like that you called him the Campus Creeper because that is exactly who he is. But, furthermore, I'm glad you are talking about this because there are more whispers than facts."

"I understand. The newspaper has excellent fact-checkers, so I encourage all of you to read about what is happening on our campus and not perpetuate misleading remarks or rumors."

"Thanks, Laura."

"Next caller."

Laura can hear a low audible voice. "Hello?"

"Hello, caller?"

Then a squeak is heard. "I wanted to call in and say that we need to come together on this. I know someone who was affected by this, and it's devastating."

"Yes, it absolutely is, and you are right. As a campus, we need to come together, all of us, and find a way to heal. I am open to suggestions and better ways in which to help."

"I wish I had some suggestions right now, but for me, merely opening up the dialogue helps. So, thank you."

"You are most welcome. Next caller, you are on with Laura."

An angry male voice quips, "I want to know what the men on this campus are going to do to get our reputation back. I can't even walk alone without someone giving me a look like I'm a creep. *It sucks.*"

Stunned by his comment, Laura has to react on her feet. Dead airtime is bad airtime. "Exactly why I feel we need to join forces to reconcile as a community. Not just as women or as men, but together. This has hit all of us. People we know and care about. The boyfriends, fathers, and friends of these women, they count, too, in all of this. For me personally, I think we need to keep this in mind. It has brought a harsh reality for everyone on this campus and for all those who care and worry about us."

"Thanks, Laura. You rock."

"Thank you for calling and voicing your feelings. We have time for one last caller."

"Yeah, Laura. When are we going to know who this scumbag is?"

"Not positive. But the judicial process is arduous and lengthy and, hopefully, for good reason. I'll be sure to keep you posted. We can all be certain of that in this time of ambiguity." She continues, "I want to thank you all for your support today. Thanks for calling in and allowing me to come into wherever you are right now. But, for now, Hawks, my hour is up for this segment of the news. I'll be back on Monday with all the highlights from the weekend. Until then, be safe, be happy, and look out for one another. From all of us at WOUR97, have a great weekend."

Laura turns off her microphone and switches off the board. Patrick gives her a surprisingly enthusiastic thumbs-up. She returns a smile. She remains in her chair awhile longer, contemplating her hour segment as she takes notes in her notebook about the callers, questions, where she might have stumbled for an answer, and what might be of continued interest for the next time. One thing is for certain; the campus is divided as to whether or not the students can move forward together.

There is a slight knock on the studio door.

"Come in," she yells, hoping it's Colin wanting to congratulate her on the show and to tell her that he supports her.

Instead, Travis opens the door with a welcoming smile. "Great job, Laura. Really great," he says with such sincerity as he closes the door behind him.

Forcing a wide smile, she replies, "Thank you. You liked it?"

"Liked it? It was great. On point, concise, and..." He pauses.

"What? You can tell me."

He now has her full attention.

"You seemed like a natural, and it surprised me." His expression is very serious.

"Okay..." Laura responds with an equally questioning countenance.

He starts to smile wide. He has an incredibly confident smile. "I didn't know how to say that without it coming off the wrong way, but I was really impressed."

"I'd rather impress than disappoint." She bashfully lowers her eyes as she fidgets with the edge of her sweater.

"Mind if I take a few pictures?" he asks.

"Um, okay," she replies as she tucks her hair behind her ear.

"Let me get a couple of you working the board," he says.

"Like this?" she asks, moving the dials.

"Perfect. Just do what you'd normally do, and I'll just snap away." And he does, making her incredibly uncomfortable. Gently folding his arms over his chest, he says, "What do you say we get out of here and talk for a little bit? I have a few things to fill you in on, and I'd rather it not be here."

Intrigued, she responds, "Okay. Like where?"

"I'll meet you down at Cool Beans, say in half an hour?"

"Perfect. I'll see you then."

"Great." Travis, without glancing back at her, pulls open the studio door and waltzes down the hall.

Laura finishes up organizing her things. Back in the main area now, she finds an empty front room, much to her disappointment. She decides to check in with Tucker. She knocks on his door.

"Come in," he yells.

Laura opens the door, gently closing it behind her. He stands and extends his hand out to shake hers. She takes it with a smile.

"Excellent job, Laura. Excellent."

"Thank you, Tucker."

"Please have a seat. I have some feedback I'd like you to take away and mull over. Maybe make some adjustments, accordingly."

"Of course," she answers as she sits in the chair crosswise from him and retrieves her notebook.

"Consider leading with the top stories and not ending with them. This gives the callers more opportunity to discuss the topics that seem to matter the most on campus. I'd also consider ending with the sports. I like the idea of an athlete of the week calling in to talk about the team, but again, save that for last."

"Agreed. I was uneasy about announcing the news about the arrest with so little information to back it. I was super nervous to open the floodgates. But, yes, I should leave more time for the major topics."

Tucker nods his head. "Yes, that was big news, which will be sure to stir things up around here. I'm just so thankful they got the punk."

"Me, too. It's a huge relief."

He pauses, glancing down at his notes. "It might not be a bad idea to tee up a few callers in the beginning, so we have enough audience participation. Ask some of your friends to call in with certain questions until this catches on and especially on the days where the news might be a little lighter."

Laura laughs. She is almost certain that Jen, Melissa, Casey, and Bree would be more than willing to call in. Abigail and Maddie might take more convincing, but if she indeed needed them to, she knows they would be there for her.

"Absolutely. I will do that."

"Great. And one last thing. Did you hear that they call him the Campus Creeper or…"

Again, she fidgets with her hands. "No, that sort of flew out of my mouth."

He laughs slightly. "Good. And tell your friend Travis at *The Weekly Blue* to give you full credit on that."

She laughs. "I will. I am meeting him shortly at Cool Beans," she adds, glancing at her wristwatch. "I think he has a few stories in the works for the next segment."

"Is he behaving?"

"Truly. He is quite kinder than he was. He's been very helpful."

"Glad to hear. After all, we are in this together with the same goal in mind."

"Exactly. He gets that now. At least, I hope it's not fleeting."

I hope not because, right now, he's the only one I can really go to with my concerns, or I might not make it through this crazy time in my life.

Laura enters Cool Beans and walks up to the counter and orders a black coffee. Travis is tucked in the back corner, his long legs spread out in front of him as he is pressed up against the wall, reading a book. He glances up and smiles. With her backpack slung over one shoulder, she balances her cup of coffee in the other hand as she approaches.

Nervously, she sits across from him. "Hi. Sorry to keep you waiting." She unzips her jacket.

As she pulls her arms out, his eyes grow wide as her ample breasts stretch her shirt. She blushes as she tosses her jacket on the empty chair next to her.

"No need to be. I was reading and enjoying the quiet away from all the clicking of keyboards I tend to hear in my free time."

She can't help but snicker at his observation. "Yeah, must be real hard on the days you've got a headache."

"Worse when I'm hungover." He chuckles with a little spark in his eye.

She smiles and takes a sip of her piping hot coffee. "I can imagine."

"Tucker have feedback for you?"

"Of course, and I agree with all of it. I need to lead with the big stories. Essentially, I must reorder my topics."

"Yeah, makes sense. The paper puts the vital ones on the cover, that's what people want."

"Exactly."

Travis glances around the room in a secretive fashion and then leans in closer toward Laura. "Listen, Wolfie has uncovered nothing about any additional attacks on campus. He is still digging as we speak, but I've got a funny feeling about this."

Laura's eyes grow wide. "What do you mean?"

"Wolfie has a few moles in the football, hockey, soccer, and lacrosse houses. But he does not want to shake the tree too much. If the male athletes on campus catch wind that we are investigating them again, it can have serious repercussions."

"Investigating again?" Laura asks with a confused stare.

"Yeah, the last guy said he was a football player. He might have used the lacrosse team as well. But, man, they did not like the fact that the paper was digging around. It pissed a lot of them off and, in hindsight, rightfully so."

"Right, I did hear about that. The Creeper saying he was an athlete."

"Your friend Tank did the best thing for the athletes on this campus. By kicking that guy's ass, he set the doubters straight again."

She smiles slightly. *He is a good guy, and boy, did he set this skeptic straight.*

"Okay, what do you believe is happening?"

"I'm not certain, but I want to pursue this as quietly as humanly possible. No one can know we are looking into this yet."

"Okay," she says, sensing there is more to come.

"But we have to stick to our story and lure this person or whatever out into the open. By continuing to act as though he has been caught and is in custody, one of two things might happen. One, this new guy might believe he is in the clear to strike again, or two, he'll be so pissed we are not buying into this fresh hell that he will eventually make a mistake."

Speechless, Laura continues to listen and sip her coffee while Travis explains the game plan he and Wolfie devised this past year. "We kept our eyes peeled at parties and especially walking home at night. We wanted to see if anyone was acting suspiciously. We even had a couple of our female staffers play decoy. But nothing ever came of it." But he does not hesitate to remind her that he feels this might be a different case.

"You keep saying that, but how can you be certain?"

"It's a gut feeling. Look, I'm not saying to be reckless or pretend the campus is a hundred percent safe, but the school might be less dangerous than we think."

"What about your contacts at the other universities? What do they have to say?"

Travis's sly smile gives Laura the chills as she watches his eyes dance all over her with obvious approval.

"What?" she asks, feeling incredibly self-conscious.

"Now, you are rationalizing like one of us." He leans back in his chair, never taking his eyes off hers.

She lowers her lashes, as his stare is too much for her.

One of them, huh? Here I thought that all I ever wanted to be was one of the radio guys, but maybe The Weekly Blue *is where I really belong. I won't get in Colin's way, schedules don't have to change, and I can investigate at my free will.*

But I love the radio; it's my home.

He interrupts her thoughts, "We can't put out any feelers yet. I'm afraid, if we do, more people will catch wind of this, and they can blow it right out of the water. We have to keep this under wraps for now."

"Okay. What next?"

"Let Wolfie do his thing, and in the meantime, see if you can book that interview with Tank."

"He said he'd do it, but I need to double check."

"Okay, and I've got a few shadow stories coming out from some of my junior writers…"

"Shadow stories?"

"Yeah, back cover, minimal words, stories that mimic others but contain different information."

"Interesting. Like what?"

"Some street reporting we do, feedback and touchpoints from the student body on the assaults—that sort of stuff. More angles in which we can shed some light on this debacle." Travis glances at his watch. "Wow, didn't realize the time. You want to grab a bite to eat?"

Laura stumbles over her words but finally slips out, "I am supposed to meet my friends for dinner—"

"Some other time," he says before Laura can consider her options.

"Sounds good," she whispers.

He starts to stand, and he gathers his book and empty coffee cup. She lets him pass and then rises as well, pulling on her coat as she does. She grabs her cup and bag and follows him toward the door, placing her empty mug atop the tray placed on the shelf near the exit.

They stroll back toward campus.

As they get to the top of the hill, he stops and turns toward her. "I'm going to head back to my place."

"You're not going to eat?" she asks, confused.

"I'll make something in my apartment."

"Oh, right. Of course."

"You did great today, Laura," he says so sincerely that it catches her off guard for a moment. "I believe we have the start of something great, a new relationship."

With that, he leans in and delicately kisses her on the cheek. Stunned, she starts to misstep awkwardly. Quickly, he reaches for her arm and steadies her.

Embarrassed, she mumbles, "Sorry, caught my foot on—"

"Good night, Laura," he says with a slight chuckle that somehow puts her back at ease.

"Good night," she yells after him as he heads down the path toward the off-campus streets that encompass the university grounds. "And thanks."

He waves slightly, and within moments, he is out of her view.

Fourteen

NEEDED ADVICE

Laura enters the cafeteria and grabs a sandwich and salad before heading over to the usual table with her floor mates. Her head is spinning with all sorts of torrid thoughts as she eyes her friends.

Bree immediately asks, "What has got you all hot and heavy?"

"What? Nothing!" she responds with too much protest.

Thankfully, Jen pipes in, "Awesome job today, girl!"

"Yeah, you were great," Casey adds. "We listened to the whole thing in Bree's room."

Laura takes her seat across from Bree and smiles. "Better sound quality?" Laura adds with a wicked snicker.

Bree bursts out loud, "But of course! You know me so well."

"Congratulations, Laura. You were incredible," Abigail adds her two cents, sporting a sweet smile. "Nathan said the whole football team listened during a team workout in the gym. A few of the guys said they'd be happy to come on and talk about the team if you're looking for other athletes."

"Cool. Love hearing that!"

"Yeah, obviously, you have full access to the soccer team, so say the word," Jen adds.

"Awesome, guys. Thank you all. I am overwhelmed today, to say the least. It's been a whirlwind. I only hope I can keep up with my job and my studies. I can't let my grades slip."

"I imagine it will be difficult to balance. But you're doing a great thing," says Abigail.

"Besides, I'm sure everyone on campus was happy to hear about the guy being caught...officially," Bree responds.

"Yeah, being close to it, it wasn't a surprise. But I'm sure you made a lot of people feel relieved today," Abigail adds.

Laura smiles. "Thanks. I sure hope that is the consensus."

After a few rare moments of silence, Jen clears her throat and announces, "Ladies, Spring Fling is next weekend. Are we all going to the soccer and football parties on Saturday?"

Melissa perks up. "I'm going to meet Logan at the football party at some point, but I'll do whatever you want to do first." She smiles wide as she envisions Logan.

The two have been dating for a few months now, and according to Melissa, he is wonderful, thoughtful, and very kind. He is also very close friends with Webber, Nathan's roommate, so the two of them tend to be seen wherever Nathan is.

Logan, the arithmetic wiz, is at OSU on some special scholarship in exchange for a mathematic formula he solved his senior year in high school. Only a professor at Harvard University had been able to solve it prior to that. When the school had found out, they'd offered him a full ride with the stipulation that he assist Professor Jenkins, who is trying to win a grant for the school with little success to date.

"Why don't we all go to the soccer house first and then the football house?" Casey asks.

They all nod their heads, except Maddie.

"What is it, Maddie?" Jen asks.

"Don't kill me, but I might go to Delta Chi. They had such a killer Halloween party, and I hear their Spring Fling is totally wild. Moon Boot Lover is playing at noon, and then Rustic Overtones is playing in the late afternoon."

"We all know how much you love Moon Boot Lover! The football house got Harpoon to play at night. Maybe we can plan to be there for the nighttime?" Melissa asks.

"Sounds good to me," Maddie agrees.

"Yeah, I'm cool with whatever you guys decide," Abigail says.

"You're the girl with the information," Bree says to Laura. "What do you think?"

Laura sighs deeply. "Honestly, I'd like to go where my friends are. I can't remember the last time I even went to a party. I feel like I'm running in circles."

Abigail slightly nudges her under the table as she watches her friend's expression turn somber. Thankfully, no one else notices. Laura barely gives Abigail a sideways glance.

After a few more bites and some more conversation, the girls wrap up dinner and head toward their rooms.

Laura sits at her desk and stares aimlessly out into the atmosphere. She knows she should be studying, but she can't concentrate.

"Hey," Abigail quietly says.

Laura spins partly toward her. "Hey. I was…"

Abigail waits for her to finish her thought. When she doesn't, Abigail says, "You want to talk about it?"

Laura's eyes mist. "I have no idea where to even begin."

"Does this have to do with work or school or—"

"I suppose all of that," she interjects, fighting back her tears.

"You're not in trouble with school, right? You're nowhere near failing, so is it merely a lot to keep up with?"

"No. I guess school is fine. It *is* fine. I'm passing everything. No concerns there."

"Okay…but?"

Laura turns and stares back out across the thawing Upstate New York campus. The buds on the trees are beginning to show signs of spring.

"It's pretty here, isn't it?" Laura whispers as if she were alone with only her thoughts.

"Yes, it is." Abigail, too, turns and faces the campus, watching a few students move in and out of the buildings spread out below.

"Have you ever wondered how we all kind of fall into things and how it can change us? As people. Change us as people."

"Change us? I suppose every decision we make leads us in one direction and not the other."

"I hope I've made the right decisions."

"Knowing you, Laura, you have," Abigail adds.

"Then, why do I feel like this?" she asks as she turns and locks eyes with Abigail. A lone tear falls on her pale cheek.

"What is going on, Laura? Please let me in. I can help you."

She releases a deep sigh. "The radio station, the news segment I'm doing—"

"You're concerned about it? But why?"

"I have to report what I know, and I'm afraid I'll be reporting on things that can affect certain people. I'm worried I'll make a mistake and upset people."

"Upset people? Do you mean Bree and me?"

"Yes, and let's say someone like you guys. Someone close to the story, too."

"Okay. But, speaking from experience, I can't be upset with someone for reporting what is, one, extremely relevant to our campus and, two, going to be reported with or without me—whether by you, by the paper, or by anyone within two hundred miles of this place. No one single person can stop what is coming." Abigail reaches over and touches Laura's leg, gently rubbing it.

"But I don't want to hurt anyone…"

"Of course you don't. Do you remember what you told Bree and me about all this?"

Laura glances up with extremely sad eyes.

"You told us, he, the Creeper, is the reason this happened, not us. That holds true from now until the end of all of this. If you stop believing it, Laura, it will show, and you can't let him win. You have earned an unprecedented opportunity on this campus to report, for the first time, the information that matters to all of us. No matter the topic, as long as you are factual and concise, no one can fault you for that."

Easier said than done. "You're saying I should plow ahead, paying no mind to others?"

Abigail leans back in her chair, contemplating her impending words. Abigail's eyes take in everything—Laura's demeanor, the roundness of her back and slumped shoulders—and then it hits her.

"You don't have to tell me names, but this has to do with someone. Someone has gotten to you. But why?"

Laura drops her eyes toward the ground. She knows she can't go at this alone. She simply can't. "I'm helping the paper—Travis actually— investigate another attack," she blurts out. Even though she promised Travis she would keep it under wraps, she knows without a doubt that Abigail will keep this close to the vest.

Abigail gasps, "What?"

"Shh, you cannot tell anyone."

"I won't, promise."

"I'm torn, Abigail. Travis says we need to be careful about the story, and Colin doesn't want—"

"Colin knows? And who is Travis?"

"Of course Colin knows; he works at the station. Travis works at the paper. He's sort of become my unofficial partner in the news segment." Laura can feel her frustration beginning to surface, to no fault of Abigail's.

"Okay, is this like an issue with the paper or the station? I'm not clear."

Of course you're not clear. I'm unclear myself, and I've been knee deep in this for a few weeks. How can I get Colin to grasp things through my eyes when he is looking directly into Joey's? He doesn't know that I, too, lived it, side by side, with not one, but two of my closest friends at school. I know how painful this has been and will continue to be. I can't tell Travis either, for fear he'll turn it into an opportunity for another exclusive interview. I can't do that to you and Bree.

"Laura?" Abigail whispers, snapping her out of her thoughts. "What does this have to do with Colin and Travis? Why would Colin care if you reported on this?"

Lying in Wait

Because Joey refuses to report her attack to the police. But Colin knows, I know about it. So if the word gets out, he'll suspect one of us at the station spilled the beans. And he's already furious with me over this whole news thing. Investigating Joey without her permission would really piss him off. Thinking swiftly on her feet, she says, "He wouldn't really. I mean, he wants to stick to the facts, I suppose."

"So, you wouldn't be sticking to the facts?" she asks with a furrowed brow. "What gives?"

"Nothing."

"You like this guy or something?"

Laura considers long and hard how to answer her. Yes, she does like him. In fact, she'll never admit how much she cares about him. But he is preoccupied, and that doesn't seem to be changing. Hard to blame him. If Joey is hurting a smidgen as much as Abigail or Bree did, then she knows Joey needs Colin more than she does right now.

"We're friends. We work together, and I suppose there could be some feelings going on, but..."

Abigail starts to grin. "Feelings?"

Laura does not return a smile. In fact, she appears quite despondent.

"But...is it timing or something else?"

"Yeah, I suppose you might say it is bad timing. They moved me into his spot to do the news, and he got moved to the late shift. I had not seen that coming when I pitched the idea. I know he's upset about being switched and that I didn't tell him myself."

"I'm sorry to hear that. Hey, sometimes, it doesn't happen overnight. He'll come around. And what about Travis? Any potential there?"

"Travis?"

"Yeah, you said you work with him, too. I'm just asking...is the guy easy on the eyes?"

Laura can feel her face flush as she reminisces about Travis leaning in to innocently kiss her on the cheek. "If you like the tall, handsome, and overly confident type, then yeah, Travis is that guy."

Abigail's eyes get wide. "But what?"

"He's not interested in some freshman girl. That guy is like the king of the paper. You should see all the chicks he's got working under him. They look at him like he is some kind of god. He is helping me because, if I look good, then he looks good. Quid pro quo."

"And Colin?"

"What about him?"

"He more your type?"

Laura pauses and remembers the day in the back room of Studio A when he sweetly cornered her to try to console her. She can picture his lofty, muscular frame approaching her, placing his arms around her slender body. The warmth of his embrace and the smell of patchouli and soap as it lingered on his skin. She breathed in his scent, not knowing she'd have such limited occasion to do so. When he kissed her, she felt her heart beat in a rhythm never tested before. A part of her wishes that day had never happened. Unfortunately for her, an even bigger part of her wishes for another day exactly like that. But what is bringing her down so deeply is that she is convinced she will never have the chance again.

Sensing Abigail staring at her, she answers, "Like I said, it's complicated. It's all about timing, and it keeps becoming apparent that I am out of sync."

Pondering her roommate's confessions, Abigail gently takes her hand. "Laura, maybe right now is the time for you to focus on you and the opportunity you have been afforded at Onondaga."

Laura raises her head. It's not as though Abigail said something so profound that she had not considered it before. It's that it came from Abigail's lips—her roommate, her friend, and unfortunately but most importantly, one of his victims. As her beautiful hazel eyes, although sad, catch Abigail's face, Abigail notes something igniting in her reverence. She looks out on the now deserted campus—the town that comes alive during the day but has been put into a deep, nocturnal slumber over the past year, out of fear.

Then, she faces her friend, tilts her head to the side, and gently speaks, "Maybe you're right, Abigail, and maybe I need to focus on why I, of all people, was given a chance to bring awareness to this on campus. I was given the open airwaves to reach the student body. I have to take that as a gift, and it is not one I'll get again, if I screw it up."

Abigail smiles wide. "That's the Laura I know. You don't let anyone get in your way from doing what is right. It's what I admire most about you."

Laura pauses. She had to press forward with Nathan, all so she could try to help a friend in need. She didn't let that little voice inside her head control what she ultimately knew was the right thing to do.

"Thank you, Abigail."

"Don't thank me yet. In fact, I owe you a lot more than some lousy advice," she says with a chuckle.

"It's good advice, and you know it." Laura sports a smile for the first time this evening.

"I'm here for you—always. Please let me know if I can help. You have my support, Bree's support, and support from all the girls on this floor who know you and love you. Move forward with that in mind, and hopefully, the rest will fall into place if it is meant to be."

Abigail is right. If I put my mind to helping others and supporting this campus the best way I know how, then no one can fault me for that, not even Colin. Having him alongside me would make this misadventure so much more doable. But, for now, I guess I'll just have to give him some space.

Fifteen

SPRING FLING 1996

"Remember, girls," Brittney, their dorm monitor, shouts over the girls huddled in the hallway, "stick together, no matter what. It's going to get crazy today. Make no mistake; this campus is still vulnerable to men behaving badly. Just because it's Spring Fling weekend doesn't mean you let your guard down. In fact, it means just the opposite. Understood?"

"Yes!" the girls all respond.

The girls devised a plan to stick together and to keep themselves in check despite the massive parties they would be attending all day.

"Have everything you need in your backpacks?" Bree asks the girls. Bree is taking zero chances and made sure to pack her pepper spray.

"Yes, I do. Bree, you want to wear open-toed shoes? The campus is full of mud," Casey says.

Bree looks down at all the girls lined up in the hallway. They are dressed head to toe in hiking boots, jeans, and an assortment of different-colored flannel shirts.

"Bree, I'd reconsider," Laura says gently.

"Ugh, fine, I'll change," Bree scoffs as she unlocks her door and goes back inside her room.

A few minutes later, she returns, wearing knee-high brown leather boots.

"Now, are we ready?" she asks.

"Come on," Maddie says as she passes by the girls. "Can't be late for Moon Boot Lover!"

"Right," Melissa adds.

The campus is filled with thousands of students traveling in packs, making their way to their perspective parties. They pass a house party with a ten-foot-tall Jenga game and watch in amazement as some guy is able to balance the massive log on top.

Once the girls arrive at Delta Chi, they hand their money to the guy at the gate and then descend into the backyard. Maddie screeches as she hears the lead singer announce the band. She grabs Casey's hand and pulls her toward the stage. Jen is close behind.

Laura, Bree, Abigail, and Melissa find a spot off to the side of the stage and each grab a can of beer out of their backpacks. They sip slowly as the band transitions into their next song.

A few beers later, Maddie rushes toward them, all flushed and out of breath. "Aren't they awesome?" she asks enthusiastically.

"Totally," Melissa adds.

"I like them more than I thought I would," Abigail says.

"Me, too. I might ask the lead singer if he'll come into the station," Laura adds.

"Oh, great idea," Bree chimes in.

"I want a front-row seat for that!" Maddie gushes.

Once the band ends their last song, Maddie, Jen, Casey, and Bree all decide to stay at the party for the late afternoon band while Laura, Abigail, and Melissa head over to the football party. With their backpacks strapped on tight, they trek through the back roads and over toward the Ridge. The crowd gathered in the front of the house is much different than the usual post-football parties they host with alumni in attendance. This party is rowdy and overcrowded.

With confidence, Abigail greets Junior, the official security guard of the football team parties.

He doesn't even hesitate to open the gate. "Ladies, welcome. Nathan is somewhere back here."

"Thanks, Junior," she says as she passes him, gently patting his massive bicep.

Melissa and Laura are close behind.

The backyard is completely mobbed with students. There is barely room to maneuver their way through the crowd, and even if they could, they'd have no clue as to which direction to go. They decide to pick a path and aimlessly wander through the mass of students while sipping on beer, stopping every few minutes to chat with someone they recognize from a class or their dorm.

Without warning, Abigail feels an arm throw its weight around her.

She tries to break loose until he whispers, "There you are. I've been waiting forever for you."

She spins around, smiling from ear to ear. "Nathan, you scared me."

Nathan leans down and seductively presses his lips onto hers while Laura and Melissa watch with wide eyes and pinked cheeks.

"Jesus, you two," Melissa says. "Can you unlock your lips, so I can ask where Logan is?"

The two part, and without glancing over at Melissa, Nathan says, "This way. Follow me."

Toward the back of the yard and near the band setting up is most of the football team along with Logan and Webber. Melissa hurries over to Logan and joins him for a beer.

Webber perks up as soon as Abigail nears. "My friend," he slurs.

He wobbles, cockeyed, over toward her and gives her a big hug. She smiles and returns his embrace.

"You seem like you are having fun," she adds with a smirk.

"I thought I was drunk the first time I was here, but nope ..I'm drunker now!"

Laura's disconnection to the conversations around her is new for her. She observes Webber, Logan, and Melissa as they chat about some video game they like to play back in their dorm rooms. Laura soon realizes that, in the span of a short time, she has consumed a few more beers. Yet she feels nothing inside. She cracks open another one.

Here's to loneliness.

She takes a sip. She glances around the party in search of no one. She lets out a long sigh, and then Melissa snuggles up next to her.

"Want a change of scenery?" she asks.

"How did you know?" she responds.

"I can tell. Let's go inside."

"Sounds good."

Melissa and Laura enter the crowded living room and grab a drink at the bar.

"What gives, Laura? You okay?"

"I don't know, Melissa. Really, I don't. I thought going out today would make me happy, but it's not working."

"I'm sorry. How can I help?"

"You are, just by being here."

She takes the cup from Laura's hand and goes back over to the bar. Laura leans on the wall, briefly closing her eyes. Contemplating nothing in particular, just the beat of the drum as the music loudly transcends over the meaningless conversations that surround her. Moments later, when she opens them, she finds Colin standing only feet from her with a straight face. No smile whatsoever.

She doesn't feel like smiling either.

He steps closer to her. "You all right?"

"I'm fine," she says through clenched teeth. She looks slightly past him, expecting that Joey will only be centimeters from him.

"Okay," he says. He, to some degree, turns and then stops.

Melissa hands Laura another drink. Quickly, Laura takes a few rather large sips.

Melissa looks at the boy standing near her friend and then back to Laura. "Everything okay here?" she asks.

"Dandy. Colin and I work at the station together."

"Oh, right. I've heard you on the radio," Melissa adds cheerfully.

He reaches his hand out, and Melissa takes his hand.

"Nice to meet you. I'm Melissa, one of Laura's floor mates."

"You, too," he quips as he veers his eyes toward Laura.

Awkwardly, Melissa adds, "Hey, I'm going to find Logan, and I'll be back."

On the tip of Laura's tongue are the words, *No, please don't go,* but instead, she says nothing.

Once Melissa leaves, Laura takes another sip of her drink, averting her eyes from landing on his. She hasn't seen him in a week, and this brief encounter alone has left a pit in her stomach. Colin goes to speak, and when he doesn't, Laura finishes her drink and brushes past him.

"Hold on," he says authoritatively.

"Yes, Colin, what?" she says with disdain dripping from her otherwise kind voice.

"You are going to leave?" In order to decrease the gap between them, he takes a step closer toward her.

She slightly staggers. He reaches for her arm to steady her. The touch of his large hand on her arm is more than she can handle.

"Please," she whispers.

"I get that you don't want to talk to me."

"Do you?"

"Laura, I don't want it to be this way."

She locks eyes with him, searching his face for a better answer. "You still mad at me for the news thing?" she blurts out.

He reaches his hand up toward her face. "If I'm being honest, I don't like the evening shift. I worked hard to get the afternoon."

Stunned by his admission, she reacts, "I'll quit then."

"Don't be ridiculous."

"Where's Joey?" she hisses in a drunken state.

"Home, I assume."

"Would you excuse me for a moment?"

She heads toward the kitchen. Laura can feel the beer sloshing in her stomach as she tries to make her way to the bathroom. She dances from foot to foot as she anxiously anticipates her turn.

About twenty minutes later, she is stumbling her way back outside and toward her friends when she halts in her path. Colin is standing near Abigail and Melissa and chatting incessantly over the loud music.

With narrowed eyes, Laura approaches. "What's this all about?"

Abigail responds with wide eyes, "Colin here was telling us how you work together." She smiles.

"Is that so?" Laura slurs.

Colin interjects before the conversation turns hostile, "Laura, I was telling your friends here that I was hoping to catch you before I left; that's all."

"Leave? Where are you going?"

"I'm—"

"Never mind. I don't want—"

"I'm going to grab some food and then head over to a friend's house," he says over the music.

Laura huffs and starts to say something when Colin places his hand on her arm, all while giving Melissa and Abigail a sympathetic glance. Laura freezes.

Colin leans in and adds, "Hey, come get some food with me. Then, I'll bring you back to your friends right after, promise."

She whips her head up at him. "You're serious?" she slurs.

"Laura," he says with shock, "yeah, I'm serious."

She looks toward Abigail and Melissa. Laura can feel the tension in her shoulders begin to relax as her two friends scoot her away. "I guess I could eat."

"I'll have her back in an hour," he says to the girls.

"We'll be here," Melissa replies.

With some reluctance, Laura follows Colin out of the gate and down the driveway toward the road. Inside, she is dying to ask him why he was at the party to begin with. They wander in silence through the crowds of students partying along the street. At some point, a rowdy group of guys streams past them, bumping Laura like a pinball in between them. She trips forward, barely being caught by Colin's firm grip. Her hand scrapes along the gravel as she tries to catch herself.

"Hey, watch it!" he yells to them.

They barely acknowledge him, nor do they say sorry to Laura.

Laura shakes her arm free of Colin as she winces in pain. She grabs her hand, and the blood begins to pool in her palm. "Great," she mumbles.

"Come on," he says. "Let me fix that up for you."

"I'm fine. Forget about it."

"Laura, please let me help you. Then, I won't bother you anymore."

For some reason, his words sting far worse than the damn scrape on her hand.

"Fine." She follows him toward his dorm.

He keys into the front door and leads her over to the elevator. She realizes she has never been in Simmons Hall and, more importantly, in his room. Something about this revelation makes her uneasy and nervous.

He opens his door. She is half-expecting Joey's clothes to be strewed about but is surprised when she enters. His room is orderly and clean with no sign of a female roommate.

"Have a seat," he says, motioning to his desk chair. "I'll be right back." He leaves, carrying a towel, and returns moments later with it damp. "Let me take a look at your hand."

She stretches her arm out toward him and slightly turns her head. He releases her fingers one by one and opens her palm, assessing the wound. He dabs the wet towel on the scrapes, trying gently to remove the gravel still stuck in her flesh. She winces.

"Sorry. Just trying to clean it out."

"It's okay," she whispers.

He kneels before her. He reaches into his desk drawer and pulls out a large bandage and gauze. "I've had a lot of skateboarding accidents over the years, so I always have a bandage handy."

"How long have you been skateboarding?"

"Oh boy, since I can remember. Probably started when I was six years old. I did some amateur competitions in high school. It used to be all-consuming to me. But you know, I wanted to go to college, so…"

"Here you are." She barely breathes the words out. She locks eyes with him but has to look away.

He slowly wraps up her hand.

"What do you say we order food in, and then I'll drop you back off at the party?"

Snapped back to reality, she says, "Whatever you want to do."

"Okay. Pizza or a sandwich?"

"Pizza is fine with me."

"Pizza it is."

He orders and then goes over to the radio and switches it on. "Want a beer?" he asks with a smirk.

"What?" She narrows her eyes at him. "You think I've had enough?" she asks.

"Well, this is the drunkest I've seen you, but it is Spring Fling, so it sort of comes with the territory."

"I will have *another* beer."

He slightly raises his eyebrows at her and then goes over to his mini fridge. He takes out two Natty Lights and gives one to her.

When she's halfway into her beer, he goes downstairs and gets the pizza for them.

He enters with the pizza and places it on the futon. He motions for her to come and sit. "You can relax more over here." He pats the couch.

She gets up and steadies herself, and then with one foot in front of the other, she makes it to the futon without falling.

She eats two pieces of pizza. The sated feeling starts to come over her. She finds her eyelids growing heavy. Colin picks up the pizza box and puts it by his trash. She motions for him to come closer. She feels her heartbeat pound within her rib cage, but her limbs are unable to move. He leans in close to her. His handsome face is only inches from hers, and she swallows, finding it difficult to speak.

"Why don't..." *Why don't you like me? Why don't you believe me? Why are you shutting me out?*

Laura, someone who speaks to hundreds of people at any given time, simply cannot find the words to say to Colin—the only one in front of her, her captive audience—and she doesn't have the courage to ask him why he can't see that this wasn't her fault.

He reaches over her head and pulls a blanket off the back of the futon. "Here. I'm going to take a quick shower before I take you back. I'll be only a minute." He smiles slightly, although one could say it is more of a sympathetic smile than anything.

As her eyes grow heavy, she whispers, "Just so you know, I'm not happy."

He turns. "I'm not happy either."

Laura rolls over to grab her pillow but feels an unfamiliar material or something under her. She slowly opens her eyes. Her head is pounding like nothing she has experienced before. Her hand throbs as she reaches forward, the bandage now stuck to the dried blood on her palm. Upon further examination of the situation, she is not wearing the shirt she had on yesterday. She peeks under the covers—the covers she does not recognize—and confirms she is clad in only a large T-shirt, bra, and panties.

She peers around the room and realizes that she has no clue where she is. There is only a smidgen of light peeking through the shade, illuminating a small part of the room. Enough light for her to roll herself off the futon. She steadies herself and stands. She starts to walk across the room but hits something in the darkness and slams her lips together before she cries out as the pain shoots up her leg.

"Hey, you okay?" A gruff voices enters the silence.

Her mouth is dry; she can hardly speak. "Yes, um, sorry."

Someone flips on a small light. She looks up as Colin is getting up off his bed, wearing only boxers. His body is some sight to behold. Laura can feel her cheeks flush.

"Oh God," she whispers.

"You okay, Laura?"

In a panic, Laura looks around the room to see who else is here. *Did his roommate witness something I can't remember? Worse, is Joey sleeping next to him, concealed by his covers? Did something transpire last night that I should undoubtedly be embarrassed about today?*

"I, um…I should go."

"Oh, okay," he says, sounding disappointed.

"Where are my—"

"Your clothes are on the chair," he interjects as he motions toward his desk.

She turns. Her clothes are neatly folded on the chair, not scattered about, as you might see after an incredible night between two people in the throes of heated lovemaking. She grabs her jeans. She starts to slip them on when she can feel his eyes on her. She has no recollection of getting undressed and is simply too embarrassed to ask him any questions. She starts to take off the T-shirt she is wearing, and as she pulls it over her head, she glances slightly over her shoulder. He is standing there, merely feet away, gawking at her. She rapidly puts on her shirt and tucks her hair behind her ears, smoothing it as she does. She takes a deep breath and exhales before turning back toward him.

He looks like a vision. He is simply gorgeous in the morning, but unfortunately for me, he's someone I cannot have.

She swallows hard. "I'm sorry if I screwed up your night or did anything stupid."

Exasperated, he runs his hands through his hair. "You don't remember?" he asks.

The confusion pulsating between them is something she cannot stand. It's too complicated, and it shouldn't be. Plus, the pounding in her head and the horrible queasiness rippling through her stomach are telling her it is time to go.

She doesn't know why she feels like she might burst into tears, but she does. "I'm sorry."

She whisks past him, leaving him standing there, mouth slightly open with a pained expression on his handsome face.

"Nothing happened," he says. "Please, let me explain."

She whips open the door, and with no sense of direction or remembrance of where the hell she is on campus, she bounds down the stairs, two at a time, and rushes out the door. She pushes open the dormitory door and enters the campus, like hundreds of others doing the walk of shame on this Sunday morning. Only she feels a different kind of shame—or dare she say, regret. She regrets not savoring waking up next to him when she had the chance, and she feels ashamed that she might or might not have done something or said something categorically stupid. Stupid enough to land on his couch and not in his arms.

Sixteen

SOMEBODY GETS IT

"Hey, Laura," Ryker says as he gently pushes open the door to the studio. "Travis is here to see you."

"Oh, great. You can tell him to come down."

"Sure."

A few moments later, Travis is at the door and knocks slightly.

"Come in, please," she says as she nervously bites on the end of her pen. She smooths down her shirt. "Find anything out?"

"Well"—his laugh is sweet—"hello to you, too."

"Sorry. Hello, Travis. How was your day today?"

"My day? The usual. Nothing earth-shattering to report from my end."

"Sorry to hear that," she says as she gives him a concerned look.

"Hey, I've had my fill of crazy days on this campus, and believe me, it's great to have a so-so day every once in a while."

"I suppose you're right. Want to sit?"

"No, thanks. I can't stay."

"Oh, okay." A disappointed feeling washes over her. She feels lonely despite being surrounded by people and can't place exactly why.

Travis shoves his hands deep in his pockets and gives her a soft glance. "Wolfie might have found something, but it's too early to call."

Laura's eyes grow wide like saucers. A chill runs down her spine. "He did?"

"Yeah. I stopped by to tell you that I'm heading to Oswego."

"Oswego? Why?"

"I have a friend there, works at the paper. I want to check out a few things that she can help me with."

She?

"Oh, okay. Well, thanks for telling me."

"You got it." He turns to leave and then says, "Be safe, okay?"

Laura swallows hard. "Something I need to worry about?"

"No, nothing like that. Just felt like I had to say that."

Laura smiles as she follows him out the door and down the hallway.

As they enter the common area, Travis, much to Laura's surprise, takes her hand and says kindly, "I'll call you when I get back."

Cheeks fiery red, she responds, "Cool."

Travis pulls open the door and leaves. Laura turns to head back to her studio. The door is about to close when she feels the slight breeze of the door opening back up. She glances over her shoulder as Colin enters with a concerned look on his face. Surprised and embarrassed at the same time, she opts not to ask him what is wrong and is glad with her decision as she witnesses Joey walking in behind him—hot on his heels, per usual. Laura continues down the hallway and closes the door to her studio.

It's been several days since she last saw Colin, standing in his room, wearing only his boxers. She should have known, at best, it was a fleeting moment between them. He did contact her after that night, but she has been too embarrassed to call him back.

She sits in her chair and spins her back to the board. She grabs her notebook and stares at the blank page.

What is Travis going to Oswego for exactly? Are the students in more danger than he is letting on? Is this she a former girlfriend? Maybe a current one? Why do I even care? Does it bother me because I can't seem to find anyone? Well, find someone who isn't currently attached to someone else. Have I closed myself off to meeting other people? Is Abigail right? Should I focus on school and my job? But everyone else appears to find a happy balance, so why can't I?

There is a knock on the door. Laura is taken out of her thoughts. She spins her chair to face the door. Before she can even say, *Come in*, the door is opening. If anything, she expects Ryker or Patrick to come in. What she is wanting is Colin. What she least anticipates is Joey.

Joey steps in and closes the door behind her. She methodically turns toward Laura. If Laura didn't know better, she could swear she clenched her fists.

She takes a deep breath in, and with venom in her voice, she says, "I know you stayed at Colin's the other night."

Laura's throat is tightening, and she feels a need to gasp for air.

"If you think for even one second that meant anything to him, you're wrong. Dead wrong. In fact, he told me what a joke you were. Too drunk to make it through your first Spring Fling."

Laura swallows hard. Her mind is racing. Yet again, she is at a total loss for words.

Come on. Speak! Fight back! Say something!

Lying in Wait

Joey continues, "He said you're pathetic, and he only tolerates you because you have to work together."

Tears begin to sting Laura's eyes as this cruel girl stands before her, senselessly beating her down. She fights them back, replacing them with resentment. "Is that so?" she replies.

"Yes."

"Maybe he should tell me that."

"I'm protecting him. Just like he is protecting me."

"Protecting him?"

"At some point, the crew here will pick sides, and they'll choose him. No doubt."

"Pick sides? What are you talking about?"

"What kind of friend would get Colin kicked out of his own spot? You've been a DJ for what, all of ten minutes? And you act as though you own the place. He'll never forgive you for what you did."

"You have no idea what you are talking about."

"Stay away from him. Got it?"

Laura, furious that she is even breathing the same air as Joey, barks, "Sure, whatever you say."

"Consider this little chat your one and only warning." Joey yanks open the door and saunters down the hallway, never even bothering to close the door.

Laura looks down at her trembling hands. She clasps them together, trying to steady herself. She wants desperately to get up and close her door but abruptly feels weak, like her body isn't capable of moving. She is frozen in disbelief. Sensing she is not alone, she slowly peers up as she continues to fight back her anger.

"What's wrong?" Sean asks as he rushes toward her.

Laura swiftly puts up her hand, trying to stop him.

"Laura, you're shaking. What the hell is going on?"

"Nothing. Please…just leave me." It's no use, fighting back her emotions anymore. She starts to sob and cannot do anything to stop it. She has never in her life been scolded by someone like she just was. Never.

Sean straightens up, and with concerned anger radiating in his voice, he whispers, "What did that bitch say to you?"

Laura whips up her head. "Nothing. Please, Sean, don't say anything. Please." She takes his hand, begging him not to go, for fear he'll barge out of the room and straight to Joey to confront her.

"It's bullshit," he declares. "This whole thing with her. You know it, and I know it."

"What?" Laura asks as she releases his hand.

"I know what's going on," he states matter-of-factly.

Laura tries to stand but is too weak. Sean goes over to the door to close it when he feels resistance.

"Oh, sorry," Patrick says. "Tucker wants to speak with you. It's urgent."

"Okay, I'll be right out," he says as he shields Laura from Patrick.

Patrick turns to leave.

Sean faces her and says, "Shit, I've gotta go. Meet me back here tonight after my show."

"Tonight? But you're on during the day."

"Things are shifting; you know that." Surprisingly, he doesn't appear bothered by this in the least.

Laura is about to say, *I know; it's because of me*, but Sean disappears before she can.

It is a crisp early May evening. The sun sets later, giving the illusion of warmth. But, in these parts of New York, it is still rather cool. Cool enough for Laura to wear her wool coat as she hurries across campus and to the station.

She didn't necessarily lie to Abigail as to why she had to go back to the station so late, but she most definitely did not tell her the complete story. Laura doesn't know the whole story, so how could she possibly explain it to anyone? With the impending mystery of her conversation with Sean lurking inside her belly, Laura takes a deep breath as she opens the door to the station. It is dimly lit with only a few desk lamps illuminating the common area. Sean comes in from the hallway.

"Hey," he says.

"Hey."

"Thanks for coming, and sorry to be secretive, but you know how it is around here. Can't have one conversation without someone walking in."

He speaks the truth. It is merely impossible.

"Happy to."

Laura leans up against a desk. Sean takes a seat in a chair across from her.

Sean, who's never been known for beating around the bush, jumps right in. "The night Joey was supposedly attacked."

Laura hyper-focuses on the word *supposedly*.

"I called Colin to come here. I never got the chance to tell him who it was."

"What do you mean?"

"He was freaked out, and he dropped the phone or something and took off to get here as fast as he could."

"Naturally."

"Laura, I swear, I swear to you, that he thought it was *you*."

Laura gasps. "Oh God, that is horrible. I mean, to not know who or what…it's terrible."

"You're not getting it. When he barged in the room, his expression, I can't explain it, but he went from horror to almost relief and then back to something, something that I haven't quite been able to put my finger on—until now."

Laura slowly drops in the open seat across from Sean. "No, I'm not getting it."

He contemplates for a moment and then replies, "Trapped."

"Trapped?"

"Yes, it sounds like a strange word to use, but it has been bothering me so much. But, yeah, he absolutely looked like he was imprisoned, and he didn't know how to get out."

"Sean, you're not giving Colin the benefit of the doubt."

She wants so badly to say, *He is a good person who would help anyone,* but not after what Joey said he'd said about her. Laura's personal feelings have been altered.

"No, that's just it. I am. I know he has to help her."

"Yes, he does."

"But don't you get it? She knows that, too."

The hair on the back of her neck stands up.

Of course she knows that. They dated for a year. She knows exactly the kind of person she is dealing with.

"Oh," Laura whispers with realization.

"Joey ensnared him into helping her, and what's worse about it, I think she made up the whole goddamn story to get him to pay attention to her."

Laura tries hard not to react. She can't let on that they are investigating this attack and if, in fact, there are others.

Is there a copycat out there, attempting to bring a fresh sense of terror to New York college campuses? If anyone can find that out, it is Travis.

"But, Sean, it is so hard to contest what we all saw. She was truly frightened."

"I don't underestimate that girl for one second."

"You don't sound like you care for her much?"

"Care for her? She's a manipulative bitch. And, believe me, she knows it."

"Tell me how you really feel," Laura says with a slight giggle.

He doesn't join in with his own smile. Instead, he simply remarks, "Oh, trust me, I'm being kind right now."

"Kind, huh?"

Well, he's not being untruthful, and he doesn't even know what she said to me.

"Strike me down if I'm wrong, but I think she's faking it, *and*"—he pauses for effect—"I'm guessing you and Travis believe there is some truth to that as well."

Goose bumps spread across her skin. He knows way more than he should, and she needs to be careful how she approaches this.

"Listen, I can't talk about what we might or might not—"

"Let me just cut you off there. I've known Colin for two years now. I've worked alongside him, and we've become good bros. I have also known Joey for three years. Same freshman class, same dorm our first year, and the whole year she dated Colin. I've seen her manipulate and quite honestly break the guy's damn heart a few times over. The last thing he needs is to get dragged into some bullshit story about his ex-girlfriend's life if—and I am saying *if*—it's all a bunch of crap."

Sean's right. Despite how Colin might feel about me or about what I did to land the news segment, I at least owe it to him to continue to pursue this. Even if he can't tolerate me anymore.

"I promise you, Sean, I'll do my best."

"I know you will. If I can help in any way possible, please say the word."

Laura reflects for a moment. "The best thing you can do to help us is to play along. He has to believe that you are on their side, and so does she. As soon as she believes you're the enemy, she'll yank him right away from you."

"Well, that ship might have already sailed."

"Why? Because they broke up a while ago?"

"Well, kind of. She knows I'm not too fond of her."

"But maybe Colin is the key. Maybe he will confide in you. Has he told you anything that Joey has said about that day?"

"Nothing. He says she refuses to talk about it."

"Okay. Well, that doesn't do us much good."

"But I'll keep trying. He acts like he could use a friend these days. Something is up with him—big-time. He is not the same Colin that he was a few months ago. You know, after he met you."

Sean smiles as Laura's face flushes pink.

"I-I..." she stutters.

"You don't have to say anything. I get it."

I'm glad you do, Sean, because I'm more confused than ever. But I think I have an idea!

Seventeen

A DIFFERENT ATTACK

Laura gets up bright and early. Abigail stayed at Nathan's last night, which bodes well for Laura, so she doesn't have to explain why she is calling a cab to take her to the police station.

Laura stands on the corner, near her dorm and waits for the yellow cab to arrive. The car pulls up and Laura, balancing two cups of coffee, climbs into the back seat. She hands one to the gentleman who introduced himself as Eddie.

"That was kind of you, young lady," he replies as he pulls onto Main Street.

"Well, I know it's early *and* I have a favor to ask."

"Sure thing."

"You won't mind waiting for me, will you?"

He pulls into the police station parking lot. "No, you bought me a coffee, and I have the paper, so I'm content," Eddie replies.

"Thanks. I won't be long." She enters the station with the other cup of coffee.

"Can I help you?" the young man behind the counter asks.

"Yes. I'm here for Officer Murphy."

"Your name?"

"Laura Chase."

"Please have a seat. I'll let him know you're here."

Five minutes pass before Officer Murphy approaches from the hallway. "Ms. Chase, I presume?"

"Yes," she replies, handing him the coffee. "Got this for you."

"Why, thank you. How kind. You can follow me."

Laura closely follows him down the hallway and to his office.

"Have a seat." He motions to a round table settled in the corner of the room.

Laura pulls out a chair and sits.

"How can I help you?"

Taking a deep breath in, she squares her shoulders to face him. "I'd like to interview you for a segment I'm doing on the college radio station."

He smiles. "I thought I recognized your name."

She nervously tucks her hair behind her ear and then continues, "I'm doing a series of interviews on campus safety. It would be beneficial to the students on this campus to hear from you specifically."

"I can clear some time in my schedule. When are you thinking?"

"Monday, three o'clock. Even though the school year is almost over, it's never too late to talk about it."

"I couldn't agree more. See, you didn't have to bring me a coffee for me to say yes." He laughs slightly as he takes a sip.

Her shoulders relax. "It's from Cool Beans. Their dark roast."

"It beats the coffee we have here."

She smiles. "I'll send over some of the questions ahead of time, so you can come prepared."

"That works for me."

"Wonderful." Laura rises and extends her hand to him. "Thank you, Officer Murphy."

"Don't thank me yet," he says with another chuckle.

"I'll see you Monday."

Laura, exhausted both mentally and physically, exits the library and into the darkness. Studying for her exams, working at the station, tutoring young math minds, and balancing her demented social life leave her barely a moment to breathe. With her bag slung over her shoulder, she reluctantly wanders toward her dorm, her mind swirling with concerned thoughts. She barely pays attention as she crosses Main Street. That is, until she notices someone step out from behind a tree, directly into the path in front of her.

"Laura?" he asks.

Her heart beats wildly, and her voice cracks as she answers, "Yes."

"I'm Wolfie. Travis sent me."

"Oh, yes, Wolfie." She exhales with relief as she looks at the portly man standing in front of her, sporting a tweed jacket over a wrinkled button-down oxford.

"Travis wanted me to give this to you. Do not share it. Understand?" He pulls out something from his messenger bag.

"Yes, I understand." Laura takes the sealed envelope and places it in her bag.

"He wants you to read it before your interview tomorrow."

"Okay, but how did he know about my interview? I thought he was in Osw—"

"It's Travis's job to know," he replies with the same arrogance Laura would expect from Travis.

"I see. Okay, I will."

"Until next time," he adds as he disappears back into the darkness.

"Do you always skulk around in the dark?" Laura yells after him with a slight chuckle.

"Only when I need to," he hollers back.

Laura, only moments before, felt drained but now has an electric-charged sensation pushing her body toward the only place she knows she will be alone at this hour. The station. She keys into the door and takes a seat. Feeling her skin prickle, she opens up the sealed envelope.

First is a note.

Laura,

Please review these before your interview tomorrow. It is your duty to question those who might or might not have had the power to change what happened.

Travis

Change what happened?
She hurriedly opens the portfolio.

Laura nearly gasps when she sees what has been given to her. The first paper in the file is an email addressed to Dean Barrymore at OSU, dated August 28, 1995.

Dear Dean Barrymore,

As you have been made aware, Oswego has had a series of complaints brought to both local and campus police regarding an influx of assaults on women. We have, to date, verified ten complaints. The attacks seem to have escalated in intensity, and unfortunately, one woman has been hospitalized for her injuries. I am writing my fellow deans to make certain your campus is aware and, more importantly, so you take proper measures to ensure your students are safe this year.

Kind regards,

Dean Finley

Laura flips to the next page and finds an outline that is attached to the email.

KEY ITEMS TO LOOK FOR AND TO MAKE THE STUDENTS AWARE OF:

Male, approximately 5'9" to 5'11"

Spiked, dark hair

Uses multiple aliases

Claims to be an athlete

Gets to know the university along with the names of professors and the classes they teach

Believe he is a native to New York, region unknown

The next document is a response to Dean Finley's email.

Dear Dean Finley,

We here at Onondaga State are sincerely sorry to hear of your campus troubles. We do appreciate your concern of OSU. With that said, my counsel and I have decided that our campus is safe, and we have no issues reported to date. We are choosing to sit tight on this information until we need to arm our students with the material you shared.

We would like to offer our guidance and expertise in security should you desire.

Best of luck this year.

Sincerely,

Dean Barrymore

Lying in Wait

Tears fill Laura's eyes as she reads the police report from the first incident on Oswego's campus. The details are horrific and graphic and mirror Bree's encounter almost to the letter.

Laura sifts through several more emails until she gets to one of particular interest. It is from Captain Frankel to Dean Barrymore, dated a few days after her email from Dean Finley.

> *Dear Dean Barrymore,*
>
> *It has been brought to my attention that one of my officers came upon a student on your campus on the evening of August 31. The officer and I both strongly feel that this woman came across someone who severely mistreated her and was, at the time, running away from her assailant. Her injuries were consistent, from what my officer could decipher, with a sexual assault.*
>
> *I would like to discuss the best means in which we can tighten security and alert the students on campus.*
>
> *Thank you,*
>
> *Captain Frankel*

"Oh my God," Laura whispers. "Are they talking about Bree?"

> *Dear Captain Frankel,*
>
> *My sources tell me that no complaints have been filed with campus security. Can you confirm this is an open investigation and that you have a report on file from this student? We typically receive numerous false claims the first week of school. These young kids are just finding their way, I presume.*
>
> *Dean Barrymore*

Young kids? Finding their way? Is she kidding me? With a sickening feeling in her gut, she reluctantly flips to the next page.

> *Dear Dean Barrymore,*
>
> *We have not yet received a formal complaint at the police station. But this is not uncommon, particularly in the beginning of the academic year. We are not currently investigating the alleged assault merely due to lack of information; however, my officers and I would like to work with you to keep the campus safe.*

Please advise.

Captain Frankel

Laura notes that almost two weeks pass in between email correspondences. *Two weeks! And nothing from our dean?*

Dear Captain Frankel,

The beginning of the school year has left me little time to respond to your inquiry. I apologize for the delay. I have spoken to our security team, and we have had no incidents reported.

Please keep my assistant, Joanne Stone, apprised of any additional information. I have copied her on this email.

Dean Barrymore

Laura anxiously flips to the next page, hoping for another email of sorts. But she finds nothing, except another note from Travis.

Laura,

I have entrusted you with these documents. Your instincts might be to run and tell someone, like a friend, but you cannot do that. You must not. Many people will lose their jobs and get in major trouble for these breaches. Please, I know this is hard, but I trust you. Please keep this between us.

When you are done with these, come by and drop them off at my apartment at 64 Winter St.

Travis

Part of Laura is relieved he wants these papers back. Having them in her possession makes her nervous. But another part of her is telling her that she might need these someday. She goes over to the copier, and without much thought of the consequences, she makes copies of the file.

She scours over her questions for Officer Murphy. Her blood boils, the more she reads the cushy and quite frankly too-kind questions for the officer. She begins to feverishly scribble her notes on the side of her paper as she scratches and rewrites each and every question she sent him. She does this for over two hours.

On the verge of sleeping in the station, she gathers the scattered papers and copies in front of her and hastily leaves the station. She is barely able to feel her legs beneath her as they carry her back to her dorm. As soon as she enters her room, she collapses onto her bed, fully dressed, clutching her bag in her hand.

She wakes in the morning to Abigail trying to remove her bag from her grasp.

Laura shoots up. "Don't take—"

"Hey, hey. You're okay," Abigail responds as she steps back. "Late night, huh?"

"What?"

"Late night? You're still in your clothes, holding your backpack." She laughs slightly.

Laura looks down at her sweater and jeans. "Yeah, too much studying."

"I hear you. Nathan and I are taking a break from all the studying today and going out for Chinese for dinner tonight. Want to join us? Melissa and Logan are coming, too."

"I can't." Laura scrambles to her feet as she notices the time. "Shit, I'm going to be late."

"Big day for you, too?"

"Yeah, I suppose."

Abigail turns to face Laura, gently placing her hands on her shoulders. "Are you okay? You seem off or something."

"I'm fine. Just tired."

"I know. Can I help?" Abigail stands before Laura, hair perfectly flowing, her big navy eyes bright, giving Laura a sympathetic stare.

For some unknown reason, Laura decides the last person who should know about the ordeal unfolding is Abigail. "No, but thank you. I appreciate it." Laura grabs her shower caddy and towel and heads straight for the bathroom.

Laura dresses quickly in black pants and a fitted gray sweater. She takes extra time on putting on her makeup. She wouldn't bother today, but since she is having an interview, she wants to look her best, and it's partly to counteract how she feels on the inside. Miserable.

As she dashes down the hall, she passes Melissa.

"You meeting us for dinner tonight?" she asks.

"I can't make it. I'm sorry I'll miss it. Talk to you later."

"Okay, no problem." Melissa adds, "And good luck today."

Laura slightly waves to her friend. She pushes open the door to her dorm, and for once, she wishes for rain. Rain would better suit her mood. The sun shining only calls for happy thoughts, and Laura has few, if any at all.

During her math class, she bites on the end of her pen and stares aimlessly out the window and across campus. Webber tries on a few occasions to talk to her, but she barely engages him, and after a few minutes, he seems to catch the hint. She is in no mood to talk. And it's nothing personal.

Quickly, she rises as their professor dismisses them. "I've really gotta run, Webber. I'll catch you later."

"Hey, of course. Big day. I get it."

"See ya." She rushes off without him.

Laura zigzags through campus and to the Union. Hoping not to run into anyone, she dodges into the station and goes directly down to Studio B.

She has less than an hour to get ready for her interview. She removes the papers from her bag. Within a moment of her sitting down, there is a knock on her door.

She hesitates and then whispers, "Come in." Surprised to see Sean enter, she says, "Oh, hey. What's up?"

Sean closes the door behind him. With a serious expression on his face, he says, "You left this." He places a piece of paper in front of her.

Laura's eyes widen as she sees her questions to Officer Murphy, the ones she made all the changes to, now placed in front of her. "Oh, yeah," she mumbles as she grabs the paper and places it under her other concealed papers.

"Something you want to talk about?"

"Nope," she curtly answers.

"Laura, you should be careful. As your friend and someone who works with you, I think you should tread lightly."

"Tread lightly? What is that supposed to mean?" Her tone even catches her off guard.

With wide eyes, he replies, "What it means is, you are interviewing a police officer."

"Yeah, and? Are they above the law?"

"Not to my knowledge."

"Well then, I made some notes; that's all, and it's…"

"You should be more careful. You can't just leave something like that lying around."

Laura realizes as he speaks what the consequences could have been, say, if Tucker or Colin had seen the paper first.

"Thank you. For not telling anyone." Although she means it to sound kind, it doesn't come out that way. The stress and pressure are growing, and she knows deep down that it has nothing to do with Sean. He is just caught in the crossfire at this point.

"You positive you want to do this?" Sean asks with a concerned expression on his face.

"Don't. Don't look at me like that. I'm nervous enough."

"Well, maybe that should tell you something, Laura."

"Damn it, Sean," she curses under her breath.

He backs up. "I'll leave you."

"I'm sorry," Laura whispers as the door shuts with a loud thud.

She shuffles nervously through the papers and notes she got from Travis last night, and then she places them in her bag. As she stands in the center of the room, she clutches her hands as she tries to calm the quaking. The faint knock on the door perks her up. She takes two deep breaths in and out, in and out.

She smiles despite herself and coolly says, "Come in."

Officer Murphy enters in his plain clothes. It catches Laura off guard at first.

"Expecting me in my blues?" He laughs.

"Yeah, something like that." She gives him a warm and innocent smile in return.

"I'm off duty."

"Of course. Please have a seat."

"Sure." He takes the guest chair on the diagonal of Laura.

He retrieves his questions and smooths the creases in the piece of paper out in front of him. Laura looks up. Patrick is ready in the booth.

"Okay, we will be on in two minutes."

"Ready when you are."

Laura places her headphones on her ears, adjusts her microphone, and waits as Patrick counts her down.

Without a hitch in her words or a tremble in her voice, she says concisely and as clear as a bell, "Good afternoon, Hawks. This is Laura Chase with what I hope will be an important segment you won't want to miss about on-campus safety and, more importantly, to dispel those rumors surrounding the recent attacks that have plagued numerous campuses in this great state of New York. Here to give us some insight and to have a conversation is Officer Murphy of the Syracuse Police Department. Welcome, Officer Murphy."

"Happy to be here, Laura."

"We are happy to have you join us today. Officer Murphy, not only are you employed in the police department, but you are also the head of campus security for the university, correct?"

"That is correct. I've been the head of security on campus for over ten years now and a police officer for twenty-two years."

Laura chuckles. "Quite a résumé. It must keep you busy."

"Yes, unfortunately more than I'd like it to this past year." He stumbles on his words and then adds, "This past year in particular. It has been a difficult one."

"To say the very least. How confident are you in the current investigation?"

"We are very confident in the current status of the investigation." He gives her a brief, hardened expression and then glances down at the sheet of questions in front of him.

"Is that because you have identified the man responsible for the attacks?"

"This is an ongoing investigation; therefore, the specifics of the case cannot be discussed."

"Understood. But why wouldn't you want to let the students on this campus right here know that they are safe and perhaps have been safe for at least a month, maybe two?"

"That has not been confirmed."

"But it has, hasn't it?"

"We have a particular person of interest, and that is all I can speak about it."

"Why not let the athletes on campus know that the police don't believe he *was* an athlete, nor was he even a student on this campus or any of the campuses he terrorized?"

"How do you know that?" he asks defensively.

"As a person whose job it is to filter the news to my fellow students, I should in fact know what I'm talking about. I have my sources, too," Laura says with an ice-cold tone.

Officer Murphy glares at her and then points down at the questions in front of him.

"My point, Officer Murphy, is that the reputation of the student athletes across numerous campuses has been scrutinized and rightfully so. But only to the point in which the facts were unclear. You, Officer Murphy, have the facts to dispel the rumors that a student athlete attacked numerous women across the state of New York."

Officer Murphy's mouth drops slightly open.

Relentlessly, Laura continues, "The facts are that he went undetected, right under the nose of law enforcement, until the night he was beat up by an athlete from OSU and was hurt critically enough to seek medical attention in February."

"I can't comment." His tone is calm but wildly firm.

"It is safe then to say that there have been no more reports of any campus attacks since February?"

"I believe, Ms. Chase, that is exactly why you asked me here today. You wanted to know and the students should know that we make campus safety a top priority."

Laura takes into mind the two women she knows personally who were attacked by the same man, and anger starts to brew inside her otherwise sweet and quiet soul. With a sinister tone, she asks, "Was this top priority of yours before or after February?"

He gasps slightly. "Ms. Chase, it has always been a priority and will continue to be. We cannot blame ourselves for the actions of one man—'

"It was in fact the actions of *one* man." Before he can respond, Laura adds, "What are you doing to improve campus security?"

Red face and all, he glances down at his paper while shaking his head. "OSU and local law enforcement plan to develop some programs next year. We plan to enlist the help and guidance of several organizations to ensure we get any and all improvements right the first time."

"And, now, what can students do *today* to feel safer on this campus?"

"Be mindful of your surroundings, travel in pairs or groups, and don't walk home alone, if at all possible. You can always call campus security for a ride home."

"Well, the phone lines are lighting up, as you can imagine. Hold tight. We're going to take a quick break, and we'll be right back for your calls."

Patrick signals to Laura, who switches off her mic. Unable to meet Officer Murphy's eyes, Laura pretends to be taking notes in her book. She feels the door open and close shut. She glances up, and he is gone. She catches eyes with Patrick, who is giving her a confused expression.

Officer Murphy storms down the hall and straight toward Tucker's door. He knocks twice and then enters. "What the hell was this? We had a deal. Questions ahead of time. Everything was all worked out!" he barks.

"I know; I know. I have no idea what has gotten into her, but I plan to handle this. You have my word."

"Damn right, you'd better! What the hell is she, some pre-law student?"

"No, math major," he mumbles.

"Ah, Jesus, Tucker." He shakes his head. "You let me get schooled by a freaking math student? Christ!"

"All right, I get it. If you want to be done with the interview, then fire, we'll end it."

He feverishly rubs his hands over his face, contemplating his next move. "I'll take a few softball calls. I want to stick to the topic. Understood?"

"Yes, absolutely." Tucker exits his office and marches down to the booth. He swings open the door and says to Patrick, "Screen all calls. Nothing about the case will be discussed or entertained. Only questions about campus security. Understood?"

"You got it, boss."

"Were you in on this?" Tucker barks.

"No," Patrick replies under his breath.

"Good." Tucker, with authority, crosses his arms over his chest and stares straight ahead at Laura.

She glances up once and immediately looks back down. Officer Murphy puts back on his headphones, and with confidence, he leans into the microphone as Laura gets her countdown.

"We are back with Officer Murphy from campus security. First caller, welcome to the show."

"Yeah, I've always wanted to know what happens when you hit those blue emergency buttons that are on all those posts throughout campus."

Realizing that his request for softball-type calls will truly mean calls with little substance behind them, Officer Murphy's shoulders relax as he takes six or so calls before the segment is over.

"Well, unfortunately, our time is up. Please join me on Thursday for another segment on campus security. Please be safe and look out for one another. See you then!" Laura reaches over and switches off her microphone. She reluctantly glances over at Officer Murphy as he slowly peels his headphones off.

"You know, I'm not the enemy here," he growls as he exits the door, giving her one final harsh stare.

"You don't understand," she whispers.

Knowing that time is not on her side, she shoves her notes into her bag, and she hurries down the hallway and directly out the door. She always hangs around after her shift to debrief with Patrick or Tucker, but if nothing else, Laura is smart and knows when she is not welcome.

With adrenaline rushing through her veins, she scurries across campus, dodging in and out of students as she comes upon the main road. She pulls out the sheet of paper Travis gave her and double-checks the address. She huffs up Russell Street and takes a right onto High Street and then a left onto Winter Street. She is at a slightly run-down white house. She anxiously knocks on the door.

She glances around her in a paranoid state. She can almost feel the shift in the air. Something is changing on this campus, and Laura is not quite ready for the revolution.

Eighteen

THE STORY BE TOLD

Travis opens the door, wearing a bright blue-and-gray plaid shirt, dark jeans, and a massive smile. "Well, well, if it isn't the infamous Laura Chase" He grins as he steps back and welcomes her in the door.

"Infamous? Hardly," she mumbles.

"Come in, come in," he adds with a chuckle as he closes the door.

Laura takes in her surroundings. His living room is relatively clean for a college apartment.

"Have a seat." He motions toward the couch.

Laura goes over, drops her bag with a thud on the hardwood floor, and sinks down into the overstuffed cushion.

He sits in the leather chair across from her. "By the look on your face, I'd say it didn't go as you'd expected?"

"I don't know *what* I expected." She sighs, allowing her shoulders to drop.

"Well, I thought you were phenomenal."

She can feel her face blush as his eyes lock with hers. "Really?"

"Yes, you were strong and deliberate, and you connected your thoughts. Not easy to do. Well, I should say, you made it sound easy."

"I did?"

"Laura, do you think you'd be doing what you do if you didn't?"

Laura hesitates briefly. "I suppose not."

Travis smiles crookedly at her and then gets up and goes into his kitchen. He returns a few seconds later with two beers. He pops the caps off and leans forward to her. "Here. Relax. You did the right thing."

Laura takes the beer and brings it to her lips. It tastes fantastic as it runs down her scratchy, tense throat. After a moment of collecting her thoughts, she peeks up at him. "You think so?"

"I know so."

"But those notes you gave me, how can all of that be true?" Her voice strains with resentment.

"Unbelievable, right? But it's true. All of it."

Laura stares ahead as she ponders everything that has transpired over the past twenty-four hours.

"Earth to Laura," Travis says. "You still in there?" He waves his hand in front of her.

Laura snaps out of her nightmare. "I'm sorry. I've had such a crazy day. I'm a little out of it."

"I can see that. Another beer?" he asks.

Laura looks down at her empty beer bottle and barely remembers past the first sip. "Why not?"

As Travis gets up and enters the kitchen, Laura leans over in her bag and retrieves the envelope she is all too glad to return to Travis.

He comes back in and hands her a beer in exchange for the envelope.

"Here are your papers back. They are all in there."

"Thanks. Pretty crazy stuff." He takes a seat on the couch next to her.

"Yeah, can I ask how you got all of that?"

"For now, it's best you don't know any more than you already do."

Somewhat relieved, Laura responds, "Okay. I understand, and quite frankly, I'm not sure how much more information my head can hold."

"It's part of the business, kiddo."

There is something about the way he calls her kiddo that makes her realize that she is *only* that to him—nothing but a kid—and she can't understand why it bothers her. Her cheeks flare.

"Something I said?" he asks.

"No, nothing," she responds hastily. She averts her eyes and takes a long sip of her beer.

"Listen," he states as he squarely faces her, "you did the right thing. Those emails and notes are real. Those people are the ones our families trusted enough to put our lives into their hands. Dean Barrymore should have, at a minimum, met with Captain Frankel. But she didn't. She ignored repeated attempts to engage her. What you did today was merely the beginning. They should know they are being questioned. The students need to know who is looking after them. And it can't be some football player named Tank. It has to be the ones who can essentially make a change."

Laura reflects on Bree's and Abigail's assaults. *Two friends. Same man. And the school knew and didn't protect them.*

"I mean," Travis continues, "you read that freaking email basically saying that an officer ran into a girl in August, and that son of a bitch wasn't caught until February!"

Tears start to fill Laura's eyes. She lowers her head, too afraid, if he notices, she'll burst into full-on sobbing. She feels his warm hand on hers. He slightly pulls on it. Laura glances up as a tear falls on her cheek.

"Oh, kiddo, what is it?"

Abruptly, Laura stands up. "I'm not a kid!" she snarls with marked frustration.

Startled, Travis gets up. Not knowing where to go, Laura scurries into the kitchen.

"Hey, come here," he says with authority in his voice.

This bothers Laura even more. *Here comes the old Travis.*

She turns her back to him and places both hands on the counter, lowering her head as the tears flow from her eyes.

She hates the silence in the room, but she can't find even one word to describe how she is feeling. Well, maybe one. *Confused.*

She can feel his presence behind her as he takes a step closer.

"Laura, please." His tone is so soft that she hardly recognizes it.

Laura straightens up and wipes the tears from her eyes, smudging her mascara across her cheeks as she does.

"Please," he repeats.

Laura slowly turns to face him.

"I know you are not a kid," he states. "My God, look at you," he adds. When Laura doesn't respond, he continues, "But something else is bothering you. What is it?"

Her lip quivers as she finally speaks, "I can't tell you."

"Before you concede to that, know that my job is to keep secrets, no matter what."

"But, eventually, you tell them."

"I wouldn't tell yours," he says as he steps closer to her.

"Why not?"

"Because, Laura, you have my word. Now, if you still don't want to tell me, then I will leave it at that." He reaches forward and wipes the makeup from her skin. "You have a little, um, make—"

Embarrassed, she says, "Can I use your bathroom, please?"

"Oh, yeah, of course, but use the one in my room, top left. My roommate doesn't clean his down here." He grimaces.

"Thanks." Laura, with heavy legs, climbs the stairs and enters Travis's room.

It's neat despite the occasional shirt or two thrown on the chair. She notes the old typewriter on his desk and the piles of papers next to it. Once inside the bathroom, she glances up in the mirror and is shocked at the sadness in her own reflection. She does not mimic the happy-go-lucky Laura who came to school ten months ago.

She exhales in an attempt to shake the blues. She tries to remove the makeup with a tissue, rubbing her face until it's red.

"Laura, are you okay?"

"I'll be out in a second."

His silence is reassuring as she finishes wiping off her makeup. She opens the door and is surprised to find him lying on his bed.

"My roommate came home, and I didn't want you to get caught off guard."

"Oh. Well, thank you. I appreciate that."

"Have a seat," he adds as he points to the recliner in the corner of his room.

Laura takes a seat.

"I brought your beer up. Figured I could at least do that."

She looks next to her and takes the beer off the table. "I'm sorry about before," she whispers after she takes a sip. She tucks her legs up under her.

"It's okay, honestly. You're not the first girl who's cried in my apartment."

"*Travis.*"

"What? I didn't say it was me. My roommate is a real asshole," he says with a huge grin.

"Funny." She can't help but crack a little smirk.

"It's good to see you laugh."

"It feels good," Laura responds.

"What's got you so down today? Because I know the show wouldn't make you cry. What gives?"

Laura takes another few sips of her beer while Travis patiently waits. He flips on his CD player next to his bed. The quiet, unmistakable whine of lead guitarist Billy Corgan of The Smashing Pumpkins fills the silence.

"Does this have anything to do with the file I gave you?"

Laura, desperate for someone to talk to, nods her head. Travis leans up off his headboard, wrapping one hand around his knee.

"I have," she hesitates, "been holding this inside for a while now. I'm not sure what to do."

"Okay..."

Laura glances up at him and finally decides to let it out. "That email, the one about the girl on our campus." She starts to weep as she confesses, "That girl is my friend. One of my best friends."

Travis releases his hand from his knee, quickly placing it over his dropped-open mouth. Eyes wide, he mumbles, "Oh, Jesus, Laura. I had no idea. I'm so sorry."

She pulls her legs in tighter and adds, "I was distraught when I read that...all of it. It's like a huge slap in the face to my friend, to all of them, and..."

Travis looks down, carefully contemplating his next words. "But, Laura, don't you see? You're exactly what they need. You can be the voice for them because it's obvious that other people weren't."

She sighs. "And here I thought, this job was going to be simple."

As though a switch flips in him, Travis pats the bed next to him and says, "Laura, you could use a hug."

Drawn by the feeling of someone taking care of her, she begins unraveling her legs before her mind is able to catch up to her thoughts. She crosses the room, and as Travis leans back and opens his long arms to her, she, like a child, curls in next to him, and he wraps them back around her. He pulls her close, and the sensation of his arms embracing her makes her feel secure.

He strokes her hair as she begins to melt into his care.

Moments later, he says, "You said you thought this job was going to be simple. But you have no control over what we uncover. You, me, Wolfie, the paper, the station—we can all help to try to make it better."

"I know telling you about my friend was not appropriate, but after seeing that email, I guess I was just flabbergasted. I've been questioning a lot of things."

"Understandable. I hope you know what you say to me stays between us."

She chuckles a bit.

"What?"

"You're different."

"Different how?"

"I don't know. Different than when I first met you."

"Are you indicating that I made a bad first impression?" He snickers.

She jokes, "Um, yeah!"

He squeezes her on the hip. She yelps as he gives her a pinch.

"That's why I'm even more convinced than ever that there was a reason you came into my office that day."

Sensing a change in the conversation, Laura, with only her eyes, glances up at him. "What are you saying?"

He releases one arm from her, and with his thumb, he wipes the wet from her cheek. "I had a feeling, when we met, that it was something more than just happenstance."

"Oh," she whispers.

"We will get through this, whatever this is. We will."

"Thank you, Travis."

"You're welcome, kid—"

Laura's body instantly tenses, and she starts to pull away. But he hangs on tighter.

"I didn't mean to say that. I call everyone that. Sorry, it's a bad habit."

Unsure of what to say, she tips her head downward, guaranteeing that he is unable to see her face.

She hears him take a deep breath in, and then he adds, "I don't consider you a kid. If nothing else, I think you're an intelligent and sexy woman…if I'm being honest, which sounds like that's what we're doing today."

"Please, Travis. You don't have to say that."

"What? That you're sexy?"

"You're embarrassing me," she whispers, barely able to glance up at his handsome face.

"I don't want to embarrass you," he says in a sultry voice.

He reaches down, now placing his thumb and forefinger on her chin, guiding her face up to meet his stare. She swallows hard. A spark passes between them.

His expression becomes serious. His eyes dance with hers, and then he says, "I want to do this." Swiftly, he pulls her around the waist and up closer to him. Grasping the side of her cheek with his hand and gingerly placing his fingers behind her neck, he leans in with fully parted lips and intensely kisses her.

Her mind swirls with confused thoughts. One being, *The great Travis Taylor is kissing me?*

His lips on hers sends a shiver down her spine, and with little warning, she finds her hand moving up his chest, finally entwisting her fingers in his thick hair. He rolls her over and is now on top of her. She desires the weight of his body, the connection that it is bringing her, and relishes in another passionate kiss from him. She senses zero hesitation from him, which intrigues her, as she, too, returns a fervent kiss to her friend and unlikely suitor.

Don't think.

He pulls his lips off hers but not before gently dragging his teeth on her bottom lip. He kisses her neck and runs his hand down her body, resting it on her hip. Then, he whispers in her ear, "Don't think," as though he were inside her head.

"Kiss me," she whispers back.

He leans over to look at her. She doesn't smile because she can't help her teeth from biting down on her own bottom lip. He takes care of that by kissing her hard, pushing his tongue into her mouth, giving her exactly what she wants.

He starts to pull up on her sweater and rolls it up over her body. His eyes are wide. Her large breasts are merely separated from him by a black lace bra. He leans up and starts to unbutton his shirt as she eases the straps off her shoulders, one at a time. He pulls off his shirt, revealing his brawny chest, and then tosses it to the side with purpose. They lock eyes as he eagerly unhooks her bra and lifts it off her breasts, revealing a full bosom. His eyes widen as he takes her in, this attractive young woman lying before him.

"You have gorgeous tits," he growls, unable to avoid remarking about her figure.

Still watching her, he runs his fingers up her waist until he finally takes her breast into his willing hand. She gasps. The noise encourages him to tease and enjoy this moment with her. And he does, taking his time to pleasure her, gradually and deliberately.

She reaches down to the top of his jeans and starts to unzip them. He moans in return. She slithers her hand down into his pants and can feel how ready he is.

Don't think, she chants in her head.

He starts to unbutton her pants, and she helps him by sliding them over her slender hips. He kisses her with purpose. He's always in control of each situation, this being no different.

Minutes later, after tasting one another with gratification, he leans up and hurries off the bed. He goes over to his drawer and takes out a condom. He pulls down his jeans and climbs on top of her. With her legs spread, he seductively crawls over her. With one swipe of his teeth on the wrapper, she watches as he gets ready for her. Then, with a need in her that she cannot describe, she closes her eyes and takes in the moment as they become an unlikely couple.

Don't think, she reminds herself as her body moves beautifully in sync with his thrusts. *Don't think. Feel.*

Sometime later, as he is lying beside her, chest heaving with excitement, is when her mind begins to supersede her lustful feelings. Her awareness opens up to the reality that has unfolded in front of her.

I'm no longer a virgin.

Nineteen

DISAPPEARING ONE

Colin hears a loud knock on his door and knows before even opening it who is on the other side. He barely gets a response out when his dorm room door flies open.

Joey enters with authority. "Can you believe her?" she barks.

"Who?" Colin responds, clearly playing dumb.

"Laura! That's who. I know you listened," she yaps.

"Oh, right. Well, I didn't know who you were talking about." He stands up from his futon. He goes over to his fridge and grabs a beer.

"A little early to be drinking," she states, hands digging into her hips.

He chuckles deeply. "Does it really matter?"

Her eyes narrow at him. "Yes, Colin, it does fucking matter. I need you on solid ground."

He twists off the cap. *Of course you need me, but what about what I need?*

Sensing her glaring at him, he scoffs, "I am."

"What are we going to do about her? You and the other guys should petition to have her fired."

Alarmed by her extremism, he shoots back, "Fired? What the hell for?"

"What for! She basically cornered him into saying that there have been no other attacks at school."

"And?"

"Colin? What about me?"

He takes a gulp of his beer and sits back down on the futon. "What about you, Joey? You haven't told me shit about what happened. You didn't file a report. No one even knows what happened to you." *Except for your roommate, Jane. I overheard you tell her about it.*

"She does! Don't you see what she is trying to do? Discredit me!"

Colin thought he once knew Laura. He would have described her as quiet, friendly, inspiring, and fearless. But, more than all those things, she had a compassionate soul. But he had to admit, her interview with Officer Murphy was uncharacteristic of her, to say the least. She was anything but friendly.

"Well then, why don't you consider filing a report? I'm still unsure as to why you don't want the police to know that there is someone else. Or worse, that maybe they got the wrong guy!"

"Jesus, Colin. Is that what this is about? You want the horrible details? Want me to expose myself for others?"

"Fuck no, Joey. That is not what this is about. You want me to be there for you, but you don't let me in."

"You want me to tell the cops? Do their job for them in the hopes of saving some other *bitch* from an attack? No, thanks."

Colin observes her say these horrible words and with little regard for anyone besides herself. He narrows his eyes at her and then boldly asks, "What did he look like?"

"What?"

"The guy?"

"Jesus, Colin."

"I'm serious, Joey. Start there."

She remains standing in front of him, unwilling to sit down. She does this when she can't settle her mind or, worse, when she feels cornered.

"If it will make you happy."

"Yeah, that's it. It will make me happy. No, Joey, none of this makes me happy. But I should know."

"Why?"

"So, I can be there for you," he lies.

A slight smirk grows across her face. "Fine. He was short, well shorter than average. He had dark brown hair. Rather plain-looking, which is probably why he has to attack women. Can't get any on his own."

Colin ignores her ridiculous comment. "Any distinct markings or tattoos?"

She glances up in the air, pretending to contemplate his question, and then convincingly says, "No, none that I can remember."

He exhales and then says, "Now, was that so hard?"

"Well, no," she adds dryly.

She starts to come over toward the futon when he adds, "Hey, I know you just stopped by, but can we finish this discussion later? I have to hand in my final project, like ten minutes ago"—he glances at the nonexistent watch on his wrist—"and I'm not quite done." He stands and goes over to his desk. He picks up a few of his school papers.

She clears her throat. He turns to look at her.

"Can I at least get a hug?" she coos.

"Oh shit. Of course. Sorry." He hesitantly strides over to her and puts his arms around her shoulders.

"Call me later." She exits his door in a much calmer fashion than she entered.

Colin plops into his desk chair and buries his head in his hands. He remembers all too clearly the conversation he overheard Joey have with Jane. She described in detail a rather tall man with a tribal tattoo on his upper arm, and yet here, today, she made no reference to such distinct markings. Confused more than ever, Colin picks up the phone and calls Sean.

"Hey, it's me. Can you meet me down at Monroe's?"

"Yeah, man. I can be there in twenty."

"Great. See you then."

Colin grabs his bag and skateboard, paces down the hallway, and hurries two steps at a time down the back stairwell and out into the crisp spring day. He rides his skateboard down to Monroe's. For a brief moment, he loses himself in the open air and propulsion of his body on his board as he glides downtown. He slips in the entryway, steps on the tail with his left foot, and catches the nose in his hand before he enters the bar. It is virtually empty at this hour in the afternoon. He clutches a few beers from the bartender in his free hand and claims a seat in the back corner while he waits for Sean's arrival.

"Hey, man," Sean says. He sits across from Colin.

"Hey, thanks for meeting me."

"Of course. What's up?"

"I wanted to ask you for a favor," Colin says.

"Shoot."

"I need to leave right after my last final. Can you cover my shifts for the next week?"

Sean gives Colin a quizzical stare. "Everything okay?"

"Yeah. Well, it's my dad," he lies. "Family issue. I need to go home."

"Sorry to hear that. But, yeah, of course. I'll cover for you. No problem."

"Great. Thanks so much, buddy. I plan to go to the station to tell Tucker but wanted to have a plan first." Colin glances down, almost unable to meet his friend's eyes, certain he'd be giving himself away. He hates lying to Sean but knows he has no other option at this point.

"Happy to help," he says with marked sadness.

"Thanks."

"How is everything else? I feel like I haven't had a chance to catch up. You good?"

"Yeah. You know, end-of-the-year crap. Trying to get through my finals. Summer cannot be coming soon enough."

"I hear you on that." Reluctantly, he asks, "How is Joey?"

"Fine, I suppose."

"She ever talk about that night she came into the station?"

"Not really."

"She ever say what happened?"

"Not really," he repeats.

"Huh. I wonder why that is."

"I don't know what else I can do."

"How do you mean?"

"That's just it. I have no idea what I'm doing…or not doing."

Sean gives Colin a pained expression. "I can't help you on that one."

"I know," Colin whispers.

"Have you talked to Laura?"

Colin whips his head up. "No. Why?"

"No reason. Wasn't sure if you've seen her since the interview."

"No, I haven't." He unknowingly grits his teeth.

"Do you ever plan on seeing her?" Sean boldly asks.

"I don't know."

"Well, you can't avoid her forever."

"Who says I'm avoiding her?"

"I am; that's who," Sean responds.

"Well, I'm…" His cheeks fill with heat.

He interjects, "You guys used to be close. What happened?"

"Ask her…*or Travis.*"

"I'm asking *you.*"

"I don't know. She's different."

"Is she? Or is it that maybe she's coming into her own, and you don't know how to handle it?"

"Screw you, Sean."

"Screw me?" He pauses and laughs briefly. "What did Joey ever bring to you but heartache, huh?"

"You don't get it."

"No, I guess I don't, Colin."

"Why? Are you on Laura's side now?" he barks.

"I was never *not* on her side. But I'm on your side, too. Do I agree with what she did to Officer Murphy? No, not really, but the more I thought about it, there has to be a reason for it. I'm willing to give her the benefit of the doubt. And you should, too."

"Do you think she purposely tried to discredit Joey?"

"I never thought I'd say this, Colin, but you're even more naive than I thought."

"What the fuck does that mean?"

"Colin, you know deep down what is going on. You have to."

Colin stands, head hanging low.

"I'll cover your shifts, no problem." Sean remains sitting. "Can I ask one thing?"

"Sure," Colin says.

"She asked you to start a coup against Laura, get her kicked out of her job, didn't she?"

Colin's fist clenches. The color drains from his flesh.

"She wants you to get the only female DJ in the last ten years kicked out because, why, Colin? She doesn't like her?"

Colin has zero retort. He meets Sean's stare and simply replies, "Thank you for covering my shifts. I'll talk to you over the summer." Then, he exits the bar.

He heads straight toward the station. He opens the door to the station and heads down the hallway, toward Tucker's office. He is halfway down when he can hear the loud voices from behind his door.

"What the hell were you thinking?" Tucker yells.

"I was doing my job." Colin knows it's Laura.

"Your job was to ask the questions we determined, not what *you* decided to do."

"I understand you're upset."

"Upset? Yes. Disappointed you didn't come to me? Absolutely. You made us all look bad. You blindsided all of us."

"But I was doing my job," she pleads.

"Jesus, Laura. What the hell has gotten into you?"

Voice shaking, she asks, "Do you trust me?"

"I don't know anymore." Tucker's response is filled with contempt.

"Do you trust Travis?" The sound of his name rolling off Laura's tongue infuriates Colin.

So, this was all his idea. I should have known.

"Yes. You know I do."

Shit.

"Then, please, Tucker. Know I'm doing this for the right reasons."

There is silence as Colin leans in closer to try to hear what they are saying. But voices and attitudes have calmed, and he can no longer make out their words.

A few minutes go by, and then he hears the door crack open. He casually leans against the wall.

Laura steps out of the office, and with one glance in Colin's direction, she asks, "Are you all right?"

"Yes." Being this close to her hurts, and he can't articulate why. Nothing these days is making any sense to him.

When he stands in silence, she gets the hint he doesn't want to speak with her.

Turning slightly before she leaves, she murmurs, "I hope you're okay."

Colin turns on his heel, frustrated and eager to get out of here for the summer. "Can I talk to you for a moment?" he says as he knocks on Tucker's door.

"Come in." He cocks his head to the side. "What can I help you with?"

"My last final is tomorrow, and I've asked Sean to cover my remaining shifts this week, if that is okay with you?"

"Everything all right?"

"Yes, I have a family matter that requires my attention," he lies.

"I appreciate you securing your backup. Will you be leaving after your final?"

"Yes, immediately."

He rubs his goatee, and Colin can tell by the flicker in his eyes that he has pressing considerations on his mind. But something in the way he regards Colin changes his decision to speak.

Instead, he quietly says, "Well then, have a wonderful summer, Colin." He pauses and searches Colin's face. Then, he adds, "Get some rest, okay?"

"Sure thing." He wants so badly to ask him about what he and Laura spoke about.

Is she in trouble? Suspended? Is Travis to blame for all this?

But, right now, all he can dwell on is making it through one more final and disappearing—hopefully, without anyone knowing.

Twenty

F NALLY SUMMER

Laura enters the station for the final team meeting before the semester concludes. She sits in her desk chair and strikes up a conversation with Patrick about his plans for the summer. Within moments, Tucker's office door swings opens, and down comes both he and Sean. An uneasy feeling glides across her skin. She tries to catch eyes with Sean, but he is doing an exceptional job of avoiding hers.

"So, everyone, great year. Lots of changes this year, and for the most part, we handled them well. I am looking forward to next year. I'll be hosting the summer camp the university sponsors for high school students interested in communications. I'll be teaching them all summer how to run this station, and I'll even let them play some music."

"Don't let them screw up our equipment," Patrick jokes.

"Yeah, last year, they messed with the microphones too much," Ryker interjects.

Tucker raises his hands in protest. "I know; I know. I'll make sure you come back to this place just as you're leaving it today."

"Thanks." Patrick's voice drips with sarcasm.

"Anyway, if you visit campus over the summer, stop into the station and say hello. Hopefully, they won't screw it up too badly while you're all gone."

"I'll show 'em how to work a board." Patrick laughs.

Tucker shakes his head and smiles. "You all have my number, so if you need me over the summer or want to check in, please do."

Everyone nods.

Tucker's expression darkens. "Also, we might have a spot open next year, so please, if you know of anyone, let me know. I don't want to wait until the last minute to fill a potential opening."

It's obvious that the excitement in the room has been sucked out, and Laura feels partially to blame for it. She glances around the room, and then it dawns on her that Colin is not here. She was so preoccupied that she didn't immediately acknowledge that he was absent. Her heart sinks. Maybe it's Colin who is leaving.

Why isn't he here? Has anyone seen him? Did he quit?

But no one asks any questions, and by the look on everyone's faces, they, too, want to get out of here and start the summer.

Sean exits.

Laura grabs her bag and hurries up after him. "Sean! Hey, Sean. Wait up!" she yells through the crowd in the Union.

With hunched shoulders, he pauses and slightly turns toward her.

Laura catches up. "Hey."

"What's up?"

"Nothing. Are you okay?"

"Me? Yeah. What's up?" he asks again.

"I was hoping you knew why Colin wasn't here."

"I think he needs his space, if I'm being honest," he admits.

"Yes, I got that feeling, too. Did I do something wrong?" she asks, feeling on the verge of tears.

Colin never even said good-bye to me.

Sean's expression softens. "No, Laura, you didn't. We all could use a break."

"Okay. I understand."

He slightly drops his head while giving her a sympathetic stare. "Look, you have my number. Call me over the summer, okay? This will all die down by then."

"I appreciate that." She stands before him, searching for words she doesn't seem to have at the ready. Instead, she adds, "Have a great summer."

There is a sadness in their encounter she cannot place. Before she knows it, Sean has walked away and disappeared into the crowd of students.

It won't die down at all. Next year will be far more challenging than this. We've barely survived these past few months. There is much more to come, and I only wish we all hadn't fallen apart so easily.

Lying in Wait

Laura wanders across campus, watching the parents and students carrying out their belongings and loading them into their cars. The first year of college is officially completed at OSU, and Laura could not have prepared herself for the whirlwind that was her freshman year. There is a part of her that is homesick and wants to be tucked away from all the drama, so she can recharge and relax in the comfort of her own home. But there is the other part of her that will miss her friends dearly. She knows she will long for the good times at the station, but unfortunately, what comes along with that is the unfinished business she can feel swarming around her *and* CSU.

She knocks on Travis's door. Her stomach twists with anxiety. She turns and gazes down the street. A few guys are hanging out on a porch a few doors down, drinking beer, blaring Rage Against the Machine. No doubt in celebration of the end of the year. Laura is about to leave when the door creaks opens.

"Hey there." He is wearing running shorts and a T-shirt that is clearly stained with sweat.

"Did I catch you at a bad time?" she asks.

"No, not at all. Come in."

Laura enters.

"Give me a minute. I'm going to take a quick shower."

"Okay," she says.

She sits on his couch as he goes upstairs. She has only seen Travis once since they were last in his bedroom, twisted like a lust-filled pretzel. She had to go to the newspaper to talk to him about her conversation with Tucker, and surprisingly, she did not feel uncomfortable around him after their entanglement. He has a way of putting her at ease. She is unclear of how exactly he does it, but he just does.

As she waits for Travis, she stares straight ahead, replaying her conversation with Sean and the fact that Colin left with little warning.

He must hate me not to even say good-bye to me. Is he mad about my interview?

"Laura, come here."

Shaken out of her thoughts at the sound of Travis's voice, she gets up from the couch and heads upstairs. She enters his room. He is standing near his dresser, pulling a clean shirt over his head. He turns. He looks sexy with wet hair. She swallows hard.

"Read this," he says as he hands her a piece of paper.

Laura takes the paper and sits in his recliner in the corner while he continues to get ready in his bathroom.

The letter is from the Associated Collegiate Press. Upon further reading, Laura realizes that the letter is indicating that, next year, Travis will be honored at a ceremony at the school for his achievement as the head of *The Weekly Blue*. He is the recipient of the College Media Liberty Award, which recognizes students for demonstrating outstanding support for college press freedom and reform.

Travis goes over toward his bed and switches on his CD player. "Immortality" by Pearl Jam fills the silence in the room. He sits on the edge of his bed. Laura glances up at him.

"Travis, this is incredible." She smiles for the first time today.

"Thank you. Appreciate you saying that."

"Well, it is. Do you know when the ceremony is?"

"Not yet, but I'd like you to be there."

Feeling honored, she says, "Of course I'll be there."

"Good," he says with a nod of his head.

"You staying here all summer?" Laura asks.

"Most of it. I'll go home for a few weekends here and there, but I have a lot to do to get ready for next year. The news never sleeps." He laughs and then adds, "But you know that."

"It's true, but I'm leaving tomorrow," she adds, although he never asked her.

"I'm glad you're not leaving today," he says as he gets up and crosses the room to be within inches of her.

She swallows hard and feels her heart beating with authority in her chest. He reaches out his hand to take hers. As he does, he pulls her up and into his arms.

"I'm so glad you stopped by," he whispers.

She glances up at him, and his expression is serious.

"Me, too," she murmurs.

He brushes a loose strand of her hair and tucks it behind her ear. With no further words spoken, he leans in and tenderly kisses her. Her tense shoulders relax. Once his lips release hers, he tugs her around the waist, spinning her toward the base of his bed. Pushing her back on the bed, he seductively crawls on top of her.

She reaches up and runs her hands through his hair as the smell of soap and cologne mix perfectly on his skin. She exhales and waits with quiet anticipation for his next kiss. Within moments, his face is hovering over hers. His eyes dance all over her figure, soaking in the trace of her beauty. He licks his lips. The shimmer across his bottom lip makes her hungry for a taste. He deliberately leans in and presses his wet lips onto hers—only, this time, it's with significantly more passion than his first kiss. She inhales sharply as he runs his hand up her shirt and squeezes her breast. He starts to moan as he begins pulling up her shirt. She reaches down and yanks it over her head. His eyes are wide yet again as he takes in the sight of her full breasts dressed in red lace. He pulls his T-shirt up over his back as he leans up on one arm. Balling it, he throws it across the room.

She wraps her arms around him and pulls him closer to her. The feel of his skin on hers makes her forget everything that is going on in her head. She can only comprehend the sensations being fired off by the hormones pulsing through her. She continues to need this distraction in her life. She desires to be wanted and not overlooked.

She kisses him back, and he allows the weight of his body to settle onto hers. No words need to be exchanged to know that they both want this equally as bad.

This is less complicated than her other relationship, and this is exactly what Laura yearns for.

Laura leans up to try to find her bra.

"What are you doing?" he asks.

"Getting dressed."

"No, not yet," he demands, pulling her body back toward his.

"Okay…" She giggles.

He tightly wraps his arms around her and then begins slowly stroking the side of her body with his fingertips.

The silence is difficult for Laura. They usually have so much to talk about with the station and the paper that this type of one-on-one is new to her. She glances up at him, hoping that the look on his face will be able to give her some kind of a clue as to what he is thinking about. She sees contentment and a relaxed Travis, which is a rarity.

"Am I too quiet?" he asks with a slight grin.

"Yes, I'm sorry. I'm so used to…"

"Me always talking?"

"Something like that."

"I'm not making you uncomfortable, am I?" he asks her so sincerely that she starts to feel badly for not enjoying her private time with him.

She could be way off, but she guesses that not a lot of people get to witness this side of Travis

Laura, too, starts to relax more. She gets out of her head as she slowly closes her eyes and allows the sensation of his fingers dancing over her skin to envelop her.

Delicately, he asks, "If you come back to the station over the summer, let me know, okay?"

"Of course. I'll leave you my address and number in case you want to write me or call."

"I'll be busy this summer, but I'll make time for you."

She doesn't even bother looking up at him; by merely the tone of his voice, she knows he is kidding with her.

"You shouldn't work so hard," she cracks out.

"I have to. It's how I'm wired, I suppose."

"Will you have any fun this summer?"

"This is my fun." He chuckles. "Besides, you know what they say; I'll rest when I'm dead and gone."

"Really? Is that so?"

"Yeah, when I'm gone, I'd like to believe people will think I did the best I could, worked the hardest I could, and was true to what I believed in."

"I'd say, you're off to a good start." She smiles, lifting her head to look up at him.

He smiles in return. "Exactly, and then one day, they'll say, *Rest in peace, Travis.*"

"Ugh," Laura moans, not realizing her reaction is outwardly.

"What was that for?" he asks.

"Sorry. I didn't mean to answer."

"But you did, so tell me."

She lowers her eyes. "You'll think I'm nuts."

"Doubtful. Try me."

She leans back up on one arm and decides to take a chance that he won't think her thoughts are silly. "It's just…rest in peace. I don't like when people say that."

"Rest in peace? Really?"

"Yes, it's cliché, and worse, it is RIP."

"RIP? That bothers you?"

"Always has. It's overused and not very personal. It's cold to me. Someone died, and the best you can come up with is RIP. No, thanks. Don't say it for me."

"Oh, believe me, I won't." He laughs. "And I definitely won't say, *Rest in peace, kiddo!*"

"Travis, that is mean. Stop it!" She playfully pinches him on the arm.

"I'm not being mean. I'm simply following your wishes. Your dead wishes."

With a smug expression, she replies, "Good. I'll expect that. And I won't say it for you either."

"I expect you wouldn't." He unlocks his arms from her and leans down to give her a long kiss. He releases her and says, "You may get dressed now."

She rolls her eyes but can't help but snicker as she leans over the side of his bed and starts retrieving her bra and shirt. Once she is dressed and standing near his door, he wraps his arms back around her.

"Curious," he asks, "what do you say when someone dies?"

She leans up on her tippy-toes and tenderly places her lips onto his. Then, she whispers. "Sweet dreams, Travis."

The smile that spreads across his face is like nothing she has seen before. She can't help but return a rosy, warm smile.

"I like that," he says softly. "I like that much better."

Twenty-One

UNEXPECTED VISITOR

Travis races up the stairs, two at a time, to his office at *The Weekly Blue*. The summer thus far has been relatively quiet around campus, but by the sounds of the message he received from Wolfie on his answering machine, things are changing.

He swings open the door to his office and finds Wolfie sitting across from his desk. "I didn't know you had a key?" he remarks with a slight laugh.

Wolfie returns a playful smirk but doesn't answer him.

Travis sits in his desk chair and folds his hands together, resting them on top. "What's going on?"

Wolfie pulls out an envelope from inside his vintage linen coat and hands it to Travis. Eagerly, Travis slides his finger under the sealed flap. He carefully takes out the paper. Inside is a photocopy of a handwritten note from who else but Dean Barrymore to her assistant, Joanne Stone. It is clear by the crumpled paper that was copied that it had previously been disposed of. Travis never, ever asks Wolfie where he gets his information. It's unspoken between the two.

It is dated May 17, 1996.

> *Joanne,*
>
> *Please solicit three faculty members for my campus security task force next year. I suggest two male and one female. I'd like them to tell people/media/colleagues or whomever that they have volunteered, but their participation will not be optional. A bonus will be paid out once*

the academic year has been completed and they have performed their duties to my satisfaction.

Secondly, we need some of the student athletes to join. The process could have gone a lot better had it been an on-campus athlete misbehaving, but now that we know it is a repeat criminal, we need to gain the trust of the student athletes again. Otherwise, boosters and alumni might begin pulling their support. A recent meeting suggested their disapproval of the way we'd been running things on campus, and donor support is down 25% in just the past semester alone. This cannot continue. Therefore, I suggest one lacrosse player, one football player, and one basketball player. No female athletes at this time.

Third, make contact with Bree Van Tousen, one of the victims. I gave her and Professor Cooper a lighter decree for their romantic fling, knowing I might play to her vulnerable side and get her to join the task force alongside me. Assume it is not optional for her as well. Do whatever you need to convince her to participate.

Lastly, I need The Weekly Blue to only run articles on this once I approve of them. Make this happen even if it means threatening their funding. Remind Professor Campbell he is on my payroll. The paper can get exclusive access to information from the administration with my approval. I need to convince them that we have been ahead of this the whole time.

Dean Barrymore

"What do you plan to do with this?" Wolfie asks.

Travis peeks up from the photocopied paper and lays his eyes on his ally. His face burns with heat and disgust, as he merely considers that these are the same people who claim to uphold the scared code of ethics that all faculty and administration do each and every day as they step onto this campus. The code is meant to establish an environment of integrity and professionalism that help to ensure each individual receives the best care and education possible within the walls of this institution.

Travis has spent the better part of the past three years making damn sure each and every student's voice has been heard but only under the guise that those representing the symbol of the OSU crest and the freedom the Hawk represents also have the best intentions of the student body. The ethical decisions that students face in an academic environment are similar to those they will encounter routinely in the professional world, yet here he sits, face bloodied by the realization that those teaching them these important life issues are in fact the same who are creating the situations in

156

which parents are spending their hard-earned money to shield their children from.

"The Student Code of Conduct was created so that faculty could conduct a fair and accurate evaluation of student performance and maintain a just and safe learning environment, yet who is evaluating those in charge? Particularly, when the person at the helm is a crooked dean?" he says.

Wolfie shakes his head. "I'm disgusted."

"The OSU code was created to arm the administration with the ability to deal more effectively with students and to work on a student's behalf both within the university and outside of it."

Yet, here, held tight in the grips of Travis's hand, is a letter from the dean to her own secretary, dispelling every idealistic notion he ever had of the perfect college experience.

He lets out a long and heavy sigh as he rubs the stubble on his chin. "Am I missing something here?" He puts the paper down.

Travis is never one to not have his next move planned. But something about this letter and its connection to Laura is halting him from making quick decisions.

Knowing Wolfie is eager for his marching orders, he can only say, "I need to ponder over this."

I need to consider a hell of a lot more than just this damn letter.

Travis pulls up to the large farmhouse and parks diagonally in an off-road spot filled with gravel. He grabs his messenger bag off the passenger seat, and with a heavy heart, he wanders up to the front door and knocks. He takes a step back on the wood steps and waits, hopeful someone is home. He shoves his hands deep into the pockets of his faded jeans.

The door opens, and an older gentleman dressed in a blue denim work shirt and khaki pants stands before him. Kindly and in a deep baritone voice, he asks. "Can I help you?"

"Yes. Hello, sir. My name is Travis. I'm hoping Laura is home."

He smiles warmly. "No, unfortunately, she is not."

"I'm a friend of hers from OSU, and—"

"But she should be home shortly. Care to come in and wait?"

With nervous relief, he replies, "Oh, thank you. I'd appreciate that." Travis steps into the large front foyer.

"I'm her father, Rick." He extends his hand toward Travis.

"Yes, of course." Travis not only read the article on Laura following in her father's footsteps as a campus DJ, but he also did some of the research on Rick himself.

"Please, come in. Would you care for a drink? Coffee, water?"

"I'd love a cup of coffee."

Travis follows her father into the kitchen.

"Travis, how do you know Laura?"

"Like I mentioned, we go to OSU together. I run *The Weekly Blue*, the student newspaper. Laura and I collaborate on her segments at the radio station."

"Fascinating," he replies as he motions for Travis to sit at the table.

"Yes, sir. I hear you had quite a radio career yourself."

"Oh, well, that was a long time ago."

"Well, it wasn't that long ago, and quite frankly, you were a trailblazer for many of my friends in the field." He pauses and adds with a grin, "I know where Laura gets her drive from."

Her father returns a wide smile as he places the cup of coffee in front of Travis. He takes the seat at the table across from him. "You don't say. How is she doing?"

"She is excellent. A real breath of fresh air for the campus airwaves. They have been lacking a voice, and she is the answer we were all waiting for."

"Wow, that's great news. You know, I ask her how it is going, and she responds the same way each time with, 'It's fine.'"

"Yeah, not surprised. It's not her style to brag."

"No, it's not. What brings you here, Travis? She didn't mention you were coming."

"I know. I didn't tell her. Something came up at school, and I want to talk to her before she returns next week."

"Everything okay?"

"Absolutely. This just couldn't wait a week; that's all. You know the business."

He rises to grab the coffee pot. He fills Travis's cup again. He starts to turn back toward the counter when he pauses for a moment and then peers out the back window. A car can be heard pulling into the dirt driveway. The smile that grows across her father's face tells Travis that Laura is home.

They can hear her singing to herself as she opens her car door. Within moments, she is close to the back door of the kitchen.

"Dad, I'm home!" she yells and then instantly freezes as she enters her kitchen to find Travis sitting at her table, drinking a cup of coffee. "Hi," she chokes out.

Travis starts to stand. "Hey there."

"Wow. Um, what are you doing here?" She glances at her dad.

He simply shrugs his shoulders, and then she turns back to Travis.

"Nice to see you, too." The sarcasm that drips off Travis's tongue is unmistakable.

Laura's face blushes a pretty pink shade. She shakes her head. "I'm sorry. That was rude."

"Surprised I'm here?"

"Naturally."

Travis gives her a friendly hug. Her father watches with quiet confusion as the two of them release their embrace.

"I'll leave you two to catch up," her father interjects as he takes his coffee to exit the room. "Happy to have you for dinner, Travis. Maureen should be home in a few hours, and she is a hell of a chef."

"Well then, I suppose I cannot say no."

"It's settled. I'll call your mother and let her know," he says to Laura.

"Thanks, Dad."

Laura is about to sit at the table when Travis says, "Is there someplace private we can go? Maybe outside?"

Her eyebrows bend with concern. "Sure. This way."

She steps back out the kitchen door, and Travis follows her toward a large deck off of the kitchen. She pulls out a wooden chair and sits in it. He sits closest to her.

"You're kind of freaking me out, Travis," she whispers.

"I know. I'm sorry. I had to come and tell you in person before next week. I need to wrap my head around this and talk it out."

As she feels a slight sense of relief, Laura's shoulders begin to relax. "Hit me with it."

Her response is exactly why he is so fond of her. She is a woman, and she is strong, eager, and full of surprises. She hones her fortitude as good as anyone he's worked with before.

"Before I tell you, you must know, for your own protection, I can't tell you where I got the information."

"I'm familiar with the drill," she adds with a smile and slight roll of her eyes.

Travis glances at the young woman sitting before him—hair tucked behind her ears, bright hazel eyes dancing back and forth as she looks at him—and he hesitates, knowing what he is about to tell her will crush her...again.

"Good. It's nothing personal, and I trust you, but you know I want to protect those around me."

"I understand."

He pulls out a pack of cigarettes from his pocket and lights one.

"When did you start smoking?" she asks.

"I smoke when I'm stressed," he replies.

She laughs. "I'm surprised I don't find you smoking more."

"I know, right?"

"Why the stress?"

He takes a long drag off his Parliament. "Did your friend Bree say anything to you about a campus security task force?"

"Campus security task force? No, not to my knowledge."

"Hmm…okay, interesting."

"And why is that interesting?"

"Dean Barrymore is forming a task force as soon as we return to school. My sources tell me the people have already been chosen to head this committee up."

"Okay, and is there a problem?"

"Well, let me ask you something. Did Bree get in some kind of trouble at the end of the year? Was she in a relationship with a professor?"

Warmth fills Laura's cheeks as she looks at Travis. "I don't feel comfortable…"

Travis immediately stops her. "Laura, you trust me, don't you?"

"I'm sorry. I meant, you know I'm not one to gossip."

"This is far from gossip."

She sighs heavily and then responds, "Yes, Professor Adam Cooper. She was reprimanded for her indiscretion, as was he. And, between you and me, they are still together, but no one is supposed to know. They keep their continued relationship a secret."

Travis shakes his head. "Dean Barrymore is using her. Using a victim to make her agenda get noticed and her mistakes disappear."

"What?" A chill runs over her skin despite the late August heat.

"Yes, she gave Bree a lighter disciplinary action, so when she requests her help with this committee, she will be certain to say yes. In fact, she won't be able to refuse."

Laura shakes her dark bob loose. "That's cruel."

"I also think, by allowing this professor off lightly, she can almost guarantee his support as well. What's shoddier is, she's going to parade athletes on this committee, so she doesn't lose the support from boosters and alumni before anyone realizes that she knew about the attacker for over six months before he was caught and did absolutely nothing about it."

"Wow." Laura shudders. "This is heavy."

"Yes, it is. I wanted to come and talk to you as soon as I got the information. You can't let your friend be a pawn in Dean Barrymore's game."

Laura's stomach churns with an uneasy feeling. "How dare she exploit a victim like this. And all because of her relationship with Professor Cooper. Asking her is just cruelty at its finest. Making Bree feel as though she is wanted on the committee. Damn her, Dean Barrymore. Now, she has gone too far!"

"I feel badly for whichever athletes get chosen, too. Oh, and by the way, she is only allowing male athletes to truly pander to the masses. No females allowed. She wants them to show they are supporting the campus security changes and that there are no hurt feelings whatsoever that she let everyone believe it was some jock misbehaving, not a real criminal wandering numerous campuses throughout New York."

"How did she screw this up so badly?"

"I don't know, but I don't intend to let her get away with it."

"Travis, what are you planning to do?"

"I'm not positive. But I *have* to do something. I have to right this wrong. Not merely for Bree and the countless other victims. Not only for the athletes disrespected. Not just for the people forced to be a pawn in the dean's game. But also for all those without the voice, still out there, believing they were safe when they clearly were not."

Twenty-Two

SOPHOMORE YEAR

Laura strains to get a better view at the mass gathered on the lawn. She can faintly hear the sound of a voice addressing the crowd. She jogs across the street and camps at the back of the pack.

Ah, yes, the welcoming committee of the new freshman class.

She remembers this like it was yesterday. She listens to the head of the Registrar's Office discuss the process of signing up for classes and where the student body can find the course catalog. Laura is entranced by the fresh faces looking around.

Did we look this young? she wonders.

She feels a presence approach from behind her.

"Joanne, I thought I was speaking first, so I could get the hell out of here," a woman barks through gritted teeth.

"Sorry, Dean. There must have been a mix-up."

Laura can feel her skin crawling with hate at the mention of the dean.

"Do I look like the kind of person who accepts that half-ass excuse?" she scolds.

Laura inconspicuously turns her head to get a good look at her. Two feet over from her stands the dean of the university, and next to her is a woman clutching a folder, pale as a ghost.

That poor woman. She looks like she wants to die.

"No, Dean Barrymore. I'll be sure to—"

"What, change it now? No, just tell me who screwed this up, and I hope it was not you."

Laura feels nauseated, even being in her presence, so she quickly turns and hurries back to her dormitory. Thankfully, she is able to put that brief encounter behind her as she enters her beloved Willis Hall. She can feel her energy rise as she steps into her room, and Abigail is unpacking.

Abigail screams as she enters, "I'm excited to see you! Isn't this awesome?" Abigail asks, motioning to their room. "Packing was much easier this time."

"It was."

"I can't believe it's our sophomore year!"

Laura smiles. "Hard to imagine we made it through our freshman year."

She finishes unpacking and notices the time. "Hey, I've got a meeting at the station. I'll catch you all later for dinner."

She hurries down the hallway, but as she passes Casey's room, she notices a new name on the door.

Laura knocks and enters. "Hey, Casey. What's with the new roommate?"

"Jen and I decided over the summer that it probably wasn't such a good idea for us to live together."

"Everything okay?" Laura asks.

"Oh, yes. We are solid. We agreed it would be best for our relationship not to be right on top of one another. But, anyway, Alex is a transfer from University of Rochester. She's arriving later tonight. Jen got permission from the school to move off-campus and into the soccer house."

"Cool. I look forward to meeting her. I've gotta run to the station. See you for dinner?"

"Yeah, cool. Looking forward to catching up!"

Laura's mind races with uncertainty as she enters the Union, too scared to see Colin there, and yet she is even more frightened to learn that he might actually be gone for good. She half-expected him to call her over the summer but wasn't the least bit surprised when he didn't. She didn't try to reach out to him either. In fact, she called no one at the station, not even Tucker. She feels badly about that now as she nears the door to the station. She takes a deep breath in and pushes it open.

Standing in the center of the room are Sean, Patrick, Ryker, and Tucker...no Colin.

"Hey, guys."

"Have a seat, guys and gal."

Tucker is about to start the meeting when the door slowly opens, and in comes Colin. Tan, more muscular, and with a short haircut. He looks amazing, and Laura has to look away, knowing her cheeks are flushing a deep pink.

"Hey, guys," Colin says. "Sorry I'm late."

Tucker begins, "I've made some changes to the lineup this year. Sean and Colin, you guys will alternate the first shift and the last shift of the day. If one of you has the early shift, the other has the evening shift. Laura, you get the midday shift, starting at three. Let's work on a schedule of guests and streamline our news segments more. Any suggestions from you guys, please come and chat with me. I want to work closely on this. Lastly, we did receive funding, approved by the dean for another head count to add a new engineer. I'm going to ask you all to help me choose the right candidate."

Laura's skin crawls at the mention of the dean and can't help but wonder what she is up to.

They all nod their heads in unison.

"Okay, well, let's have a great year! Laura, can I speak with you in my office, please?"

She can feel Colin eyeing her as she follows Tucker to his office.

"Close the door, please."

Laura does and takes a seat across from his desk. "I wanted to talk to you privately about your news segments this year."

"I know. I figured that, and like I said, I'm sorry about—"

He cuts her off, "Listen, if you are working on something, you need to fill me in. Bottom line. You're going to need all the support you can get. And, in order to do that, you'll need my buy-in."

"I understand, Tucker, and thank you."

"So, what do you have planned?"

"Well, I'd like to interview Tank McPherson about the night the Creeper was caught. I'd also like to cover the trial. The Campus Creeper is being tried in Onondaga County."

"Go on."

"I have a few more things in the works. I need more time to iron them out. In the meantime, I'd like to start off the year on a lighter note. I've lined up a few of the guys from Moon Boot Lover to come in as well as Rustic Overtones and Thanks to Gravity. Give the local bands a little wink."

"I like it. Okay, keep me posted, and I want a copy of questions prior to each interview."

"Of course. And sorry I didn't check in this summer." She fidgets with her hair, tucking and untucking it behind her ears.

"I get it. We had the interns this summer to help fill in the gaps. Next year, if you're interested, I'd love for you guys to help keep this station alive in the summer."

Laura smiles. "Well, you can count me in next year for certain."

"Good, and I'm glad you had a nice summer."

Laura rises and opens the door. From the dimly lit hallway, she senses a figure in the distance. As she comes into the common area, she notes Colin is standing by his desk. He turns toward her. His expression is indescribable.

Laura lowers her head and starts to head straight for the door.

"Laura," he whispers.

She stops and waits.

"Can I talk to you?"

She glances up at him. Her pulse reacts. "Okay."

"Can we go somewhere more private?"

"I'll follow you."

He pushes off his desk and crosses the room. The heat from his body so close to hers confuses her. She allows him to pass and follows him out the door. He exits the Union down near the mailboxes and takes her to a secluded bench behind one of the academic buildings. The sun is shining brightly, and the touch of it on her skin is welcoming. She sits, tucking her legs up as she wraps her arms around her knees.

He sits next to her.

Barely able to push the words out, she asks, "You have a nice summer?"

He exhales deeply and then replies, "It was okay."

She waits for him to speak again.

"How was yours?"

"Went by fast, too fast."

He nods in agreement. "I was kind of hoping you and I could come to some agreement about how we handle the situation on campus," he blurts out.

Laura drops her arms from around her knees and turns slightly toward him. "Agreement? About what?"

"About your interviews and the impact they have on others…"

"You mean, the impact they have on Joey," she replies, clearly irritated and not trying to hide it.

He has some nerve, coming to me after not speaking to me in months, only to ask me to come to an agreement with him.

"Well, she is one of them."

"And I'm very sorry about that, but I can't base my interviews off of one person, Colin."

"Not even if I'm asking?"

A barrage of feelings rushes through Laura as her eyes squint in the sunlight. A vision of red flashes before her senses as she replays the last conversation she had with Joey. In order to commit to anything, she deserves to know the truth.

"Can I ask you something? What is going on with Joey? You obviously care about her, or you wouldn't be here asking for my help."

His eyes show great pain as he glances at Laura. He starts to speak and then immediately stops. She holds steady, awaiting his answer.

"I'd care about anyone in her situation. Can't you see that? Don't you know that about me?" he whispers.

"And what situation is that?"

Like a broken man, he adds, "I'm not confident. But, over the summer, she told me she went to counseling. How can I not believe that something is wrong if she took the time to seek help?"

"My point exactly. If you're not confident how can you ask me to back off?"

"I thought we could start off the year on better terms."

Sadly, she has to stick to her investigative nature and all the work she and Travis have already uncovered.

She stands and takes a deep breath in. "Colin, if you wanted to start off the year on better terms, in my opinion, the last person you should have come to, to ask for help with Joey is me."

His mouth drops open in disbelief, but she presses on, "If you're uncertain of what is going on, then that should tell you something. I am trying to do what is right for this school, for the women on this campus, and the women all over New York impacted by the events last year. But what I won't do is bow to a girl who so clearly does not care for me. I'm sorry if you and I can no longer be friends. But I'll understand if your loyalties lie with her." She pauses, hoping for a reaction but gets nothing. "You seem different, if I may say, since she has come back into your life. I hope you are okay, and...I still care about you, for what it is worth, but I sense from my last conversation with her that you do not feel the same about me."

"What?"

Her lip begins to quiver. "It's water under the bridge."

"What conversation?"

Not wanting to get into the terrible things he said about her she replies, "You know, Colin, the truth is out there, and it could very well set you free. You just need to find it. I can't help you do that."

With that, Laura turns as the tears well in her eyes. She hurries across campus before she starts crying. She doesn't turn back despite him repeatedly calling her name.

She can only think of one place to go. Travis's apartment. She knocks on the door and steps back, hoping he will answer. She can hear someone inside. A guy she does not recognize opens the door.

"Hey, is Travis around?"

"Yeah, he's upstairs. Come in."

"Thanks. I'm Laura."

"Cool. I'm his roommate, Chris." He motions for her to go upstairs, so she does.

She can hear "The Day I Tried to Live" by Soundgarden blaring through his speakers. She knocks.

"Come in!" he yells.

Feeling on the verge of tears after her conversation with Colin, she exhales deeply and then opens the door. Travis is lying on his bed, surrounded by papers and folders. He scrambles when he realizes it's Laura.

"Hey there. Wasn't expecting you."

"I know. I'm sorry. I just didn't…" She starts to tear up.

"Oh, what is it?"

"It's nothing. Silly really."

"Can't be silly if it's gotten you this upset."

Embarrassed, she nears him as he pats the edge of his bed.

"What happened today?"

"I went to the station for our meeting, and the vibe is way off."

"Okay, we can fix that."

"Tucker asked to speak with me about my role this year and how I need to keep him in the loop. I had to lie to him. I had to. I can't tell him what we are doing. He'd put a stop to it."

"Now, we don't know that yet. He has surprised us thus far, hasn't he? Maybe we test the waters with him a bit."

"You think?"

"Maybe. I want to check with Wolfie on a few things first."

Laura lowers her gaze. She senses Travis's movement, and he gently places his finger and thumb on her chin, raising her face.

He searches her eyes and then adds, "But there is something else bothering you. You can tell me, Laura. Always know that."

She watches his blue eyes soften. She decides to take a leap of faith and tell him. "Colin asked to speak with me after my meeting with Tucker. He asked me to reconsider my interviews and my approach with the Campus Creeper."

"Why?"

"Because the girl he used to date, she was the one who claims she was attacked in April. Long after the guy was caught. But she didn't file a report or anything, and in the meantime, she's got him following her around. He is at her freaking beck and call. And I'm so torn!"

"Torn how?"

"Torn because I don't believe her. Pissed off that I don't believe a woman who says she was sexually assaulted. What kind of monster does that make me?"

"You are far from a monster. Besides, we said we were going to stick to our plan, remember? We stick to our story and lure this person or whatever out into the open, and maybe that person ends up being her. One of two things can happen. He might think he's in the clear to strike again, or she'll be so pissed that we are not buying into her attack that, eventually, she'll crack."

"It sounds cold."

"Of course it does. Either way, it's screwed up, right?"

"Yeah, and if Joey plays him all through this, that is the ultimate messed-up thing to do."

Travis's expression is one that Laura is unfamiliar with. She can't place his demeanor either.

"Have I helped you at all?" he asks.

"Yes. Of course. I knew I could come and talk to you."

"Good." He places his arm around her shoulders and pulls her in toward him.

The calming beat of his heart soothes her mind as she listens intently. She closes her eyes. She feels so comfortable in his arms, in a way that she is truly unable to explain. It's as though he is teaching her about life on many levels, taking her under his wing, and there is something beautiful about it. She's never asked him how he feels about her. Something in their unspoken partnership is enough for her. She'd rather not have this defined, for fear that words would only complicate things.

She opens her eyes, gazing up at Travis. He searches her face—for what, she does not know. He leans in and brushes his lips upon hers. A shiver runs over her skin as his fingertips trace the curve of her side. He pulls her body up toward him as he leans back on his bed. Their faces now inches from one another, he gives her a look that tells her he is no longer in the mood to talk. Lucky for him, neither is Laura. He undresses her as though he were peeling away the layers of her, seeking that desirable flesh underneath. With each touch, with each kiss, he tries to pull her away from her melancholy.

Pushing her shirt off her shoulders, he drags his teeth over her skin. Her complexion pinks. He's encouraged by her lust for more. So, he toys and teases her with his tongue, watching her head tip in approval. He knows how to make a woman feel like she is the only one in existence.

But, unfortunately for Laura, her mind continues to be one of her greatest weapons, yet it has an indecisive and hasty trigger. But she'd never admit it. So, as she moves on top of him, enjoying the fullness he brings her, she can't help but curse herself for fantasizing about Colin.

Get out of my head!

Twenty-Three

THANK YOU, TANK

"Tank, thank you so much for joining me today," Laura announces into the microphone.

"My pleasure, Laura," his deep voice booms.

"Can you take us back to that night in February?" she asks, wasting no time in diving into the interview.

He sighs and appears slightly uncomfortable. "Since this is an ongoing investigation, I'm currently not allowed to speak about the specifics. But I do remember this horrible, gut-wrenching feeling in my stomach. I have to admit, adrenaline aside, I, too, was scared. It's not a situation I ever want to be in again."

"I can only imagine. Was there any doubt in your mind that the person was up to no good, if you will?"

"Never a doubt. I've never doubted it."

"You saved someone that night?"

"Yes, had I not been there, I can't even fathom what might have happened."

Although the audience cannot see his expression, Laura takes in the full anguish on his face. She is trying to remain like a stone, or she'll never get through this interview either.

"I suppose saving one meant saving countless others, as we are learning through police reports. So very sad."

"I can't argue with you on that."

"What has it been like, being an athlete on this campus, taking into account the past year?"

"Well, to be honest, there has been a lot of negative light shed on the athletes at OSU. The stigma surrounding athletes is one thing, but to be so misrepresented at this university has been disheartening. I speak for all my teammates when I say, we deserve our reputation back."

"Do you believe the administration has done enough to help you and the campus?"

"No, I don't. There has been so much talk and very little action."

"Have you heard from anyone in the university administration? Perhaps Dean Barrymore?"

"No."

"Not at all? Not even to say thank you?"

"No, but I'm not looking for one."

"Of course not. What about the police?"

"Yes, they have been very complimentary and easy to work with. I'm sure this can't be easy for them. It's a lot to process."

"Have those in charge opened their eyes?"

Leaning in closer to his microphone, Tank replies, "They didn't have a choice."

"You could say it was an epidemic."

"Exactly."

"Hard to ignore at this point," Laura boldly pronounces. "Do you, Tank, consider our campus safe?"

"That is subjective but probably safer than it was before."

"We will be hearing more from you and others as the trial begins later this fall."

With a saddened expression, he simply replies, "Yeah. Unfortunately."

"I want to thank you for your openness. And, now, to this season, what can we expect from the Hawks?"

He perks up at the mention of his beloved team. "We have a killer team. Everyone is back from last season. We elected Marcus as our captain again. Nathan is our assistant captain. I, personally, am really proud of QB One. He had such an incredible freshman year."

"Yes, he did. And so did you."

"Yeah, you know, I did pretty well, too."

"Yes, you were nominated for Rookie of the Year."

"Yes, I was."

"Well, you are off to a good start this year. First win under your belt."

"Yes, but we have a tough opponent coming up. Georgia Tech is always a hard one for us."

"I'm predicting a win." She laughs.

"I like your prediction."

"Well, Tank, I'm not afraid to reach out and say thank you on behalf of all the women, students, athletes, and surrounding community. Thank you for being there that night to finally catch the Campus Creeper."

"I wish I didn't have to, but…I appreciate the thanks and for having me on today."

"Of course. For all my listeners, come out this Saturday to Menton Field at one to support our impressive Hawks football team. Stay tuned, and I'll be right back."

Laura switches off the microphone and peels the headphones off her ears, resting them around her neck.

Tank's smile tells her all she needs to know. "Thanks, Laura, for what you're doing."

"You were great, Tank. And you know it goes without saying how personal this is for us. I'll do whatever I can to make this better."

"Yeah, and we might be in a lull now, but once this trial starts…well, the pain is gonna start all over again for them. Not looking forward to it."

"I hear you. Wish we could avoid it altogether, but we both know that is not possible."

He shakes his head and then leans in to give Laura a friendly hug. "Well, I have to get to practice. I'll see you later."

"Absolutely, and thanks again. Oh, tell Coach we appreciate him letting you do the interview."

"I will."

As Tank closes the door, Laura eases back into her chair. She stares out the window into the Union and watches the students linger about. She wonders if they truly understand the impact Tank had on this campus. The relationship between Abigail and Tank is and will remain the reason this terror all came to a screeching halt. That might be the one and only indisputable fact in this entire mess.

Twenty-Four

LET ME TELL YOU HOW I FEEL

Laura enters her dorm and takes the stairs to her floor. She pushes open her door and finds Abigail lying back on her bed, reading a textbook.

She glances up. "Hey, how are you?"

"Oh, fine," Laura replies, plopping her bag on the floor.

"I heard your interview," she says with a slight sadness to her voice.

"And?"

"Well, it was good. You were great. Tank was great."

"But what?"

"It's hard to hear a story when you know it is about you."

"I understand. I do." Although it has dawned on Laura a thousand times how close to home this all is, she can't even begin to fathom what it must be like for Abigail and Bree.

"But that's life, and we can't hide from life." Abigail puts her book down on her bed and swings her legs over the side to face Laura.

"No, we can't." Laura fumbles with her hands.

"Hey, Bree called and said she wanted to talk to you."

"Oh, okay. I'll go try to find her. Dinner later?"

"Yes, come grab me."

"Cool." Laura exits the door.

She knocks on Bree's door, and she hears her yell, "Come in!"

Laura opens the door and finds Bree sitting at her desk, watching the campus below as the students move fluidly from their afternoon classes back to their dorms. Others are sprawled out on the lawn, enjoying the breathtaking fall afternoon.

"Hey, Bree!"

"Hello," she replies coolly.

This gives Laura an uneasy feeling as she takes a seat in the desk chair next to her. "What's up?"

Bree deliberately turns and regards Laura.

She swallows hard. "Abigail said you wanted to see me?"

In a hoarse voice, she says, "Yes, I did."

"What's wrong, Bree?"

"You know I'm an up-front kind of person, so I have to say my piece." Her large brown eyes flicker with fervor.

Nervously, Laura nods her head.

"Before we left for school last year, you did that interview with Officer Murphy."

"Okay…" Laura begins to feel the skin on her arms prickle and not in a good way.

"Then, today, you did one with Tank."

"And?"

"Well, I take personal offense to the fact that you attacked Officer Murphy and now Dean Barrymore."

"I've attacked them?" Laura's voice rises an octave.

"Yes, your interview with Officer Murphy was way off, Laura. I wasn't going to say anything, but now that you've thrown Dean Barrymore under the bus, as your friend, I have to tell you how I feel."

Laura's head starts to spin. She envisions the letter written from Captain Frankel to Dean Barrymore and knows unequivocally that both the police and the school didn't act quickly enough to prevent these horrible events from continuing on campus.

The best the police could do was write an email? Maybe Officer Murphy was a casualty caught in the crossfire, but why did he not fight harder?

But she can't tell her that. She is sworn to a secrecy that must remain buried deep within her. She, too, carries a pain she cannot release. They have that in common.

She attempts to stick up for herself. "I did what I thought I had to do in regard to my interview with Officer Murphy."

"Really?" she scoffs.

Laura is getting a bitter taste of the Hamptons' Bree.

"Do you know him at all?"

"Well, not exactly, but I—"

"Precisely. You don't know what he did for me." Bree closes her eyes, forcing back her tears.

"Bree, I am sorry if I did something to hurt you."

"Well, you did. I consider Officer Murphy to be my savior. Someone who cares for the students on this campus, and you made him out to be a real *asshole*."

Laura gasps. "I had no idea you were so upset about it." Tears sting her eyes as she realizes she has done the unthinkable.

"Like I said, I was going to let it go. But then you did the same to Dean Barrymore. She, too, has taken a special interest in me."

Laura wants to vomit at the mention of her name. "Bree, you have to understand that I…" But Laura simply lets her words fall off. She can't tell Bree why she is doing what she is doing.

"Understand what? That I have to explain to the dean that my best friend at school, the girl on the radio, is slamming her for protecting this campus?" Her voice is heightened. "And when should I do this, Laura? At the campus safety committee that I'm helping her lead?"

"What?" Laura can't help her reaction.

"Campus security task force. I'm on the committee."

"Bree, you can't be on that," she blurts out.

"What? Why the hell not?"

"I have my reasons. And, as your best friend, I'm asking you to trust me," she pleads.

"Just like that? Nothing else to go on? You want me to drop out of the committee?"

"Yes." Laura notices the trembling of her hands as she tries to reach out and take Bree's.

Can you see I'm trying to tell you something? Don't you know this is not me?

Bree yanks her hands back. "Well, I can't do that."

Laura's face twists with anguish. She is bordering on saying too much, and she knows she can't afford that. She speedily contemplates her next move. She has no choice but to walk away…for now. "Well, I can see that I've hurt you, and I am very sorry." Laura abruptly stands, and on the verge of tears, she leaves her room.

She shuffles back down to her room and enters.

One look, and Abigail asks, "You all right, Laura?"

She sighs. "No, as a matter of fact, I'm not."

Abigail's eyes grow wide. "Okay, how can I help?"

Laura shakes her head. "It's nothing you can help with. I need to clear my head."

"Want me to go with you?"

"No, but thank you," she says as she grabs her bag, shoving jeans, a T-shirt, her ID, and keys into her backpack.

"You need clothes for that?" she asks with an undeniably concerned voice.

"I'm sorry. Please don't worry about me. I'll call you if I don't come back." She exits the door before Abigail can get another word in.

Twenty-Five

NOT TONIGHT

Laura passes Monroe's and instead enters the bar next to it—The Cookie. She can't stomach the thought of seeing anyone from the station and knows this place will be much quieter, particularly at this hour of the evening. She shows the bouncer her fake ID, the one Wolfie made for her. He eyes her up and down and then motions for her to head in.

She takes a seat at the bar and orders a beer.

She orders another beer.

And then another.

She glances at the clock. It's seven o'clock, and she's already missed dinner with the girls.

It's probably for the best. I don't want to upset them more than I already have.

The bartender places a bowl of pretzel sticks in front of her. She's too upset to have an appetite, but she slowly eats them anyway.

"Can I get you another?" he asks.

"Why not?" she grumbles.

The bartender places the beer in front of her. She senses someone sit next to her at the bar. She doesn't acknowledge them.

The bartender asks, "What can I get you?"

"I'll have what she is having," he says in a low voice.

Immediately, Laura gets a sting down her flesh. She'd recognize his voice, no matter what, and so would most people on campus.

"I swear, I didn't know you were here," Colin says.

With blurred vision, Laura slightly glances over at him. "I came here specifically to get away," she slurs.

"Me, too." His tone is sad, and it makes her turn slightly toward him.

"What are you running from?" she boldly asks, knowing full well he will tell her nothing.

"Joey," he whispers.

Laura whips her head up to regard him. "Really?" she questions.

"Yeah."

"Have a lovers' quarrel?" Laura manically laughs.

"We're not lovers," he replies through gritted teeth.

Laura quickly sobers up in the words he spoke. She has no idea how to respond to that.

"I haven't touched her in half a year or probably more. Who knows? I don't think about it," he adds. He takes a sip of his beer.

Laura swallows hard. Her mind races with questions. There are so many things she wants to ask him but can't find the words. She takes a gulp of her beer. She watches as he peels the label from the beer in his hand. Neither says a word.

He finishes his beer and starts to stand. Something in her now feels worse than she did before he walked in.

"Don't go," she says. She looks up at him, sadness in her eyes. "Stay for one more."

Slowly, he sits back down on the barstool. The bartender brings over two more for them.

"I'm surprised to hear you say that," he says.

"I surprised myself."

"I'm sorry about the other day."

"Wait, you're not with Joey?" she asks again.

"No, Laura, I'm not *with* Joey."

"But I don't get it."

"Get what?"

"Why are you doing this then?"

"Doing what?"

"Helping her?"

"Do you hear yourself?" he asks.

"You know what I mean."

"No, I don't."

"Why help her if you don't like her any—" But she stops.

"Why help someone I'm not sleeping with? Jesus, Laura. What has gotten you so jaded?"

"Jaded?"

"What the hell am I supposed to do? You saw her that day. Fuck, don't you get it? I fucking ran there that day because I thought it was *you*, Laura."

"You thought it was me?" She's way too drunk to be having this conversation with Colin. But she remembers Sean's observation of the situation. It can't merely be a coincidence.

"Yes, I never thought she'd be at the station, asking for me."

"Oh." She takes a pull on her beer, averting her eyes from his stare.

"She needed my help. I'm trying to help her."

"Then, why are you here today?"

He exhales and slightly lowers his head. Finally, he says, "Because I feel as though I can't stop helping her. I can't step away from the situation without feeling like a total jerk. Is that what you want to hear me say? I'm trapped with no way out." Exasperated, he runs his hand through his hair. "Can I get a shot of tequila?" he asks the bartender.

"Trapped," she whispers.

"Yeah, I don't know if she is telling me the whole truth or not, yet she is demanding all of my time, and I don't have much to give anymore. To her...or anyone."

"Oh. Well, have you asked her?"

With eyes closed, Colin plays back the conversation he had with Joey last semester. "Yeah, I've tried." He throws back his tequila shot, wincing as he swallows. "This happened to my friend in high school..." he whispers.

"What?"

Tired beyond comprehension, Colin hangs his head to where his chin is almost resting on his chest. He peers over at Laura. She notices the red rings around his eyes.

He sighs, and then in barely a whisper, he says, "She was my good friend, and unfortunately, she dated this real prick. One night, she climbed in my window at three in the morning, distraught and shaken to her core like nothing I had ever seen. She looked terrible. But all I could do was hold her to try to calm her. That was it. That was all she wanted from me. She wouldn't let me call anyone or help her beyond that night. She never spoke about it again, and it still haunts me to this day. So, there is a part of me that needs to help Joey to try to make up for the fact that maybe I didn't do enough for my friend in high school."

"What happened to your friend?"

"After that night? She went back to him and pulled away from me. She stopped talking to me, and I never said anything to anyone. But I fucking should have. I should have reported that asshole to the police. I mean, God only knows what he is doing now, right?"

Laura places her hand on his arm. "I'm so sorry to hear that. It must have been awful for you. And your friend. Anything I can do?"

"Oh, now, you want to help me?" he says sarcastically.

"Hey, not fair. I've got my own shit going on, too."

"Yeah? Like what?"

"Like stuff I can't talk about," she says under her breath.

"I get it. We're not really friends anymore, so I don't expect you to tell me."

Hurt by the truth, she adds, "Then, why would you tell me your shit?"

"Because I'd like to still be friends with you."

"Right. We work together. Totally get it."

"No. Well, there is *that*. But I'd like it in general. Can't you see it in me?"

"If we are being honest, then I have to say this. I'm hurt about what you said about me to Joey, and to be honest, I can't be around you when you're around her. I simply can't."

"You said that the other day, but I still have no idea what you are talking about."

His eyes show great concern, and Laura can't help but start to believe him.

She sighs and then mumbles, "She said you thought I was pathetic, and you only tolerated me because we had to work together."

He slams his beer on the bar. He looks up at the bartender. "Sorry." Then, he turns toward Laura. "She said that to you? When?"

"Right after Spring Fling."

His eyes narrow. "Is that so?"

"Yeah."

"What else did she say?"

"It's not worth repeating, and quite frankly, it hurts to."

"Laura, I can assure you, I did not say any of those things to her."

"Really?"

"Yes. Why the hell would I talk to her about you? Isn't it obvious why she doesn't like you?" Laura starts to respond when he says, "It's because she is jealous of you and me."

"Jealous of you and me? There is no you and me!" Laura cries with exasperation.

"Exactly," he says as the realization of the past several months washes over him. He pauses and then continues, "But I can't deny what she told me happened to her. Unless you can prove that she is lying. You can see now why this is so difficult for me."

"Are you asking me to find out if she lied?"

"What you said to me the other day hit me hard. The frustration I felt and you felt was enough to make me question all my recent decisions. Watching you walk away from me sucked, Laura. I hated it so bad."

"Well, I don't like any of this either."

"Yeah, I guess I am asking for your help. Just me this time."

Travis flashes in Laura's mind.

"I'll have to think about it."

"I understand."

"Can I ask you one thing?"

"Sure."

"Why approach me the other day and ask me to drop all of this, only to change your mind today?"

"I wanted to talk to you, but it sort of turned into something else. You seemed angry with me, with her, with the situation, and I guess I didn't know what else to say."

Laura was confused when she came into the bar today, but now, she is even more muddled. "Well, yeah, you don't say good-bye to me before the summer, I don't hear from you—"

With a sad voice, he replies, "I didn't hear from you either."

"I know. I feel bad about that. But, when I do finally see you, the first thing you want to talk to me about is helping her, and…well, I snapped a little."

He smiles slightly.

"What?"

"I got a diminutive taste of pissed-off Laura."

"You're damn right you did." She can't help but smile. She watches his face light up. She realizes how much she has missed his friendship.

Hiccup.

"Oops, excuse me."

He chuckles. "You've had a few. Let me at least walk you home."

She is sad to think their time has ended. But, really, she couldn't drink another ounce.

He motions to the bartender and hands him some money.

"No way. I've got it," she says as she tries to balance herself and reach for her bag.

He gently touches her arm. It is a welcome feeling. "I've got it. It's the least I can do for making you believe I thought those terrible things about you."

She stands and steadies herself on the bar. "To be clear," she proclaims, "she did that and not you."

He motions for her to go in front of him. Once outside, her head twirls as the fresh air hits her lungs. She concentrates hard to put one foot in front of the other. They hike back up the hill toward campus.

"You still in the same dorm?" he asks.

"Yep…but I, um, can't go there right now. I'm too drunk. I might go to the Union or something."

"No. Not letting that happen. You can't be drunk in the Union, Laura. You could get fired."

"Shit, right. It is a good thing you ran into me." She giggles.

"Sober up at my apartment."

"Apartment?"

"Yeah, I'm a junior now. I live off campus."

It dawns on Laura in the moment how little they have connected recently. She completely forgot he was a junior now.

"Right, slipped my mind."

"Come on," he says with a slight smile. "This way."

Laura is secretly hoping he does not live on the same street as Travis. He can't see her this way. She surmises Travis might be wondering if she is slowly falling apart as the events on campus come swiftly crashing around her. To know she is wasted at eight at night will do nothing to convince him she can handle her role in all of this.

They turn onto Merrill Street.

As they walk up the driveway, Laura asks, "Who do you live with?"

"My roommate from the dorm, Stef, and two other guys we know, Austin and Brandon. We skateboard a lot together, so we thought, *Why not just live together?*"

He keys into the main door and enters into the living room. His roommates are all sitting on the couch, playing video games.

"Guys, this is Laura. One of the DJs at the station."

"Hello," she slurs. She is wildly disappointed with herself for undoubtedly making a terrible first impression.

They all turn from their game and say hello, naturally checking her out in the process.

Colin whispers, "We can go hang in my room."

Relieved, she follows him upstairs and down the hall and to his room.

"I'll go grab you some water," he says as he opens his door and allows her in.

His room is typical. Several skateboards leaning on the far wall next to his desk. Bed partially made, clothes tossed randomly throughout the room. He has a Pearl Jam poster on one wall, one Laura has never seen before.

He comes back in the room.

"That Pearl Jam poster, 'Dissident.' Where did you find that?"

"Ah, that was a sweet find of mine this summer at a record store. I had to beg the guy for it. But, in the end, I traded him a Ben Harper bootleg. So, we both made out okay."

He hands Laura the water.

"Thanks."

"Have a seat. Relax," he says as if the two of them being alone in his room were normal. This is a far cry from typical. "Music?" he asks.

She nods her head. "Mind if I call my roommate? I told her I would."

"Of course."

She goes to his desk, picks up the phone, and reluctantly dials her number.

She's surprised to hear a male voice answer, "Hello?"

"Nathan?"

"Yeah. Hey, Laura. Abby went to take a shower. Told me to answer the phone in case you called."

Laura's heart sinks. With everything going on, the last thing Abigail needs is to worry about Laura. "Tell her not to worry."

He quickly adds, "She is worried about you, Laura."

"I know. Tell her I'm fine, and I'll see her later. Promise."

"Okay…" He pauses.

"Nathan?"

"Are you okay, Laura?" His voice is sincere and genuine.

"Yeah." She turns and glances at Colin. "Just trying to figure some stuff out; that's all."

"Understood. I'll tell her you called."

"Thanks, Nathan." Laura gently puts the receiver down.

She turns back to Colin as he is pulling his T-shirt up over his back. *He looks incredible.* She blushes.

He takes another shirt out and puts it on. She takes a seat in his desk chair, facing him.

"You make this tape?" she asks.

"Yeah, I'm the king of mixed tapes."

She laughs. "Challenge accepted."

He laughs, too. "Challenge accepted?"

"Yep, because you're looking at the queen of mixed tapes. I make you one, and you make me one. May the best person win."

"What are the stakes?"

"Let's see…how about concert tickets? Show of the winner's choice."

"I like it. You're on." He crosses the room to shake her hand.

As he gets closer, she leans back. He touches her hand, and a tingle washes over her body. He doesn't let her hand go.

"Colin," she whispers.

His eyes are firmly locked on hers. He pulls her up. Her body feels weightless as he does. He takes his other hand and tucks a strand of hair behind her ear. She drops her eyes toward the floor and leans her head into his hand. Her heart is beating faster as he strokes her cheek with his thumb.

He leans down as he draws her face up. "Do you have any idea how hard it is to be close to you?"

She has no response. She doesn't need one as his lips press firmly onto hers. She's melting into the carpet. She releases her hand from his and wraps her arms around him. Her pulse reacts to each kiss he gives her. He responds, spinning her body toward his bed and guiding her backward to the edge. With long, muscular arms cradling her, he lowers her onto his bed, resting his body on top of hers.

Her thoughts spin with indecision and disbelief. She convinced herself they would never touch again. But the hunger between them is undeniable.

His passionate kisses are pulling her away from her reality, away from Travis, and she can't stop it.

That is, until he does.

"I can't," he breathlessly interjects.

Laura's face pinks with embarrassment. "What?"

"Laura, I can't."

"I, um…oh," she stammers as she tries to slink out from under him.

"Listen, you're drunk, and I can't. I don't want this to be a mistake."

She averts her eyes. *I don't want to make another mistake either. I don't want to hurt Travis. He is my dear friend whom I care for deeply. Although it is undefined, I know in my heart he is someone I'll always have feelings for.*

Oddly relieved, she leans up, and as she does, he lightly kisses her.

"You're okay?" he asks.

"I'm okay."

Am I? I feel rejected but not in the way I think I should feel. But I know I don't want to hurt you. By being here, it's confusing us both. I know this, but somehow, I can't walk away. And, believe me, I have tried to forget about you.

He pushes himself up off of her and sits on the edge of the bed. He sighs deeply. She gets up off the bed and resumes her position in his desk chair. She waits for him to look at her, but he currently appears to be deep in thought, somewhere else than here with her. Sadly, her pulse slows, and her body returns to a much less heightened state. She tucks her legs up under her, hugging her knees.

He snaps out of it and says, "I heard your interview with Tank."

"And?"

"Thought it was good."

"Okay, now, really tell me."

He's contemplating something.

"Just tell me."

"It's more of a question. I get the feeling you think something else is going on."

Trying not to react but needing to retort quickly, she simply replies, "Right now, we are doing all we can." She takes a big sip of water. She can feel her exhaustion taking over. "Can I use your bathroom?" she says, hoping he'll drop this, so she won't have to outwardly lie to him anymore.

"Course. Down the hallway, on the left."

"Thanks."

She staggers as she stands. He gets up to help steady her.

"Sorry," she says.

"You need help." He laughs.

"No, I can manage on my own, but thanks."

When she returns from the bathroom, Colin has turned off all the lights in the room, except the small lamp near his bed. He is leaning back on his headboard, and with no warning, a wave of anxiety rushes over her as Travis reenters her mind. But the force she feels when Colin motions for her to come over is one she is unable to ignore. She kicks off her shoes and climbs in next to him, burying her head on his chest. The beat of his heart begins to lull her to sleep or pass out. Whatever it is, sleeping or passing out, she is completely mesmerized by him.

Don't think. Tomorrow will come, and you can sort it all out then. But not tonight. Not tonight.

Twenty-Six

WHAT IS WRONG WITH LAURA?

Laura not coming home last night and Bree calling Abigail to ask to speak with her leads Abigail to believe something is stirring with her friends.

Abigail catches a knock on her door. Expecting Bree, she yells, "Come in!"

The door swings open, and Abigail turns from her biology textbook to greet her friend. She is shocked to find a guy standing in her room.

"Oh, hello. Can I help you?" she asks.

His stature is intimidating as his muscles bulge through his tight T-shirt. He has tattoos up and down his arms. But what Abigail can't ignore are his piercing green eyes and tan skin. She can feel herself blush at the sight of him.

"My mistake," he says in this low, husky voice. "I'm looking for Alex."

"Alex?" Then, it dawns on her that Alex is Casey's new roommate, whom Abigail and Laura have yet to meet. Abigail stands. "Oh, right, Alex. She's new here. I haven't met her yet," she stammers. "But she lives with my friend Casey on the opposite end of the hallway."

His eyes dance up and down her, and something about his stare sends a shiver down her spine. He reaches out his hand to shake hers. "I'm Kelly."

"Kelly, I'm Abigail."

"Nice to meet you, Abigail." He releases her hand.

As he does, Bree comes waltzing down to her room. She starts to enter Abigail's room. "Oh, sorry to interrupt," she says. Bree's eyes get wide as she gets a good look at him, too.

"Bree, this is Kelly. Kelly, Bree."

"Hello."

"Hello to you as well. Sorry again to disturb you. I'll go bug Alex now."
He lends a smile to both of them. As he passes by Bree, he says kindly,
"Are all the women on this floor beautiful?" And then he wanders down
the hallway to Alex and Casey's room.

Bree and Abigail stand still for a moment.

Until Bree breaks the silence. "Who the heck was that?"

Abigail exhales. "No idea."

"Is he hot or *what?*"

"Either that or the temperature in here rose about a hundred degrees."
Abigail fans her face with her hand.

"Wow."

"Precisely."

Bree closes the door and takes a seat next to Abigail. "Hey, I wanted to
talk to you about the upcoming trial and about Laura, too."

"Okay."

"I guess I'm surprised by how antiestablishment she is coming off as.
First, the interview with Officer Murphy was somewhat disturbing to me.
Why she had it out for him, I can't figure out."

"I'm glad you said something because I, too, felt it was
counterproductive. He's not the bad guy. If anything, I get the sense they
are doing all they can."

"I wasn't going to say anything to her until the Tank interview. She
mentioned the school not doing enough and even called out Dean
Barrymore. I was personally asked by the dean to be on her campus safety
task force. When I mentioned this to Laura, she got really upset and told
me not to join the committee."

"She did?"

"Yeah, and she was adamant about it."

"That is strange."

"Granted, I wasn't going to budge on my end; you know how I can
be," she adds with a slight frown. "But she couldn't tell me why."

"She had no reason for asking you?"

"None. Just that I had to trust her, which I do, but I can't back out of a
huge commitment with the school because my friend simply tells me to."

"She doesn't know Nathan is on it then; otherwise, I'm assuming she'd
say something to me. She didn't come home last night, and I have no clue
where she was. She did call, but Nathan answered the phone while I was in
the shower. He said she sounded off."

"She was upset when she left my room."

"I know she is on the radio today at three. I'll see what she has to say
then, and maybe, after that, we can decide if we approach her or not."

"She didn't come home last night? Interesting," Bree adds.

"She talk to you about any guys she might be dating?"

"No, nothing. She mentioned that guy she works with, Colin, but I gathered that was over before it even started."

"Right. She never mentions him at all."

Bree stands. "Well, I've gotta run to class. Dinner later?"

"Sounds good," Abigail replies.

Once Bree leaves, Abigail decides to head over to the Union to listen to Laura's show from the study area near the fireplace. She gathers her belongings and locks her door. As she strolls down the hallway, Casey's door is open. She can hear Casey talking. She knocks.

"Come in!"

"Hey, Casey."

"Abigail, oh, good. You can finally meet Alex." As Abigail enters the side with their beds, there is a girl sitting on the floor, dressed in high-top Dr. Martens boots, ripped jeans, and a tight black tank top. She has several tattoos on her arms. She has short, spiked bleached-blonde hair and has a ring in her nose.

"Hey, Alex. Nice to finally meet you."

"You, too. I've heard a lot about all of you guys."

"All good stuff," Casey adds with a smile.

"Did Kelly find you?" Abigail asks.

"Yes, as a matter of fact, he did," she replies with a wide smile.

Lucky you.

"Oh, good. Well, I'm off to the Union to study and listen to Laura. Will you guys join us for dinner?"

"Yeah, cool," she replies. "Awesome that your roommate is a DJ."

"She does love it," Abigail confesses.

"See you later," Casey says.

"Bye." Abigail exits their room and heads to the Union.

She settles into a table across from the station with her cup of coffee. Laura enters her booth, and within moments, a tall guy enters, whom Abigail does not recognize. It's clear they are having an intimate conversation. She can tell this by the way Laura anxiously fiddles with her hands. Then, someone else comes in the room. Abigail can see the tension rise.

She is different. Something has changed with her, and I'm not so sure it's for the better.

Twenty-Seven

SITTING DUCKS

Laura enters the station.

"Hey, guys," she says to Ryker and Patrick.

"Hey, Laura."

"I'm going to get ready," she says. "I'll see you down there in a few." She directs her words toward Patrick.

"You got it."

Laura opens Studio B and settles into her chair. She is jotting down notes in her notebook when she senses the door open. She glances up as Travis enters.

"Hey," he says.

"Hey."

"You okay?" he asks.

She swallows hard. "Me? Yeah. Totally."

"Oh, I see."

"Are you okay?" she hesitantly asks.

"Yeah, I waited for you at the coffee shop last night, and when you didn't show, I got concerned."

"Oh shit, Travis. I'm sorry. It completely slipped my mind." She stands "I-I can't believe—"

"Where were you?" he asks.

"I was—"

Unexpectedly, Colin enters the room. The wind is knocked right out of Laura's lungs.

"Hey," he says.

"Hey," she chokes out.

"Travis." Colin acknowledges him with a hint of irritation in his voice.

"Colin." Travis looks between the two of them and then adds, "Laura, stop by later, okay? We have some items to review for your next segment." His tone is cool, much like the Travis she first met and couldn't stand.

She is wildly uncomfortable with the two of them in the same room as her. Travis passes by Colin without saying another word and leaves the studio.

Colin cuts the tension by saying, "I wanted to stop in to say hello."

"Hello." She averts her eyes, pretending to look for something on her board.

He clears his throat. "You think Travis might have some information regarding any recent attacks?"

Shocked by his question, Laura responds, "I'm not positive. Do you want me to ask him?" *But the answer is yes. I know he must have information.*

"Maybe."

Maybe? Are you changing your mind about all of this?

"Okay, well, you can mull it over and let me know."

"Okay, I will."

Although the other night still remains foggy for Laura, she does distinctly remember him saying he was trapped and that he needed to get out. He takes a few steps closer to Laura. He leans in, brushing the scruff on his face onto her cheek as he kisses it.

"I suppose I'm afraid to find out it is true. Maybe that is my hesitation," he confesses.

His omission is just the motivation she needs to continue to try to help him. "I understand. Let me see what I can uncover. I'll tell you only what you need to know."

"Appreciate it." He smiles for the first time since he entered the studio.

"Can I call you later?" she asks shyly.

"I was hoping you would."

He turns toward the door but not before glancing back at her. "Good luck," he adds.

Luck? Yeah, I'm gonna need it all right.

Laura's show was relatively uneventful, which she needed. She had a dozen-plus callers with very little news or updates to report. Her classes were uneventful, too.

As she exits out of her Geometry class and heads toward the office of *The Weekly Blue* in Rounds Hall, she can't help but feel the same shift in the air she felt at the end of last semester. Something is brewing, and she is unsure of what.

She enters the newspaper office and greets Wolfie, "Hey there. How are you?"

"Just dandy," he says as he rises. "I'm going to join you and Travis. There is a ton going on, and we are going to need to put our heads together and come up with a game plan."

"Hmm, you have my attention now."

She follows Wolfie into Travis's office. Travis looks deep in thought as they enter his domain. He doesn't glance up from his paper as he says, "Please, close the door."

"Boy, you guys know how to make a girl feel nervous." Laura laughs as she sits in the chair opposite him. It's her words that finally make Travis look at her. He is not smiling. Nor is Wolfie. "What's going on?" she asks nervously.

Travis begins, "We have reason to believe that Dean Barrymore knows a lot more than we originally thought. She is up for tenure and is doing her best to make certain she keeps this campus in a frenzied state, so she can affirm to the board that they need her to settle these issues. The task force is only the beginning for her."

"I don't understand."

"She wants the police to come off incompetent, not her. By pointing the blame at them and making it appear as though there are other attacks on campus are to her benefit. As sick as that might sound, she will end up looking like all the other campuses around OSU. Like a sitting duck, waiting for the next tragedy to strike. What the people don't know is, she was warned well in advance and did nothing about it."

"Are we sitting ducks?" Laura asks, pupils dilated larger than normal.

"Maybe. And here is why. I got word that any and all articles written about the trial must be approved by Professor Campbell."

Wolfie yells, "You have got to be kidding me!"

"No. Wish I were. She even threatened to pull funding if we sidestep the process. Obviously, Campbell didn't say it came from her mouth, but I know it."

"And what about the attack?" Laura asks.

Wolfie turns toward Laura, and as though he is speaking in slow motion, he says only one word. "Staged."

Laura swallows hard. "Staged?"

Oh, Colin, what am I going to do?

"Yes, she is trying to hide amid the chaos. I'm convinced of this," Travis says.

"But how does that make her look good?"

"It doesn't necessarily, but she becomes a sympathetic player in a dark game. She can't be accused of ignoring things if those things are still going on."

"We received an anonymous letter," Wolfie says, pulling a folded piece of paper from his tweed coat pocket. He hands it to Laura.

We need your help. Dean Barrymore has created a hectic scenario to make the campus continue to appear unsafe despite numerous attempts by local law enforcement and campus security to develop and perfect improved safety measures. She deliberately undermines their work and has even, to my direct knowledge, asked a few students to fake attacks on campus to keep the confusion heightened. In exchange, she promises scholarship money.

I am not in a position to do something about this. But you can. Dig deep, and you will uncover the truth.

"Who the hell wrote this?" Laura asks after reading it.

"We are not confident. But whomever it is has a direct line to the dean if in fact what they are saying is true."

"You believe it's true?" Laura asks Travis.

He hesitates and then says, "Yeah, unfortunately, I do."

"As do I," Wolfie proclaims. "No one knows what we are working on, so to get this is too much of a coincidence in my world."

"Indeed. But, Laura, what I need to know from you is, do you trust the guys at the station?" Laura opens her mouth to speak, but Travis immediately interjects by asking, "Trust them like you trust us?"

Laura leans forward in her chair. "I do, Travis. I completely trust them. They might not know what we know, but they have been there for me this entire time—taking calls, listening to my interviews, watching people suffer. I've seen their faces. Their painful expressions tell me they are sickened that this has become their community. I know they'd do whatever they could to help."

"Good, because we are going to need some assistance."

"Okay. What next?"

"We give her exactly what she wants," Travis says with a devilish grin. It sends a shiver down Laura's spine. "She wants chaos? We'll give her chaos. Here is the plan…"

Twenty-Eight

CHAOTIC PLANS

For the past two weeks, Laura has put her life on hold. She has kept her nose clean, keeping a low profile as she continues to work side by side with *The Weekly Blue*. She also helped Tucker prepare the team there for what is coming.

It is now the day before the trial, and Laura hurries out of her dorm room and to the station. She is exhausted from staying up all night, stuffing fliers into every single mailbox on campus. She can't stop for a moment to think about how tired she is. She has much to do today, and it will even entail skipping all her afternoon classes.

She enters the studio and finds Sean, Ryker, Patrick, Tucker, and Colin all waiting for her. Nervous expressions on all their faces, even Tucker's. They gather around him.

"I trust you guys to do what is best. Now, please be careful and look out for one another," Tucker says.

"We will," Colin says as he gazes at Laura.

"Okay, now, the equipment is in the back. All ready to go. Patrick, you're with Laura. Colin and Ryker, you team up. Sean and I will stay here. We only have an hour. Please use the time wisely." Tucker motions for all of them to get going.

The other thing Laura has avoided is her twisting relationships with Colin and Travis. Luckily for her, Travis knows how to compartmentalize his feelings and can focus on the task at hand. Colin, in contrast, has been truly sweet and patient, slightly keeping his distance. This aloofness is purely planned as they look into whether or not Joey is lying. The question they ponder is, *How can they confirm she made it up?* Colin needs to remain close to Joey if any of this is going to work. It is a sacrifice both Laura and Colin agreed was needed.

"Hey," Colin says as they are about to leave the station. "Please be careful." His eyes soften.

"I will, promise."

"I'll keep an eye on her," Patrick adds.

"Thanks, buddy." Colin pushes open the door to the side entrance of the Union and is shocked by the number of students already gathered on the center lawn.

Some of them are holding signs while a girl in the front speaks into a bullhorn.

"I'll take the left side," Laura says. Her heart beats hard within her chest. Her respiration is kicking into overdrive.

Colin grabs her hand and pulls her toward him. "Be safe," he stresses again.

"I will, and you, too."

Laura heads to the other side. She spots a young girl holding a sign that merely says, *We are not safe.*

Laura asks her, "Hello. Mind if I ask you a few questions on the radio?"

"No, not at all," the girl responds confidently.

"Great. Let me get up and running." She motions to Patrick, who switches on the equipment. "Sean, it's Laura. You ready for me?"

Clear as a bell through her headphones, she hears Sean say, "We are ready."

"Hello, this is Laura Chase, live from the commons lawn outside of the Union. I'm here with a student. Your sign caught my attention. Can you tell us what it says?" She pushes the microphone toward the girl.

"Yeah, it says, *We are not safe.* And we are not. There is still stuff going on right on this campus, and the school is not doing enough about it."

"You blame the school?"

"Yeah, I blame the school. Aren't they the ones who should be keeping us safe?" The crowd roars a little as she raises her hand in the air. "What more evidence do they need in order to take action?"

Laura asks, "What are you hoping to accomplish here today?"

"We are protesting the security measures at this school, the lack of police presence. We need someone to listen. Someone has to pay attention! That guy was allowed to roam on this campus, undetected, and no one did a thing about it!"

"But you saw in the paper that the dean has formed a task force to improve campus safety. Isn't that a step in the right direction?"

"The right direction but too little and way too late."

As the girl starts to speak again, Laura catches a glimpse of Abigail and Bree in the distance, walking to class. She doesn't know if she expected them to show up for the protest or not, but by the way they are not even acknowledging the large group gathered, this leaves Laura with a sinking feeling that they are not impressed with this congregation, nor do they have any intention in participating in it.

A girl bumps Laura back into action. She reaches for Laura's microphone. "I'm here for the LGBT community. The women on this campus have been treated poorly for too long. We have just as many rights as any man. Yet no one wants to talk about how this all makes us feel. This attacker knows no boundaries, and the violation of such is a travesty to us all. We all need our voices to be heard, and I'm here to say, we are sick and tired of being the last to be spoken about."

Laura, never at a loss for words, struggles to find the right ones to say. *How would Casey and Jen react?* "I personally can assure you that we have your back at the station."

The girl responds, "Thank you, Laura. Wish the school had our backs. I mean, look at what has happened around here. How are we not more outraged?"

"Do you think that is why people have gathered here today?"

"Yes. The trial starts tomorrow, and that cannot be the end of this discussion. The school needs to do more, or they'll be sure to repeat their mistakes."

Laura is about to comment when her eyes suddenly grow wide as she catches a glimpse over the girl's shoulder. Up on the horizon, a mass pack is invading the lawn. Students dressed in school colors. Many holding signs as well. The closer they get, the quicker Laura realizes they are student athletes.

Laura waits for them to get closer. "Sean, I've got a massive crowd coming at us. Athletes. Let me see who I can grab."

"Got that. Ready when you are."

Laura spots Marcus, captain of the football team. "Marcus, can I ask you a few questions?"

"Absolutely, Laura."

"Great. I'm here with the Hawks football captain. Marcus, why are all these athletes here today?"

"We are as much a part of this campus as anyone else. What happened is a tragedy to us all. Not only have some women been mistreated, but so have the male athletes on this campus. We, too, have been victimized by the Campus Creeper and by the school administration."

"Can you elaborate?"

"Nothing has been cleared that he was not a student athlete, but rather a pathetic human who preyed on women at numerous campuses and in the name of decent student athletes. Not just here. But he claimed to represent us, and we want our reputation back. What has the school done for us?"

Perfect. Hit her in the donor pockets.

"Are you saying you don't feel as though the administration has supported you?"

"No. Not at all. In many ways, we feel like we are on trial, too."

Slightly stunned by his admission, Laura adds, "It sounds like the athletes on this campus are looking for some redemption from all of this as well. I appreciate you talking with me."

"Anytime, Laura."

Colin jumps in by talking to the woman who is the leader of this protest. "I'm here with Sasha, chapter head from OSU's AAUW—American Association of University Women. Sasha, can you tell me why you are here today?"

"The fact that the school has only disclosed two percent of sexual assault incidents on this campus is a farce. We are in the throes of an epidemic. You can't create the illusion that students are safe if we are not. The people gathered here want to show this school and the administration that it's time to listen. It's time to do something to help the students heal. *All students*," she reaffirms.

"I understand. What has your organization done to help this campus?"

"We empower women by providing a safe place to come and talk about the issues affecting them. We meet weekly, and it is open to all who are interested. Our information is posted in the campus paper, and we welcome all to join and help those who feel helpless. We know that just because they caught one guy doesn't mean there aren't others out there like him."

"What is next, after today?"

"Look, there will be others next year and ten years from now. So, unless we stand together today and let those predators know that this campus is not the place to come to, then what good is all of this? Because tomorrow will come, and we all need to be ready for it."

"Well said, Sasha. How can people get involved?"

"Come here tonight. We plan to gather again at midnight to show our solidarity to the women who have to testify. We want to be as supportive and discreet as possible, as this is a very sensitive subject and one that we do not take lightly."

"Thank you again. Appreciate your time."

Colin shuts off his mic and looks around, hoping to catch Laura in the sea of people gathered. There has to be at least a thousand-plus people filling the lawn, chanting, and holding up signs.

And Colin is even more impressed that this was all Laura's idea.

The protest lasts a few hours, and eventually, people begin to disperse. Laura, Colin, Patrick, and Ryker head back into the station.

"Brilliant." Tucker beams as he claps his hands together. "You were both fantastic!"

Feeling emotionally exhausted, Laura drops into her desk seat and desperately gulps down a bottle of water. "I'm exhausted," she says in a harsh tone.

Colin stares at her in wonder. *She is amazing.*

"If you guys don't mind, I'm going to cut out. I've got another long day tomorrow," she adds.

"Of course," Tucker replies. "Get some rest."

She looks at Colin and thinks back to the time they first met—when working side by side was simple, carefree, and easy. Now, with all this campus turmoil, she has little time to focus on anything else, let alone her relationships. She has only a limited window in which to see Travis before tomorrow, too. She has more to do than she'd like, but she has to stay ahead of the curve.

She waves slightly at Colin and then leaves, bag slung over her shoulder. She dashes across campus toward Travis's house. She knocks on his door. His roommate opens it.

"He's upstairs, working," he says.

"Thanks, Chris." She heads straight up the stairs. She's not in the least bit surprised to find Wolfie in his room as well.

Travis smiles wide when she enters. "Laura, you were incredible. Spot on."

"You think?"

"Wolfie?"

"Spot on, Laura," he says matter-of-factly.

"Good. Was the quality okay?"

"Yes, could hear every conversation clear as a bell."

"Good. Any word?"

"Yes," Wolfie says.

Laura takes a seat on Travis's bed, next to him, and they both face Wolfie in the chair.

"Word is, she is livid. She called for an emergency meeting with the faculty on the safety committee. They are supposed to be meeting in her office at eight."

"She must be pissed," Travis says with a smile.

"She is furious. In light of the opening remarks tomorrow at the trial and now this being broadcast on the radio, she has to be shaking in her shoes."

"Good," Laura says with a nod of her head.

"Aside from the station, no one knows that you planned the protest, right?" Travis asks.

"Of course not."

"Good."

Wolfie rises from the chair. "I have some more work to do. I'll see you guys tomorrow."

"Thanks for your help," Travis adds.

It's the first time Laura has noted a level of appreciation in his voice toward Wolfie. In the past, he's always had that *I'm your boss* type tone. But not this time. Something is different.

Wolfie closes his door.

"I know you're tired," he says tenderly as he runs the tips of his fingers over her leg.

She gazes up at him and can't help but smile. "What are you up to now?" she asks.

"I think I might go pay the dean a little visit. Disrupt her so-called private meeting."

"Travis, you think that is a good idea?"

He smiles. It's warm yet confident, and it reminds Laura of why she cares for him so deeply. He has taught her to be more self-assured and to grab what is rightfully hers.

If the students on this campus only knew how lucky we all are to have someone like Travis, looking out for us and protecting the truth.

"I think it is a great idea." He chuckles.

He pulls her in close to him. He smells woodsy with a hint of tobacco dusted on his shirt. She breathes in his scent. She exhales slowly and closes her eyes.

"I am tired," she whispers.

"I know. But we are almost there," he reassures her.

"But what about my friends? You think they'll ever forgive me?" she says in a hushed voice.

"I know they will. How could anyone stay mad at you? Your intentions are too good to be misconstrued for anything other than genuine."

"I don't know. I think Bree is pretty mad at me."

"For starters, you can't blame her."

Laura sits up immediately at his confession.

"Bree is a smart girl, and to have this happen to her, it is going to sting. You'll have to take the punches when she swings—for now. Eventually, the truth will come out, and the full picture will be in everyone's view. Until then, you are going to have to suck it up."

His brutal honesty is something Laura can't help but admire. Before she can let her head get ahead of her heart, she smiles at him as she leans in and kisses him. He tightly wraps his arms around her waist and pulls her back on his bed. She kisses him again. And again. Each with more passion.

After the day Laura just had, she feels a sense of empowerment come over her. She is lucky that she can be in control of her situation and make choices based on what she wants right now, in this moment, with zero reservations of who or what she is. She is a woman with a brain who is able to make any decision she wants, and that includes her level of commitment to Travis *or* Colin. She is able-minded and won't allow herself to feel badly for putting herself out there and enjoying the pleasure of a man's company. She doesn't need to define a relationship in order to enjoy the benefits

Twenty-Nine

EVERYONE TAKE CHARGE

Laura steps off the elevator to her floor. She is not surprised to hear the buzz of hair dryers and music being played loudly as, no doubt, her floor mates are getting ready for a night of partying. As Laura tries to sneak past Bree's room, she notices the door is open, and both Bree and Abigail are standing inside.

"Hey, Laura," Abigail chimes.

Laura stops in her tracks and leans back into the doorway. "Hey, guys." One look from Bree tells her all she needs to know. She is still angry with her. "Everything okay today?"

Reluctantly, Bree says, "Yeah, I suppose it went as well as it could."

"That's good," Laura says.

Abigail gives her a worried expression.

"Sorry I couldn't be at the trial."

It's the first time in a long time that Bree's expression mimics one of great disappointment. Laura hates this more than anything. She'd rather Bree be mad at her than disappointed. Before she can say another word, they hear someone from down the hall call Bree's name.

"Bree, Bree, we have a makeup emergency," Melissa yells.

Clearly not in the mood for continuing this conversation, she yells, "Coming." She brushes past Laura and wanders down the hallway to Casey's room.

Laura spins on her heel and marches to her room with Abigail right on her tail. She pushes open her door and tosses her bag on her desk with a loud thud.

Abigail closes the door. She bluntly asks, "Where have you been?"

Laura spins around, eyes tired as hell, and replies, "I've been working."

"Working on what?"

"My show at the station."

"Your show. Boy, it's had you out awfully late these past few weeks." She searches Laura's face. When Laura drops her eyes, Abigail continues, "I feel like I haven't seen you at all this year. Here we are, at the end of September, and we haven't even hung out once."

"Is this a guilt trip?"

Clearly agitated, Abigail responds, "Guilt trip? Is that what missing our friendship means to you?"

"No."

"Then, what is it?"

"I'm busy, and I'm..."

"Too busy to be there for us today?"

Ouch, the truth hurts...and badly.

"No, I couldn't make it today."

"But why?"

Desperate to tell someone what has been eating away at her, she lowers her shoulders and drops down into her desk chair. As Abigail takes the seat next to her, Laura contemplates her choices. Laura knows unequivocally that she is keeping secrets because she has to, and equally, they are sucking the life out of her.

"I'm trying to help someone, and I'm not doing a very good job of it."

"Who?"

"I can't tell you."

Abigail's eyes show sadness.

"But it's not because I don't want to tell you. I can't. You understand, right?"

Abigail nods her head.

"You remember, last year, when you had to keep something from everyone because you felt deep down it was the right thing to do for Tank? But..."

"It starts to eat away at you."

"Yes," Laura exclaims. "Exactly."

"But you also remember, by me keeping those secrets, I pushed away Nathan, you, Tank, and anyone else who ultimately got in my way. And only because I couldn't decipher where I was going anymore."

I know she is right. But I'm doing it regardless.

"I know."

"Tell me. And I promise I'll keep it close to me. No matter what."

Shit, of all people to tell about the dean of the school and Bree's involvement in the committee being a pawn in her game...the worst person I could tell...is Abigail. It is too close to home. Besides, the information Wolfie and Travis have obtained could expel them both. It is a sure way to ruin any chance Travis would have of managing a newspaper when he graduates.

Abigail can sense her hesitation. "Does this have anything to do with Bree and the committee?"

Caught off guard, the only thing she can think to say is, "Maybe…"

"I think I know why…"

"You do?"

"Yes. Because you want to help her, and by Bree joining the committee, it only throws her right back into the mix of it all."

Laura sighs deeply. She hates lying to her friends, but she has no choice. So, she continues her downward spiral. "Exactly. I guess I have wanted so badly for her to run from it all."

"Much like I have," Abigail whispers.

"I know, and I've been a lousy friend."

"I feel like things are changing somehow."

"I know."

"So, can I ask where you have been staying?"

"Staying?"

"Yeah, when you don't come home. It worries me."

Of all people to not be forthcoming with, the worst is to a person who has been through what she has. Has she been sitting here at night, wondering if I'm safe or struggling for my life? God, I feel worse now.

"I suck so badly," she confesses. "It never occurred to me that you'd be worried, but of course you'd be worried. I would be, too. I kind of had this…" *Go ahead, Laura. Dare you to try to define it.* "This friendship that kind of came out of nowhere and at a time when I needed serious direction. I needed a purpose, and he helped me to accomplish what I thought would be impossible."

Abigail's eyes light with enthusiasm. "Really?"

"Yeah."

"This doesn't sound like a typical crush."

"It's not. It's not that at all."

"Really? He makes you happy?"

Laura's mind drifts in between Colin and Travis. Stuck between two very different men who have undoubtedly caught her attention this past year. Something that is not accomplished easily. But do they make her happy?

Travis makes me relaxed and confident and I've undoubtedly developed deep feelings for him. Colin, on the other hand, excites me in a way I haven't been able to get ahola of.

"I need to focus on some other things right now besides my relationships."

"Relationships?"

"Yes, I'm all over the place," she admits.

"Put you first," she says as she gently touches Laura's leg. "You owe that to yourself."

"Thank you. Can I ask how today went?"

"It was hard, knowing he was in there. But I don't plan on going back until I have to."

"When is that?" Laura kicks back into her reporting mode and away from her social life.

"A week from today."

"And Bree?"

"I know she is scheduled after I am. But that is all I know."

"At least a week?"

"Yes, at least."

Shit, that doesn't give us much time. Only a week to expose the current evil lurking among us. I have to let Travis know.

"Dean Barrymore," he yells as he hurries down the hallway.

She turns, squinting in the darkness. "Who is that?" she asks.

"Travis, from *The Weekly Blue.*"

Even though it is dark, her shoulders hunch at the sound of his name.

"I'm in a hurry, Travis. What is it?"

He catches up to her. "Working this late, Dean?" he says in an uncharacteristically sweet tone.

"Yes, I'm always working," she quips back.

He peers past her, into her office, and notes the faculty in there.

"How can I help you?" she says as she tries to shade his view.

"I have some ideas for this week's paper I wanted to run by you. Campbell mentioned I should talk to you to get your buy-in."

"Now is not a good time."

"When would be a good time?"

"Contact my assistant, Joanne. She will set something up as soon as possible."

"I will do that," Travis adds. He waits for her to shut the large wood door to her office before turning to leave.

He steps outside and lights a cigarette. Travis leans on the side of the building and takes a drag of his cig. He is about to exhale when he hears a crack of a tree branch toward his back. He whips around.

"Jesus, you taking a page out of Wolfie's book?" he asks.

"Sorry," Laura replies. "I wasn't expecting you to be standing right here. I thought I'd catch you on your way out," she whispers.

"The dean didn't have much time for me. But I'll get an appointment tomorrow or the day after."

"Good, 'cause we are running out of time."

"How so?"

"Abigail is testifying a week from today and Bree shortly after."

"Shit. Okay, I'll circle back with Wolfie. But, in the meantime, you have to act normal. You need to cover the trial, fair and balanced. We can't let on to what we are doing."

"I know, but I…"

He reaches down, and with his fingers on her chin, he draws her face up. "We are almost there, and you've done a goddamn good job, Laura Chase."

"Have I?"

"Absolutely. Wolfie and I could not have done this without you. I know it, and he knows it."

A warm feeling envelops her. "I appreciate you saying that."

"No appreciation necessary." He stomps out his cigarette on the ground. "I'll pick you up tomorrow…if you want." He hesitates, and Laura wishes she could catch his expression better, but the darkness shadows his face.

She needs him, but she can't say it. "That would be great."

"Okay, eight sharp."

"On the dot." She laughs.

He drapes his arm over her shoulders and, with a chuckle, he replies, "Come on. I'll walk you back."

From the window high above the spectacular campus that lies before her stands Dean Barrymore. The heavy wood door closes as her guests depart for the evening. She can hear Joanne approach from behind.

"Are they gone?" she asks.

"Yes," Joanne whispers.

Dean Barrymore locks her hands together in front of her. "We need to get this back on track. We are losing ground. This trial is going to drum up all kinds of feelings for people, and we need to silence those feelings."

"Understood."

The dean watches as Laura and Travis pass by a lamppost, wrapped in each other's arms as they venture back toward the dormitories.

"Travis Taylor. I don't like that he was here tonight. Something is not right," she whispers. "Set up a meeting with him as soon as possible."

"Yes, of course," Joanne replies.

"And the loudmouth girl, too. They both need to be set straight."

"Yes, Dean." Joanne exits the door, closing it behind her, leaving the dean to stew in her own thoughts.

"They need to be reminded of who is in charge," she whispers.

Thirty

DENIED BUT NOT OUT

Travis is not surprised when he pulls up in front of Willis Hall at ten of eight, and Laura is already standing there, holding two cups of coffee. He can't help but smile as he catches eyes with her, and more importantly, he can't help his heart from beating quickly as he takes in her beauty.

"Good morning," he says as she opens the door and slides into the seat.

"Morning." She hands him the coffee.

"You look well put together," he remarks. He can't help but admire the tight black pants she has on and even more so, the tight black shirt she is wearing.

She reddens. "Thank you, Travis."

They drive about twenty minutes to the courthouse, chatting mostly about what they think they can expect from today. Travis can tell Laura is nervous because she is fumbling with her hands and can't seem to rest them on her lap.

"Don't be nervous, okay?"

"I can't help it," she stammers.

"I know, but I'll be right there with you, and we can get through this, promise."

"He's hurt so many people…" she whispers.

"I know, but what we need to remember is, he won't anymore." He knows she is thinking of her friends, and in many ways, he can't help her there. It's a tragedy that cannot be erased, no matter if there is a trial or not.

Travis parks his silver Honda Civic in the courthouse parking lot. Across the way, a gathering of reporters, students, and protestors has convened. They enter the mass chaos unfolding in front of the courthouse steps.

"I'm surprised you are here," a deep voice whispers to Laura.

She whips around. Officer Murphy is standing before her in full uniform. Travis watches the color drain from Laura's face.

"I'm not sure I have a choice," she says, barely able to meet his eyes.

"We all have choices. Some make bad ones, some make good ones, and others make ones that have consequences. Isn't that why we are here today?"

"Yes, and I'm so sorry..." She chokes on her words as he glares at her. "I..."

Travis feels the need to save her. "Officer Murphy, my name is Travis Taylor. I'm the student editor for *The Weekly Blue.*"

Officer Murphy averts his eyes off Laura and looks toward Travis.

He takes his extended hand. "I'd love an opportunity to interview you for the paper."

"I appreciate that, but I will respectfully decline. I've had my quota of OSU interviews."

"I understand," he says. "But new year, new beginnings. Please, consider it."

He eyes Travis up and down and then adds, "It was nice to meet you, Travis. Laura." He nods in her direction and then blends into the crowd.

Laura exhales. "You had to ask him for an interview?"

"Sorry. Too soon?" he replies with a smug expression.

She slaps him on the arm. "Yes, way too soon."

"Come on. We don't want to be late."

"God forbid," she mumbles under her breath.

"I heard that," he adds as he makes his way through the crowd and into the courthouse.

They take the stairs to the second floor. Waiting outside the large wood doors to the courtroom is Wolfie. His face shows concern.

This cannot be good.

"What is it?" Travis asks.

In a whisper, Wolfie says, "We are not allowed in."

"What?" Travis says, trying to tame his reaction.

"Really? Why?" Laura says.

"Something happened. I don't know what...yet. But I'll find out."

"Goddamn it."

All Wolfie needs to do is give Travis one glance for Travis to know to keep his cool.

"Okay, got it. What are you going to do?"

"I have a friend in the courthouse I plan to reach out to."

Lying in Wait

"Okay." He looks at Laura. "We can head outside and see what we hear."

Trying not to let her sense his defeat, Travis leads the way back out of the courthouse. The students are milling about. One woman is holding her own court as she shouts about the administration's failure to stop a reported attacker from entering campus grounds. Others seem more interested in the case in general, holding signs about a flawed investigation that included victim blaming. Some chant about rape not being a part of their education. Travis and Laura stand in the middle of it all. Finally, Laura decides to get her recorder out, and she begins taping the madness as it unfolds in front of them.

Laura reluctantly interviews a few people for the station while Travis talks to a girl who is heading up the largest team gathered.

After about an hour, Laura is at her limit. Travis watches her from a distance as she wanders back toward his car, alone, head hanging low.

"Will you excuse me?" he says to the girl he has been interviewing.

He zigzags through the crowd, back toward the parking lot. Laura is leaning on the back of his car, head in her hands.

"Hey," he says quietly. "You okay?"

She raises her head, makeup running down her wet cheeks. He feels his heart stop beating.

"Can we go?" she says.

Travis nods his head, too afraid his words are not useful in this moment; if anything, they might further cloud the day. They drive home in virtual silence. At some point, Travis reaches over and gently takes her hand. She doesn't move hers away. He is relieved by this.

Travis drives up the main road toward campus. "Do you...where do you want me to bring you?"

"I have to drop the equipment off at the station," she whispers.

"Okay," he says as he takes a left turn.

He pulls into the faculty parking lot behind the Student Union and kills the engine. He pulls the latch to pop open the trunk. She is not moving.

"Want to talk about it?" he asks.

She starts to cry. "This girl sought me out and said she was willing to be interviewed for the station."

"And?"

"She then started to say that I was not supporting the cause but rather hurting it. That my interviews were the reason her friend cannot heal and that I was more supportive of the male athletes on campus than the women. She accused me of being a woman hater and that the LGBT community was going to rally against the station to have me fired!" she cries.

"What? That is nonsense. I won't let that happen." Travis squeezes her hand.

Something changes in Laura. There is a darkness behind her tired eyes. "Ever since I got involved in all this secret stuff…" She trails off. She bites into her bottom lip, stopping herself from saying what is truthfully on her mind.

"Laura," he whispers.

"I'm sorry, Travis. I appreciate you driving me, but if you'll excuse me…" She opens the car door and gets out. She grabs her equipment and closes the trunk.

He is frozen. He can't make a move either way. But then he decides to let her go. He watches as she treks toward the back entrance, and without looking back, she goes inside.

He puts the car in drive and heads straight toward Wolfie's apartment.

Wolfie opens the door. "Come in," he says.

Travis enters the dimly lit apartment. "Mind if I smoke?" he asks.

"No."

Travis lights a cigarette and sinks down in the chair at the kitchen table. "What did you find out?"

"Dean Barrymore pulled all student media passes."

"Son of a bitch," he says, slamming his hand on the table.

"Yeah, the dean got ahead of us on this one."

"That bitch."

"I can try to get you in another way. My guy said he might have a seat in the gallery."

"Let me brood over how I want to play this. For right now, I need you to work on something else for me."

"Name it."

"Laura."

Wolfie perks up. "Laura?"

"Yeah, I need you to monitor her."

"The usual?" Wolfie asks.

"Yeah, the usual."

"Consider it done."

"Aside from that, we need to get our other plan moving faster. We are running out of time, and right now, we can't count on Laura. We're going to have to handle this one ourselves."

Lying in Wait

Wolfie leans forward in his chair. "I was hoping you'd say that. I know just what to do."

Thirty-One

GRAFFITI PARTY

Laura drops her equipment back off, and in a rush, she forgets to destroy the tape in her recorder of that horrible interview with Jane. She never caught her last name, and more importantly, she hopes she never runs into her again.

"I'll pick all this stuff up later," she yells to Tucker. "I really need to leave."

She rushes past the desks, and as she is about to make it out, safe and clear, Colin pushes open the door in the exact moment she is about to exit.

Startled and on the verge of tears, she pushes past him.

"Hey, how are you?" he asks with a huge smile.

As though her feelings were completely disconnected from her, she bursts into tears, and at full speed, she runs down the hallway of the Union and outside, all while Colin yells frantically after her.

She sprints across the campus and enters her dorm. Once inside her room, she shuts the door and locks it. Without turning on a single light, she buries herself under her covers as she listens to her phone ring over and over again.

Colin leaves her a message. "Laura, it's me. Please call me back. I'm worried about you. You ran off. You seemed so upset. Please, call me back. I..." He hesitates and then adds, "I can be there for you, if you'll let me. I want to be." Then, he hangs up.

Travis leaves her a message as well. His is more formal, but she expects that from him. She calls neither of them back. Instead, she remains balled up, hugging herself, trying to decide what the hell she should do next.

She feels a tug on her sleeve. She slightly rolls over, opening her eyes as she does. Standing at the edge of her bed are Abigail and Nathan.

"Hey," Laura squeaks out.

With a questioning countenance, Abigail says, "Are you all right? Where were you?"

"I can explain," Laura says, scrambling to get up. "They wouldn't let us in. We had passes, but then they pulled them."

"Who pulled them?" Nathan asks.

Laura shrugs her shoulders and nervously tucks a strand of her hair behind her ear.

"Oh," Abigail replies as she sits on the edge of the bed.

Not wanting to talk about what happened outside the courthouse, she adds, "Yes, so we left."

"You've been sleeping this whole time?"

"Yeah, I was feeling…I don't know. But I'm feeling much better now. I needed some rest."

Abigail glances at Nathan, who in return gives her a slight nod. "Why don't you come out with us tonight? It's the weekend. Time to put this behind us until Monday, right?" she asks. "Please. We've hardly hung out at all this semester."

Laura lets out a deep sigh. "I don't want to impose—" she starts to say.

Nathan stops her. "A bunch of us are going out. You should come. It will be fun. Who doesn't love a good graffiti party?"

"Graffiti party?"

"Yeah. We have an extra white T-shirt for you, and everyone writes messages and such on your shirt. It's fun!"

She gazes up at Nathan and realizes that, if she doesn't say yes, they will never leave her alone. "Okay, sounds like fun."

"Cool!"

"Great. Get ready, and we will come back and get you," Abigail says.

"Where are you guys going?"

"To get some Chinese food, and then we will be back. Extra T-shirt is on my desk. Want us to bring you something back?" she asks.

"Nah, I'm not really hungry."

"Okay. We'll come back to pick you up."

Laura undresses and puts on her robe, heading toward the bathroom. She takes a long, hot shower, letting the water run down her skin and watching it slip down the drain. Once she is out, she goes back into her room. She doesn't feel up for anything, yet she decides, as she draws eyeliner around her weary eyes, to pay attention to how she looks. Maybe, if she looks good, it will fool people into thinking she feels good. She applies blush and bronzer and dabs bright pink lipstick onto her pouty lips. She pushes her hair back off her face and tucks the bob tightly behind her ears. She places large silver hoop earrings in her ears.

Before she sits down at her desk to put on some music, she erases all the messages on their machine, as she knows exactly whom they are from. She waits for Abigail and Nathan as she stares out the window across the darkening campus, listening to Temple of the Dog.

Within half an hour, Abigail and Nathan are back from dinner.

Nathan is concealing a six-pack of beer in his bag. "One before we go?"

"Why not?" Laura says.

Abigail says to Laura, "You look gorgeous."

Feeling warmth hit her heart, she smiles. "Thank you."

Nathan sits at the desk next to Laura while Abigail touches up her makeup and brushes her hair.

Laura faces Nathan. "You guys are off to a heck of a start this year, huh?"

"Yes, undefeated so far. And we've had a tough schedule. It's looking good for us this season."

"That is great, Nathan. I have to get down to a game. I've been so busy at the station…"

"Believe me, I get it. There are plenty of things I'd like to do, but football takes up all my time…and that committee."

Laura feels a stabbing pressure in her chest. "What committee?" she asks him.

"The one Bree is on."

Shit. Oh, the dean is good. She knew exactly who to pick to play this right. Pick the beloved star quarterback whose girlfriend was the sole reason the guy got caught, and she comes out smelling like roses. She has no shame.

Feeling the urge to dig deeper, she asks, "What made you join that?"

Abigail steps into the room and gives Laura a questioning glance.

"Well, for one, when the dean asks something of you, it's hard to say no, and two, I wanted to try to do my part."

"No, I get all that, but like you said, you don't have a lot of time. And is this where they want the quarterback spending his time? You'd think your coach would want you to—"

"I do have some free time." He takes a sip of his beer, and unbeknownst to Laura, he shoots Abigail a concerned look.

Laura pushes on, "How many meetings have you had?"

"Four, I'd say."

"Is the dean at these meetings?"

"Yes, she is."

"What do you talk about?"

"Are you going to report on this? On the radio?" he asks.

"No, I'm just curious."

"Okay, 'cause there are a lot of layers to this, and we are in the early stages, so we mostly talk about security measures, increasing campus safety, and how this can extend to off-campus events and parties where the school has limited jurisdiction."

Laura sighs deeply. While this all sounds good and with the right intentions, it's the fact that the dean is covering for her costly mistakes that still eats away at Laura. Plus, she is using her friend, re-victimizing her and now propping up Nathan, the ultimate picture-perfect college student to do her bidding for her.

Laura downs the rest of her beer. On an empty stomach, she most definitely starts to feel the effects. "You guys ready?" she asks as she stands, not meeting their eyes. She opens the door and waits in the hallway.

Abigail says, "We have to stop and grab Bree and Melissa."

The sound of her name makes her throat tighten. She hasn't spoken to Bree in a week. She knows why Abigail didn't mention this before. She knows Laura would have declined. She knocks on her door, and immediately, Bree opens it. When she locks eyes with Laura, she knows Bree is not thrilled to see her.

Laura pushes out, "Hey, Bree."

"Hey, guys," Bree says to all of them.

Melissa follows her out. "Hey, guys!" Melissa says in her typical cheery voice, oblivious to the tension felt by all.

They head to the graffiti party while, thankfully, Melissa chats the entire way about the movie *The Usual Suspects* she watched with Logan the other night.

They enter the party, which has black lights lit all around. The walls have been painted with colorful paint, glowing in the darkness and illuminating the rooms. Everyone is wearing white T-shirts with writing all over them. It is very cool and a little trippy.

Laura heads right for the bar. She impatiently waits in the line and finally is served. Nathan and Abigail are close behind her. She takes her drink and waits for the others. She gulps it down, and before Nathan can step away, she asks him to grab her another.

She turns to find Bree standing within inches of her. With the music pumping loud, it is all but impossible to have a conversation. This bodes well for Laura.

That is, until Bree leans in and says, "Were you ever going to come talk to me to say you're sorry?"

Stunned but somewhat expecting it, she replies, "Why didn't you tell me Nathan was on the committee?"

"Really? We haven't spoken in over a week, and that is what you ask me?"

"Yeah, I guess I'm more curious, to be honest. Why the secret?"

"It's no secret, Laura. It has to do with the committee, and I know you're against it."

"I have my reasons," Laura says.

Bree's eyes get wide. "So, there's your answer then."

Laura gulps down her second drink and is about to spill the beans to Bree and tell her everything. She owes her friend that much. "Bree, the reason…" She feels someone come up behind her.

"There you guys are!"

They whip around. Casey and Alex are standing behind them.

"You guys sign your shirts yet?"

"No."

"What are you waiting for?"

Laura and Bree hesitate, and then Bree says, "Turn around. I'll sign the back."

Reluctantly, Laura turns while Bree writes on the back of her shirt. Once she is done, Laura draws a peace symbol on Bree's sleeve.

"Hey, guys, will you excuse me for a second?" Bree says.

After she leaves, Casey asks, "She okay?"

Laura, knowing it is her presence that is upsetting Bree and rightfully so, can only shrug her shoulders. Then, she says, "Want to get a drink?"

"Why not?" Alex says as she pushes her way through the crowd.

Although Alex is a transfer student, she is blending in well among the floor mates. It is a good thing for Casey to live with a roommate who is not Jen. The two of them dating and living together is way too close for comfort, and the last thing anyone wants is either of them being unhappy. With Jen's soccer team taking up a lot of her time, it also gives Casey someone to spend time with when Jen is busy.

Out of the corner of her eye, Laura observes Bree talking with Nathan and Abigail. No doubt, they are trading stories about their recent encounter with Laura and the discussion around the committee. This makes Laura extremely uncomfortable.

But knowing she is only upsetting them, she says to Casey and Alex, "Want to venture downstairs?"

"After you," Casey replies.

The deafening beat in the basement pulses through Laura's brain. She can barely hear her own thoughts as they step into the massive horde of graffiti-clad students. A few people write on their shirts as they make their way through the crowd to the back room. Once inside, they watch as Alex cozies up to the pool table and hustles a few guys who think, for some reason, it's a given to beat a girl. She proves them wildly wrong. Obligated after their defeat, they bring the girls another round of drinks.

For the first time since she can remember, Laura is having a good time. She is forgetting all her issues, one sip at a time.

"You know those girls?" Alex asks.

"What girls?" Laura replies.

"Over there. They have been staring at you for the past twenty minutes."

Through blurred eyes, Laura glances across the room. Standing in a huddle, like a pack of misfit bullies, are none other than Joey and her friends. As Laura searches their faces, she is struck by Jane's face, the girl who said horrible things to her at the courthouse, staring back at her. She tauntingly waves at Laura.

Her whole life, Laura has been the girl who everyone counted on. Counted on to be a good friend, a good listener, the understanding one, and the friendly one. Yet something is changing. As she stands across the room, beholding the faces of the girls who have continued to gibe and poke at her moral fibers, she realizes she can no longer be silent. She refuses to play the part of the girl who is too afraid to stick up for herself.

She turns to Casey. "I've got to take care of something. Do me a favor and follow me out."

With a concerned look, Casey replies, "You okay, Laura? You seem…I don't know."

"Trust me, okay? I'm going to say hello to my *friends*, and then we should go find Abigail."

A smirk grows across Alex's face.

She gets it. Laura gives her a slight wink.

"Come on, Casey," Alex says, pulling her toward the doorway.

Laura casually heads around the pool table and toward the girls. Jane reaches out her hand to shake hers. A smile flits across Jane's lips as she takes Laura's hand.

Laura leans in and speaks with full conviction right in Jane's ear, "Don't ever fucking say hello to me again. You got that?"

Jane whips back, trying to drop her hand, but Laura remains holding it tight, staring straight into her eyes.

Joey pounces in. "What the hell, Laura?"

Laura, dropping Jane's hand, turns to Joey, who has no idea what they are even talking about. "And you," she snarls, "stay the fuck away from me. You are a horrible human being. Stay clear of me!"

Joey is shocked into silence after Laura drops a bomb, and then walks away. As she nears Casey and Alex, she can hear Joey start to yell after her.

Laura whips around and hollers as clear as a bell, "We all know you lied, Joey!"

Joey shuts her mouth entirely.

With adrenaline pumping through her body, she marches through the crowd and straight up the stairs of the basement and into the cool, crisp fall evening. Casey and Alex are hot on her heels.

"What the hell was that about?" Casey says.

Breathing heavy, Laura says, "I got tired of them pushing me around. Saying things about me that aren't true."

"Like what?" Casey asks.

Laura leans in, and through the darkness, she says to her friend, "You know I love you, Casey, and that means everything about you."

"I know that, Laura. I would never question that."

"Some people do."

"Bitches," Alex remarks. "I knew the way they were glaring at you that they were no friends of yours."

"No way. They are no good to—"

"What the heck is going on?" they hear a male voice ask after the opening and closing of the basement door.

Startled, they turn around.

Colin strides over. "Well?"

Laura stumbles for words, as she had no idea Colin was even at the party.

He turns to Casey and Alex. "Are you guys here with other people?"

"Yeah."

"Good. Can you go find them and tell them I took Laura home?"

Laura begins to protest when he cuts in, "You have any idea how pissed she is? Trust me, I'm doing you a favor."

"You know them?" Alex asks.

"Yeah, you could say that."

"Sorry to hear that," Casey says as she spins on her heel and heads back toward the basement. "Come on, Alex. Let's go find Abigail and Bree."

Before Laura can comprehend what is happening, she is being escorted by Colin back onto the street.

"Mind filling me in on that altercation back there?" he asks, his tone less accusing than before.

"You have no idea how they treat me."

"I have a little bit of a clue."

"Then, why do you seem mad at me?"

"I guess I expected you to take the higher ground."

"Higher ground? But why? So they can continue to stomp all over me and treat me like crap and all because of what? *You?*"

"Ouch, that stings."

"Does she plan to torture me simply because I work with you?"

"It is a little more than that."

Somewhat surprised, Laura turns and looks at him. "Doesn't she know we hardly talk to one another?"

"It's not the talking that bothers her. And, besides, didn't we agree we needed to keep up this charade for now?"

Laura swallows hard.

He stops and faces her. Gently placing one arm around her waist, he says, "Come on. I want to show you something."

He drops his arm and starts to move again. She quickly catches up. In silence, they make it through campus and over toward his apartment. She's too afraid to ask questions, for fear this is simply another confusing night, alone with Colin.

He keys into his apartment and heads up the stairs. She follows, like a puppet on a string. Only he goes past his room and to a window at the end of the hallway. He opens it and climbs out onto the roof, taking the blanket that was on the floor with him. He reaches back for her hand, and she, too, climbs out. He steps onto a ledge and then up onto the peak of the house.

He spreads out the blanket and sits on it. He motions for her to sit next to him. She does, and as she lowers, he lies back, resting his head in his hands. Hesitantly, she lies back.

"Now, look up," he says.

The stars that fill the night sky before them are undeniably majestic. But it's hard to comprehend in this moment that the universe exists beyond his rooftop. Because, somehow, in the midst of this all, there is still something on Laura's mind despite how hard she would like her thoughts to simply disappear. She sighs.

"Want to talk about it?" he asks.

"Not exactly."

"Does this have anything to do with what happened today? When you stormed past me and left the station in a hurry?"

"I was having a bad day."

"I'll say. Does this have to do with the interview with Jane?"

"How did you know?" Too afraid to look at him, she remains lying down, but her heart is beating fast.

"Tucker asked me to put your equipment away and go through the tapes. So, I did."

Her heart sinks further. "I don't know what to say."

"It was awful, and she should be ashamed of herself. They all should."

"Did you tell Tucker?"

"Absolutely not."

"Thank you."

"Can I ask what you said to her tonight?"

"I asked her to leave me alone. I'm trying to do something good, and I can't have them getting in the way," she whispers.

"I'm proud of you for speaking up for yourself. I'm sorry if I'm the root cause."

She releases a heavy sigh. "You're not. But where were you tonight…at the party?"

"I saw you through the crowd and was coming to say hello. I was struck by what unfolded in front of me and figured the last person either of you needed coming onto the scene was me."

"It all comes back to you," she whispers.

He props himself up on one arm, glaring at her through the darkness. "Does it? Because, so far, I'm not feeling it at all."

In confusion, Laura replies, "Not feeling it at all? I don't know what…"

"What I mean is, if it all comes back to me, then why am I the one sleeping alone every night?"

"I didn't know you were," she says as she swallows hard.

"Of course you did," he quips.

"*Colin.*"

"Laura."

Feeling feisty, Laura jabs back, "No, I didn't know that. I just know you're not sleeping with me."

"Ha," he growls. "You're blaming me?"

Regretting her words, she mumbles, "No, of course not."

But he isn't going to let her off easily. "So, Spring Fling, I should have taken advantage of you? And a few weeks ago…just screwed you to get it over with, out of my system? Is that the type of guy you want me to be?" She starts to answer, but he continues, "That's not an actual question, Laura."

If he could see her cheeks burning red, he'd know for certain, he's caught her at her weakest.

Quickly, he gets up.

"Where are you going? Be careful."

"Have I not tried, Laura?" he barks.

"What?"

He stands on the roof like a giant before her, yet his slumped shoulders tell her he feels small. "I know that this has not been ideal. Believe me, you don't have to tell me twice. But, one minute, you're in my bedroom, and then the next minute, you're practically running away from me. Only I don't hear a word from you in between. Nothing. Radio silence."

Right when I thought this day, night, could not possibly get any worse. Add Colin to the list of people I can't seem to get it right with. It's a long list. Longer than it's ever been for me. I'm barely hanging on. I'm in my own head and with a complete loss of words for the living and breathing in front of me. I have nothing left.

Laura watches in disbelief as Colin makes his way off of the roof and back into his house. She sits on the blanket, pulling her knees up to her chest, rocking slightly, like a child wishing away the pain. As she closes her eyes, a flash runs across her memory bank, back to the first time she met Colin. The passionate blows he bestowed upon the papers and his desk at the station. The sadness she felt in the room. He looked shattered, like the broken glass on the floor.

He carries the same expression tonight.

The hurt that we do to each other, the ones we claim to care for the most, but why? Is it because we are merely humans? Humans with expectations that cannot be fulfilled? How is it that we expect ourselves to be so perfect, without a flaw, yet we are surprised when that is all we are? Flawed.

Laura carefully stands, folds up the blanket, and makes her way back through the window. She hesitates as she nears his door.

The ring of the phone pierces the silence of what might be the best night's sleep Travis has had so far this semester. But being disturbed is par for the course for him.

"It's late," he says into the receiver.

"I know," Wolfie replies.

He assumed the only one to call him this late would be Wolfie. "What's the latest?"

"Thought you'd want to know that Laura was at the graffiti party and got into an altercation of sorts with Joey and her roommate from the protest. The one she interviewed."

"Jesus Christ." He makes a deep sigh into the receiver and then asks, "Is she all right?"

"Yes, she seemed fine. Probably overdue on her part."

"Yes," he grunts. "I tend to agree. She's been heading down that path for quite some time. Where is she now?"

Silence.

Then, finally, Wolfie finds the courage to speak the unspeakable, "She's with him."

There are the sinking feelings in life that are unexpected. Then, there are the ones you expect to happen, and those tend to hurt more because, all along, you saw the truth right in front of you, and you knew it was only a matter of time until those dreadful fears become your reality.

"Okay, thanks for the intel."

Lying in Wait

Wolfie, not willing to end the conversation, replies, "We are almost there. Maybe it will be different in the end."

"Maybe." Travis lets his breath go and then places down the receiver and turns on his side, staring at the empty spot beside him.

I know what I need to do. I've known it all along. It's time to let her go.

Thirty-Two

ARENT WE ALL FLAWED?

Laura steps into the doorway of his room. There is a dim light on next to his bed. Colin is sitting in the chair. He glances up at her, only he does not speak. His eyes tell her all she needs to know. He is angry with her, and she knows exactly why.

She leans on the frame of his door and releases her breath. "I'm flawed. This has become inevitably clear to me over the past few months. My whole life, I've been the one everyone could rely on, and now, I'm simply not. I've made mistakes, lots of them, and I've done things merely because I've had to. I've held on to secrets so tightly that they have been slowly eating away at me, yet I am no further along than I was on my first day of college."

She shifts her feet and then continues, "I wanted to audition for the station because I wanted to make a difference, be the voice for countless who didn't have one." She enters his room and sits on the edge of his bed. "My roommate, Abigail, she was the reason the guy…the Campus Creeper got caught. Tank, he was protecting her," she reveals. "But what is worse about the whole damn thing is that my friend Bree, she was attacked her first night of college by the same man, and the school knew about it and didn't do a damn thing about it."

His breath catches. "Laura, what are you saying?"

She notes his reaction and feels an obligation to not hold back. "Everything I've done this past year has been to keep one secret or another. I have alliances that I need to maintain."

Like Travis and Wolfie. They could both be expelled for the information they have obtained on the dean.

"And, now, I'm telling you all of this, and I expect you to keep my secrets, so I'm basically doing the same thing to you." She pauses, and then, in a whisper, she says, "And that is what I was trying *not* to do."

"I can handle it," he whispers.

"Can you? Because it's like holding a ticking time bomb. I have no idea when this will all self-destruct, but it will."

"I had a feeling there was much more to what you were doing."

"There is, and please believe me, there are details I wish I could divulge, but I can't. I could cause serious destruction to people I care about."

"I'm starting to understand that."

"It's not because I don't want to tell you. Believe me, I'd love nothing more than to unburden my soul and rid myself of all of this, but we're almost there. We've made it this far, and I have to hold steady. I have to. They are depending on me."

Surprisingly, he smiles. "I know, Laura. I'm not blind."

"Neither am I. You've spent the better part of last year helping someone who, in the end, will betray you not once, but twice."

He lowers his head. "I've felt like such an idiot. There were days I couldn't even stand the sight of me. This self-loathing has torn me to pieces, yet she is still in my life."

"Don't let her."

"I know. I've tried harder this past month, but she can manipulate with the best of them. She played Jane right into the mix, and in the blink of an eye, she strikes when you least expect it."

Needing to hear him say it once and for all, she asks, "You're really over her?"

His expression softens, and he replies with such conviction, "Yes, and I have been for a very long time. To be honest, I think we were never right for one another. We weren't good together, even on our best days. It just took me too long to realize it."

"You're too good for her." Laura's words flow out of her mouth.

"I don't want to discuss her. I want to talk about you. Tell me what you need from me."

She glances over at him. She can finally tell him how she truly feels. No shields up. She has zero hesitation in this moment, so she goes all in. "I need *you*."

She watches his body react. He slowly and deliberately gets up from his seat. He crosses the room like her knight in shining armor and sits down next to her on the bed.

"You have me," he whispers as he reaches up and gently caresses her cheek.

"I didn't know…"

He looks deeply into her eyes. "You know, when I saw you through the crowd tonight, I thought to myself, *that is one gorgeous girl, and if I try to make it right with her, she might actually like me back.*"

Shocked by his admission, she replies, "Really?"

"Most definitely."

"We've had such a rough start."

"Believe me, I know. Between the station shifts, all the other stuff, it's not been easy. But, somehow, we keep coming back to this."

She can feel her pulse react to his words. Just words, and she knows more than ever that he is the one for her.

"I'm sorry, Colin, for everything. For what I said tonight. That wasn't fair and—"

He cuts her off, "Do you honestly think that I haven't wanted to sleep with you? Laura, my God, it's more of a fear in me that I'll somehow screw it up and not be able to go back."

"Really?" she gasps.

Inopportunely disrupting their newly found love is the horrible ring of the telephone on Colin's desk. Startled, Colin drops his hand from her face and strides across the room toward his desk.

"Who is calling me?" he grumbles. He grabs the receiver. "Hello?"

Laura can faintly hear a girl's voice.

Colin's face drops a shade whiter. "Jesus Christ, what is going on?" Then, there's silence while he listens. "Okay, yes, I understand. I will get there as soon as I can." He places the receiver back down and stares ahead for a moment.

"Everything okay?"

He hesitates, and Laura can feel the lump in her throat.

"Colin?"

"It's, um…it's Joey. She's in the hospital. She took some pills…" His voice fades.

Laura's mind races as she replays her altercation and what she said to her. She feels a sickness roll through her stomach. "Oh my God," she whispers.

"I don't—"

"You should go," Laura says as she stands and takes his hand. "Go, Colin."

He finally locks eyes with her. His pupils are dilated, and there is mist in his eyes. "What have I done?"

It's not what you've done. It's what I've done, Colin. I am sorry. I never should have lashed out at her in front of everyone at the party.

"You've done nothing."

"I should go. I should ensure she is okay." He puts his wallet in his back pocket.

"Yes, you should. I'll walk myself home. You go to her," she replies with deep sadness.

"No, it's late. Let me drop you off."

"Okay," Laura whispers, not wanting to argue with him.

Colin grabs his keys, and with little warning, he exits his room. Laura is quick on his heels, feeling the sense of urgency pulse through him. He drives her to her dorm in silence.

As he pulls up front, she whispers, "I'm here if you need me, okay?"

"Okay, and thank you."

"I'm truly sorry, Colin."

"So am I."

With that, Laura pushes open his Jeep door and climbs out. She watches as he pulls back out and speeds down the road. Her heart sinks as she considers the pain he must be feeling and, worse, the pain a person must feel to be distressed enough to cry out.

Thirty-Three

TIME TO LET YOU IN

Bree opens her tired eyes, rubbing them to wake up. She sits up in her bed and swings her long legs over the side of the bed. She gingerly steps onto the plush carpet below her feet. She undresses and then wraps her posh robe around her body. Eager to shower off the party from last night, she heads down the hallway and to the bathroom. She takes her time in washing her hair and shaving her legs as she hums to herself.

Twenty minutes later, she pushes open the door. She drops her razor on the floor as she balances her shower caddy into her room. She kicks the door shut behind her as she bends forward to pick up her razor. She hastily tosses her caddy on the top of her dresser. She disrobes and pulls on a pair of jeans, a silk cami, and a long wrap sweater.

As she glances at her reflection in the mirror and piles her wet hair on top of her head, she freezes. She spins to look over at the other side of the room. There is a large envelope on the floor.

That was not here a minute ago.

She steps forward and reluctantly picks it up.

Her name is inscribed on the front, and below it, it says, *For your eyes only!*

A chill rushes over her skin. She sits in her desk chair, and with trembling fingers, she tears open the envelope. There is a typewritten note on plain paper securely attached to several other papers.

> *It is with a heavy heart that I share these documents with you. You have endured enough, yet I firmly believe what you are about to read will, in many ways, further your cause and that of all the other women who were victimized by the school.*

The school? What the hell does that mean?

> *The following documents were sent to me by an anonymous source. Their authenticity has been confirmed. Nonetheless, for me to be the one to come forth with them would be of consequence to those I have helped build a deeply respectable community with. My voice is esteemed and heard across this campus and must remain intact if we are to bring down those in power. Those who had the power to stop what happened and didn't. Those who have continued to manipulate all of us and remain doing so today.*
>
> *But then there is you. You have the power to stop them and to bring an end to the reign of an ill-equipped administration. An administration just as dangerous as the Campus Creeper. Your day in court is vastly approaching, and I am asking you to put an end to all of this. They don't know you have the clout. But I do.*
>
> *Sincerely,*
>
> *Your watchful friend*

Bree eagerly flips to the first page. But, as she begins to read the email, she is immediately struck by a stabbing pain in her chest. She reads the next one. And the next one. Each email is more painful than the next. Each holds a very specific jab to her inner being. Each hurts a little more than the one before. The notes compound the pain she has already felt this past year.

With tears streaming down her face, she shoves the contents back inside the envelope. She grabs a bag and stuffs a few items of clothing into it. With a sense of urgency and with her car keys tightly gripped in her hand, she exits her room.

She drives an hour to her boyfriend's cabin. She pulls in, parks, and runs up to the door, pushing it open with force. Adam is crouched over the fire, putting another log on it. Her rapid entrance startles him.

"Bree, you scared me." But then he gets a good look at her face. "Jesus, are you all right?"

He hurries over to her. Without warning, she drops her bag and throws her arms around him as her chest heaves from her uncontrollable sobs.

"Are you hurt?" he asks with fear in his voice. When she doesn't answer, he pulls her back, trying to take a good look at her. "Bree, please talk to me," he pleads.

"I…I didn't know what else to do," she cries.

"Please, tell me what is wrong!"

Her lips quiver as she tries to form a sentence. He slowly leads her over to the couch and gently lowers her down. He strokes her cheek, and then, with soft fingers, he guides her face up to meet his. He locks eyes with her. The sheer sadness held within her eyes is something he has not seen in quite some time.

"Is someone hurt?" he asks.

She shakes her head.

"Okay, good. Well, that is a start. Something happened today. What is it?"

Her bottom lip trembles as she finally speaks, "I...I got an envelope, and I can't believe what was inside..." Her sobs come on strong again.

"Do you have it with you?"

She nods her head.

"Where?"

She averts her eyes toward the door where she dropped her bag.

"Okay, can I get it?"

Again, she nods her head. He releases her and goes to retrieve the envelope from her bag. He comes back to her and sits next to her. She turns slightly away. The pain is resurfacing as she hears him pull the papers out of the envelope. She peeks over as she watches his face drop as he flips to the first email after reading the cover note.

"Jesus Christ," he whispers. "Bree, is-is that you?"

She nods as a tear drops onto her cheek. He continues reading all of the documents, trying hard not to make comments, although she knows he must want to.

Once he is finished, he hangs his head, no doubt gathering his thoughts. Finally, he speaks, "They knew all along and did nothing about it until it was too late?"

"It appears that way."

"The police warned them, yet they stood idle and let chaos consume our campus. Dean Barrymore did nothing. Took no action, and you and others paid the price. It simply can't be."

She wipes her tears on the edge of her shirt. "Officer Murphy, he-he tried so hard to help me, and I refused his help. I can't imagine what that must have been like for him. To know they tried but got nothing but resistance from the administration and all the way down."

Bree thinks of the time she finally had the courage to go to the police station to meet Officer Murphy and identify the man Officer Murphy knew about well in advance.

After they spoke, his final parting words were, "In general, people are good and want to help others. You just have to let them in."

Bullshit. From what I've read today, people have their own agendas, and regardless of consequences, they plow straight ahead.

"She gave you and me a lighter punishment for our relationship merely so she could come and convince you to join her committee to help fluff her falling feathers. Could Dean Barrymore be that cruel?"

"She is. I can't believe she played me right into her hands, and Laura..."

"Laura what?"

Bree pauses, searching Adam's face. He is already far too involved than he should be. She knows that Laura can get in a lot of trouble for sharing these with her. Each move she makes from here on out must be completely thought through and vetted by her father.

"Laura is my best friend at school, and she knows nothing of this but has been—"

"Reporting on it at the station, trying so hard to piece this all together to make the campus better," he interjects. He grabs her hand. "Man, am I pissed that Dean Barrymore played me."

"Now, wait, Adam. To be fair, in our circumstance, it did keep your job intact, and I was able to remain enrolled at the university, which we both know was not a guarantee. So, it goes without saying that I'm glad she did...in a twisted way."

"I don't discount that, but I'm still angry with her. But I have a feeling her day will come, and I'll no longer have to worry about her opinion."

I have a feeling her day will be coming very soon.

Thirty-Four

IT WAS GENUINE

Laura knocks on the door to Travis's house.

Travis opens it. "Hey, stranger," he says rather oddly.

She forces a smile. "Hey, can I come in?"

"Of course, please do. I was wondering when I might see you again," he says.

"Yes, I know. About the other day, I'm sorry I got so upset after we were at the courthouse. I haven't been in touch. I'm sorry." She drops her bag on the couch.

"I understand. I do." His eyes soften. "I was hoping I'd catch you before the trial concluded."

She cocks her head to the side. "Okay, what's up?"

"I plan to go to the trial on Wednesday. Wolfie got me a pass. So, I'll be there."

"Okay, Wednesday is when Bree testifies."

"I know. I could only get one pass, but I wanted you to know I'd be in attendance."

"Okay, well, that is good news. At least someone should be there."

"I wish I could have gotten two, but the paper had to pull hard to get one, and I couldn't ask…"

"I understand; I do. It's probably better I'm not there."

"How so?"

"I've been kind of a shitty friend lately." *To lots of people, including you.*

"It will all work out. I have a feeling."

"I hope you are right." She sighs.

He winks and then adds, "I'm usually right, aren't I?"

Laura smiles for the first time since entering his apartment. "Yes, you are."

He steps closer toward her and smiles warmly. He locks eyes with her and then softly asks, "We're friends, right?"

"Of course we are." She tips her head with a questioning countenance.

"Good. I want you to know I'm always here for you…as a friend." He stresses the word *friend*.

Part of Laura is relieved to hear him say that, and there is a little part of her that is undeniably sad.

She responds, "You know I'll always be your friend, too. You're a hard person not to like." She smiles. "Once you crack through that cocky, pompous exterior."

He dramatically gasps, placing his hand over his heart. "Pompous? Cocky? Me?" He laughs in return.

She gives him her renowned sarcastic smirk, but little does she know, it drives him wild.

Laura grasps for the door and starts to pull it open. But, before she can open the door, he reaches for her and pulls her into him. Travis leans her back in his arms, and with no warning, he kisses her so deeply that she sincerely questions every kiss she has had up until this very moment. She imagines they must look like something out of a movie scene. When he finally releases his lips from hers and pulls apart from her, her eyes remain shut for just a moment longer. Then, he helps steady her upright, finally letting her go. Her cheeks are as rosy as a spring tulip.

Her eyes flitter open, and she whispers, "Friends."

He doesn't say anything. Instead, he reaches over her head to open up the door.

She steps out onto his front steps. "Call me after the trial on Wednesday, okay?"

"You'll be the first one I call."

She goes to step down the stairs.

"Your bag." He laughs as he holds it up.

"Oh, right. Forgot." Clearly frazzled, she leans forward and takes it from him.

He leans in the doorframe, and before she is down the last step, he says, "Oh, hey, did I tell you I bought a motorcycle?"

"You did? Aren't you full of surprises?"

"I try to keep it fresh," he jokes. "I'm picking it up tomorrow. It's a beater, but I plan to fix it up."

"You love to stay busy."

"Can't sit still." He chuckles.

Laura gazes up at him in the afternoon sun. His handsome face looks back at her, and she has zero regrets that he was the first person she ever slept with. The only person in fact. She grants him one last glance and a wave. Then, she turns with a slight swing in her step and casually wanders down the street. She can't quite articulate it, yet somehow, she feels that words would be an injustice for exactly what Travis means to her.

Travis watches Laura disappear down the street.

His heart, while completely heavy, is happy to continue to love her from afar. Like most relationships, only a few stick around for the long haul. A fleeting romance, although he wanted it to last longer, can almost be poetic when it falls short. The writer in Travis finds comfort in the tragedy of his adoration of her because only then does he know it to be true.

Thirty-Five

TOGETHER AGAIN

Laura hurries over to Colin's apartment. He was expecting her over twenty minutes ago, but she wanted to pick him up a pizza since he'd spent the past two days in the hospital, waiting by Joey's bedside.

She knocks and Stef, his roommate, answers.

"Hey, Colin is upstairs. It's cool if you go up," he says.

"Thanks, Stef."

She heads up the stairs to his room. She can hear the soft hum of music pulsing through his door. She knocks, and when he doesn't answer, she opens the door.

Colin is lying on his bed, eyes closed. Her heart softens at the sight of him sleeping. She steps into the room, placing the pizza and drinks on his desk. She lowers herself on the bed and gently touches his arms. She can feel his muscles twitch to life as he begins to stir. His eyes flit open. The color of his irises mixed with the fading afternoon sun strikes a chord with Laura. She reaches up and touches his face. Then, she runs her hand over his tightly sheared hair. When they first met, he rocked this longer side hair that many skateboarders have, but when he came back this year, it was buzzed, and with his tan skin and bright eyes, he is even more handsome.

"Hey," he says with a raspy voice.

"Hey," she whispers back. "How are you?"

He props himself up on his elbow. "I'm okay. Exhausted actually."

"I brought you pizza."

"My savior," he says with a slight smile.

Laura has not had a chance to speak with Colin since the night he dropped her off. He has remained by Joey's side the entire few days.

"Can I ask how she is?" Laura's voice quivers, for fear the news will not be good.

The past few days have been hard enough as she reimagined the events of that night at the party over and over in her head. She can't help but feel as though her encounter with Joey and Jane might have pushed her over the edge. While not specific, she is convinced Joey knew exactly what she was referring to when she said she was lying.

Colin sits up and rubs his eyes. He lets out a long sigh and then says, "She is okay. I mean, she will be. Her family is here now, and the doctors say she will recover."

Laura has to turn her head, and surprisingly to her, the news is more than she can handle. "I'm so sorry, Colin."

"Oh my God, Laura, what is wrong?" he asks, placing his hand on her shoulder. "Look at me, please."

Refusing to turn, she says, "I really hope she recuperates."

"Of course, and I believe she will." Colin pauses.

He contemplates whether he should tell Laura about his visit with Joey. Maybe some details should remain sealed. Like, for instance, when he went to the nurses' station to call Joey's parents before their flight to give them an update on how she was doing, only to return to find Dean Barrymore standing over Joey's bed. The look on her face was puzzling at best. She seemed angry, and Joey, while pale and drawn, looked frightened by her visit. Colin waited back in the hallway while the two spoke. The dean did not sound pleased in the least. Joey, on the other hand, sounded like a child being scolded by her mother.

Once the dean left, Colin waited only a few minutes before reentering her room. She did not mention the dean's visit, nor did he ask. Something in her demeanor told him now was not the time to ask her such things, considering her fragile condition.

"I've been thinking about what could cause a person to try to harm themselves, and right now, what we need is to support each other in any way we can. What happened the other night at the party was not of consequence. I assure you. She is troubled. We both know that. But, now, at least her family will have a clue as to what is going on with her, and she can get some help."

"I'm glad to hear that. I have been worried, and I want her to be okay. I don't wish her ill."

"I know. What happened between all of us is college-life drama. We could not have foreseen this coming. No one wants this."

"You said her family is here?"

"Yes, her parents and I have always gotten along, so everything is good there. They appreciated me being by her side while they could not."

"Thank God. Her poor parents. They must be so worried."

"They are managing and working with the hospital, so she gets what she needs."

"And you?"

"I'm starving," he says with a fleeting grin.

Laura gets up off the bed and brings over the pizza box, placing it between them. She watches as Colin devours slice after slice.

Finishing his last bite of the pizza, he asks, "Tomorrow is Bree's testimony?"

"Yes, unfortunately."

"Do you wish you could be there for her?"

She has thought long and hard about this, and every time, she comes to the same conclusion—*yes*. Yes, she should be there for her friend. She's one of her best friends at college, and the thought of her looking out into a group of unfriendly faces, who are there merely for the entertainment value of one of the most publicized trials in the last ten years, makes Laura's stomach twist with anguish.

"Yes, I should be there to support her. But I can't get in."

"That is a shame."

She blurts out, "But Travis will be there. That is a good thing."

Colin's smile is genuine, and it catches her off guard. "You guys are good friends, aren't you?"

The opportunity to be able to acknowledge her relationship in front of Colin warms her tired heart. "Yes, we are. He has been very kind to me. He cares for me, and I care for him. He has taught me a lot this past year, and I owe much of my success at the station to him."

Colin continues to smile.

"What?" Laura asks.

He laughs and says, "I have a confession. I was always a little jealous of the guy."

"Really? Why?"

"He got the chance to hang out with you when I wanted it to be me. Hard not to be jealous of that."

A smile forms across Laura's lips. She bashfully glances away from him. Without warning, he tosses the empty pizza box on the floor.

"Come here." His voice is low and very sexy.

She squeals slightly as he pulls her into him, rolling her on her back. He leans above her. The weight of his body feels incredible on top of hers. With one hand, he brushes back her hair from her face. Eyes locked on hers, he leans in, and with warm, soft lips, he gently brushes them across hers. Her heart beats wildly. Their sobering kiss pulsates through her body.

He pulls back. "I've been waiting so long to be with you."

She smiles. "Me, too."

"I hope you know that I never stopped thinking about the day in the studio when I kissed you."

"Me, neither. And I'm sorry for all those drunken nights. I felt like such a fool. I was embarrassed and could never remember what I might have said…"

"Spring Fling, you told me you weren't happy. I told you I wasn't either. I told you that I'd wait for you, no matter how long it took, and then I held you in my arms—"

"You did?"

"Yeah, I didn't want to let you go. I couldn't. I would have rather been alone in my room with you on Spring Fling than at some party, looking for you. Wishing things were different. I had you, and that was all I needed."

"Oh, Colin. I'm so sorry. About everything."

"Me, too. Believe me. I wish we could start all over again."

She wraps her arms around his neck, pulling him closer. "I'm a serious pain in the ass, aren't I?"

He places his arms around her body and smiles. "As long as you're my pain in the ass, I'm fine with it."

She is about to protest when he leans in, and with a deeper passion, he kisses her mouth. He starts to move his hips, pushing them into hers. She runs her hands up his back, drawing his shirt up as she does. He pulls it over his head, tossing it on the floor. His eyes are asking her for more as he deliberately takes his time in unbuttoning each button on her shirt.

"I don't want to wait any longer," he says.

She notices his sultry eyes come to life when he opens her shirt and finds her ample breasts waiting for his touch.

"Neither do I."

He eases her shirt and bra straps off her shoulders. He reaches behind her while he kisses her hard and unhooks her bra. He runs his hand up her waist and to her bra, pulling it off her. His hands caress her alert breasts, and she can hear him moan with satisfaction as the mere size of them fills his hands with her beautiful body.

"You're gorgeous," he growls as he releases his lips from hers and begins a trail of kisses down her neck and to her breasts.

She runs her hands over his head. The feeling of his short hair on her fingers is stimulating to her senses, but what is more exciting is the feeling of his lips and tongue all over her body. Her breath catches. He starts to unzip her denim that hugs her figure perfectly. With his assistance, she slips out of them. He glides off of her and stands at the foot of the bed, taking in the beauty lying before him. She loves how his eyes dance all over her body. Without even touching, she is completely turned on.

He locks his door and then unzips his jeans. He reaches for a condom out of his drawer. Like a sultry lion, he climbs on top of her, starting all over again. Kissing her legs and belly and then caressing her breasts, moaning with each touch they land on one another.

"I want you," she breathes.

His teeth rip the wrapper, and he eagerly readies himself. He climbs in between her legs. Then, with released anticipation, he thrusts himself inside her. She moans loudly, and he shuts her up with a hard kiss. He pushes harder and harder into her, and she reacts more and more with each plunge. He kisses her firmer, masking her groans.

She digs her nails deep in his back, and he acknowledges it by gently pulling on the back of her hair. She lets him know she likes it with a devilish stare, and in this moment, she realizes that he's thought about their time together as much as she has.

It is well worth the wait.

He grunts louder and louder as he brings himself to the point of no return. She smiles, knowing he is worth every second apart if it means they can be here now, as one.

Laura dresses while Colin is down the hallway, showering. When he comes back into the room, it takes all her might not to pounce on top of him as his body glistens from the water still on his skin. He smiles wide at her. Without a word, he strides toward her. He leans down and intensely kisses her. She can feel her body tingle. All too soon, he releases her. She could stay in his arms forever, if he'd let her.

He drops his towel and playfully dresses in front of her. He knows exactly what he is doing, and she admires that about him. He is sexy, and he owns it. It is a complete turn-on.

She smiles as she leans back on his bed and watches him. Finally, he turns, and he can't hide his smile.

"You were awesome," he says sincerely.

Ugh, melt my heart, why don't you? Good in bed, sexy, and not afraid to talk about it. Could he be the complete package?

She smiles bashfully and replies, "So were you."

He slips his shirt over his head. "Call me tomorrow, okay?"

"I will. Good luck at the hospital. I hope everything is getting better for her."

He crosses the room, leans in to Laura, and kisses her again. "Thank you. I appreciate you saying that."

They leave together, and as they walk out of a place as a couple, for the first time in a long time, Laura is smiling ear to ear.

Before he drops her off at her dorm, he grabs her hand and squeezes it. "I wish I could wake up with you tomorrow."

"Soon." She leans over, planting a kiss on his cheek.

She pushes open his Jeep door and climbs out. She knows he is watching her, so she takes her time, enjoying the admiration from him. She puts her key in the door, glances over her shoulder, and gives him a sultry smile. He beeps his horn and then pulls out onto Main Street.

Oh, how college life is such a whirlwind of events and relationships. You never know when you might be closing the door on one relationship and opening the door to another…again.

Thirty-Six

OUR SECRETS

With pleasure in Laura's heart, she takes the stairs up to her room. She is not the least bit surprised her floor is quiet on a Tuesday evening. Not much happens in the dorm midweek. Either people are studying or in the lounge, watching TV. She hurries past Bree's room. She has not seen her since she wrote in Spanish, *No olvides quiénes son tus amigos,* on the back of her shirt at the graffiti party. She later, with the help of a friend, found out it meant, *Don't forget who your friends are.* It stung. But Bree had known it would.

Her door is cracked open a smidgen. Inside, Abigail is lying on her bed, reading one of her science textbooks.

"Hey," she says.

"Hello!"

Abigail glances up from her book. "You sound cheery."

Laura hugs herself. "I feel cheery."

"What's up with you?" she asks with a wide smile.

Laura plops down on her bed. With a long sigh, she says, "Colin and I might have finally found our place in all this craziness."

"Colin from the station? Colin from last year?"

"Yep, that Colin." She chuckles.

"By the look on your face, I have a feeling he makes you happy."

"He does. I've been wishing for this...but you know, timing was never quite right."

"That is the official theme at OSU."

They both laugh as Laura kicks off her shoes.

When she looks back up at Abigail, her demeanor changes. "What's up?"

"Um, Bree left this for you." Abigail gets up from her bed, crosses the room, and retrieves a piece of paper. She hands it to Laura.

By now, her heart is beating double time with anticipation. With trembling fingers, she reaches out to take it. "She left this for me?"

"Yes. She went to stay in the hotel with her parents for the night. They plan to bring her to the courthouse in the morning."

Laura eagerly opens the letter.

Dear Laura,

It would mean a lot to me if you could be in the courtroom with my family tomorrow. My lawyer has given your name to security. You will need to bring identification. If you can be there at eight a.m., the court proceedings will begin promptly at eight thirty a.m. I appreciate what you did and know it could not have been easy.

With love,

Bree

Appreciate what I did and know it could not have been easy? What does that mean?

"Do you know what this is about?"

"She wants her friend by her side. That is what this is about. Nothing more."

Laura's face burns with heat as she recaps the past few months and the distance that has grown between her and her closest friends this year. "I haven't been a good friend to her," she whispers.

Abigail sits and gently places her hand on her leg. "Listen, remember, last year, when I went through all that stuff with Tank and Nathan?"

"Yes."

"What compounded it the most for me was that I'd pushed away my friends, my best friends, and it only made what I was going through worse."

"I remember. I was worried about you."

"And we are, too. Whatever this is that you are going through, you need to let someone in."

Laura pauses, only to remember the pain she watched Abigail and Bree endure. Yet here she sits, having learned virtually nothing from her friends' experiences. She has repeated history, but she should have learned from it. She tips her head as she looks into Abigail's eager face, and it reminds her of how she once felt.

Let me in!

Lying in Wait

She, much like Abigail now, only wanted to help her friend through whatever it was she was going through. Yet she senses a hesitation, much like Abigail did. She decides to be as transparent as possible.

"I have confided in someone. I wasn't given a choice as to whom I could. I have had a lot to protect, and I've chosen to do so. And, by doing that, it limited me to whom I could talk to, and that includes both you and Bree."

Abigail's eyes grow wide. "But you have talked to someone?"

"Yes, and I have trusted him. His name is Travis, and he is my friend. But, Abigail, if I can ask you, for now, please do not repeat his name. It is all I can say today. I'm sorry for that."

She watches Abigail's eyes. While deeply troubled, there is a glimmer of hope in them.

"As long as you know you can come to me for anything. But I do understand what it is like to keep someone else's secrets. I had to keep them for Tank in order to get past it all. It hurt a lot along the way, but I know now that I did the right thing."

"Thank you. I love you so much. I hope you know that. You've been an incredible friend, and I want you to know I appreciate you."

"I feel the same. We all have good intentions, and I know that college life is confusing and not without moments that make us all have to look deep within ourselves. It will make you see who you truly are."

"That is the truth if I've ever heard it." Laura laughs and then hugs her friend deeply.

She knows that Abigail and Bree have no clue that the school did not protect them enough, and it hurts Laura more so than ever as she imagines herself entering the courthouse and taking her place next to Bree's parents. Knowing what she knows, it will be more difficult than ever to sit there idly.

But I must, for their sake. I love my friends enough to put it aside and wait for further instructions from Travis. After all, he is the man with the plan, and I am the girl who will do anything to help. And I can only hope that, someday soon, it will all come to light, bringing this chapter in our lives to an end.

Thirty-Seven

JOEY

Colin knocks quietly on the doorframe before entering Joey's hospital room. Her parents stand at the foot of her bed and grant Colin a halfhearted smile as he joins them.

"Hello."

"Hello, Colin."

He turns to a sleeping Joey. "How is she doing?" he whispers.

"She is okay. We don't know what caused her such distress," her mother adds with tears in her eyes.

Colin's shoulders hunch. "Do you know when she will be discharged?"

"Hopefully, in a few days." Her father grabs her mother's hand and gently squeezes. "Would you mind if we went and grabbed something to eat?"

"No, of course not," he says.

He pulls up the chair next to her bed as her parents exit the room. He leans forward, resting his arms on the edge. He looks at her frail body and can't help but wonder about her. Wonder how they got this far apart from where they once had been. He reaches up and touches her hand. She begins to stir.

She turns her head, and with sunken eyes, she opens them and tenderly smiles at his presence. "Hello," she says with a groggy tone.

"Hey there," he says, returning a small smile. "Your parents went to get something to eat."

"Good. They have been hovering over me for hours."

"They are concerned. We all are." He squeezes her hand. Tears well in her tired eyes. "What is going on, Joey? Can you talk about it?"

With sadness, she chokes out, "I can't."

"Please, you can trust me. You should tell someone."

"That's not me, Colin. You should know that."

"Maybe it's time we change?" Colin replies.

He notices Joey exhale deeply, as if she had been holding her breath for months. She sits up in her bed.

Colin's eyes grow wide. "Can I help?"

"I might have gotten caught up in something I shouldn't have," she admits. "But I feel like it's best you know nothing."

Feeling as though all the women in his life have secrets, he lowers his head and replies, "But I can handle it. I can try to make it better for you."

"I know that, but I care about you too much to hurt you anymore."

"Hurt me?"

"Yes, I know what I've done to you. Even before all this happened. I screwed up and couldn't stand the thought of not having you as mine."

"Let's not worry about that now. We all make mistakes."

"I know, but I've made a costly one."

"Joey, what are you saying?"

He notes how her body stiffens, and her jaw clenches slightly. She turns on her side to get a better look at him. For the first time in a very long time, Colin catches a glimpse of the old Joey. The Joey he first met years ago, sprawled out on the lawn of the dorm she lived in. A girl full of conviction and spunk. She caught his eye, and within seconds, she motioned for him to come over. He would have kept walking and simply admired her from afar. She, on the contrary, would have no such thing.

"I want you to know that I never stopped caring about you. Despite my behavior..." She pauses as she wipes a tear from her eye. "You might just be the one who got away, Colin. But, until I can put all this behind me and try to get better, I am asking you to not come and visit me anymore."

His mouth drops open, and he is about to protest when she cuts him off, "Please, do this for me."

He releases his breath. "If that is what you need."

"Yes, more than anything. I need you to be far away from me. The less you know, the better you will be."

"The less I know?"

"Yes, we both know I lied. But you must pretend like you know nothing more than what I've told you."

"Joey, are you going to be okay? This is a little scary."

"I will be...promise. Let's just say, I have an insurance policy on me getting out of this mess." She drops his hand and rolls back onto her side.

Colin slowly rises from his seat, and with hesitation, he walks toward the end of her bed.

There has remained a burning question in his mind over the past few days. He can't shake it and needs to know once and for all. "Joey, why was the dean of students in *your* room?"

Her voice cracks when she replies, "Please, don't ask me that."

"Why?"

"You don't want to get involved with her. Trust me." He notes the rigidness of her tone and realizes quickly that he will not get the answer he is searching for. "Now, please, go back to your life. Get out of this situation while you can." She motions for him to leave.

He drops his head and shuffles toward the door.

As he reaches for the handle, he hears her say, "Colin?"

He eagerly turns. "Yes?"

She picks her head up to get a better look at him. She can't mask the sadness as she whispers, "I'm going to be leaving school when I'm discharged. Please don't tell anyone. But I wanted you to know in case it's a while before we see each other again."

"Will you come back?" he asks.

She faintly smiles. He waits for an answer, but instead, with heavy eyes, she rests her head back on her pillow and mouths, *Good-bye, Colin.*

He tips his head and observes her. Then, with an indescribable feeling wrenching in his gut, he leaves Joey, and he wonders if it is for the last time.

Thirty-Eight

FACING HER FEARS

Laura can feel her pulse react when the bailiff enters the room and stands before the packed courtroom.

"Please rise. The Court of the Second Judicial Circuit, Criminal Division. The people of New York versus Jeremy Gordon is now in session, the Honorable Judge O'Connor presiding."

With shaking knees, Laura promptly stands along with the others and waits as the judge walks up the stairs to his seat. He scrutinizes the crowd before he sits down.

"You may be seated," he replies in an authoritative tone.

It sends a chill down Laura's spine.

He wastes no time at all. "Counselor, your first witness?"

"Yes, the state would like to call Aubrey Van Tousen to the stand."

The back door opens, and Bree comes waltzing through the courtroom. Her tall frame, while slightly hunched, is more determined than Laura expected she would be. Although, in all honesty, Laura has no idea what anyone in this situation would be like. She watches out of the corner of her eye as Bree's mother, father, and brother clutch one another as she passes down the hallway, through the wood gate, and toward the stand.

The bailiff says, "Please raise your right hand. Do you solemnly swear to tell the whole truth and nothing but the truth, so help you God?"

"I do," she says.

"You may be seated."

The counsel for the state, Claire Marion, stands and buttons her suit coat. She clears her throat and then begins, "Ms. Van Tousen, are you a student at Onondaga State University in Syracuse, New York?"

"Yes."

"When did you enroll in the school?"

"The spring of my senior year in high school, 1995. I was a freshman at Onondaga State University in August 1995." Her voice quivers as she mentions her freshman year.

"Where were you the night of August 31, 1995?"

"I went to a party on North Adams Street."

Laura listens intently as Bree answers the questions as though they were traveling back in time, hour by hour, all leading up to the moment that changed Bree's life forever. Although she appears poised, Laura notices she is vehemently rubbing the symbol on her necklace. As though she is rubbing it for good luck.

"Your new acquaintance went to get a drink. You remained upstairs. But you weren't alone for long, correct?"

"No."

"Whom did you meet next?"

Bree dabs the corner of her beautiful brown eyes with the tissue she has been clutching tightly. "A guy struck up a conversation with me when he sat next to me on the couch."

"Did he introduce himself?"

"I never got his name. The conversation was casual, and I was really not interested in talking to him."

Laura quietly smiles at Bree's jab at him. *Good for you. Let him know you weren't interested. Get in all the punches while you can. This is your time, Bree.*

"Did he say anything about himself?"

"What I remember is, he said he lived in Troy, New York, and was a lacrosse player at OSU. He asked me what dorm I lived in. Said he had a girlfriend who lived in Willis and was a biology major."

Amazing. Sounds exactly like Abigail's description of her night. This guy had the whole school and the students figured out. How horribly calculated he was.

"And what dorm do you live in?"

She chokes, "Willis."

The prosecutor pauses for effect, and Laura can tell it is working. The expression on the jurors' faces is sympathetic at a minimum.

"Then, what happened?"

"I didn't want to be there anymore. I excused myself and went down to try to find the girl I had gone to the party with. When I couldn't locate her, I decided to leave."

"You didn't tell anyone you were leaving?"

"No, I didn't know anyone to tell."

"You didn't tell Missy, the girl you had come with, or any other person you might have met or—"

"Objection!" the defense lawyer boasts. "It is clear she did not tell anyone."

"Your Honor, I'm trying to establish that the defendant knowingly stalked Ms. Van Tousen."

"Approach the bench."

Through hushed voices, the lawyers argue. From where Laura sits, she can vaguely hear them.

"Your Honor, I'm trying to establish the timeline here. The defendant had to have stalked her in order to determine when to leave to get her alone outside."

"Let's get to the point on this line of questioning," he says. "I'll allow it."

Laura can recollect about a hundred law shows she has watched on television, but being here, watching this unfold, is surreal. They both move away from the bench. You can almost smell their distaste for one another

"Ms. Van Tousen, as I was asking you before, you did not tell anyone that you were leaving the party?"

"Correct."

"How long did you look for Missy?"

"About twenty minutes."

"In the time you were at the party, how much alcohol did you consume?"

"I had one drink. Punch. I think there was vodka in it."

"Have you consumed alcohol prior in your life?"

"Socially. I'm not a heavy drinker compared to maybe other college students, I suppose."

"From the time you left the defendant to you exiting the basement door of the party, approximately twenty minutes passed? And in the entire few hours you were there, you consumed one drink?"

"Yes."

"And then what happened?"

With a shaking hand, she raises the tissue again to her eye and dabs the tear off her cheek. It takes all of Laura's will not to burst out crying—or worse, leap across the benches and strangle the defendant herself.

"I heard someone call, 'Hey, Hamptons.'"

"Hamptons?"

Laura watches the coward whisper something in his lawyer's ear, as though he had any defense at all.

"Yes, I told him where I was from after he said he was also from New York."

"This made you turn around?"

"Yes, I could tell someone was calling after me."

The prosecutor, with sympathetic precision, requests Bree to recount in full detail the events that happened to her after she turned and saw the defendant, Jeremy Gordon, approach her.

No doubt rehearsed but needing to remove all emotions to get through the horrendous details in front of a room full of mostly strangers, she narrates her story. Laura's heart feels on the verge of bursting as she watches her friend push the final sentence out of her.

"And then I ran toward my dorm."

"When you ran toward campus, you didn't make it straight home. Is this correct?"

"Correct. I ran through the back roads and behind the Student Union."

"What happened next?"

"I ran into a person and spilled his coffee all over him."

"Did you know this person?"

"No, and I was terribly frightened. I tried to get away from him."

"How?"

"He asked me numerous times if I was okay, and by the expression he had on his face, I knew I appeared as though I needed assistance."

"How did you know he could help?"

"He told me he was a police officer."

"You ran right into a police officer as you were running back to your dorm?"

"Yes."

"But he was not able to help you. Why?"

"I was confused, scared, beat up—mentally and physically—and wanted to go somewhere safe."

"Somewhere safe?"

"Yes, where I could lock the door."

"And you assumed your safest place was on campus, back in your dorm room, where you could lock your door?"

Little did she know, Laura thinks. *She wasn't going to be protected at all back at school. She was running straight into the lioness's den.*

"Objection, Your Honor."

"Is there a point here?" Judge O'Connor asks.

"Your Honor, I'd like to enter in Exhibit C1." The prosecutor opens her file and pulls out some papers. She approaches the bench with them and hands them to Judge O'Connor.

Laura notes the judge scowls as he reads the pages.

"I'll allow it," he says with a slight shake of his head.

The prosecutor hands the defense lawyer a copy. "What is this, Your Honor?" he wails.

"Your Honor, I am trying to establish a timeline of events here, and these documents clearly corroborate and develop an accurate picture of the happenings that evening and up until the defendant was apprehended by police."

"You are walking a fine line here, Counselor," he scolds. "But I will allow these into evidence."

The defense lawyer sits and shakes his head as he scours through the documents again.

She hands the paper to Bree. "Ms. Van Tousen, can you tell me what these papers are?"

Bree's eyes dance over the papers that were handed to her by the lawyer. Her voice trembles as she says, "Yes, these emails were put under my door the other day."

"Can you clarify what you mean by, put under your door?"

"Yes, I went to take a shower, and when I came back, there was an envelope in my room. I assume they were slid under my door."

"Do you know who put them in your room?"

"No, I do not."

"For the court, can you please read the highlighted sentences?"

Bree slightly raises the paper, and with a sickened tone in her voice, she begins reading.

> *"Dear Dean Barrymore,*
>
> *"It has been brought to my attention that one of my officers came upon a student on your campus on the evening of August 31. The officer and I both strongly feel that this woman encountered someone who severely mistreated her and was, at the time, running away from that person. Her injuries were consistent, from what my officer could perceive, with a sexual assault. I would like to discuss the best means in which we can tighten security and alert the students on campus.*
>
> *"Thank you,*
>
> *"Captain Frankel."*

Laura gasps. She feels a spine-tingling sensation wash over her.

"Does that sound at all familiar to you?" the lawyer asks.

"Yes."

"Thank you, Ms. Van Tousen. Can you continue to read the next highlighted section, please?"

Bree clears her throat.

> *"Dear Captain Frankel.*
>
> *"My sources tell me that no complaints have been filed with campus security. Can you confirm this is an open investigation and that you have a report on file from this student? We typically receive numerous*

false claims the first week of school. These young kids are finding their way, I presume.

"Dean Barrymore"

Laura can feel the hair on her neck stand at attention as Bree reads word for word the emails that were given to Laura months ago. She feels her body heat rise and a churning sensation in her stomach. She watches Bree as she, for the first time with her eyes, acknowledges Laura is in the room.

What is happening? Is Bree really reading these emails out loud in front of a courtroom full of people, on the record? What is going to happen to all of us once they know we were involved in this?

Laura's instinct tells her to run, run far away, and distance herself from this before they get in trouble. She frantically searches the courtroom for Travis but can't find him in the crowd.

Travis will know what to do, won't he?

"Can you tell me who the person in the email from Captain Frankel was referring to?"

Bree chokes out, "It was me."

A slight murmur fills the courtroom, and the judge bangs his gavel. "Quiet in my courtroom."

"Are you certain?"

"It was August 31. I ran right into Officer Murphy near the Union, and I did not report the assault until after the defendant was caught. Officer Murphy came to my dorm room and implored me to file a complaint. He said that he couldn't stop thinking about me *and* that night."

"He came directly to you to file a complaint? Why do you think that is so?"

"Objection. Leading the witness," the defense lawyer says.

"I'll allow it," the judge says. "Please continue, Ms. Van Tousen."

"After that night, he tried to find me before in my dorm to talk about campus safety and if I knew how to report a crime. He said he was going around to all the students, but I was wise to him. I knew by the sadness in his eyes that he was trying to help me."

"According to these documents, he did in fact try to help you."

"Yes, he is a very kind man."

Laura's heart sinks as she recounts her radio interview with him and how she attacked his character. She hates that she did that to him. But, in her mind, she was trying to show her listeners that somebody should have tried harder to help, whether that was the police or the school. Not enough was done, but she let her feelings about Bree's and Abigail's situations get the best of her. She knows that now.

"What happened to you after that evening?"

"I left school."

"You left school?"

"Yes, I went away because I was scared and felt unsafe."

"Did you miss your first day of school?"

Bree begins to cry. "Yes, I did. I didn't want anyone to see my face."

"Your Honor, please note Exhibit C2. These photos were taken by Dr. Tamburino, a plastic surgeon in the area. The date of the photos is September 1, 1995. The day after the alleged attack." The lawyer places one of the photos in an easel at the front of the courtroom for the jury to observe.

Laura, now completely sick to her stomach, can't take her eyes off the picture of her friend's swollen face and terrified eyes that are on display. Tears roll down her face. She dabs the corner of her eyes with a tissue.

"Ms. Van Tousen, you mentioned earlier that you ran away from Officer Murphy because you wanted to be somewhere safe. Your dorm room, where you could lock it, yet the next day, you left. What made you return?"

"I had to. I had to get back to school. It was my dream to attend OSU, and a part of me could not let him win. I returned, but I never felt safe."

"How did you cope?"

"Objection. What does this line of questioning have to do with the case?"

"Your Honor, again, I am trying to establish a timeline."

"Please get to the point, Counselor."

"Thank you, Your Honor. Ms. Van Tousen, how did you cope?"

"I got an internship in the marketing department and poured much of my time and energy into that."

"This is a coveted internship, correct?"

"Yes, I beat over forty people for the position."

"Well done. But this caused some issues for you, no?"

"Yes, I had a relationship with someone at the school, and it became an issue for another student."

"Was Dean Barrymore aware of this?"

"Yes."

"And what was the outcome?"

"I repeated the class even though I'd gotten an A. After my punishment, the dean requested my assistance on a task force on campus safety."

"Campus safety? When was this?"

"This September."

"September? The alleged perpetrator was caught in February, and the dean started a campus security task force seven months later. Can you read the second highlighted document? And can you note the date at the top?"

"Yes, it is August 28, 1995."

"Three days before your attack?"

"Yes."

"Please continue."

Through tired eyes, Bree reads the email.

"Dear Dean Barrymore,

"As you have been made aware, Oswego has had a series of complaints brought to both local and campus police regarding an influx of attacks on women. We have to date verified ten complaints. The attacks seem to have escalated in intensity, and unfortunately, one woman has been hospitalized for her injuries."

Bree's lips quiver when she reads this, and mist forms in her eyes. She continues:

"I am writing my fellow deans to make sure your campus is aware and, more importantly, to ensure your students are safe this year.

"Kind regards,

"Dean Finley"

"Please let the record show that the email is from Dean Finley at Oswego. Please continue."

Bree flips the page and reads:

"Key items to look for and to make the students aware of: male; approximately five-nine to five-eleven; spiked, dark hair; uses multiple aliases; claims to be an athlete; gets to know the university and the names of professors and the classes they teach; believe he is a native to New York, region unknown."

"Let the court show that the defendant fits the exact description according to the women who filed reports and have testified earlier."

"Objection, Your Honor. The description is vague at best and describes almost every male college student in the tri-state area."

"Overruled."

"Can you read the response, please?"

Lying in Wait

"Dear Dean Finley,

"We here at Onondaga State are sincerely sorry to hear of your campus troubles. We do in turn appreciate your concern of OSU. With that said, my counsel and I have decided that our campus is safe, and we have no issues reported to date. We are choosing to sit tight on this information until we need to arm our students with the material you shared.

"We would like to offer our guidance and expertise in security should you desire.

"Best of luck this year

"Sincerely,

"Dean Barrymore"

"Guidance and expertise in security. Interesting. Only seven months later would they form a task force on campus security. Why is that?"

"She found out about my attack through the incident with my internship. I was reprimanded for my indiscretion, but it has come to my attention that she targeted me with a lighter reprimand, so she could later use me to campaign for her task force. She's never wanted to help us. She doesn't want everyone to find out that she knew all along and had the opportunity to stop it but didn't. She ignored the warnings, and many women have paid the price for it."

"That is a serious accusation, Ms. Van Tousen," the judge warns.

"I understand that, Your Honor, but these documents were sent to me for a reason, and I can't sit idly by and simply ignore them." She glances over at her mother and father. "We believe we are enrolled in a school that will, at a minimum, make their students' safety a top priority. But the dean ignored it. I can't help but believe that it was *he* who felt safe enough to come and go on campus as he pleased."

The courtroom guests mumble a response, causing the judge to bang his gavel again. "Silence."

"Ms. Van Tousen, I have one more question for you today. Do you recognize the man in this courtroom who attacked you on the evening of August 31, 1995?"

One tear drops on her pinked cheek. "Yes."

"Could you point him out for the court?"

With a slight squaring of her shoulders, Bree turns and points directly at Jeremy Gordon.

"Let the court acknowledge that Ms. Van Tousen pointed out the defendant, Jeremy Gordon."

Thirty-Nine

MORE THAN FRIENDS

Laura rises along with Bree's family and exits out of the uncomfortable booth she has spent the past several hours sitting in like a statue. Outside the courthouse, Bree is waiting inside a black Range Rover with tinted windows, parked near the back entrance of the courthouse. There is a gentleman of rather significant size standing guard in front of the vehicle.

Once we get closer, he opens the back door, and Bree gingerly slides out of the back seat. While her exterior is in stunning condition, her eyes tell Laura her interior is suffering. One look at each other, and they're immediately embracing, like long-lost sisters. Sobbing words are exchanged that only they can understand. Finally, they depart.

Bree, holding tightly on to Laura's hand, whispers, "Thank you for giving me those papers. You completely changed my perspective on the whole thing, and I needed to see this all through a new lens."

Laura, completely dumbfounded and too caught up in their reunion, gazes upon her and then goes in again for another deep hug. A hug that not only does Bree need, but that Laura also desperately needs from her.

"Aubrey, darling, we do need to go and finish up some things with the lawyers," her mother kindly interjects.

Laura releases her hug and looks at her friend. "I'll see you back in the dorm, okay?"

Bree smiles and replies, "Of course. My family and I are having dinner at Adam's later. Tell the others I'm okay, will you?"

"I will."

Laura gives Bree's parents and brother hugs and then stands and watches as the dark Rover pulls out of the lot and onto the road. She turns toward the guest parking lot. She isn't the least bit surprised to find Travis leaning up against the door of his Honda, waiting, no doubt, for her.

She stands before him. His arms are folded over his chest, and he is brimming with confidence. She steps closer. She waits for him to speak first, but she knows he won't. It's not his style at all.

"What made you decide to do it?" she asks.

He, trying his hardest not to, cracks a smile. "Who says it was me?"

She, too, returns a well-deserved smile. "I'm not easily impressed, you know."

"I know."

"What's the deal anyway? Is Wolfie on some kind of payroll of yours that I don't know about? I mean, this guy—"

"Is the best guy to know."

"There is nothing he won't do for you."

"Yeah, and he's damn good at it, too."

"Obviously. He got in and out of the dorm in what, under ten minutes?"

"Seven."

"No shit." Laura laughs.

Travis nods his head.

"It can't be traced back to you?"

"Can never be sure of that. But whoever has been feeding me information will at some point be the one to save us all. I have this feeling I can't shake."

"Is that why you did it? Made sure she had all of that?"

He pauses for only a second before replying, "No, I did it for you."

"For me?"

"Yes, you. Your friends need this to come to an end. I knew I had to help you more. The way I look at it, there are two people who need to go. Jeremy Gordon and Dean Barrymore. Only then can this campus get back to how I remember it."

She sighs with a full heart. "Thank you, Travis. You stuck your neck out for a lot of people, and they don't even know it. And, for that reason alone, I..."

"What?" he asks with a hushed voice.

She blushes slightly and then says, "It's just one of the reasons that I feel..." She hesitates. "Don't kill me for saying this."

"I won't."

She steps even closer and takes his hand, looking him square in the eyes. "I feel so privileged to be your friend. And I know we've never talked about our relationship, but you're a good friend. My good friend. You were my first." She pauses, placing her hand over her heart. "And no one ever forgets their first. You'll always be very special to me."

His smile is infectious. And she knows in that moment that she said what he wanted to hear. But, more importantly, she wanted to say it.

"You're special to me, too. Always know that." Like nothing has changed, he reaches forward and tucks a strand of hair behind her ear. "I've always loved doing that," he adds.

She dips her head and smiles.

He gently touches her cheek. "You did good, Laura Chase, really good. Now, go kill it on your show tomorrow. Have no mercy."

"You've taught me well, and it's the least I can do for you, considering what you've done for me."

Travis opens his mouth to say something, but nothing comes out. He wants to ask her to come home with him, spend one last night together, but he knows he can't put that on her. If Wolfie said she's moved on, then she has.

Sensing his demeanor shift, she changes the subject by asking, "I thought you'd be riding your motorcycle."

He pulls out a cigarette and lights it. "She's not ready, but when she is, then *adios*. I'll be on the open road, free and enjoying the ride."

"She?"

"Yeah, she's got a name."

"What is it?"

"I'll tell you when she is ready. How does that sound?"

Laura laughs. "Fair enough."

"You need a lift back to campus?"

"No, I've got a ride "

Travis doesn't bother to ask because he simply does not want to know. He pulls open his car door, and before climbing in, he says, "Bree was brilliant today. It was a good day."

"Yeah, she was." As he starts to close his door, she adds, "And so were you." But what she wants to say is, *You were better than good, Travis. You were magnificent.*

Through the glass window, she can make out his smile.

Colin is waiting by his Jeep toward the front of the courthouse. He gives Laura a warm and much-needed hug. "How did it go?" he whispers.

"As good as it could."

"Good. I'm sure you're anxious to get out of here."

"Definitely," Laura says as she climbs into his car.

He closes the door for her and then goes around the front of his Jeep and climbs in. He pulls out of the lot. "I've got an idea," he says.

"Really?"

"Yeah. It's what you need right now."

He drives past the campus and about fifteen minutes down the road. He pulls his Jeep off to the side of the road. "Come on," he says.

She opens her door and follows him down a slight path. She can hear the rushing of water as they get closer to the clearing.

"Ever been to Livermore Falls?" he asks.

Her eyes grow wide as she takes in the water lapping over the rocks. Colin takes her hand and leads her down to a large boulder right on the edge of the water. He pulls her down with him, cradling her in his arms.

"This is majestic."

He responds by pulling her in tighter and giving her a squeeze. She closes her eyes and breathes in deeply. Moments of silence pass by them like the running river below their feet. Laura is relaxed for the first time in what feels like a very long time. But, with unfinished business lurking around her, her mind begins to pull toward the darkness.

She sighs. "Did you hear what happened today?"

In a low, husky voice, he replies, "I wasn't going to bring it up, but there was quite the buzz circulating by the media and the groups out front."

"I have a confession to make." She unlocks herself from his grasp and turns slightly to face him.

His expression turns from contentment to concern. "Okay, what is it?"

Laura pulls in a deep breath and then releases it. "I've known about all of this—the emails, the dean's involvement, the attempt by the police to help..."

"For how long?"

"A while."

"Jesus, Laura," he says with pure sympathy.

"I read all those emails. They even had a description of him, and it was exact. I knew all about what the school had known last year." A tear falls on her cheek.

"They had a description of him?"

"Yes, his modus operandi was eerily exact. To know that my own school would be that careless with the lives of their students is beyond my comprehension."

"Mine, too. I wish I had known, so I could have helped more."

"Believe me, I wish that, too. But those were some of the secrets I had to keep, and now, you know why."

"Yeah, getting secured emails is a big deal. Whoever copied those could get in serious trouble."

"Exactly, and thankfully, I had nothing to do with that. But there is someone out there who really wants the dean to pay for her incompetence."

"From what I heard today, she should."

"Yeah, reporting on all of this has been crazy. It's kept me up many nights, wondering if I was doing the right thing or getting in too deep."

"I think we are all in pretty deep at this point. Speaking of, you ready for your show tomorrow?"

She channels Travis and the fact that he put his neck on the line for many people. "Yes, I am. I'm going to show no mercy."

"That's my girl," he says with a slight grin.

"Too many people were hurt under her, and she needs to know the students on this campus will not stand for it any longer."

Colin has a sinking feeling in the pit of his stomach that he can't get rid of. He remembers the dean standing over Joey's bed, the cool tone of her voice, and the scared, childlike behavior Joey exhibited.

With a sudden sense of urgency, Colin replies, "There is something I need to do. Can I take you home?" He rises from the rock and extends his hand to her.

Concerned, she takes it and allows him to pull her up. "Of course. You okay?"

"Yeah, I am. Promise." He draws her in and deeply kisses her as she wraps her arms around his waist. He releases her, glancing at his watch while he does. "Come on." He takes her hand and guides her back through the trail and to his Jeep.

Laura watches out of the corner of her eye as he drives, glaring straight ahead at the road with a furrowed brow. Deep in thought.

Something is going on with him, but I respect him enough not to ask. I, more than anyone, know what it feels like to just need to take care of something. And, by the determined look on his face and the silence in the car, he's on a mission to solve a problem.

Forty

LAST KISS

Colin drops Laura off in the front of her dorm. "I'll call you," he says.

She leans over, kisses him on the cheek, and climbs out of his Jeep. "Bye," she says with a slight wave of her hand. She pushes the door shut and watches as he drives down the road.

His heart is beating faster and faster as he finally pulls into the parking lot. With a sense of urgency pulsing through his veins, he jumps out of his Jeep and hurries toward the main entrance of the hospital. He passes the nurses' station, having been here plenty of times in the past week. His heart sinks when he gets to Joey's room, and the bed is empty, remade and tidy for the next patient. He rushes back to the nurses' station.

Merely out of breath, he asks, "When was Joey discharged?"

The nurse, familiar with Colin, replies, "She left about ten minutes ago."

Before she can even finish saying another word, he is running at full speed back down the hallway and toward the lobby. His pulse quickens as his eye catches a young woman up ahead. He dodges in and out of a few people in the hopes of catching her. She is steadying herself on the door of the car as she tries to slowly climb into the back seat.

"Joey! Joey!" Colin yells. The sliding door eases open as another person passes through them. He yells again, "Joey, wait!"

Startled, she looks up. Colin runs through the sliding doors and right toward her car. She steps back onto the curb.

With a heavy breath, he says, "I'm glad I caught you. I need to talk to you!"

He takes in the girl before him. Once sexy and beautiful, she now looks pale, thin, and somewhat broken.

Concerned, she replies, "Colin, are you all right?"

Her mother opens the car door. "Is everything okay?"

"Yes, Mom, give me a minute." She closes her car door, as does her mother.

Colin steps away from her car. Joey cautiously follows.

"Colin, I thought I told you not to come here."

"I need to ask you something, and I need you to be one hundred percent honest with me."

She pauses, knowing full well she has told her fair share of lies to Colin. She sighs deeply as she takes in his eager eyes. "I suppose I can do that."

"Good." He fidgets with his hands, knowing the subject matter in itself is personal and cuts deeply. "Why did Dean Barrymore visit you in the hospital last week?"

Joey's eyes immediately fill with tears.

Colin steps closer and takes her hand in his. "You can trust me. You know that, Joey."

"I know I can," she whispers. "It's just that…I'm scared."

"But, if you tell the truth, you will no longer need to be scared. I believe that."

"She'll come after me."

"No, she won't. She won't have that option."

A tear drops on Joey's cheek as she replays the memory of that day and how that one meeting changed everything. Finally, she speaks, "She knew you and I dated and that Laura was starting to make waves on the radio. I received a message that she wanted to speak with me…"

"The dean will see you now," her assistant, Ms. Stone, announced.

Joey rose from the leather couch across the dean's door and stepped forward. Her nerves, not easily shaken, are toying with her as she entered. The dean stood before the window, peering out at the campus below.

"Have a seat," she bellowed.

Joey does as she was told.

"I've been watching your academics, and I must say, this past year has not been the best for you," she stated.

"I know. I've taken some harder classes, and…well, I've had some personal issues to contend with as well."

"What does school have to do with your personal life?" she asked.

Joey swallowed hard. "It's just—"

The dean turned. She interrupted when she said, "You seem like a very confident and independent young lady. Is that not whom I'm speaking with now?"

Feeling challenged, Joey said, "No, that is who I am."

"Good." She stepped closer to Joey. Her icy stare was dramatic. "I need your help with a campus matter, and I know you have connections to the radio station. This is an

important assignment, one that could only be trusted to the likes of someone resembling you." The coolness in her voice sent a shiver down Joey's spine. "This is a paid job. If you take the money, you are acknowledging that you are responsible for your part. Understood?"

"Yes, Dean Barrymore."

"Good." She sat in her chair and began what would be one of the worst decisions Joey has ever made.

"She told me that the police weren't doing anything to stop the wave of panic captivating our campus and that, in order for them to start to pay attention to her repeated attempts for assistance…"

"What did she ask you to do, Joey?"

Colin has known for quite some time that Joey was lying. But what he could never quite put his finger on was why someone would ask her to do it. When he saw the dean in her hospital room, he finally put the two together. Unfortunately, with her cry for help and the state she was in, he could never get himself to push her to tell him. And now? He simply needs to hear her say it in order to put this behind him.

"In exchange for a five-thousand-dollar stipend, she asked me to fake an attack and to make sure you, Laura, and everyone else at the station would know about it." She hangs her head in disgust.

"Jesus," Colin whispers.

"I know, and I am ashamed I took it, but at the time, she made me believe I would be helping the school, not hurting it. She was so convincing that she had tried to get the police to pay attention, but without hard evidence, she said they were doing little to nothing to help."

"And she knew, if you came running into the radio station, it would have to be news."

"Yes…and she promised me no one would get hurt." Colin goes to speak, but she cuts him off, "I know what I did to you, Laura, all the guys at the station, and my friends was really fucked up. And, once I saw the impact it had on real victims, I couldn't go on. I didn't want to…"

"Oh, Joey."

"I am sorry. More than you'll ever know."

"When she came to you, what did she say?"

"She first scolded me, threatened to expel me for not keeping my shit together. She didn't want me to report my so-called crime to the police because that would have legal consequences. Within minutes of her being in my room, she changed her mind and told me that my demise might actually help the school. That, somehow, my cry for help would show everyone that the police were useless. She was going to prop me up and tell everyone she begged the police for assistance, and they were too busy investigating other schools to pay attention to OSU. That's when I knew I needed to leave this school. I can't be a part of this. I need to get my life together. Her being so easily able to influence me made me realize a lot of things about myself that I don't love. I did a terrible thing to try to get you back."

He steps in and gently places his arms around her, tightly hugging her. His heart is heavy with concern, disgust, and sheer sadness. "Listen, I will do all I can for you, I promise you."

Still holding him, she says, "As long as I don't ever need to come back, do what you need to do, Colin."

"I will, Joey."

They release their embrace and step apart from one another.

"Can I ask you for one favor?" Colin requests.

"Of course. I owe you."

Colin, thinking on his feet, asks her for one final parting gift. She agrees. Then, with her head hanging low, Colin watches her go back toward her waiting car. She climbs in, and as the car rolls past him standing on the curb, she blows him one last parting kiss.

Forty-One

THE WORD IS OUT

Laura enters the station and immediately heads to Tucker's office. She knocks on the half-opened door. Tucker picks up his head, and with wide eyes, he smiles at Laura.

"Close the door," he says.

She does and sits across from him.

"You have been up to quite a bit, now haven't you?"

She doesn't know how to take his question; therefore, she simply responds, "Yes, I have."

"It has most definitely stirred the pot around here."

"I can imagine. But I'm not sorry," she adds with a slight smile.

He smiles in return. "Nor should you be. And all I ask of you today is that you report the facts, and if a caller gets too out of line, I have instructed Patrick to immediately cut them off. You can say you're having issues with the lines or what have you, but we can't create more chaos."

Laura slides back in her seat, nervous for the first time since day one of her show. She watches Tucker's expression turn stern and knows he means business. "I will."

"Have a great show, and all we can do is hope for the best."

Laura enters Studio B and begins her ritual of adjusting, moving, and getting set up for her show. Patrick enters the glass booth before her and waves slightly. He then enters the room, which he rarely does.

"Hey. What's up?" she asks.

"Wanted to get a pulse check on you and see if you're okay."

"I'm a little nervous."

He grimaces. "This won't help then." He points to the closed blinds facing the Student Union.

"What?"

"Maybe you should look."

Laura, with a shaking hand, reaches over to the string on the blinds and slowly pulls them open. She tries to shield her reaction, but it's too jarring for her to mask. The Union is filled with hundreds of students standing before the studio, as though they were about to see a concert. When they catch a glimpse of Laura, the Union erupts with loud hollers, cheers, clapping, and fist-pumping in the air.

"We're live in two," Patrick reminds her.

She stands before the glass in disbelief. "What is all of this?" she asks as she turns to face him.

He rarely smiles, but this time, he does when he says, "It's you, Laura. They need to hear from you."

She sits down in her chair, leaving the blinds wide open. She places her headphones on her ears, and with a countdown from Patrick, the On Air light illuminates.

"Good afternoon, Hawks. This is Laura Chase, bringing you our campus and community news. I'd say by the gathering of students outside my window in the Union that buzz surrounding this past week's trial has gotten many of you concerned as to what exactly is going on. Please call me up."

She notes every single line is lit. She presses the first button.

"I'll take the first caller. Hello, caller, you are on the air."

"Hey, Laura. Do you think they'll find this guy guilty or what?"

"I'm not on the jury, but I'd say, with the amount of evidence stacked up against him, the chances are good. I'm hopeful. And I believe those close to the trial are hopeful, too. Next caller."

"We owe Tank McPherson a huge debt of gratitude for being there that night and risking his career by getting into a fight with the guy. He could have gotten hurt, and who the hell knows where the Hawks football team would have ended up? From the sounds of it, this guy was cruel and would stop at nothing to hurt someone."

"I could not agree with you more. I hope Coach Bromley is listening. Tank deserves some kind of recognition from the program for his efforts in hopefully sending this guy to jail for a very long time. Thanks for the call. Next caller."

"I heard a rumor that, yesterday, at the trial, some documents were leaked about the university's involvement in hiding some of the events that happened. Is that true?"

Laura watches as the mass of students outside the window lean in closer, awaiting her response. She glances at Patrick. He gives her a questionable shoulder shrug.

Feeling a heightened sense of anger roll through her as she considers Abigail and Bree, Laura does little to mask her feelings. "I heard something similar."

"You did?"

"Yes. In fact, I was in the courtroom when the papers were admitted into evidence."

"You were? What did they say?"

"For the sake of the integrity of the trial, I will hold off on talking about the papers until we know more about them. But I will say, they were compelling and quite damaging to the defense and our school, unfortunately."

Patrick signals to her that he dropped the call.

"Next caller, you are on the air."

"What I heard was that the dean ignored all the signs and did nothing to help our school be safer. How can that be?"

"Without knowing all the details, I can't be certain."

"But she didn't help us. She hurt us."

"Again, with the information so fresh to all of us, we must not jump to conclusions." Laura's anger rises as she attempts to defend the horrible dean of OSU. "We need to keep reminding ourselves about the victims and those who were truly impacted by the events of the past year. Everyone will have their day in court, and we have to let the system work for us. Next caller."

"Laura, I heard that there were going to be several lawsuits against the school for failure to protect the students. What will that mean for our reputation as an elite university if we have several lawsuits pending against us?"

"Thank you for calling. But, first, to my knowledge, there have been no suits filed. This is the first I'm hearing of it."

"But there could be. Wouldn't you sue the school?"

"I can't put myself in the victim's shoes. I don't think that would be fair to them. And, about your second point, the integrity of this school can only be measured by the success of the students and those who contribute to society once they leave here. Nothing that happens within the administration can take away the value of the degree we will someday hold in our hands."

With each additional caller asking similar questions pertaining to the trial and the administration, Laura feels the energy drain her weary soul. During a quick station break, Laura gulps a cool glass of water, trying to loosen her tightening throat.

"You okay?" Patrick asks.

"Yeah. This is exhausting."

"Only ten more minutes, and you're done."

She glances outside the window. The crowd has grown since her last glance.

"How am I going to get out of here?" she asks, not expecting an answer.

"Your guess is as good as mine."

With a quick countdown, they are back on the air.

"We are back. I'd like to take the last few minutes, if I may, to remind all of you listening today that we still must remain diligent about our surroundings. We are not free of danger, nor will we ever be. I'd be remiss not to mention that there are numerous free services provided to us on campus to help talk about the issues or things that might or might not have happened to us or to someone we care about. When the trial is over, the pain will remain for many of those impacted by the crimes. I thank each and every one of you for your continued support. I'm going to take one last caller before I end my segment."

Laura inhales a deep breath. "Next caller."

"Laura," a deep male voice bellows, "those people gathered outside the studio are expecting you to be the voice for us. How are you not more outraged?"

"Outraged?"

"You said yourself, you were in the courtroom. You know for a fact that those documents clearly stated that the police warned our university of attacks on numerous campuses across the state, and they did nothing to help us."

Laura's face burns with heat. She glances at Patrick, and he frantically tries to disconnect the call.

"They even went so far as to describe the attacker, almost to a point where he should have been caught far sooner than he did!" The caller's voice is filled with anger.

Laura, speechless for the first time, sits in her chair, unable to move, as the crowd outside the studio becomes rowdy and begins chanting words she cannot herself hear through the window.

Then, in a deep, almost disguised voice, the caller says, "The dean knew, and she did nothing." Then, the line goes dead.

Patrick signals Laura to end.

With a rushed and ill-planned exit, Laura simply says, "This is Laura Chase. Until next time, Hawks." She switches off her microphone and pulls the headphones off her head.

Tucker comes into the studio. He goes over to the blinds and closes them. "Why don't you stay put for a bit? Until this all dies down."

"I swear, Tucker, I wasn't trying to stir anything, I, Patrick—we did all we could to keep it on track."

"You did fine, Laura. They are simply looking for answers."

Lying in Wait

Laura leans over the board, and runs her fingers through her hair, resting her hands on the back of her neck. With eyes closed, she can feel the pulsating chant of the students right outside the glass separating them.

This campus needs answers! Once and for all.

Forty-Two

JOINING FORCES

Colin knocks with trepidation on the door. It's late. He steps back and waits a few moments. He hears the footsteps from behind the door draw near. The door cracks open.

Clearly surprised, Travis says, "Hey. Wasn't expecting you."

"I wasn't expecting to be here," Colin replies.

"Come in." Travis motions through the entryway as he pulls the door open.

Colin steps in and finds himself in the living room.

"Have a seat."

He sits on the couch.

Travis takes the recliner across from him. "How can I help?"

"Let me start by saying, I don't want to be any more involved in all of this than I already am. But I didn't know where else to go. I know Laura trusts you, and…well, that's good enough for me."

"Okay."

"You don't have to divulge any more information to me. I've put most of it together on my own, but I have something you might be able to use."

"I see."

"I know you, or someone close to you, gave Bree those emails. Laura would never do that, for fear it would come back and hurt you. That I get. It's who she is."

Travis nods his head, although it pains him to hear Colin speak of her in the context of how well they know one another.

Colin pulls out a piece of paper from his pocket. He takes a deep breath and then slowly releases it. "I don't know what Laura has told you, but I dated a girl, Joey, and she and I had a falling out. However, in April last year, Joey claimed that she was attacked on campus. This threw many of us—"

Before Colin can continue, Travis raises his hand. "I know all about it. You do remember my job is to investigate any and all leads I might hear about?"

Colin, feeling slightly stupid, replies, "Of course. But, regardless, her lack of facts about that event made me question a lot of things, and it pulled me in a direction that hurt people. But that is neither here nor there and solely my burden to bear."

Travis leans back in his chair.

Colin continues with a marked sadness in his voice, "This piece of paper is proof that Dean Barrymore paid Joey five thousand dollars to fake the story of her attack."

Travis leans forward. "Really?"

"Yes, she told me herself. She didn't expect people to start digging into her claim, and when she couldn't prove anything and I started to question her and pull away, she ultimately became unglued and started down a path of serious self-hatred. The dean got word of her attempted suicide and threatened her in the hospital. She said she would expel her and ruin any chances she had of attending another school if she didn't continue to cooperate."

Travis feverishly rubs his face. "Jesus Christ," he mumbles.

Colin hands Travis the paper.

"What is this?"

"This is a copy of Joey's school tuition account. It states that, on the day before her alleged attack, five thousand dollars was subtracted from her tuition bill. It says work stipend, and it was signed off by the dean. There is no such thing. It is a payoff, plain and simple."

Travis reviews the document and then replies, "How can I help?"

"Joey is gone. She left school and does not plan to return. I can't involve Laura in this, and I'm certain you'd agree with that. You were the only other person I could think to go to."

Travis scans the paper. Then, he glances up at the ceiling and mumbles something to himself. "Is this your only copy?"

"Yes."

He again looks at the ceiling and says something incoherent to himself. His eyes fall back on Colin. "I'm trying to decide how to play this. The dean wants to speak to me tomorrow. I have a meeting with her at ten in the morning. If I show her all my cards, it could backfire. I need to ponder over this one. May I keep this?"

"Yes. Like I said, I want no further involvement than I already have."

Travis smiles for maybe the first time since Colin walked in his door. Colin cocks his head and gives him a quizzical glance.

"Oh, don't act innocent," Travis says in a nonthreatening manner.

"Innocent?"

"Yeah, I haven't given you enough credit."

Colin can't help but return a sly grin.

"You knew, if you called from one of the station lines, it would confuse Patrick enough and make it merely impossible for him to hang up on you."

"What gave it away?"

"The fact that only a select number of people knew the attacker's description was noted in those emails. That was only in the emails and read in court. Not a single source reported on it."

"Good catch."

Travis lends Colin his cockiest grin. Colin rises to his feet and heads toward the door.

"I can imagine Laura has mentioned that not a lot gets past me."

"No, she's never mentioned that," Colin says with a grin.

Travis pulls open the door and pats Colin on the back. "Ask her. She'll love to tell you about it."

Colin chuckles as he steps out onto the cement steps. "I'll be sure to ask her," he replies with full sarcasm.

Travis leans in the doorway. He holds up the paper given to him and simply says, "Thanks."

Colin nods and bounces down the steps and onto the street. As he walks away, he can't help but think, *There's something about that guy I like, as strange as that might be. He's arrogant, but I get the feeling he's earned it.*

Forty-Three

FACE-TO-FACE

Laura, after an hour or two, was able to leave the station without being swarmed by students. She tried on a few occasions to call Colin but was only able to leave him a message.

She opens the door to her room and finds Abigail, Alex, and Casey sitting on the floor in between the beds, studying.

"Hey, guys," Laura says with a massive yawn.

"Oh my God, we've been dying for you to get back!" Casey says.

"What happened today? We heard there was a huge mob in the Union, and everyone was chanting and yelling…"

Laura plops on her bed. "It was insane. I had to wait at the station for it to die down just so I could leave in peace. And I'm exhausted because of it."

"I can only imagine." Abigail grants her a sympathetic glance.

"You should get some rest," Casey says.

"Yeah, you've earned it, girl," Alex adds as she climbs to her feet.

"Thanks, guys. Sorry to break this up…"

"No, not at all. I'm tired myself." Casey leans in and kisses Laura on the head. "Try to sleep," she says as she and Alex leave the room.

"I hate to be the bearer of bad news, but the dean's assistant called and the dean would like to meet you tomorrow at nine."

"Oh shit. Really?"

"Yeah, kind of got the feeling from the message that it was not optional."

"Of course it's not. She plays the part of a woman who always gets what she wants." Laura moans slightly.

Abigail tilts her head and gives Laura a questioning expression. "Why do you say that?"

"Just everything that has gone on…"

Laura slips off her shoes. Too tired, she pulls back the covers on her bed and climbs in without undressing. Laura has come too far to stop now. She owes it to Abigail, Bree, Travis, Colin, Joey, Wolfie, and countless others. Particularly those who have no idea what has been going on at Onondaga State University for the past year.

"Good night."

"Night."

As she feels her body attempt to succumb to sleep, she can't help but stare at the wall with dread, as she knows that nine in the morning will be here before she knows it. And she'll be face-to-face with Dean Barrymore. The one woman she would do anything to avoid.

"Yes, I know what to do, Travis. But are you sure?"

"Yes, I'm positive. Stick to the plan. Get in and get out."

"Okay, I will."

"I'll talk to you later, all right?"

"Yes. Bye, Travis." Laura places the receiver down and grabs her bag.

She hurries across the bustling campus. She enters Speare Hall at about a quarter of nine.

"Dean Barrymore will see you now," her assistant, Joanne Stone, announces.

She gives Laura a sympathetic glance as Laura stands and straightens out her silk blouse. She nervously tucks a strand of hair behind her ear and steps forward toward the large wood doors that separate the dean from the rest of civilization. Laura turns the knob and pushes it open.

Dean Barrymore is sitting casually at her oversize wood desk, scribbling something on a piece of paper. She barely glances up at Laura as she says, "Take a seat, please."

With guarded movements, Laura lowers herself into the hard wood chair with the OSU crest chiseled into the back of it.

She peers up from her paperwork and barely grants Laura a smile. "Hello, Ms. Chase."

"Dean Barrymore."

"I have been keeping track of your career this past year at the station, and it's been interesting, to say the least."

Laura, trying to keep even ground, says, "Yes, it has. It has been an honor to be the first female DJ in over a decade. I think that says a lot about the school."

"You do now?"

"Yes, particularly these days."

"Some might beg to differ." Her eyes narrow.

Laura swallows hard. She is dying for a glass of water, something to ease her clenching throat. She keeps her eyes steady on the dean. "How, um, how can I help you, Dean?"

"Help me," she replies with a coolness that makes Laura shiver. "You seem to have a way of being one step ahead of the information on this campus. I'm curious, how is that?"

She tilts her head. She knows now is the time that she needs to play dumb. "I'm not sure what you mean."

"Your news source?"

"Oh, sorry. I misunderstood." She moves forward in her chair, feeling more confident. "As you know, I'm a math major, so this job at the station was a real leap for me. I had to find a resource I could rely on."

The dean leans in closer, intertwining her fingers. "Yes, and?"

"I believe you know this, but I work closely with *The Weekly Blue*. Professor Tucker introduced me to Ainsley Atwood. We work well together."

"Ainsley?"

"Yes, you must be familiar. An excellent writer. An award winner."

The dean's cheeks glow an unflattering shade of red. "Well, I would be remiss if I didn't say that there have been some incredibly harsh accusations thrown around about the administration at this school. This not only hurts our reputation, but the donors will also soon pull away. This could be catastrophic!"

Laura ponders her life over the past year, like a record playing over and over again, skipping as it spins, yet no one has been able to reach over and pull the tonearm off.

Without realizing she is speaking, she says under her breath, "Catastrophic?"

The dean leans forward.

Laura jumps back into reality. She abruptly stands and faces the dean. Before Laura can stop herself, she barks, "What is catastrophic is that countless women all over this state were assaulted by the same man. And, for some reason, reasons I'll never quite get, you call me, a lonely DJ on a college radio station in the middle of New York, to ask me how I get my information? Are you serious? I pay to go to school here, Dean Barrymore. Last time I checked, that is what pays your salary, so if you'll excuse me, I have to get to class."

Laura spins on her heel, and with a vengeful stride, she storms out of her office. Leaving the dean, no doubt, with her jaw hanging somewhere on the floor.

That felt good. I've held my tongue for far too long.

Forty-Four

CONFESSIONS

Exhausted after her meeting with the dean, Laura hurries back across campus and makes it right in time for her Trigonometry class. Her heart races like a thoroughbred throughout the entire class, as she anticipates that she will be summoned out of her class and told, in a Shakespearean dramatic fashion, that she is expelled from the university for yelling at the dean of students. But it never happens. Instead, she stares aimlessly ahead at the chalkboard.

Finally, the clock strikes eleven, and Laura is free to go back to her dorm. She strolls up to the sixth floor and finds Bree's door slightly ajar. She knows Bree is in one of her darker moods when she hears The Smiths playing from her speakers. She cautiously knocks. When there is no answer, she knows that Bree expects whomever it is to know her well enough to know whether or not to come in. Complicated? Yes. True? Indeed.

Laura enters. "Hey."

"Hey." Bree is sitting on the floor, albeit on a lush carpet, surrounded by Egyptian pillows, curled up, watching one of her favorite movies, starring her friend Eve, titled *A Love to Remember*, with the sound off no less.

Oh boy, it's one of those days.

"What's up?"

She hits pause on the movie. She fidgets with her well-manicured hands for a moment. Laura takes a seat next to her.

"My parents—actually, my dad and his people—have decided to sue the school for negligence." She blurts this out in true Bree fashion. No sugarcoating, whatsoever.

Laura sighs, "What can I do?"

"Please, do not repeat this, even to your friends at *The Weekly Blue*. All the money, we plan to return right back to the school. Penny for penny. We don't need the money. We need to make a statement."

"Wow, okay. Do you know about any of the other girls?"

"No, but I won't blame them for taking what they can get. I just know what I plan to do with it. I don't want that to sway anyone else. As you know, I've been rather fortunate in my life. I say that, but it doesn't excuse or erase what that scumbag did. I just know that it would make me feel better to give the money back."

"I understand."

Thinking aloud, Bree states, "Quite honestly, I hope the others take what is owed to them and do whatever they want with it. I only know that keeping it would be a reminder, and I no longer want that."

"Hard to argue with that."

"Adam does have something to do with it. I want him to have a place to be proud of, and that means something to me. We built up that curriculum so much last summer and got such traction that I'd hate to think one guy...asshole can ruin that." Laura is silent. Bree continues, "I can't believe the dean was involved in all of this."

"Can you believe she had me in her office today to grill me about my sources?" Laura snaps her mouth shut.

"That bitch. But aren't you the source?"

Laura lowers her head. It's clear she is unwilling to make eye contact.

"Laura..."

At this point, almost all her cards are on the table, and she knows, more than anyone, that she can trust Bree wholeheartedly.

"It wasn't me..." she says in a low whisper.

"What? What the hell, Laura?" Bree sounds more scared than angry.

"I know; I know. I didn't know about it until later at the trial, but, hell, the guy is good."

"What guy?"

"I have a friend, friends actually, and they have been the ones feeding me all this information from day one."

"Friends you say?"

"I got involved in the paper in the beginning to kick-start my news segment, but then it started to evolve."

"Evolve how?"

"Travis and his partner, Wolfie—who is kind of my friend, too—had been investigating the whole Campus Creeper thing from the beginning. I'm talking way back to SUNY Oswego, Buffalo—you name it, and these guys were all over it. Until Jeremy came here. Then, it got real for them, and it was not good. They had inside info into the athletic teams...digging deep to see if this guy was who he said he was..."

"Okay, but how did your friends get to me?"

She replies with blushing cheeks, "Travis and I became close, and I was deep in all of it. When I read those emails, it was hard to disguise that I didn't know the person they were referring to."

Bree reaches her hand out and gently touches Laura's leg. "He was there for you when you needed someone."

She glances up. "Yes, desperately. Honestly, Bree, he has taught me a ton. I truly care for him. It's deeper than I thought it would ever be. He means something to me."

"I can see that."

"When he brought me those emails, I thought I was going to be sick, Bree. Literally. To read how callous the dean was with my friends' lives made me angry and pissed off and mad at everyone."

"Including Officer Murphy."

"Yes. I was mad at him for not trying more, but I had no idea what he had done for you, trying to save you. I feel like such a dick for how I treated him."

"He'll forgive you once this all comes to light. I know he will."

"I hope so."

"Who came to my room?"

"Wolfie. Travis is too recognizable, and honestly, the dean is keeping a close eye on him. On both of us. But I didn't even know they gave the papers to you. I knew I couldn't do it, and I'm guessing they knew that, too."

"I know that must have eaten away at you, and as I sit here, I can't say for certain I would have given them to you either. Those were really hard to read."

"I'm really sorry, Bree. So sorry you went through what you did."

"Me, too. It sounds like you had some support. I'm grateful for that."

"Between Travis and Colin…"

"Colin?"

She smiles. "I totally fell for him last year."

"You did?"

"Yes, but then lo and behold, his ex, Joey, claimed she was attacked, and there went our relationship, right out the window."

"Did she have something to do with the dean?"

"Colin confirmed that the dean bribed her to fake an attack to throw Colin, me, the station, the paper—you name it—on a wild goose chase. And the poor girl broke. She tried to hurt herself from the guilt of it all."

"Jesus!" Bree claps her hand over her mouth. "She will stop at nothing."

"She is awful, and that was why I wanted you to distance yourself from her. I wanted you to not be involved with her agenda and let Travis, Wolfie, and me figure this all out."

"Travis did the right thing by giving me those papers."

"You can never tell anyone where you got them from."

"I said what I said in court, and my story will remain the same." She gestures by locking her lips and tossing the imaginary key over her shoulder.

"Thank you. I appreciate that, and I know they do, too. But they wanted to expose her and knew the best way to get the ball rolling was to have those papers read in court."

"How the hell did they get them?"

"That is something none of us know. He received a few anonymous letters, and that's the end of that."

"Sounds like we have a few unsung heroes among us."

"Yeah, we definitely do."

Bree shakes her head. "Boy, did she fool me."

"She fooled us all. That was her job. To fool us one by one into thinking she had our backs. She never did and never will." Laura pauses and gingerly asks, "Are you still going to her committee?"

Bree's shoulders relax. "Look, I get that you were trying to warn me about her and that you couldn't tell me why. But what the school is trying to do will help this campus move forward."

"But how can you be in the same room as her?"

"I have a feeling, after the trial is over and the lawsuits come flying at her, she'll no longer be welcome."

"When is your next meeting?"

"Next week, on Wednesday."

"Closing arguments are today, and then it could be only a matter of days until..." Bree's voice starts to quiver.

This reminds Laura of the day she knocked on her door late at night, and Bree collapsed in her arms and wept like a child. Not the woman who elegantly sauntered the catwalk of campus, but more like a young girl still in her teenage years, scared and broken.

Laura quickly puts two and two together. There is a chance, although a small one, that this guy might walk free. He might never be encased in the four concrete walls he's meant to spend the rest of his life in. And it is scary. It is scary to all of them.

Laura embraces her friend. "I'm sorry about all of this. This year has been crazy. I hope, in the end, we'll all feel a little better."

"We will." Bree pauses and then adds with a slight smile, "I'm certain we will."

Forty-Five

INSIDE JOB

Confidently, Travis approaches Joanne Stone's desk. "Good morning. I have an appointment with the dean."

"Yes." She averts her eyes toward the book on her desk. Her hand shakes slightly as she crosses off his name on her schedule. "I'll let her know you're here." She then returns to her computer and types something. Then, she slides out from behind her desk, and with trepidation, she knocks slightly on the dean's door.

An angered voice yells, "Come in!"

Joanne barely pushes the door open. "Your next appointment, Travis Taylor, is h—"

"Send him in," she squawks.

Travis is already standing behind Joanne when she turns. She is startled, to say the least.

"Please, you may go in now."

"Hard not to hear her," he whispers with a wink. He gets Joanne to smile.

Travis enters and promptly closes the door behind him.

The dean is standing in front of one of her large pane-glassed windows overlooking the campus. Her slight frame leans toward the glass as the students move in and out of buildings, chatting, playing hacky sack, and enjoying what is left of the autumn days.

Travis stands before her desk but does not sit. He clasps his hands together in front of him and waits for her to speak.

She slightly clears her throat. "Twenty-seven years."

Once a moment of silence passes between them, he asks, "I'm sorry, Dean?"

"Twenty-seven years, I've been an administrator of higher education. A loyalist for sculpting young minds. Watching them grow to their fullest potential." She remains still, gazing out across her once-beloved institution.

She doesn't know he is smiling, but he is. He is grinning ear to ear. He watches her on her perch, her posture upright and confident. Like a woman who has not a care in the world.

He sighs outwardly and replies, "Fourteen months, seventeen days, and eleven hours."

She tips her head up toward the edge of the tall window, and with deliberation and determination, she turns to face her nemesis. Her stare is icy cold. She waits. But Travis simply returns her glare, waiting for her to ask.

"For what?"

He steps in front of the wooden chair recently occupied by Laura, and without taking his eyes off of her, he lowers into the seat. "It took me fourteen months, seventeen days, and eleven hours to conclude without an ounce of uncertainty that you, Dean Barrymore, are, at a minimum, an incompetent administrator, but, at your worst, you are a selfish woman whose need for institutional accolades supersedes the health and well-being of the students you claim to care about."

Her laugh is deep. "Ha! Is that so?"

Travis does not flinch. He remains as cool as a cucumber. "Yes."

She takes a seat in her chair. Her slight frame is now enveloped by her oversize desk and chair, as though it were swallowing her whole.

"Your reputation as being arrogant and overly confident might hurt you in the end."

"How?"

"I have the power to expel students as I see fit at this institution."

"Would you recommend doing that before or after the ceremony I am scheduled to attend for the College Media Liberty Award at the school? You know, the one that recognizes students for demonstrating outstanding support for college press freedom and reform?"

"It seems you have a few award winners among your minions at *The Weekly Blue*. Ainsley Atwood apparently is someone I'd like to meet, and maybe she could take over for you when you're gone."

Travis doesn't even flinch. He feels the paper in his breast pocket burning a hole in his argument, yet he can't quite get himself to play that card yet. "With all you having going on right now, I should be the least of your concerns. I report the news, plain and simple. Information is brought to me, Dean Barrymore. I am not an investigator, a PI, or any of those things. Did it ever occur to you that someone wants you gone from here? Out. Removed. I can assure you, that idea did not come from little old me."

Her face turns a new shade of pale. It's as though, for the first time, it has occurred to her that this is an inside job. Someone wants her gone. But who? And why? Before all this, she was revered—or so the students all thought. Karma can be a real bitch, and that simple fact is hitting Dean Barrymore pretty hard right now.

With that in mind, showing the document about the bribe that was transferred into Joey's account is not the right move at this juncture. Travis does not want the dean to ponder, even for a minute, that he is insinuating the inside job is Joey. The poor girl tried to overdose on sleeping pills—at least, that's the rumor running around the inside track at the paper—just to get away from this all.

She takes a sip of the water from the cup on her desk. Despite her nervous appearance, her hands remain steady.

Travis leans forward in his chair. "Dean, someone leaked those emails. Did it ever cross your mind that I might be able to help you?"

A sly smile spreads over her face. "You wouldn't help me."

"You said yourself, you have the power to expel me. I'm merely seven months from graduating with honors, and I want *this* hanging over my head? I might be arrogant and overly confident, like you said, but I'm also not an idiot. Reckless at times, yes, but I'm not stupid."

"Your associate from the radio."

"Laura."

"Yes. She appears to have a rather crude opinion of me."

Travis rubs the scruff on his face. "Jesus, Dean—and pardon me for saying this—but did it ever dawn on you that not one, but *two* of her friends were attacked on campus?"

For the first time ever, the dean drops her perfectly neat hair and shakes it. But then she peers up at Travis with narrowed and hate-filled eyes and says, "Of course it did. Everything occurs to me." The coolness in her tone is alarming.

Travis soon realizes he is up against more than he might be able to chew off and spit out.

"If I walk out this door," he says, "I will try to find the source."

"What do you want in return?"

"That you leave Laura alone. The only things she knows are what my team feeds her. And that stops today."

"And Ainsley Atwood? She stops her relationship with the station?"

"Of course. Consider it done."

The dean rises from her faux throne and reaches her hand out toward Travis. Being a master at his craft, he doesn't bat an eye as he, too, rises and shakes the hand of the one woman on earth he despises the most.

"Now, behave yourself," she warns.

"Believe me, I will." With that, he spins on his heel and treads to the door. He opens it and leaves, hastily shutting it behind him. He slips his hand in his pocket, and then, with kindness, he steps in front of Joanne Stone's desk. "Ms. Stone, thank you for setting up the meeting." He reaches his hand out to shake hers. "I'll see you soon."

"Of course, Mr. Taylor. The dean enjoys visits from her students."

Boy, does she ever.

Forty-Six

THE START OF THE END

Laura enters the Union, which is already packed. She can barely make her way to the coffee shop to grab a cup before her shift at the station. She finally gets up to the counter, and the barista, the young girl she has seen more times than she'd care to count, smiles warmly at Laura.

"I hope we all get good news today," she says as she hands Laura her usual. "This one is on me. Good luck today."

"Thanks. Appreciate it." Laura takes the cup, leaves a few dollars in the tip jar on the counter, and gently pushes her way in and out of the horde of students.

Once she is in the open area by the fireplace is when it hits her. This has no longer become a radio show. This has become a live-studio-audience show. The curved stairwell to the upper section of the Union—where the basketball courts, art studio, and administrative offices are—is completely jammed. Students are sitting with their legs hanging over the side, so their friends can get closer to the edge, too.

Laura fumbles her way into the station door. Everyone is standing there, waiting for her.

"Jesus, you guys, too?" she says with an uneasy laugh.

"Thought you might want to hide under your covers today." Tucker grins.

"Not a chance," Colin quips. "You were made for this," he says as he gently drapes his arm over her shoulders.

"I agree. This is what we've all been waiting for."

"Sean and Ryker are at the courthouse, at the ready." Tucker claps his hands together.

"Okay, let me get set up, and we'll be ready to go." Laura's voice is confident, but inside, she is shaking.

Her stomach is tied in knots, and she feels on the verge of tossing her lunch all over the floor. She looks up at Colin.

He smiles and says, "I'll come down in ten to check on you before you go live."

"Cool, thanks." She gets on her tippy-toes and kisses him on the lips.

Patrick and Tucker witness this for the first time, solidifying their relationship status to their coworkers, and by the smiles that spread across their faces, it is safe to say that they are more than happy for the two of them.

Laura opens the door to Studio B. She flips on the lights and places her bag and coffee down on her desk. She does her usual ritual, attempting not to waver from her routine, for fear the change will send bad energy her way. Once she is sitting down at her chair, she turns away from the door and lowers her head, resting her hand on her chin, and closes her eyes.

She envisions half an hour ago. As she left Abigail, Bree, Melissa, Maddie, Alex, Casey, and Jen all gathered in Bree's room. Laura takes herself back to those seven women, and with all her might, she silently prays for justice. But Laura has this fear she can't shake that, as they gather around the radio in the dormitory, awaiting the announcement, she might not give them what they want.

The world has been cruel thus far. Will it actually stop now?

A quiet knock can be heard on her door.

She spins in her chair as she wipes the wet from her cheeks. "Come in."

The door slowly opens.

"Hey," he says.

"Travis, what are you doing here?"

He smiles, knowing she doesn't mean it in the way it sounds. "I have something for you."

"Me?"

"Yes."

"Okay, what is it?"

"I need a favor, and you are the only one who can do it for me."

"A favor? But I'm about to go on…"

"I know." He reaches into his pocket and pulls out a folded piece of paper. "After the verdict is read, I need you to read this statement. Word for word." He reaches forward and gives the paper to her. "Don't open it now, okay?"

"Travis, you're kind of freaking me out."

His smile is content and warm. "You've come to trust me over the past year, and in turn, I'm asking you for this courtesy, Laura. You know I always have the best of intentions, and today is no different."

She cocks her head to the side, taking in the tall, intelligent man who stands before her, and she is swiftly brought back to their first night together. How he held her so tightly, as though he had feelings for her for much longer than she realized herself. And how, ever since that moment, he has done nothing but been kind and considerate of her.

"Yes, of course. I will do this for you."

He steps forward, opens his arms, and motions for her to come into him. She does quickly as, today more than ever, she needs the warm and loving embrace of her friend, her partner, and her mentor.

He breathes in deeply as he holds her. "You'll do great today. You got this."

"All because of you," she replies without hesitation.

He kisses her on the head and then releases his embrace. Without another word, he steps back and out through the door.

Laura tucks the paper in the back pocket of her jeans and takes her position in her chair. Patrick comes in the booth and begins his preparations. There are five minutes until she is live.

Colin comes waltzing in. "Laura, anything I can get you before you start?" he asks.

"Thanks, but I'm good." She shakes her hands free. "Why am I nervous, Colin?"

"Because you're about to deliver the news that everyone has been waiting for; that's why. I have faith in the legal system. This guy is going down. I have no doubt about it."

"Good. Keep reminding me of that."

"Now, give all those students out there a look at the voice that has transformed this station from a CD-playing machine to the voice of a new generation of programming."

Before she can protest, he pulls up the blinds to the huge window overlooking the fireplace area of the Student Union. Shouting and clapping erupt as she comes into sight of hundreds of students, waiting eagerly for her to go on air. Her face pinks as she slightly waves at her fellow students. Colin backs out from the room, blowing her a kiss as he does. She glances up at Patrick as he signals to her that she is live in…

Three, two, one.

Unbeknownst to Laura just the evening before, Travis had waited under the cover of darkness with only the lit end of a cigarette to warn anyone that approached that there is an actual person standing beneath the shaded tree. He flicked his ash, and as he did, he sensed a shadow in the midst. He whistled once.

The shadow came closer.

He took a long drag of his cigarette and then stomped it out into the dirt.

"Thank you for meeting me," he said.

"I was wondering when you might reach out to me," she replied.

Travis, while the dean's back was turned as she glared out the window, took out the small notebook he kept in his breast pocket and wrote a brief note to Ms. Stone. Upon leaving, he kindly shook her hand, transferring the note to her. He'd had an inkling when he saw how nervous she was upon encountering him that she was in fact the one who had sent the documents.

"I'll be honest, it took me a lot longer than normal to figure it all out. But, when I saw you the other day, it dawned on me. Those closest to the situation tend to be the ones who blow the whistle."

"I couldn't let it go on anymore."

"Of course not, Ms. Stone. You did the right thing."

"That I don't doubt. What I do want to be clear about is that it can't come back to me. I'll lose my job, my pension, everything I've worked for. Forty-one years at this school. I graduated in 1955, and I've been a faithful and proud employee of this university ever since."

"I commend you. I guess I'd ask you why you did it, but any person with a heart would have."

In the darkness, Travis could see her hang her head.

"She once did, too. But she kind of, for lack of a better phrase, got too big for her britches. That saying might be somewhat old for you."

Travis chuckled. "I understand the meaning."

"She used to have a connection and wanted to be involved with the students and faculty. But then she became this power-hungry, almost egotistical person I didn't recognize anymore. When the donors started to drop and the complaints about her style and involvement with the students and faculty came pouring in, she became so focused on making the campus seem perfect. Her lack of compassion for the safety of my beloved university was more than I could stand. I didn't want to be a part of it. But, sadly, I was." Her voice cracked.

"Listen, I've only been in the presence of the dean a few times, and she is ice cold. I can only imagine what it has been like for you to have to work alongside her. It must be horrible."

"My only saving grace will be if they convict him tomorrow. That is what this campus needs. And that is what I have prayed for every night."

"Me, too," Travis whispered.

"You have what you need to get her fired. Please, I hate to rely on you to do this, but I knew you'd be the one person with the gall to stand up to her."

"That you are right about," he said with a chuckle. "But I've had some help this year."

"I know. You kids have done this school a great justice."

"Not yet."

She sighed. "She mentioned to me there was a breach in the computer system and that you were going to try to look into who sent those emails to that poor girl."

He lit a cigarette. "Ms. Stone—"

"Please call me Joanne."

"Okay, Joanne. You have my word, I will be doing all I can to keep the dean off our trail and, more importantly, believing that I am on her side. Until we meet again." Much like Wolfie, Travis dipped back into the darkness and strolled back through the path in which he came.

Now, I need to convince Laura to read the dean's note without further implicating her in this mess. She means too much to me. It's time to keep her at bay. As hard as that might be for me.

Forty-Seven

THE VERDICT

In a solemn tone, Laura leans into the microphone. Today is different. Much different than the other one hundred thirty-eight some-odd times she has been live on WOUR97.

"Good afternoon, Hawks. This is Laura Chase. By the mass of students gathered in the Union and to all of you listening in your dorm, apartment, home, car, what have you, I'm here with you for the rest of the afternoon until we get word regarding the recent trial." She pauses. "With that said, the guys at the station and I have decided not to play music, not to take calls, and to simply be here with you as though we are all under one roof, unified, together, until the time comes for me to report to you. For all of you in the Union, thank you." She looks out the window, and the students raise their hands in solidarity. "Thank you for being here. Thank you for all the support you have shown.

"I'd like to give a special thank you to Professor Tucker for taking a chance on me and allowing me to bring you the news on air. I'd also like to thank all those who took part in my segments, whether that was through your calls, interviews, requests, or what have you. You have all been a part of this journey, and I appreciate it.

"To the guys in the station, thank you for allowing me to crash your bro show." She laughs. "You've all made me feel like a real part of the station family."

She pauses, allowing the silence to resonate a little as her intention is not to ramble on during the time, just to fill the quietness. She also doesn't want this to be solely about her. But it felt good to thank everyone for welcoming her and accepting her through the good shows and the bad ones.

Laura glances at the clock on the wall—3:32 p.m. The jury deliberated for two days, and finally, the campus got word they would be back in session this afternoon. Laura glances up at Patrick as he grabs the phone in his booth. His face turns a ghostly shade of white. Laura swallows hard.

He places the receiver down and leans into the booth microphone connected to Laura's studio. "The jury has entered the courtroom."

It's not that what he said is prolific or unexpected even, but the chill that emanates down Laura's spine and the hair that stands up on her arms would lead anyone to believe his words were weighty. Laura reaches over to her receiver that connects her to Sean via his communication transmitter. She hits the silence button on her microphone for a brief moment.

"Sean, can you hear me?"

There is significant static and then, "Yes, Laura, I'm here."

"Great."

"It's unbelievable. The amount of news stations that are here from all over. This is insane."

"I can imagine."

"The jury is in, and they are about to read the first of several counts."

Laura switches on her microphone. "I have received word that the jury is in the courtroom, and the first of several counts are about to be read."

She couldn't say either way if she expected an eruption of cheers, but she is definitely not prepared for the complete silence that remains in the Union. Not a peep out of one person. In fact, many bow their heads, as if they are silently praying. She places her ear back to her receiver to listen for Sean when, all of a sudden, she can hear the loud yelling in the background.

Finally, with a heavy breath, Sean bellows from his end, "Count one, guilty!"

Laura can barely hold her own excitement and turns to the microphone. She eyes the crowd as she says in a shaky voice, "The jury has made a decision. Count one...guilty!"

Now, the Union bursts at the seams. People are hugging, jumping up and down, high-fiving, embracing, cheering, yelling, all at the mere fact that Jeremy Gordon is guilty of only one of many counts.

"Sean, what else?"

"Jesus, I can hear them yelling from here! Hang on."

Silence for a minute.

The crowd leans into the glass in front of her booth, anxiously awaiting the next announcement. Sean continues to give her updates.

Laura immediately relays it to the listeners. "Counts two and three, guilty!" She feels her energy rise, but something inside her is sensing a pull toward Bree, Abigail, and the girls. In many ways, she wishes she were there with them.

For the next fifteen minutes, Laura relays each count. "Count fourteen, guilty. Count fifteen, guilty. Count sixteen, guilty—"

"Wait, hang on, Laura." Sean's voice is strained.

"Hold on, everyone," she says. "Sean, you there?"

"Yeah, count seventeen—I can't believe it—not guilty."

"Are you positive, Sean?"

"Yeah, confirmed."

The color in Laura's face drains. "Count seventeen, not guilty."

The Union vents with anger.

"Hold on, everyone. We don't know what that means. Please remain calm."

Laura returns to the receiver that connects her to Sean. "Sean, what are you hearing?"

"You've got to be kidding me! Eighteen is not guilty, too!"

"Jesus Christ," Laura says. "Can you get me more information on that as soon as possible?"

"Yes, hang on."

The crowd outside her window is getting restless. The phone lines are all lit up like a Christmas tree.

The silence is killing her.

Finally, Sean reports back in, "The district attorney did a press conference on the courtroom steps."

Laura relays the information back on the radio.

"Go ahead, Sean."

He is breathing heavy into the line. "Counts seventeen and eighteen, the jury felt the prosecutor did not present sufficient evidence to convict for sexual assault and battery, but the DA said, despite all that, the sentencing tomorrow should in fact incarcerate him to the maximum time in prison for each count, which is seven years per count."

"Thanks, Sean. Appreciate it."

"Tell Tucker I'm going to stick around longer. See what I can get."

"Thanks. I'll let him know." She turns back to her microphone. "Everyone, he was found not guilty on counts seventeen *and* eighteen. They did not have enough evidence to convict for sexual assault and battery, but the DA said, despite all that, the sentencing tomorrow should in fact warrant him the maximum time in prison for each count, which, in New York, is seven years."

She pulls out the note from her back pocket. She tears open the envelope and scans the title.

"I have a note I'd like to read to all of you. It is from Dean Barrymore. She says:

"In light of recent events, I'd like to extend my deepest condolences to all those throughout our community who have been impacted by the events of the past year. As you know, the administration has and continues to put the safety of all our people as a top priority. If you or someone you know needs assistance, please do not hesitate to reach out to the campus safety task force or any one of the caring faculty and staff who makes OSU one of the greatest schools in the country. My door is always open, and I will be with you as we continue to heal from these tragic events."

Laura is downcast to say the very least. *How could Travis ask me to read that piece-of-shit note from the dean? He must have a reason, but what could it be?*

Laura can feel herself churning with anger inside her. She leans back into the microphone and says with a softness in her voice, "Now, if you would all excuse me, I have some friends I need to be with. Thank you all for the support, and if you run into Tank tonight, buy that guy a beer! Until next time, Hawks."

Laura shuts down and pulls the blinds on the window. She allows herself a good cry. A much-needed one.

Colin comes bursting in. He doesn't have to say a word as he wraps his arms tightly around her. They stand together as one and hold on for dear life. She can feel his chest heave, and she knows he, too, is finally releasing all the sadness inside of himself. The victory he never got for his friend in high school and for Joey, wherever she might be.

As Laura squeezes her eyes shut tight, she tries to allow the triumph of today to come forth, but unfortunately, the sadness she feels from the years of pain this has bestowed upon her friends is immeasurable.

"We have everything?" Travis asks.

"I double-checked it, and then I checked it again. It's all there," Wolfie replies.

"Okay, and one is…"

"Going to the president of the university," he says with a sinister grin, "the other to Officer Murphy, and the last one to the district attorney's office."

"Nothing with Joanne's name or email address on them?"

"Not one."

"Where are you mailing these from?"

"I'm overnighting them to my confidant in the city. They'll never figure out how they got there."

"Good. I don't want our zip code associated."

"It won't be."

Travis hesitates and then adds, "I could not have gotten through the last three years at the paper without you. I hope I've shown you that."

Wolfie chuckles. "Sometimes. But it was a pleasure working alongside you regardless."

Travis smiles. "What do you plan to do without me?"

"I might finally get my chance to run the paper." Wolfie grins.

"Really?"

"Nah. I like being the no-name, the underdog, the guy no one is quite sure of."

"You play that character flawlessly."

"I've perfected it." Wolfie buttons his tweed coat.

"Yeah, you have. You're exactly what this school and the paper needs."

"Who knows? Maybe, after I graduate, I'll come work for you again."

Travis smiles. "I'd like that."

Wolfie grabs the envelopes and stuffs them into his bag. "I'll see you tomorrow."

"Tomorrow."

Travis shuts the door to his apartment and drags his tired legs up the stairs. As he collapses on his bed and rests his hands behind his head, he can't help but feel a huge sense of accomplishment for never giving up. No matter how hard the days got or how many toes he had to step on, he always had one goal in mind. Getting that son of a bitch caught and behind bars.

One more day, and I will be able to say unequivocally that I've succeeded.

Forty-Eight

A STORM IS COMING

Laura rushes back toward her dorm despite the numerous people who try to stop her to talk about the news. She hurries up the stairs to the sixth floor. The silence is alarming. She jogs past each closed door until she reaches Bree's door. She knocks.

She hears a resounding, "Come in!"

Laura pushes open the door and finds the room almost exactly as she left it. All the girls are huddled in the room; only, now, Professor Cooper is in the room, tightly holding Bree. He rarely makes his presence known around the dorm—and for good reason. But there isn't a soul who would have the audacity to question him today.

Laura is at a loss for words as she surveys the scene in front of her. Beer bottles tossed about, tissues barely in the wastebasket, and sad and happy faces all pooled into one. She takes in each and every one of their expressions. Casey is crying while Jen holds her hand. Maddie is sitting on the floor, arms wrapped around her knees, rocking back and forth. Melissa stares back at Laura while she takes a long sip of her beer. Alex is leaning against the wall in near shock. Laura can only guess that she had no idea when she transferred a few short months ago that she was walking into this. Bree's face is buried deep in Adam's chest.

Then, Laura's eyes lock with Abigail's. Those large navy eyes are bloodshot and tired. She looks drained. She immediately jumps up and rushes over toward Laura. She throws her arms around Laura and sinks deep into her. She doesn't speak. She doesn't have to. She just cries. But, for some reason, the way she is weeping is different than the others. There is a sense deep inside Laura that is signaling to her that something is very wrong. Yet she can only hold on to her.

No one is speaking, and it's probably best for now. Tomorrow, this will be over. *Really over.* And, hopefully, with that will come a sense of relief and the closure they all need.

The next afternoon, Laura returns from the station and finds Abigail alone, enjoying the quiet confines of their dorm room.

"You're back." She smiles.

Laura plops on her bed. "I'm looking forward to celebrating that jerk's incarceration."

"Is it weird that we are all reveling in it?" Abigail asks.

"As long as you or Bree or anyone else doesn't feel it's weird to go to a party, then I think it is awesome," she replies with a darkness in her mood.

"No, I guess it's a good thing, just feels odd in some aspects."

"No, it's definitely odd." Laura tosses her notebook on the edge of her bed.

"But something else is bothering you. What's going on?" Abigail asks, placing her book on her lap.

Her face turns red as she blurts out, "Someone vandalized the soccer house last night."

"What? What do you mean, vandalized?" Abigail asks.

"They don't know who or if it was more than one person, but they wrote some…" Her voice fades as she lowers her head.

"What did they write?"

"What do you think?" She is visibly upset.

"What?" Abigail whispers.

"Lesbo, dykes, all kinds of horrible stuff…"

Abigail's eyes grow wide. "No. Who would do such a thing?"

"Monsters. We are surrounded by them," Laura adds with anger.

"Good God! Is no one human anymore?"

"It feels that way."

"I'm so sorry for them. You think this trial had something to do with it?"

"Hard to know," Laura states.

"How are Jen and the girls doing?"

"They filed a police report, but obviously, they don't feel welcome or safe."

"You know Jen can stay with us. I can even crash with Nathan."

"I'll definitely let her know. I have to go talk to Travis about this. I'll stop by to see her after."

Lying in Wait

Abigail glances at the clock on their wall. "Shoot. Time flew by. We should probably go down."

"Right."

They enter the lounge area and flip on the television. Laura takes a seat next to Abigail on the couch as they eagerly wait for the news reporter to announce that court will be in session.

"We are going live in the courthouse," the woman from Channel 8 News announces. The judge has allowed cameras only in the court for the sentencing phase. "The judge should be entering the courtroom momentarily."

The lounge room starts to fill up with students from her dorm as the minutes tick by.

Laura notices Abigail shudder at the mere glimpse of Jeremy Gordon as he is escorted in, shackled in handcuffs and leg cuffs. She grabs her friend's hand.

The bailiff stands before the packed courtroom. "Please rise. The Court of the Second Judicial Circuit, Criminal Division. The people of New York versus Jeremy Gordon is now in session, the Honorable Judge O'Connor presiding."

Everyone promptly stands and waits for the judge to take his seat. He carefully eyes the crowd before sitting down.

"You may be seated." He pauses. "Would the defendant like to make a statement?" he asks his attorney.

"No, Your Honor."

Coward.

"Very well then. Let's not delay this any longer. Please rise, Mr. Gordon. The State of New York has found you guilty of sixteen out of eighteen counts of battery and sexual assault. After careful consideration of your case, I've noted the three-strikes statutes for which you have not been convicted of any felony or misdemeanors in your short time on this earth."

Laura swallows hard. She can feel the beat of her heart pound within the cavity wall of her chest.

He continues, "While I've taken that three-strike into consideration, I've also looked at the disproportionately harsh crimes for which you have been convicted of. This, by most standards, would be considered a crime spree. Therefore, for the sake of the safety of others and by the power bestowed upon me by the State of New York, I am sentencing you to seven years, the maximum allowed for each count, for a total of one hundred twelve years to be served consecutively."

The roar can be heard in the courtroom, the dorm lounge area, and practically across the campus. Abigail, fixated on the back of Jeremy's head, watches his knees drop as his lawyer tries to hold him up.

The judge bangs his gavel. "Order in my court."

The courtroom hushes.

"You may be eligible for parole in ninety-eight years."

Considering he is only twenty-two years old, he'll be a hundred twenty, which tells them he won't see a parole hearing.

Abigail rises to her feet and pushes her way through the crowd of cheering students, and with hunched shoulders, she makes her way back up to their room. Laura is quickly on her heels. Once inside, they both drop into their desk chairs, side by side, and gaze out across the campus.

"I can't help but feel a relieved sense of safety, knowing he is behind bars, but with the horrible news about the soccer house, it's hard to imagine we are in the clear," Abigail confesses. She drops her head in her hands and closes her tired eyes.

"I know; I know," Laura whispers.

They sit in silence. Watching the crowds of students spilling out of the buildings to celebrate on the campus lawn. Unfortunately for them, the phone rings, jolting them back to reality.

"It's probably my parents," Abigail states as she reaches for the receiver.

"Hello?"

"Abigail?"

"Yes?"

"It's Claire Marion, counselor for the state."

Abigail clears her throat. "Oh, yes, of course. How are you?"

"Much better after today. More importantly, how are you?"

"You know, it's been an emotional few days."

There is a long pause, making Abigail's stomach turn with an uneasiness that is becoming all too familiar to her.

"Yes, I understand. I wanted to speak with you about a few items, if I may?"

"Of course." Her voice shakes.

She can hear the counselor ruffle some papers in front of her. "Yes, I wanted to call you personally, now that the sentencing is behind us, to inform you that the two counts he was found not guilty pertained to you."

Abigail tries to breathe in, but it feels as though the wind has been knocked out of her.

"Me?" she chokes out. "But how? It was Tank—Thomas was the one who caught him, and I was the..."

"I understand completely. It was a surprise to all of us."

"I don't understand." Tears well in her eyes.

Laura grabs on to her arm, a concerned expression on her face.

"The sexual assault charge was hard to prove since there were no physical markings, if you will, besides the ones from what they believe was the altercation with Thomas and you and him on the ice. Understanding that this was, of course, by accident. Plus, your medical records showed a fall and hospital stay not long before. The second count of sexual battery was again hard to prove without a reasonable doubt. The jury believed it was tough to prove with little physical evidence. They felt it was, despite his history and the other counts all being guilty, that two people left a party, Tank got jealous, and an altercation took place."

Abigail gasps in sheer disgust.

"I know. It is heartbreaking—"

"Heartbreaking? It's a lie! I never left with him. I never did anything to warrant his advances…"

"Ms. Price, no one doubts your story at all. My team and I fought to have this overturned. We believe that is why the judge was harsh with his sentencing. Mr. Gordon could have gotten the minimum of forty-eight years and been out at the age of seventy. If he makes it that long. Prison is hard. It will be extremely hard for him."

Abigail hangs her head. "Does Thomas know?"

"Not yet."

"Okay."

"Listen, I believe it is best if I call your parents. I can explain the process and answer any questions they might have. Are you okay with this?"

"Yes, please do. May I go now?"

"You have my number. If you need anything, please call me, and in the meantime, if anything changes, I'll be in touch."

"But it won't."

"I will speak to your family lawyer about a civil suit, but otherwise, most likely not."

"Thank you for calling," Abigail whispers.

"Take care, Ms. Price."

Abigail places the receiver down, and like a moth to a flame, she flutters to her bed, climbs in, and pulls the cover tightly around her.

Laura rushes to her side. "What is it?" Laura asks.

As she squeezes her eyes shut, a myriad of thoughts runs through her head. She opens her eyes as she feels the weight of Laura's body sink onto her bed.

"Please tell me, Abigail. I'm freaking out here," Laura pleads.

Abigail bursts into tears as she retells the conversation she just had.

Minutes later and with a sick feeling churning in her gut, Laura places her cold hand across her beating heart, wishing for calmness to come over her. But that's the funny thing about being in college; there never actually is a calmness, and more importantly, most never feel the storm coming.

Forty-Nine

TRAVIS

What feels like countless other times before, Laura heads up the steps to Travis's apartment and knocks on the door. The door is slightly ajar.

She pushes it open. "Hello? Travis?" She hears a loud bang coming from near the kitchen. She steps through the doorway. "Travis?"

With a wincing voice, he yells, "Out back!"

Laura enters through the kitchen and out the side door to his backyard. "Never been out here before," she remarks as she steps out.

"Wouldn't have a reason to be unless you were doing something stupid like this." He grimaces as he rubs the top of his head.

"What did you do?"

"I hit it on the stupid pipe, trying to fix it." He glares at the motorcycle in front of him. Mostly intact with a few parts spread out on the ground near his feet.

"Writer, newspaper editor, mechanic, and now, I suppose I can add sly detective to your repertoire?"

He can't help himself. He smiles, his eyes sparkling in the fading sun. "Why would you say that?"

"Why would you make me read that note from the dean?"

He glances at his watch. "I'm surprised it took you this long to confront me. You're losing your drive, Laura. That can't be good." He rubs the grease from his hands on a rag.

"Me? You're out here, fixing this beat-up thing, when we still have work to do."

He grants her a fabulous smile. Maybe even better than the ones she was privileged enough to witness after a roll around in the sheets.

"What?"

"You honestly think that I, Travis Taylor, have been sitting around, doing nothing?"

"Well?"

He comes closer to her and wraps his arm around her shoulders. "Come inside, have a beer with me, and we'll talk."

She laughs as they walk inside. He takes two Natty Lights out of the refrigerator, pops the caps, and hands one to her. He leans up against the counter. His tall frame takes up most of the space, floor to ceiling. Laura hops up on the counter and waits for him to talk.

"First, thanks for not freaking out on me…"

"You asked me for a favor. I wouldn't go back on that. I knew something else was brewing in order for you to ask me to read that."

He smiles. "As you know, I saw the dean after you did, and she was not impressed with my detective work—if that is what we are calling it. She threatened to expel me."

Laura nearly chokes. "That bitch. Of all the shitty things she's—"

"Now, hold on. I'm about to get that award in a month, and she wouldn't dare expel me when her precious school is about to be recognized. Unfortunately for her shortsighted agenda, she never considered that she had a mole in her house of cards. She asked me to find that person. In return, she promised to leave you alone."

"Me?"

"Yeah, you," he says in a cocky tone.

"But what does that mean for you?"

"I'm good. She has to tolerate me for seven more months, and— boom—I'm out of her hair and making a damn good name for her school in the process. She knows I'm going to go on to do great things, and I'll have OSU written all over it."

Laura appreciates his arrogant attitude because he has in fact earned it. "Damn right! So, okay, why the note?"

"To keep her off my back, and it lets her know that I have you on my side, willing to help me as I need. That you have no specific agenda other than to have that asshole behind bars. She thinks you are my puppet on a string. I'm the mastermind behind all these stories, not you. I have only fed you the information. She is very satisfied with that. Success. Case closed."

Laura narrows her eyes. "Oh, you are good."

Another smug grin. "I know."

Laura laughs and takes a sip of her beer. "How will you find the mole? And, if you do, you wouldn't tell her—"

"Already did."

"What? How the hell did you figure that out?"

"Deductive reasoning. And a nervous demeanor."

Laura tips her head, contemplating her words. "Nervous? But who?"

"Think about it. Close to the source, a lot to lose but something to gain."

Laura pauses. She takes another sip and thinks some more. She eyes Travis, who gives the hurry-up motion with his fingers.

"Have I taught you so little?" He laughs.

A light goes off. Laura lightly taps herself on the forehead. "Duh, of course. Makes total sense. Access. Knows her movements. Hears everything, yet many times is probably in the background, storing it all away."

"Loves this school. Hates working for her. Knows what she did. Can't let it go on…"

"Oh, poor Ms. Stone. I feel bad for her. She could have gotten fired big-time. Life ruined."

"I assured her, she would be as far from this as possible."

"You'll do right by her "

"She broke this thing wide open. We owe her a lot. This whole school does."

"So, what next?"

"Wolfie is sending out papers to some major players, the district attorney, the police, and the president of the university. After they get a look at what we've put together, I can only assume that the dean will be, at a minimum, asked to resign, and worst case, she'll have charges brought against her. Of what I'm not positive, but those getting the files will ensure that she doesn't work here anymore. Or any other school for that matter."

"Hopefully." Laura sips her beer and watches as Travis relishes in his accomplishments. Then, it pops in her head. "Hey, what about the soccer house being vandalized?"

"It's sickening. Wolfie is checking out a few leads."

"My friend Jen lives there."

"Jesus, so sorry. We are making it a top priority." Travis finishes his beer, placing the empty bottle on the counter. He glances at the clock. "I'd better get back to fixing her before I run out of daylight."

"Thank you. Let me know how I can help." Laura hops off the counter and puts her beer bottle in the sink. "You coming to the party tonight to celebrate the incarceration and our victory?"

"Nah." He smiles. "Much more your scene. You and your friends should have that time together. You've all been through a lot."

"Okay. You'll be missed." She winks.

"Got some work to do." He motions toward the backyard.

Travis starts to escort her to the front door. He opens his arms, and without hesitation, she leans in and squeezes him tightly.

"You're the best," she whispers.

He laughs. "I know."

She releases her embrace, and a smile spreads across her face from ear to ear. She steps off the porch as he stands there in silence.

She abruptly turns back toward him. "You never told me what you named her."

His smile, while somewhat sad, is pleasant nonetheless. "Ruth."

"Ruth?" She chuckles. "Huh, unexpected. Why Ruth?"

"It means…friend, a vision of beauty."

Laura smiles warmly. "After you fix her up, she will be."

He continues to smile as she waves and walks down the street toward campus. "The name reminds me of you," he whispers.

Fifty

THÁNATOS

Laura steps onto her floor. The blaring beat of music, the blow-dryers on high speed, and the yelling across the hallway asking to borrow these jeans or that white shirt are par for the course on a Friday night at OSU. Only tonight is an invite-only party, hosted by the football team at the Ridge to revel in the fact that the Campus Creeper is no longer. At this soiree you won't have to pay to get in, and you don't have to drink sticky red punch out of a Tupperware bin.

Bree steps out into the hallway as she catches sight of Laura. "Where have you been?" she inquires.

"Oh, Bree. Jesus, what a day. How are you?" she says with a hug.

"Better than I could have hoped. So glad that jerk is going to jail."

"Me, too!"

"But enough chitchat. We can talk at the party." She checks her watch. "That you're going to be late for. Get going!"

"I know. Give me half an hour, and I'll be ready."

"I'll give you twenty-five," she says in her typical Bree fashion.

Laura tips her head back with a laugh. She pushes open the door and finds the room empty. *Abigail already left for the party?*

Laura knows what kind of state she is in and fears she is taking out her bad mood on alcohol. She hopes she will at least relish in the fact that Jeremy Gordon is going to spend the rest of his life in prison.

With a sense of urgency running through her, she changes into the outfit she already planned to wear tonight. She slicks her hair back tight, tucking it behind her ears She applies heavier eye makeup, dusts her cheeks with a pale peach blush, and then dabs a nude lip gloss on. She inspects her tight black button-down shirt, her well-fitted jeans, and her black boots in the mirror and is pleased with how she did in such a short period of time. She sprays on her favorite perfume, grabs her purse, and heads out her door, locking it behind her.

Laura and Bree walk, linked arm in arm across campus. They arrive at the party.

"Where is Abigail?" Laura asks as they meet up with their friends in the backyard.

"Inside. Said she wanted to hang in there."

"Really? She okay?" Laura asks Melissa.

"Seems fine to me."

"Cool."

She is hoping Abigail is in better spirits than anticipated. Since no one else seems concerned about her, Laura remains outside with her friends and Colin. Hours go by as they watch game after game of beer pong.

Nathan passes by and places his hand on Laura's shoulder. "I'm going to grab Abigail and head out. Need to get some sleep before the game."

"Tell her I said good-bye. Time flew by, and I didn't make my way inside."

"I haven't seen her much at all either. She probably struck up a conversation, had a few drinks, and hopefully, celebrated," he says with his usual killer smile.

"I'm sure."

"By the way, Colin is a badass pong player." He laughs, glancing over his shoulder.

Laura chuckles. "He's not bad."

"See you later, Laura."

"See you later, Nathan, and good luck tomorrow," Laura says as she watches Colin sink another ping-pong ball into a Solo cup. She gives him a winning smile.

He immediately places his cup on the table. "Guys, thanks so much, but I've gotta go."

The party is nearly empty. Most of the players left to get some semblance of a good night's sleep before the afternoon game tomorrow. The rest are stragglers, finishing their last drinks and wishing more than anything that the pizza place downtown is still open for a late night meal. She clasps Colin's hand as they exit out the side gate.

Within a few short minutes, they arrive at his apartment and make their way up the stairs to his bedroom.

He pulls his sweater and T-shirt off at the same time, and before he can even toss it onto the floor, Laura slips her hands over his waist, pulling him in toward her. He throws his clothes onto his chair. She stumbles as she kicks off her shoes. He leans his tall frame down toward her, taking her body into his. She can feel his breath on her face, and then, as soon as they lock eyes, he eagerly kisses her. She moans as his tongue promiscuously explores her mouth.

He takes his time in unbuttoning her shirt. The seductive manner in which he pops each button tastefully exposes her flesh underneath. He clutches her full breasts as she runs her hands up and down his body. With agile fingers, he unhooks her bra, and in one swift motion, he frees her bosom, so he can fully enjoy them. He teases and licks them. She tips her head back, relishing the moment and, more importantly, his undivided attention. She reaches for his belt and zipper, undoing them as they stagger toward his bed.

He playfully pushes her back as he leans down, slowly unzipping her jeans. The sexy grin that plays across his full lips is intoxicating to her. She wants him more than he could possibly imagine. He slowly pulls down her jeans over her hips and then her thighs, and then he eases them over her feet, massaging them as he does.

She resembles a 1940s pinup girl as she rolls onto her belly, her full breasts resting on his comforter and her legs elegantly twisted at the ankles. He leans over, running his hand over her backside. She moans as she tips her head toward the bed. His hand grazes her neck, rubbing and massaging her supple skin. He senses her muscles unwind.

"Does that feel good?" he asks. The tenor of his voice is sexy.

Instead of responding, she moans a little louder.

She peers over her shoulder at him. Just looking at her eyes, he knows she is ready for him. He slides out of his jeans and crawls onto the bed behind her. He uncrosses her ankles, letting his hands run down the backs of her legs, sending a tingle down her spine. He gently taps her backside. She giggles and blushes with approval. He does it again as he pushes his knees in between her legs, raising her hips up and back.

"You ready?" he growls. He rips open the condom wrapper with his teeth.

"Un-huh," she purrs as she leans up on her forearms, seductively glancing behind her to meet his gaze.

With one look, she pushes herself into him. He groans loudly, tipping his head back as he does. With one hand now on her shoulder, he pulls her back with each thrust. Forcing them together again and again. He grunts and groans along with her moans, each one bringing them closer and closer together.

Unfortunately, he can't hold on much longer. In a climactic state, he hollers her name, and then with complete satisfaction, he collapses on the bed. He pulls her into his arms, twisting his long arms around her body. His breathing is quick, but as the two lie there, entangled in one another, the sound of silence magnetically lulls them both into a deep, gratified slumber.

Bang!

There is a loud knock on the door. Laura stirs and then rolls over on her side. She must be dreaming. Colin doesn't move. Then, as though the moment never happened, the heaviness of sleep washes over her again.

Bang, bang, bang!

The sound resonates up the stairs. Colin sits up, tipping his ear toward his closed door. He waits for another sound.

Laura, sensing Colin's uneasiness, leans toward him. She grabs his hand. "Did you hear that?"

"Shh, wait a second."

Bang, bang!

It echoes up the stairs.

He glances at his clock. "Who the hell is at the door at this hour? It's six twenty-three a.m. on a freaking Saturday. I swear, if someone is playing a joke, I'm going to be pissed," Colin barks as he stands and pulls on his boxers.

He whips open his bedroom door and looks both ways down the hallway. His roommate Brandon's door is open, which means he didn't come home last night. Stef's room is at the end, and he sleeps through everything. Austin's door is closed, and he hears no signs of life. Nobody is moving.

Bang, bang!

Colin bounds down the staircase with authority, mumbling to himself as he gets to the door. He unlocks it and pulls it open.

Standing on his porch is a young man, dressed, oddly enough, as an older gentleman would. He is wearing a tweed sports coat, khaki pants, and loafers. His eyes are red and hollow. The scruff on his face is at least a few days' worth. His hands are shaking. He clasps them together, attempting to calm his nerves.

"Can I help you?" Colin says unkindly.

Despite his disheveled appearance, he replies very delicately, "I need to speak to Laura."

Colin's eyebrows crease as he cocks his head to the side. "Who are you?"

He keeps his eyes locked with Colin's. "It's important. Can you please get her?"

Colin slightly closes the door. He hesitates at the end of the hallway, but as he peers up the stairs, Laura, clad in his sweatshirt, is standing at the top with a pained expression on her face.

Not wanting to disturb the entire house, he whispers up the stairs, "There is someone here for *you*."

"What? Me?" She takes a few steps forward.

Colin motions for her to come down. She moves down the stairs as though her feet were detached from her body.

She lands in front of Colin. "Who is it?"

"I have no idea."

"Really?" Her curiosity is at an all-time high as she brushes by him.

She nervously smooths her hair behind her ears. She grants Colin one last glance and then pulls open the door. He is standing with his back facing out toward the driveway, but she would recognize that figure, no matter the time of day.

"Wolfie?"

He turns his head only halfway but doesn't face her. She steps onto the porch, closing the door behind her. She can tell by his mannerisms that he has to tell her something top secret. He wouldn't be here at this hour if he didn't.

"What's going on?" she whispers.

Like a slow-motion movie being played without sound, she cautiously approaches him. He reluctantly turns to face her. His lip quivers, and his eyes, bloodshot and wet, alarm Laura. Wolfie is the epitome of emotionless.

"Wolfie, talk to me," she pleads.

A lone tear falls on his cheek, and Laura, within an instant, knows this cannot be good news.

"Travis," he stutters.

Anger fills her voice. "Travis what, Wolfie?"

"He..." His body starts to shake. "He passed away."

Laura's senses go numb. She loses hearing first. Secondly, her heart stops with a hard thud in her chest. Lastly, her arms and legs lose sensation. Then, nothing. Just the world spinning uncontrollably.

"Motorcycle accident last night," she thinks she hears him say.

Without warning, a horrific scream bursts through her lips. When you hear the words that someone you care for deeply has died, the permanence of the truth is almost impossible to grasp. It takes days for that to sink in, if not months, and unfortunately for many, it can take years. *This* immediate news is incomprehensible.

Laura starts to collapse, Wolfie grabs her in a panicked embrace. She holds on to him for dear life as they cry in one another's arms. She knows his loss is significant, too.

"I-I don't believe it. Tell me it's not true!" she wails into the deepness of his shoulder. She pounds her fist on his chest. "Dead? He's dead? But I just saw him! This can't possibly be true!"

He reaches up, hand shaking, and holds her head into his chest. "It is, Laura. He's gone."

She slightly pulls back. They still hold each other as she asks, "What happened? When?"

"Last night. All I know is it was a motorcycle accident."

"No, not Travis!" Laura's cries are loud. She hears the door open to Colin's apartment.

Startled by the scene in front of him, he rushes over.

"Laura, what's going on?" He gently grabs her shoulder and spins her around to face him. Once he does, he comprehends the anguish displayed on her face. "Jesus Christ, what's happening?" he replies out of sheer panic.

Laura falls to her knees, her bare skin hitting the pavement, but the pain shooting through her is welcome because it is a much better pain than what is tearing through her heart. She buries her head in her hands as tears flow through her fingertips.

Colin glances at Wolfie. "What is happening?" he asks. "Please, someone, tell me!"

Wolfie, silenced with grief, reverts back to Laura as he wipes his own tears on the sleeve of his coat.

Colin bends down, trying to hold Laura. "Talk to me, please..."

She peeks up through her soaked lashes. In a harsh whisper, she admits, "Travis is dead."

Colin stumbles back himself, but then he tries to get closer to her on the ground and envelops her in his arms. "Oh my God...I am sorry. I am so sorry," he repeats over and over as he rocks her broken soul. He looks up at Wolfie. "What can I do?"

He chokes out, "His dad called me about an hour ago. I need to go tell Professor Campbell. The school should know."

"Okay. If I can do anything, anything at all, please let me know." Colin's own eyes become misty.

Wolfie simply nods. "Laura, I don't want to leave you."

"Let me come with you," she blurts out. "I need to."

Colin pulls her back. "You sure?"

"Yes. Please. I-I need to go with him."

"Okay, come get dressed." He pulls her up in his arms and steadies her as she weakly treads to the door. "Come in, please," Colin says to Wolfie. "I'll make some coffee."

Laura is barely able to make it up the stairs. She holds on to the railing as she heaves with sadness. She enters Colin's room. Her mind is empty, but her body is filled with a tremendous amount of pain, and she can barely catch her breath. She staggers, trying to find her clothes. Her eyes blurred with tears, she assembles herself and then drops on the edge of Colin's bed. Her hands are uncontrollably shaking as she tries to survey the room. *Do I even have my clothes and are my shoes on?* No, her shoes are by the end of the bed. She reaches for them, straining just to stretch in front of her. Without warning, she collapses on the floor.

The loud thud sends Colin sprinting up the stairs. The door flies open, and he finds Laura unconscious in a heap on his floor.

He rushes to her side. "Laura, Laura!"

He gently shakes her. She does not respond. Her skin is ice cold and pale. He cradles her in his arms.

Stef bursts into the doorway. "What the hell is going on?"

With tears stinging his eyes, Colin looks up, and with authority, he says, "Call 911."

Fifty-One

SIX MONTHS AFTER

The spring air in April gives hope that, with the rain, there will again be blossoms flourishing across the now dreary campus. The large white tent set up on the lawn across from Rounds Hall is filled to capacity. Numerous people are waiting outside the tent, clutching umbrellas, as they pray for the rain to stop.

Laura is off to the side, shaded by a divider set up to give some separation from the crowd. The president of the university is finishing his remarks when Laura feels a presence next to her. She turns and smiles. "Ainsley Atwood. I was wondering when you were going to show up."

"Very funny. Now, you know why anyone who gives a shit about me calls me Wolfie."

Laura chuckles. "I like Wolfie better, too." The two, not much for small talk, always get right down to business. "The dean's suspension?"

"Upheld, indefinitely."

"Good. Any word from Officer Murphy on the accident?"

"He is looking into a few more items. Said he'd get back to me when he could."

"So help me God, if she had anything to do with—"

He grabs her hand. "I've got this. Don't worry."

She sighs. "I know. And your role at the paper?"

"Like I've said, I prefer being the guy in the background. The one no one *needs* to know about. I've still got work to do."

"I like it that way, too. You are a master at solving problems at an exceedingly fast pace and with an unusual efficiency." She playfully winks.

A rare smirk graces his face. "Why, thank you. And I like that you're the one giving the speech today. You are the voice of this campus, Laura."

She briefly reflects back upon the past six months leading up to today, and with a comfortable sadness, she adds, "It is my pleasure."

"He would have wanted it to be you." He touches her hand again and then pulls it away, drawing the collar of his tweed coat up as though he is going to go back out into the rain.

"You're not staying?" she asks.

He turns slightly, and then with the same arrogance and mystery of their late friend, he says, "Nah, not my thing."

Laura smiles, and before she can respond, she hears the president say, "It is with great pleasure, I introduce Ms. Laura Chase."

The crowd claps as she approaches from behind the divider. She glances at her friends, Colin, Tucker, and all the guys from the station sitting in the front row, and she exhales, releasing her nerves.

She places her paper on the podium in front of her, adjusts the microphone, and says in her precise radio voice, "Good afternoon, Hawks. It is my great honor to be standing before you today to accept the Associated Collegiate Press College Media Liberty Award on behalf of my late friend, Travis Taylor. As I gaze out into the crowd today, I ponder two things. One, Travis would have loved the recognition for his work. I don't doubt that for a second. But, more importantly, I look out at a lot of faces of people who didn't truly *know* Travis. Not many of us did. He was arrogant, complicated, driven, fearless, and calculated. Those qualities did not leave much for those around him to care for. That is, unless you were lucky enough to truly get to know him."

She pauses. "I had that distinct pleasure." She quickly dabs the corner of her eye with a tissue before continuing.

"His idealisms were based solely on his future. He had grand plans to run his own newspaper someday, and that left little playtime for him. Hence, his tight inner circle. He would do anything for those close to him and stop at nothing to tear down an undeserving opponent." She pauses again. "I came to admire this about him.

"He taught me to believe in myself. To stand strong when times were difficult and, more importantly, to never let anyone get in the way of the truth. His integrity was second to none, and many of you are here today to pay your respects to him for simply *that* quality alone. He never backed down, even when his own college career lay hanging in the balance. He refused to let that uncertainty stop him.

"His loss is something that this university will never forget. No doubt, his colleagues at *The Weekly Blue* and the radio station will never be able to replicate the hard work and dedication Travis had to uncovering the truth."

Laura breaks. It is apparent she is trying to hold back a flood of tears. She sighs and continues as she places her hand over her heart. "And, for me, it's quite simple. Every time I reflect back on my time at OSU I will forever and always remember *my* dear friend Travis Taylor."

The impact of her statement resonates with her friends sitting in the crowd, especially Colin.

With tears stinging her eyes, she recites, "Thank you to the Associated Collegiate Press for recognizing Travis's continued demonstration for college press freedom and reform. You have chosen a worthy recipient, and I accept this award in his memory. On behalf of Travis's family and his friends, thank you to the university for the plaque outside the doors of *The Weekly Blue*. It will be a reminder to us all that, when our days feel long and we just can't possibly push ourselves an inch more, if you do, you, too, will *earn* your success.

"Thank you all for coming here today. And…" She pauses, glancing up from her notes. The rain has stopped, and she feels a warm rush of air pass her despite the cloud of her breath telling her it is still cold. She tucks her hair behind her ear and smiles, remembering the last time he smiled at her. "If I may, to Travis, wherever you might be…sweet dreams."

What Is Next?

The saga at Onondaga State University is far from over.

Laura is hospitalized over her grief from losing her dear friend Travis Taylor. As her intimate memories of Travis haunt her, she hesitates to resume her life at the radio station without him. Will her relationship with another friend take a sudden turn, throwing a wedge between her and Colin?

When Tank discovers Abigail made a major decision without consulting him first, his hurt turns to anger. Yet again, these two friends find themselves on opposing sides. The only difference this time is, her boyfriend, Nathan, is not there to support her. As Nathan's popularity consumes him on campus, Abigail pulls further away from the football team. Will Nathan and Tank's behavior push Abigail into the waiting arms of the mysterious Kelly Conrad?

Continue the journey with Abigail, Laura, and their friends at Onondaga State University as they close the book on their complex sophomore year and start their junior year off with an unforgettable bang!

Acknowledgments

To my family and friends—Thank you for supporting me these past few years.

To all of those who read *Last Goodbye* and *Longing to Be*, my sincere thank you.

Thank you Jovana, Letitia, Lindee, Judy, Catherine, Cat, Kel, Zara, and Mila for your continued guidance, feedback, and help.

About the Author

Laurel (Kupillas) Ostiguy was born in Queensbury, a town sandwiched between Lake George and Saratoga Springs in Upstate New York, where she still visits with friends and family. She attended Plymouth State University and graduated in 1997. She also received her master's degree from Northeastern University in 2003.

She is now married to her college sweetheart, Jeff, and they have two sons. She currently lives outside of Boston, Massachusetts. When she is not working, she loves to spend time with her children, ski, practice yoga, write, or just enjoy the beautiful New England seasons.